Worlds To Conquer

A Klondike's Circus Novel

By

Nathan Woolford

ISBN: 978-1-917129-11-4

About the author

Nathan Woolford is a newspaper journalist, sub-editor and author.
Born and raised in Swindon, Wiltshire, his journalism career began while he was still at school with a weekend job at BBC Wiltshire Sound.
He also wrote articles and features for various local papers and magazines.
Nathan graduated from University College Falmouth with an honours degree in journalism and has worked as a writer and copy editor for more than 20 years.
He is the author of the Klondike's Circus novels, which began in 2022 with Trail Dust.

DAILY SENTINEL FRONT PAGE. MARCH 1, 1961…

SUPERSTAR CIRCUS HEADS TO EUROPE!

It's official! America's favourite circus is leaving our shores and heading across the pond for a tour of Europe.

Hot off the back of last year's ATV spectacular Superstars and Stripes, Klondike's Circus is now venturing into a new market with its bold move to play to continental crowds.

It is a brave and exciting development for the troupe, headed by former knife thrower turned circus manager Kal Klondike, who built the business up from scratch.

But his promotion has been on the up for years now, going from a West Coast outfit touring California, Arizona and Nevada to a national institution, playing at every major city in the US.

There have also been a string of TV specials over the past four years, culminating in the unforgettable Superstars and Stripes extravaganza last summer.

Klondike can now boast the hottest talent in America today, headed by legendary trapeze artist Gino Shapiro, master ventriloquist Roddy Olsen and motorbike stunt team The Daredevils.

Many experts have said the natural next step for Klondike and co is to head abroad, where new fans and exciting venues await in glamorous cities across Europe. The opportunity to maximise revenue and capitalise on the so-called "Americanisation" of Europe would appear to be a pull too strong for the circus boss to ignore.

In a press event yesterday announcing the upcoming tour, Mr Klondike said: "We have a deep respect for circus fans around the world, and would dearly love to reach as many as possible. This tour is a way of accomplishing that.

"Now, fans across Europe have an opportunity to be a part of our show. And we sure hope they like it."

The tour will take in London, Paris, Antwerp, Berlin, Geneva and Rome. The troupe will then return to the US for its standard national run of 22 cities.

But will it be a success? Few American circus companies have ventured into Europe down the years.

The so-called “forbidden gate” has remained firmly closed for many. But, once opened, it is largely unknown what wonders, or woes, might unfold.

One thing is for sure. It will be one hell of a ride!

CHAPTER ONE

"And so on to Europe! And the new frontier."

Kal Klondike said the words majestically, with a theatrical flourish, as he pulled back a sheet of felt that had covered a large board on an easel.

Beneath the fabric sat a giant map of Europe, a red line projecting across it like a disjointed arrow.

"Gentleman," he continued, "I give you the Klondike's Circus European Tour, 1961. Our greatest achievement yet."

He was standing at the head of a large conference room in the monolithic headquarters of Addison Incorporated, a giant skyscraper dominating San Francisco bay. From up here on the 25th floor, you could practically see forever through the dramatic floor-to-ceiling windows that formed the room's perimeter.

Before him sat Daryl Addison, his former principal investor and now a partner in his circus, under the title of consultant. Addison now ran a huge, far-reaching conglomerate that specialised in financial advice and public relations.

Gordon Walters, his attorney, sat next to him around the needlessly large mahogany conference table that dominated the room.

Both sat spellbound as Klondike explained his latest venture. The circus boss was forever the great showman. A tall and lean man with craggy looks and jet black hair and eyes, he was dressed in a dark brown suit, with his trusty fedora and silver-topped cane deposited on a chair beside him.

"As I'm sure you are aware," Klondike was saying, "this is by far our grandest, most audacious excursion yet. A gamble, yes. But the risk is justified. Every angle taken care of by my contacts overseas. Venues booked months ago. Work crews signed up. Media coverage guaranteed." He smiled at them, a twinkle in his dark eyes. "All we need now is for the people to come in their droves, like they do here."

Addison nodded, clapping his hands together in a show of praise. "Well done, Kal. I salute your plans. Such a grandiose scheme. I can scarcely believe it."

The old banker rose and wandered over to the map laid out on the board before them. He was a small, wiry fellow, with close-cropped grey hair and a pencil moustache.

Klondike's Circus had helped generate mighty profits for his company, ever since its breakout season in 1958. He had used the capital to diversify into an intriguing catalogue of different business ventures, making him fabulously wealthy just as he had been considering retirement. The fame and success of Klondike's Circus had been the turning point. And he had never forgotten that.

Addison studied the map, following the felt-tipped red line that showed the route.

"This really is something else," he muttered, turning to Klondike. "London. Paris. Antwerp. Berlin. Geneva. Rome, for Chrissakes! This will be a culture shock for everyone, surely?"

Klondike joined him by the map. "By why not, eh partner? Last season, we broke records everywhere. Superstars and Stripes on July fourth was the biggest circus spectacular of all time. Why not branch out into Europe, like Barnum did back in the day? Create a worldwide entertainment empire."

Addison looked back at Walters, then at the map again. He shook his head. "I need a drink." He wandered slowly to a huge oak-panelled bar in the room's corner, where a leather couch and several armchairs were scattered.

"Cognac, Kal?"

"You bet."

He poured a balloon snifter full of the deep, golden brown liquid, and then fixed two Scotches, handing one to Walters. "What do you say, Gord?"

The lawyer, a balding man with huge, horn-rimmed glasses, looked up at the map on display before him. "Well," he mumbled, "this isn't exactly my area of expertise, gentlemen. It would appear, though, that there are plenty of risks involved." He eyed Klondike. "I mean, what do you even know of all these far-off places? Isn't this a great step into the unknown?"

Klondike accepted his cognac gleefully, took a sip, then placed the large glass on the conference table. Addison grinned as his old friend pulled a giant cigar from his breast pocket and lit up, blowing a waft of purple smoke towards the ceiling. It was like a performance.

"Risks are everywhere," Klondike mused, staring at the panoramic, vertigo-inducing view of San Francisco bay outside. "I've had them since day one. Daryl too. And every risk we've faced, we've battled through and come out trumps. In many ways, the problems we've faced down the years – which have been plentiful – have actually inspired us to success."

The thought floated through the men's collective conscience.

Addison, drink in hand, paced the room, his eyes darting back to the map every few seconds. He looked down at the conference table, where Klondike had emptied a satchel full of promotional materials, posters, press releases and general paperwork. A billing sheet sat to one side. Addison studied it.

"So, you've got 100 Gs from me for this escapade?"

Klondike nodded, cigar in mouth. "That will be about a third of the outlay. I'm putting up the rest."

"That's a lot of green, Kal."

"Well, it's a big adventure, Daryl. But think, just think, about the potential rewards. Offers from across Europe. Annual tours and appearances. An endless stream of revenue from across the world, dammit! If we pull this off, we can truly start to think of ourselves as the world's greatest circus." He stepped forward, his eyes wild and alive. "Addison Incorporated are our main sponsors. Your firm will be everywhere. Programmes, billboards, media coverage. Hell, before you know it, you could get calls coming in from all over the place."

Addison half-smiled. "Now, that part I like."

Walters had finished his Scotch. "There are still a few issues I can't look beyond, Kal. Maybe you can oblige me."

Klondike grinned at him and perched on the edge of the table. "Go ahead, Gordon."

"Well," the lawyer said weakly. "Again, I'm no expert, but… well, what about the language barrier? You have songs in your show, dialogue. That puppet guy. How will anyone understand any of it in, say, Antwerp?"

Klondike nodded. "It's a good point. The honest answer is, we don't know. But what we do know is the Americanisation of culture in Europe is raging. Our TV shows, our pop stars, who are now touring there frequently. All of this will no doubt help."

Walters did not seem appeased. "Such a gamble. And these cities you have chosen. Why them?"

"Because market research has shown they are circus towns, where people come out in their droves to see the show. Historically, these are the places where tents pitch up. We are continuing an old tradition."

Walters ran a hand across his bald head. "And what of this ship you've bought?"

"Leased," Klondike corrected him. He fumbled through the papers on the table and produced a large photograph the size of a poster, placing it on the easel in front of the map.

"I am calling it the Floating Top!" he proclaimed. They all studied the picture. The ship photographed was a long, white and blue painted freighter with a light superstructure and massive deck.

Klondike lectured his audience. "It was originally a Transatlantic freighter serving the automotive industry, carrying cars abroad. Then, it was sold to an entertainment supplies agency, who used it to ferry props and sound systems to film sets and movie locations around the world. I leased it from them a few months back. It is perfect for this venture. We have stable blocks for the horses, a garage for the motorbikes. Hell, there's even a practice area we've created in an old storage room. It's comfortable and... there's something about it. It has a certain seaworthy charm."

While Walters looked at him blankly, Addison had to smile.

"And so, this Floating Top is docked at New York now? As we speak?"

"That's right, Daryl. We'll all transfer across to New York in three weeks for departure. On the train. Performers, equipment, props, the midway stalls. Everything. We're all set, partner."

Walters shook his head. "But I still say you're going in blind, Kal. You don't know anything about the European circus scene."

Klondike smiled knowingly. "Well, I've got us a little help on that score."

Addison nodded. "That's right, you have haven't you? I thought this contact of yours was joining us up here..."

"He's waiting in reception. I said we'd call him in."

Walters was alarmed. "What are you guys talking about?"

Klondike grasped his cane and twirled it as he spoke. "Our European consultant. Jack Bannion. Born into the circus. They say he started out as a roustabout as a teenager in an outfit on the English south coast. Worked as a rigger, hawker, midway hand. Ended up working the trapeze rings, became a god damn superstar. Then he suffered a bad fall and busted his knee. He worked as a talent scout and foreman after that. These days, he works as a freelance promoter, helping big tops across Britain."

"You mean he was a flyer?" Walters blurted.

"Right. Called himself Union Jack Bannion."

The other two laughed. Addison held up a hand and pressed a button on his intercom at the head of the table.

"Susan, please show Mr Bannion in."

Seconds later, the doors at the far end of the great room burst open. A tall, painfully thin man with thick red hair and wearing a pink flowery shirt – that looked hopelessly out of place in the boardroom – waltzed in.

Klondike shook his hand warmly and made the introductions.

Bannion stood beside him, his eyes widening as he took in the immense city views that enveloped them.

"Mr Bannion," Addison was saying, "thank you for joining us. I hope you are enjoying American hospitality."

"Very much, thanks," said the Englishman.

Walters cut to the chase. "So, what do you think of this tour, Bannion? Do you think it will work?"

"Of course! I wouldn't have come on board if I thought otherwise, my sir."

Addison studied the newcomer. "You believe European audiences will take to our show?"

Bannion shuffled over to the table and picked up some of the promotional materials. "The English public cannot get enough of America right now. TV Westerns are booming, dominating the ratings. Films too. Rock n roll is everywhere. Elvis. Cochrane. Avalon. Ricky Nelson. Everybody goes crazy for these guys. A show like this…" he held up a circus poster. "Dynamite. Anticipation is growing already. This will be the first American circus to hit England in years. These posters are up across

London right now. The idea of American performers is capturing the imagination."

Klondike nodded, backing up the appraisal. "We're giving the show a true American theme. The Range Riders will help with this. Their segment will be a cowboy extravaganza of horses, riding and roping. And…" his eyes took on that twinkle again. "This year, they are getting a helping hand from one James 'Duster' Williams."

Addison's eyes widened. "Duster Williams! Is he still around? I saw his act years ago. In LA. Jesus! He must be pushing 60 now."

"He's 58. Or so he says. But his lasso act is still first class. A king among cowboys. And a true cowboy. Hell, he says his father was a gunslinger in the old west."

"Wait a minute," Addison mused. "Didn't I hear he'd become a drunk? Stuck in rehab somewhere?"

Klondike smiled thinly. "He got cleaned up. Now, he's making a comeback."

Walters looked like a dog sensing danger. "I don't like this one bit. A drunk?"

"Just leave it to me," Klondike said quickly.

"Alright, alright," Addison said, moving into the middle of the gathering. He looked up at Klondike and winked. Then, he turned to Bannion again. "And so I understand you have set up a train to get the circus across Europe?"

"Yes, sir. On loan from the Imperial Circus, out of Guildford, Surrey."

They all looked at him blankly.

The Englishman grinned. "It can be transported by ferry across to France. From there, it's all straight rails."

That seemed to satisfy the others. Addison nodded slowly. Then, he stared directly at Bannion, eyes serious and alive.

"In your opinion, Mr Bannion, can Klondike's Circus be a hit in Europe?"

Bannion licked his lips as he looked the assembled men over. "Sir, I study the international circus industry as a job. Klondike's Circus simply has a winning hand. Gino Shapiro is the world's most famous trapeze artist. Roddy Olsen is perhaps the most talked about performer in world circus today. The Daredevils have the most death-defying, most audacious act imaginable. Throw in the cowboys, the showcase revue-"

"The freak show!" Addison blurted.

"Er, yes, the freak show. Throw all these elements together, and you have a winning show, guvnor."

Klondike slapped him on the back. "Damn straight!"

Addison grinned, like a wise old bobcat. Hands behind back, he continued pacing the room.

"We've seen much success with your circus down the years, eh Kal?"

"You bet."

"You've always delivered. For me. For your people. For the fans. And now this. Europe! It's all so completely fantastic. What can I tell you, Kal? I'm delighted to be onboard."

Klondike chuckled. "Thank you Daryl. None of this would have been possible without you."

"And now what?" asked Walters, still seated. "A new chapter?"

Klondike wedged his cigar into the corner of his mouth. Using his cane, he pointed its tip at the window, towards the mighty Pacific that spread out below and before them.

"Onwards and upwards. We head into these strange and distant lands, far from our comfort zone." His eyes fixed onto a point far out at sea, and he squinted. "For there are new horizons to cross. And new worlds to conquer."

At that, they all cheered.

CHAPTER TWO

Buried deep within the luscious hills and endless prairies of Napa Valley sat a true hidden gem of tranquility and beauty, a faraway outpost known as Rio Cristo.

Originally a garrison and army barracks built in a large open field surrounded by forestland and hilltops, it had served as a hideout and, indeed, a home for early western settlers as they battled for land against marauding Commanche tribesmen. Generations of Oregon Trail travellers had used the fort as a base and holding camp, creating corrals, livery stables and barns over the years.

Decades later, the site was bought out and redeveloped by a wine magnate and land baron, who used Rio Cristo as his California lodgings and pleasure den.

Now, the old fort was a vacuum of vibrant excitement, colour and energy in its current incarnation – as the headquarters and winter camp of Klondike's Circus.

A large whitestone structure sat in the centre of the compound, known as the pavilion. It held a conference room, canteen, bar and several executive offices and suites. The pavilion was flanked by two rows of cabins used as lodgings for the staff and talent.

Beyond that, laid out across a sea of gravel and cedar shingles that stretched to the base of the hillsides, sat trailers, huts, several marquees and a mini open-air performance stage.

A tarmac practice grid in one corner was used by the motorcycle stunt riders. In the opposite corner sat stable blocks, outside which a team of fine golden palominos grazed happily in a large corral.

Just beyond the camp sat a small hut known as the station house, which was located next to the old branch railway line, a route into the outside world for the circus troupe, and the starting point of a new adventure each season.

As the circus crew and teams of roustabouts went about their daily business in the warm spring sunshine, they were watched from high above by a woman sat on the balcony of the pavilion.

With flaming red hair, cinnamon complexion and startling violet eyes, she could have passed for a movie star or fashion model. Instead, she had spent much of her working life promoting and advising such celebrities in her role as a public relations guru.

Lacey Tanner idly flicked through the glossy magazine she was eyeing, before dropping it onto a large pile of journals she had been going through all morning. As she picked up another from a box next to her, her gaze took in the endless activity all around her. A string of roustabouts were working on the circus's midway stalls down in the gravel below, painting the wooden outboards and fixing various holes and cracks.

"Romantic, isn't it?"

The deep voice from behind momentarily startled her. Then, she smiled.

"In a way, it is. Try as I might, I can't look away. All my glamour magazines here… I just can't concentrate on them."

She turned in her armchair and looked up as a large, brawny man waded onto the balcony. He was tall, heavyset and wore a cherubic face under thinning brown hair. Henry 'Heavy' Brown, the circus ringmaster and de-facto second in command.

"Well," he murmured, taking in the scene below, "it's like I always say, Lacey. You got the sawdust fever. You got it real bad." He laughed softly to himself. "We really made a circus gal outta you. It got into your blood. To know it is to love it, as Barnum once said."

She smiled. "I can't deny that, Henry."

Heavy chuckled again. "I know what it's like. Hard to stop watching all the guys down there, bringing out all the wonders and beauty of the big show. Like watching pieces of a watch all come together."

Lacey leant back, lighting a cigarette. "What's the latest, Henry?"

He leant his mighty frame against the edge of the whitestone balcony wall. "Kal is on his way back from Frisco. With our, er, English adviser. He just called. Predictably, old man Addison loved the whole pitch. There were no unforeseen issues."

Lacey blew smoke into the light breeze. "Incredible."

Heavy studied her. "I suppose it is. But Daryl knows the circus turned his empire around. He trusts us. All the way. Hell, Kal could pitch anything to him, I say he'd go for it."

"But this…" she breathed. "This adventure. Into Europe. And all that it entails. I can't imagine anything more unpredictable. I'm nervous, Henry."

"Well, we all are to an extent." He grinned again. "But what a ride, eh? And just think…" his eyes widened. "This could be our finest hour."

Lacey nodded slightly, lost in thought. She went back to studying the movements of everyone spread out in the yard before her. "Like watching the inhabitants of a city," she whispered. "Everyone going about their business. Their routine. All striving to get us ready for roll-out day."

They both looked up, to the far side of the camp, as a wandering group appeared from behind a large tent. There were several men in suits and two women in smart dresses, all led along by a dark, swarthy-looking man dressed extravagantly in an orange tracksuit. He was obviously conducting a tour, pointing and gesticulating as the group nodded and looked around with vest.

Heavy shook his head. "Another of your public relations coups, Lacey. Talent-led press tours."

She watched with interest. "The reporters love it. How many people can say they have been shown around the Klondike's Circus winter camp by the great Gino Shapiro?"

Heavy smirked as he watched Shapiro talking to the group. "Someone better tell those ladies they're swimming in a shark pool."

She rolled her eyes. "They love him." She watched the enigmatic showman decked in orange down below. "Hell, everyone does."

"And here, ladies and gentlemen, is where I practise my trapeze work. It is like a miniature big top. Without the screaming fans calling my name!"

The reporters all laughed as Gino Shapiro led them into the tall red and blue tent, where a small trapeze rig was lodged in the summit. There was a ring dangling down and two platforms sitting atop great wooden pillars.

Shapiro wandered inside causally. "Me and my handler Penny practise every day. Four hours in total. It is all about practice, my friends. That is what makes us the best."

The press pool all looked up as one, studying the rig above. Then, slowly, all eyes fell back upon their host.

Shapiro was outrageously handsome, with jet black, oily hair and smooth, olive skin and giant brown eyes. He was of Mexican/Italian heritage, and came from a long line of circus entertainers.

A lean, lithe figure, he seemed to bounce around like an over-excited puppy as he happily explained the history of trapeze to his audience. He paused for questions.

"Mr Shapiro," one of the females asked, "what about all the injuries you've sustained doing this trapeze all your life?"

"Ha! Bumps and bruises. Nothing to me, signora. Nothing can hold me back."

A young man in a bright suit spoke up. "What about that shoulder? It was ripped out at that Vegas show a few years back."

Shapiro looked at the man coldly. "You are mistaken, my friend. Nothing so dramatic."

The youngster wasn't finished. "I saw it on TV. You were almost killed."

"Pah! You exaggerate, amigo. I am the king up there on the rings. What could possibly kill me, eh?"

Another man, who appeared to be a cohort of the youngster, stepped forward. "That dame. What was her name? Jenny Cross, right? The femme fatale of the circus."

The woman who had asked the first question seemed to jump. "Oh, yes! Jenny Cross! What on earth happened to her, Gino?"

Annoyed, Shapiro seemed to bristle in his fireball outfit. He smiled politely. "Madam, I am sure I do not know." He made a great sweeping gesture with his hand, trying to move the party on. "Now, let us move on, my friends. The next stop on the tour is the horse blocks. Who wants to see some real cowboys, eh?"

An older reporter cried "Yee-hah" and raced out of the tent, while the others trundled out slowly, disappointed.

Shapiro manoeuvred himself back to the front of the group as they wandered slowly in the afternoon sunshine.

"The great thing about Klondike's Circus," he proclaimed loudly as he strolled ahead, towards a path between two lines of trailers, "is that worlds of wonder come to life here. We have everything. Cowboys. Daredevils. Acrobats… a wall made of human beings. Giants. Monsters. Clowns. Singing and dancing. And, of course, magic."

They all walked between the rows of trailers.

"Why do you still do it, Gino?" one of the reporters called out. "You've been with Klondike since the beginning, right? They say you've worked in movies down in Hollywood. What keeps you performing in the circus?"

Shapiro looked around himself majestically. "Why?" he snarled. "That is the easiest question yet. It is in my blood, signora. I had a calling into the circus like some folks get a calling to be a priest. You understand? The circus is my life. My soul. The bright lights, the roar of the crowd, this is what your Gino lives for. For you see my friends, I…"

He broke off abruptly as a bizarre screeching sound reverberated across the camp grounds. With an irritated scowl, he recognised the noise as the sound of young girls squealing in delight.

The tour group all turned as a fabulous scarlet Cadillac convertible rumbled across the gravel, past the cabins and towards a small garage block next to the whitestone buildings. A maddening tribe of about 20 teenage girls was in hot pursuit on foot, racing after the slow-moving car as if in a trance.

As the car stopped, its driver climbed out quickly. He wore stylish black sunglasses and a Hawaiian shirt. He looked barely older than the pursuing group, and was quickly mobbed by them.

"What the hell is that all about?" one of the reporters cried as they all watched the commotion.

Shapiro started to speak, but was quickly interrupted by one of the women reporters. "Oh my god! It's Roddy Olsen!"

The press team all seemed to gasp together, before storming off towards the Cadillac. And the screeching.

Shapiro suddenly found himself alone and forgotten. He eyed the chaotic scene before him with cold eyes.

"Santamaria," he muttered.

Roddy Olsen happily signed autographs for the group of youngsters, shaking hands and posing for pictures as they all jostled around him excitedly.

Many had been waiting for his arrival outside the camp gates, and had simply followed him in. Others were summer workers at the camp who had been eagerly awaiting his appearance.

All waited patiently to meet him and get the all-important signature.

As the crowd slowly dispersed, Olsen removed his sunglasses. He looked barely out of his teens, with thick amber hair, a golden California tan, sky blue eyes and immaculate white teeth. He looked every inch the teen idol, and fitted the bill, seemingly generating excitement in everyone he greeted.

As the youths all slowly backed away, Olsen walked forward, with the press team now taking their turn to mob him. Questions were fired at him with wild velocity.

"Roddy! Where you been? Hollywood? Las Vegas?"

"Hey, Roddy! When are you on TV next?"

"Do you think the audiences in Europe will like your act, Rod?"

Olsen looked the group over in dismay. "Woh. That's a lot of questions, guys. The official Klondike's Circus press call is in New York next month. I'll be answering all your questions then. For now-"

"Come on, Roddy!" one of the older men snapped, pen and notepad poised before him. "What about Europe? Are you excited?"

Olsen smiled. "Of course. Performing overseas is a dream come true. Particularly London. Y'know, one of the world's greatest ever ventriloquists is from there. His name is-"

"Is it true you're going to be appearing on the Jim Russell Show?" another voice cried. The press pool all rounded on him.

Olsen looked around awkwardly. "Well, er..." He smiled. "You're remarkably well informed, pal."

The impromptu press conference was suddenly interrupted by another high-pitched wail, this time from a young girl wearing a denim dungarees, who raced from the pavilion and straight into Olsen's arms. They embraced warmly.

The reporters all grinned like alligators.

"Who's this, Rod? Your girlfriend?"

"What's your name, sweetie?"

"What's it like dating the Puppet Master?"

Suzi Dando released her arms from around Olsen and looked about innocently at the army of newcomers. Several of the teeny boppers nearby were now glaring at her. She gulped heavily.

"Friend," she said in a squeaky, irritated tone. "Not girlfriend. Friend."

Suzi was the circus's resident songstress, known for her beautiful high voice that closed out each show. Like Olsen, she could've passed for a teenager, and had childlike features and a neat bob of hazelnut hair.

"Me and Suzi have been close pals since day one. In fact, since minute one," Olsen explained. "Ever since I first wandered into the winter camp. Three years ago."

He looked down at her. They both smiled.

"What do you think about the European tour, Miss Dando?" a journalist asked.

She baulked. "Well, er, I don't really know much about Europe. But I'm sure looking forward to it. I never thought I'd ever be able to go abroad. The circus, and Mr Klondike, have made all these things possible."

The young man in the bright suit pushed his way to the front.

"I think the big question is… is Rusty Fox looking forward to the trip?"

Everyone laughed.

"I have a question!"

They all stopped and turned at the shrill, accented voice from behind. Olsen rolled his eyes. Shapiro marched forward, into the centre of the reporters. His fiery eyes were glaring at Olsen.

He continued in a rasping tone. "Do you think our friends in Europe will take to your horseplay, eh Roddy? The man who talks to his dolls. You think this will sell over there? Do you?"

Olsen tried to smile. "Hello Gino," he said. "Thank you for the warm welcome. Good to see you too."

The press pool looked on with utter glee. The rivalry between Gino Shapiro and Roddy Olsen was legendary. Each seemed to have a deep, unsaid respect for the other, but clearly both men saw themselves as the promotion's top star. Shapiro's name was still at the top of the bill, and he was still the highest-paid performer at the circus. But Olsen had enjoyed a meteoric rise to prominence over the years, and was the darling of west coast circus-goers. Everyone knew the young ventriloquist's popularity had irked the great Gino terribly. But few saw them verbally sparring up close.

"It is good to see you back at camp," Shapiro was saying. "You finally decided to join us, no? And you brought this group of schoolchildren with you…"

As was the standard protocol now, Olsen bit his tongue. "Somebody must have told them I was arriving today."

Shapiro frowned even more. "So… are you ready for Europe?"

"Can't wait. It is a fantastic opportunity for the circus."

"Of course," Shapiro proclaimed loudly, as if addressing a stadium full of people, "I am a veteran of European circus. My father ran a troupe in Italy for many years. Me and my brother Nicky performed for him. I know what the European audiences embrace and love." He glared at Olsen now with cold, mocking eyes. "I look forward with interest to seeing what my friends abroad make of your dolls."

The press pool parted, like schoolchildren making way for two unruly pupils ready to fight in the playground. Suzi defensively stood before Olsen.

"You and your big mouth, Gino," she blurted. "Don't you ever learn?" Her eyes narrowed. "Your jealousy is just insane."

All of the reporters began scribbling notes frantically.

Shapiro laughed out loud in an exaggerated roar. "Child, you are blind! Like all of these other children. They who worship the doll master!"

"That's Puppet Master!" she hissed.

"Alright, alright," Olsen said impatiently. He eyed Shapiro with an equally cold, icy stare. "You've been busting my chops for three years, Gino. I've been back five minutes, and already you've started. When is this all going to end?"

Then, Shapiro stepped in close, so that they were just feet apart. Both men stared at each other intently, anger the overwhelming emotion. Both chests puffed in and out rapidly, in unison. The journalists, the teeny boppers, stewards and roustabouts working nearby, everybody… all held their collective breaths.

"Hold it!"

Again, a new voice interrupted the gathering, seemingly diffusing a volatile eruption.

They all looked towards the pavilion, where a middle-aged, athletic-looking man in yellow pants, a black T-shirt and rainbow-stripped bowler hat came bounding over. Although barely recognisable without his facepaint, Corky the beloved circus clown still attracted attention and acclaim from anyone who saw him. Like Shapiro, he was a legend of Klondike's troupe and a seasoned veteran of the industry.

Now, he pushed his way into the group and forced himself between Shapiro and Olsen. Then, with a joyful flourish, he produced two sets of red roses, seemingly from his sleeve, and handed one to each of them.

"And then we all kiss and make up!" he bellowed. He turned to the press group. "All part of the show, folks. They wind each other up and then, hey presto, old Corky saves the day. Hoorah!"

He held his arms aloft and a tiny round of applause broke out among the watching crowd.

"OK folks," Corky was saying rapidly. "So, you've seen the stars. Now, the tour continues. Where to next, my dear Gino?"

Shapiro's eyes were still locked onto Olsen's. A few moments passed.

"The horse blocks." His voice was dry, his lips unmoving.

"Fantastic! Go see some real-life cowboys, folks." Corky took his hat off, raised it, then deliberately pushed Shapiro forward. Finally, the trapeze artist moved on, the press pool reluctantly following. Though all eyes looked back at Olsen.

The show was over.

As the crowd moved around the row of trailers beyond them, Corky spoke under his breath. "For Chrissakes, man. How many times do we have to tell you? None of that nonsense around the press. It could break us!"

Olsen watched the group disappear. "How much of this garbage am I supposed to take, Corky?"

Suzi nodded angrily. "He shouldn't push people around like that, Corky. It just ain't right."

Corky huffed. "Yeah. Don't I know it." He looked Olsen over and they finally shook hands. "Good to see ya, kid."

"You too, Corky. It's good to be back."

Corky nodded at the Cadillac. "Go get unpacked. I'll catch you tonight."

He smiled as the youngster wandered back to the magnificent car, Suzi hopping excitedly beside him.

"That was some nice work, Corky. And the season hasn't even begun yet!"

Corky turned at the sound of Lacey's smooth voice. She was walking down the pavilion steps with Heavy close behind.

The three of them stood there, watching Olsen unload his bags and trunk from the car.

"That was too near the knuckle for the press," said the clown.

"I dunno," Heavy said, grinning, "the public seem to lap it all up. Especially where those two are concerned. They probably just gave the people what they want."

Lacey nodded. "It's true. A lot of journalists ask about what happens backstage."

Corky fiddled with his bright bowler hat. "Y'know, folks. I love being here. Love the show. Being a part of it all." He frowned. "But, lately, I can't help but see myself as a referee. Always trying to separate Kal's two golden boys."

They all laughed.

Then, Olsen approached the front steps, Suzi helping with his bags. He stopped when he saw Lacey, eyes widening. A point not lost on any of the others.

"Lacey…" he breathed.

She smiled widely. "Welcome back, champ. How was Fresno?"

He gawked, looking barely older than 16. "It was great. Er, well, that is, great to have a look around there again. Been a long time."

"I'm sure. So wonderful to see you."

He strode over, suddenly embracing her in an awkward hug, before shaking hands with Heavy.

Then, Olsen and Suzi wandered inside with the luggage.

Lacey watched him enter the main building, all smiles, seemingly lost in thought.

Corky whispered in her ear. "You look like you just won first place in the beauty pageant, dear."

"Yeah," Heavy muttered. "What gives, Lacey?"

She shook herself all over. "Same as always, boys. I'm just thanking god that super-talented young boy walked into our camp three years ago."

They slowly headed back into the pavilion.

CHAPTER THREE

The business district of Central Rome, Italy, had been known since the 1930s as Esposizione Universale Roma.

A bustling, swarming metropolis of taxi cabs, scooters and humanity. All wrestling with each other to get to their destination in the gentle spring sunshine.

The buildings around them were beautiful examples of baroque architecture, soft walled with giant, medieval-like windows. All joined together to form a labyrinth around the city centre.

One of the tallest structures among the ensemble of prime brickwork was a great yellowstone tower that seemed to rise to the heavens.

At street level, a giant, curved sign hung over an arched, old-fashioned doorway. It read: Courtinio and Co Intrattenimento…

Home to Circo Grande.

In a penthouse office suite near the very top floor of the behemoth, a small, heavily tanned man with thinning brown hair and pointed features sat at a large mahogany desk.

The office was immaculately decorated, with Oriental rugs, leather armchairs, vintage artwork and a full library on the far wall. To the side of the desk, a fire place showcased a full blaze, sat burning slowly, emitting a warm glow over the room.

But none of this seemed to bother the man at the desk.

Carmine Courtinio was reading an international newspaper, a rueful glare on his bronzed features. He shook his head slightly, in irritation.

A booming banner headline in English read:

KLONDIKE'S CIRCUS COMES TO EUROPE…ROMA AMONG STOP-OFFS FOR SENSATIONAL NEW TOUR!

He began re-reading the article below, his beady eyes narrowing with each line.

Suddenly, he looked up at the sound of the doors opening, and idly dropped the newspaper.

A tall, slim man with reddened skin was approaching. He had thick, tossed black hair that looked like it had been styled with a tar brush, and soft, almost feminine features.

Conrad Handel. Courtinio's chief associate. Many years ago, Circo Grande had bought out Handel's German circus, Wunder Welt. As part of the deal, Handel had stayed on as a chief operating officer.

He was followed by an enormous bull of a man. Six feet six and over 300 pounds, the giant Tarz hailed from Hungary and was the circus strongman of Courtinio's outfit. Bearded and with a large, cube-like head, he cut an uncompromising figure.

The pair approached the desk and stopped, as if to attention, as Courtinio appraised them.

"You sent for us, Duce?" Handel asked quietly.

Courtinio watched them silently, squinting amid the glow from the fireplace beyond. "Good morning, gentlemen," he said with little warmth. He nodded at the newspaper, the International Herald Times. It was open on the page he had been reading. "You have seen the news, no?"

"Si, Duce. It seems the great Klondike is coming to Europe. Who would've ever thought?"

The seated Courtinio continued to study the newcomers. "I have long feared this day, Conrad. The coming of the Americans. With their hot dogs, popcorn and this so-called cotton candy they all love. Here! In our sacred land."

As Tarz stood silent, arms folded, Handel looked around absently. "He is looking to build an empire, methinks. Like the dynasties of old. Clearly, he thinks he is ready."

Courtinio finally stood and paced around his desk, glaring at the raging fire. "We have ruled the circus world in Europe, Conrad. Particularly in our native countries. What is it now? Eleven years?"

"Almost twelve, Carmine."

"Years of success. Constant touring. Each new season all the more exciting than the last. Giving our fans what they crave, no?"

He came to rest on the mantelpiece above the fireplace, looking up at a giant, theatrical poster from his glorious 1956 season. They had played every major city in mainland Europe. He looked back sadly. "Gentlemen," he said in a weak tone. "My life, my very existence is enshrined in circus folklore. I am dedicated to the traditions, morals and history of our beloved industry." He moved back to the desk, holding up the newspaper page, so the others could see the main picture of the American troupe. "Yet, I am confused and bewildered at what it has become."

Handel shrugged. "I'm afraid I do not follow, Duce."

"Look at this picture!" Courtinio snapped. He thrust the paper aloft. "Motorcycle riders doing stunts, preparing to kill themselves in this so-called Sphere of Death."

"I have heard about this act."

"Yes, well, it perfectly showcases my point, Conrad. We are circus people, no? We have clowns, dancers, flyers, monkey tamers, fire-eaters, the animal acts, good old Tarz here. We are traditional... we have old-fashioned acts, seeped in circus history. But this..." again he waved the newspaper before him. "This! This is, how can I put it... ah! Otherworldly! Like, I don't know, a glimpse into the future of our industry."

Handel nodded slowly. "You are concerned by their impending arrival?"

"Of course!" Courtinio roared. He cooled quickly, pacing again on the soft rugs. "A development like this could ruin us. Not just ruin us, but render our attractions – our lifeblood, our whole operation – render them... extinct!"

The German frowned. "I hadn't thought of it like that."

"Of course," Courtinio said angrily. "You fail to see the bigger picture, Conrad. This is a threat. A danger. These Americans... if this tour of theirs is a big success, what do you think will happen then, eh? It will only be the beginning. And, mark my words, it will put us out of business. More of them will come. Bigger, bolder and better. We can't boast the talent these big American companies have growing on trees. Our talent programme is bleeding dry, searching for stars in places like, argh..." he shuddered visibly, grabbing at a small glass of grappa and downing the lot. "Bucharest. Sofia. My god, but to visit such desolate places. And for what? To see jugglers who can't juggle. High-wire walkers who fall. Who fail! No, I can see already how this will all play out. Once the fans see these big American firms, they will want only that. Big, stars and stripes extravaganzas. Just look at what has happened with the movies, with rock n roll…"

The giant Tarz finally spoke. "Yes. This is happening, Duce. Kids everywhere love American stars."

Courtinio pointed at him. "You see? Even our monosyllabic friend, the mighty Tarz, knows it."

Handel finally moved, walking to a small bar in the corner and pouring himself a grappa. He sipped it delicately. "And what do you propose we do about this Klondike's Circus, Duce?"

Courtinio, irate, did not even hesitate. "Whatever you have to."

"Excuse me?"

"Listen, I have their schedule mapped out. I know everything. We'll make our move accordingly. Just like two seasons ago. You remember, no? That fancy troupe from England?"

"Little Oscar's Circus of Stars," Tarz spat the words out.

"Ah yes," Handel said, his eyes wary. "I remember very well."

Courtinio nodded enthusiastically. "Now you're getting it, Conrad. Do what you have to."

Handel shifted slightly. "You're sure you want to go to all that trouble, my Duce? Just to scare off some Americans?"

Courtinio moved swiftly to the bar to confront his old associate. "Now, you listen to me, Conrad. I have indulged your fantasies and nonsensical schemes for years. At great expense! Have you any idea what we stand to lose if Klondike is a success and proves to be a pioneer… inspiring others to follow across the ocean into Europe? The whole thing could cripple us." He seemed suddenly incensed. "And it is all wrong, dammit! He is opening the forbidden gate."

Handel backed off, raising his palms. "OK, Duce. I understand. It… it just seems like a lot."

Courtinio looked back at the fire. "We are seeing off an epidemic. Stopping a plague at the starting point."

"What if he refuses?"

The older man bristled, though his eyes seemed to sparkle in the light of the fire. "I have ensured the cards are stacked in our favour."

Tarz seemed to have enjoyed the last part of the conversation. "This man Klondike. What do we know of him, boss?"

"I know everything," Courtinio whispered, strangely in awe. "I have studied him. A former knife thrower. Served in the Marines. World War Two. Here, in Italia. Tough. Strong-willed. He built his outfit up from scratch, they say. And now… now he has the most celebrated circus acts in the Americas."

Handel looked at Tarz, then back at the older man. "Sounds like he won't be an easy man to fight."

"You are absolutely right, Conrad," he breathed. Slowly, as if grasping for a much-cherished heirloom, he reached towards a shelf behind his desk and pulled down a framed picture of a woman. She was beautiful, with twirling black hair and a sultry, cheeky expression, and was dressed in a bright leotard, posing on a circus ring.

"But, of course," Courtinio continued slowly, "there are other ways. Other, beautiful, mystical ways. Of getting what we want. What we all want."

He began to laugh. A slow, disturbing laugh that filled the room.

Handel and Tarz glanced at each other in quiet dismay.

"And, er, what is it we want?" Handel asked.

Courtinio stopped laughing at once. He eyed his associate with an evil, twisted grin, his eyes wide in horror. He spoke in a chilling, deformed tone.

"To see Klondike's Circus implode."

CHAPTER FOUR

A solitary light illuminated a far corner of the canteen, where two men sat in silence playing cards.

It was 6am. All was silent at Rio Cristo at this hour. No roustabouts roamed the grounds. The roar of the motorbikes had yet to begin. The only sound heard around the courtyard was the chatter of bluejays singing happily.

The two figures had been in the canteen for some time. After coffee and a hearty breakfast, which they had cooked up behind the serving bays themselves, they had settled into a game of five card stud. Their favourite.

Kal Klondike had arrived at the camp before dawn, having caught a cab from Santa Marina station with Bannion. While the Englishman had gone to his newly appointed cabin, the circus boss had wandered into the canteen to start his day in style.

As if sensing his presence, Heavy Brown had quickly joined him for breakfast. The two had been best friends since childhood. They had met at their first home, an orphanage, decades earlier in Brooklyn, running with a street gang for many years. Both had enlisted with the Marines at 18 and served in the war, fighting across Europe. Returning to the US in 1945, they had joined Ribbeck's World Circus. Kal had found great fame as a knife thrower, while Heavy worked as a booker and manager. Then, both had become talent scouts and promoters for old man Ribbeck. But everything had changed when Klondike decided to break away and form his own troupe several years back, immediately enlisting Heavy as his principal lieutenant.

Now, they drank coffee and studied their cards, the conversation gentle in the gloomy canteen building.

"Yeah, I told them," Heavy was saying, "there's no knowing how five days on a ship will affect a man. Particularly the acrobats. That first London show is two days after we land. Maybe it is too soon."

Klondike shook his head. "Hell, half the guys probably just want to go off sightseeing. Like a bunch of regular tourists."

Heavy studied his old friend over his hand of cards. "You remember our last time in England, Kal?"

"How could I forget? June of '43. Operation Falcon. Dropped into the Netherlands overnight." He smiled, lost in thought. "All those Brits. Jesus! They were like gentlemen at a society ball, so polite and aloof. We were flying to possible death and destruction. It was incredible."

Heavy nodded vaguely, though a haunted look fell over his green eyes. "And our last time in Germany?"

Klondike looked down. "I guess there's some things no man can ever forget… no matter how hard we try." He shook the memories off with a mighty shrug. "I'd rather remember those dashing, daring Brits."

A grim silence fell over the table.

Heavy folded his cards in disgust after much deliberation. "I'm out," he mumbled. Then, he sat back. "And our Brit? This Union Jack Bannion. What of him?"

"He's been first class so far, Heav. Has already arranged work crews at each stop. All from his list of contacts, which sure is plentiful. He's also hired publicity teams to send the press releases and get the posters up."

Heavy chuckled. "Hell, Lacey won't like that!"

Klondike's ears perked up at a familiar sound. The clattering of high-heeled shoes along the wooden floorboards. "Speak of the devil."

He turned and his eyes lit up as Lacey Tanner waltzed in. He shook his head. Not even seven in the morning, and she looked like a countessa at a Venetian cocktail party. She wore a dazzling purple and green frock and smiled beautifully at them.

Just behind her, somewhat unnoticed, walked a small, balding man with spectacles, the circus finance manager Richie Plum.

"Welcome back Kal," Lacey gushed, arms wide.

"Lacey," he stammered, embracing her. "Are you a sight for sore eyes or what? You look truly beautiful."

She looked him over with a haughty look. "Why, thank you tiger. We were all beginning to get worried without our beloved leader around here."

Everyone seemed to suddenly notice Plum standing awkwardly to one side. "Hell, Richie, how are ya!" Klondike cried, shaking – and crushing – the little man's hand.

"Thank god you're back, Kal," he said softly. "I have a thousand questions about the tour. And need answers fast!"

Klondike nodded as he poured two fresh cups of coffee from a pot on the side. "And you'll get them, buddy. We got a lot of planning to do. You guys need to bring me up to speed on everything."

They all sat at the table, Heavy brushing away the cards and poker chips to one side. They would resume the game later, of course.

Lacey spoke first. "What did Daryl say, Kalvin?"

Klondike could not stop smiling. "Hell, he loved it. All of it. His legal team too. We're good for the dough. He'll give us even more if we's to ask, I reckon. Just make sure his branding is on everything, huh?"

She nodded. "I'll give it my own personal attention."

"Er, Kal," Plum said nervously. "I've been studying the books and, well, there are a few things I don't understand."

As Heavy rolled his eyes, Klondike frowned. "Like what, Richie?"

Plum gulped nervously, and looked around the deserted canteen. All was silent. "How in god's name did you manage to lease that ship?"

Klondike chuckled again. "Well, I'm not going to lie. It took a large chunk of our profits from last season, but I didn't expect to find a liner that so suited our needs."

The small man made to continue. "And then there's this train in England…"

"Alright, Richie, alright." Klondike patted him on the shoulder. "We'll go through everything, every single expense, later on tonight. I promise." He looked at the others, an inspirational gleam in his eye. "For now, we've got our staff meeting at nine. Anything I need to know?"

Lacey sipped her coffee. "I think everyone seems to be comfortable with the idea of Europe now. For many, it has taken some getting used to. Fortunately, a lot of the guys have been out there before. Some, like Gino of course, originated out there."

Heavy nodded, as he began shuffling the cards, a long-time habit. "Yeah. There are a lot of questions everyone keeps asking me."

Klondike squinted at him. "Like what?"

Heavy gave him a comical look. "Where the hell is Antwerp?"

Klondike laughed. "The jewel in the continental entertainment crown right now, my man." He looked mishchevously at his old friend. "Anything else?"

"Something's really bugging me," he mumbled.

"And what's that?"

"Do the TV networks in Europe cover baseball?"

Klondike shook his head, took off his fedora and shoved it playfully over Heavy's face.

They all laughed.

A mighty cheer went up as Klondike and his management team entered the central marquee at the camp, which served as the main talent meeting hall.

Although many of the performers had stayed at Rio Cristo all winter, most spent the off-season away from the circus, performing where they could, or involved in other enterprises.

Klondike had not seen many of them in weeks. He spent several minutes chatting with his troupe, exchanging pleasantries and offering warm welcomes.

Shapiro gave him an exaggerated bearhug, while Corky offered a pink handkerchief from out of his sleeve of tricks.

Then there were the Range Rider cowboys, seven men decked out in stetsons, jeans and western shirts. The Rocking Robins song and dance team, all girls in their 20s wearing sparkling red tracksuits and leotards. The Flying Batistas, a family of ground acrobats from Mexico. The Showcase Revue stars were also there – Gargantua, the 400lb 'human blob'; Goliath, the 7ft 3in giant, and Rumpy Stiltskin, the expert stilts walker and acrobat.

Newcomers for this season were the High Tops, an all-female team of gymnasts who created shapes and towers by climbing on top of one another. It had to be seen to be believed, Klondike often thought. Like everything around here.

He had a short chat with Tip Enqvist, the leader of the Daredevils, his motorcycle stunt team. In the space of two years, the Daredevils had established themselves as one of the circus's most popular acts, beloved by youngsters up and down the country. Their showpiece finale, the Globe of Death, was known as one of the world's most spectacular stunts acts, involving all six riders racing around inside a caged sphere.

Klondike also spoke briefly with Olsen and Suzi, who, as usual, entered the marquee together and sat side by side at the front.

With Heavy and Lacey seated behind him, Klondike finally waded out front, standing before the gathering.

"Alright," he called, holding up a hand and bringing the meeting to order. He was dressed in his "uniform" of brown leather jacket, black slacks and fedora. "Thank you for the kind words, folks. I hope you're all enjoying our private little utopia up here in the hills. And I trust everyone is well rested. I sure as hell hope so, cos pretty soon it's time… time to blow some trail dust!"

A small cheer and plenty of laughter broke out through the tent.

"The guys here tell me everybody is ready. That's great. The express train rolls up in just over two weeks, and then we're off to New York harbour, and our new temporary home… the Floating Top!"

A mild cheer ran through the assembled group.

"You know the schedule by now," Klondike continued. "London. Paris. Antwerp. Berlin. Geneva. Rome. And then, just like that, we set sail for home. All the better for our excursions abroad. And all set for the American season!"

"You're sure getting your money's worth out of us all," Corky quipped from the front row.

Klondike grinned. "Just remember, folks, we're gunna be a long way from home. In faraway lands. And we must never lose sight of the fact we are representing America. Every step of the way."

A general murmuring swept the room. Then, as if on cue, everyone started making excited exclamations.

"I can't believe I'm going to see Paris!" Suzi shrieked.

"Wait till they get a load of us," one of the cowboys cried.

"Thank you, Kal, for making this dream come true." This from Marion Kramer, leader of the Robins dancers.

Klondike nodded happily. "You all should have met Jack Bannion by now." He pointed to the Englishman, who stood against a support post at the side of the group. "He is our European consultant. Anyone has any questions about the cities we're playing, or about the people, the language, the culture… hell, anything. Jack is your man."

A sea of faces turned to Bannion. He smiled and gave a nod.

"What about ticket sales?"

Klondike looked back to the front and groaned slightly. Enqvist was standing, a slight sneer on his face. The stunt rider had come over from Norway with his crew in '56. An outstanding performer, he was unfortunately something of a trouble-maker and had an attitude. With his premature white hair and thick black stubble, he looked a hard case.

"They're selling," Klondike said. "For all dates, as far as we know. Whether we will enjoy the sell-outs we are used to here, well, there's just no saying or knowing till we get out there, Tip."

Enqvist looked around ruefully. "The better the ovation, the better we perform. That's what me and the boys have found."

Lacey joined Klondike at the front, as she often did in these moments. "Tip, you and your boys are a national sensation," she gushed. "And, might I add, soon to be an international sensation. Everyone will be mesmerised, as they always are. Everywhere."

This seemed to appease him. He sat down again.

He was replaced on the deck by Shapiro, who jumped up and turned like a Shakespearean actor performing a climactic scene.

"Chairman," he cried, "I think I speak for everyone, all assembled talent, when I say we are all thrilled by the tour. By the chance to perform for an international audience. I for one salute your grand vision and spirit of adventure. Bravo, chairman, bravo."

Klondike tried not to laugh. "Thank you Gino."

"Just you wait," the flyer was saying, chuckling to himself. "Just wait until we hit Roma, my chairman. The people will see their Gino again. After all these years. Santamaria! I wish papa were alive to see it. A moment that will live with me forever."

"As always," Klondike said, "we are honoured to have you, Gino."

Goliath stood next, a look of confusion on his face. The giant was known for his feats of strength, but was ultimately a hillbilly farmer who had not left his home state of Arkansas until he was 28.

"I'm scared, Mistuh Klondike," he mumbled in his deep south accent. "Travelling all over America is one thing. But this! Europe! I just can't… I can't…" he couldn't finish the sentence.

Heavy leapt up beside Klondike. "Relax, big guy!" he cried playfully. "You'll be worshipped and adored over there. I bet no one in Europe has ever seen a real giant. You won't want to come home!"

Goliath chuckled and looked around. Everyone smiled up at the big man.

Klondike held up a hand. "OK folks. That's it from me for now. Glad to see there are no big issues here. Now, I'll be checking in on each and every one of ya in the days ahead. Any grievances you may have, that's when I want to hear it. But, for now, keep practising and stay focused. Lacey will have some press duties for you all. Other than that, enjoy yourselves."

He thought for a moment, as the sea of faces waited curiously. He held his arms aloft. "Viva Europe!"

Everyone laughed. The performers slowly rose and slipped away, the mood jovial and relaxed. Just as he wanted it.

As the talent left the tent in a great flood of humanity, Klondike turned to Heavy and Lacey. He winked. "Let's get to work."

Several hours later, Lacey was in her cabin going through her mass of press materials. The releases were all sorted into separate folders, one for each city. Early copies had been sent out a month ago, but a second version was to be despatched via airmail tomorrow.

She had a long-time habit of rechecking every press release, over and over again, until time ran out.

Now, she sat back in a leather armchair in the corner of her small living room and absently groped at a cup of coffee as she read one of her pieces for the umpteenth time.

So engrossed was she in her work, she failed to hear a light rap on the front door, which then creaked open.

"Hope I'm not interrupting?"

Lacey looked up in shock, then smiled slightly as Olsen peered in. She put the paper down. "Of course not, Roddy. Come on in."

The youngster slipped inside, silently closing the door. When he faced her, he simply stared, as if breathless.

She studied him awkwardly. "Anything wrong, champ?"

Theirs was an unusual relationship. Lacey and Roddy shared a mutual, unspoken attraction with each other. But both were frightened that any romance would kill their unique business understanding. Lacey had been directly responsible for Olsen joining the circus several years earlier, and had taken on a personal management role for the ventriloquist in the years since. Olsen was all too aware that the ace publicist had masterminded his rise. Neither wanted to jeopardise such smooth success with anything untoward – despite the fireworks. Both were also well aware of the near 20-year age gap between them.

Olsen finally spoke. "It's just… well, y'know, some things I just want to run by you, Lacey. And only you. Y'know, like you always said I should."

She stood and approached him, a motherly concern clouding her beautiful features. "Of course. What is it, Roddy? The tour? Europe?"

He nodded innocently.

Slightly unnerved, she guided him into a desk chair and perched on a dining table, leaning over him.

"Tell me."

He looked at her. "Can you guess?"

She thought for a moment, then raised an inquiring eyebrow. "The language barrier?"

"Right. And not just the language. Or languages. But everything. The culture. The manner." He shook his head suddenly. "Hell, Lacey, I just don't know if these people are gunna get my act at all. What if no one understands a word I'm saying?"

Lacey absently lit a cigarette, as if in a trance. "It's a valid point. I must admit, it has given me plenty to think about. But, then again, the whole show is in English. Everyone has the same problem."

"Yeah, but no one else's act involves them standing on their own for 20 minutes talking. And singing!"

"But Roddy," she breathed, her eyes imploring him to listen. "It is your skill that makes you a star. The fact you bring your puppets to life. The way you create lifeforms out of dummies. Your voice manipulation. Audiences will be amazed wherever you go. Just as they have been here."

"I just don't know," he mumbled, looking downwards.

"Your act on this tour is going to be more song-based. The songs you'll be performing with the puppets are hits everywhere. Everyone in the world knows them. And they will be mesmerised seeing them performed by… Rusty Fox, Napoleon and Tony Tan. Of course they will!"

He seemed to lighten up, just as he always did after a talk with the publicist. Her hold over him was quite extraordinary.

He grinned, looking every inch the teen idol again. "I sure hope you're right, Lacey."

She eyed him sternly, feeling him squirm under her glare. "Now… was there anything else, champ?"

He looked downwards. "I'm real glad you're coming on this trip."

"Of course I'm coming!" She stood opposite him and smiled thinly. "And I just cannot wait to see you do your thing in all these exotic places."

Olsen smiled with glee. Both looked into each others' eyes. Then, almost subconsciously, they joined together in a mighty embrace. As they hugged, she patted him lightly on the back.

"You're the best, Roddy," she whispered in his ear. "The best. The best. The best."

Outside the cabin, Suzi Dando had been wandering around the camp absently, looking for Roddy.

Suddenly hearing his voice, she had peered through the window of Lacey's cabin, just as the embrace unfolded.

Suzi watched, stiff as a statue, and heard Lacey's silky voice as she held him. "The best…"

Looking no more than a child, Suzi looked downwards glumly. Then, she jumped out of the soil pathway encircling the cabins and ran.

Racing through the central garden and past the trailers, she headed for the hillside.

It was getting dark when Klondike ducked out of his small bungalow at the top of the camp later that day.

The crickets were just starting to chirp, a pulse-like sound that would punctuate the still atmosphere until dawn.

He wandered casually across to the old wooden fence that encircled the entire camp. It made the place feel like a ranch from days gone by, as if his kingdom had been corralled off from the rest of the world.

Klondike pulled a Virginian cigar from his inside breast pocket and lit up delicately, relishing the smell and taste as a cloud of purple smoke rose into the evening haze. He looked around idly, at the horse blocks to his right. The endless rows of trailers and huts. The tall hills encircling them.

Home. His true home was on the road. But, four or five months a year, this was his sanctuary. And boy did it feel good to be back.

His temporary reverie was interrupted by the sound of approaching footsteps. He turned towards the horse stables, and saw a figure emerging from behind the trailers, heading his way.

Lost in shadows, the person looked like a gunslinger from the old west. Decked out in rawhide boots, leather chaps, buckskin shirt and white stetson, the newcomer completed the vintage look by hauling a saddlebag over one shoulder.

Klondike stared at him in shock as the two figures took stock of each other in the evening haze. Then, he smiled.

"Duster," he said happily. "You made it."

The stranger stepped forward, out of the shadows, and smiled. He had leathery skin, twinkling blue eyes and greying hair.

"You betcha, Kal. Sorry it took me so long. I rode in on my appaloosa Jezebel. The old girl got a bit ornery down in the valley, so we had to have a day's rest."

Klondike shook his head. James 'Duster' Williams was a cowboy of the oldest school. Still riding around the country on horseback. Sleeping under the stars. Unphased by fame, money or just about anything else.

"It's good to see ya, Duster," Klondike said. "And we are honoured to have you, a genuine cowboy legend, here with us at our big top."

The older man cackled. "Hell, don't believe what folks say about me. I'm just a simple country boy."

They shook hands warmly, Klondike marvelling at him as he gazed into his blue eyes.

"No, this is a great moment for our circus. I can't thank you enough for joining us for the season."

Williams looked around at the camp. "From what I hear, son, this is quite a season you got yourself planned."

Klondike nodded. "Across the pond, into Europe. The new frontier, I'm calling it."

"Haven't been to Europe in several years now. The folks out there seemed to get a kick out of my act. Back then." His eyes took on a sad, melancholy look. "All seems like a lifetime ago now. When I think about all that's happened since those days…"

"People loved you then, Duster. And they will do again."

The old cowboy huffed. "I sure as hell hope so, Kal." He took on a solemn look. "Listen, I appreciate you giving me this chance, son. I really do. I've straightened myself out these past few months, I just needed that chance to perform again. You've given me that, Kal, and I won't let you down."

Klondike patted his shoulder. "Forget about it."

Then, he began leading Williams back towards the centre of camp.

"Now, let's get you started, Duster. I've got a trailer for you to stay in. If you unpack your, er, saddlebags, get comfortable, then head on over to the canteen in the pavilion down there. Cookie will fix you something up. Just tell him Kal sent ya."

Williams licked his lips as they walked down the path in the growing darkness. "Treated like a king! You're too kind."

Klondike laughed. "You are a king… king of the cowboys!"

CHAPTER FIVE

The following morning, there was a sea of activity across Rio Cristo as preparations began in earnest for the big departure. The famous Barrowman Express train was coming next week, transporting everybody to New York, where they would set sail for England.

Everyone seemed to have a spring in their step as they went about their business in the beautiful spring sunshine.

The luscious green hills that encircled the camp seemed almost to shine as the sun rays illuminated the meadows.

Teams of roustabouts, many of whom had been at the camp all winter, were transporting equipment across the grounds to holding stalls close to the branch railway, so they could easily be placed on to the train.

Back and forth the workers roamed, led by the circus foreman, Jim McCabe. A great bull of a man, never seen without his porkpie hat, McCabe was like a trail boss of old times, whipping his men into shape and barking out orders incessantly. A fine leader of men, he waded around briskly, checking everything, a clipboard in one hand as he ticked off tasks and duties.

None of the surreal sights of the circus, that seemed to bloom all around, bothered him in the slightest. Cowboys rode around on horseback. Men bombed along on unicycles, juggling pins or balls. Clowns rushed around like children at a birthday party. Acrobats vaulted past, practising their routines. And women in bright leotards performed aerobics routines in a long line out in the gardens.

McCabe watched as a flatbed truck rumbled past him, carrying the circus's shooting gallery stall.

Heavy Brown eased himself beside him and looked up with glee at the shooting targets as they rolled past in the truck.

"Ready for Europe, Jim?"

The foreman was impassive. "Ain't no different to what we do every summer, the way I see it. Just got a long boat trip first."

Heavy smiled. "You, er, ever been overseas, Jim?"

McCabe snorted, annoyed. "Not since the war. You?"

"The same." He watched as a group of roustabouts, none of them older than 30, all walked across to a small stone platform, ready to unload the shooting gallery.

Heavy squinted into the sun. "You think we'll still be able to get hands signed up in all these cities?"

McCabe remained utterly placid. "If there's one thing I've learnt down the years, Brown, it's that wherever there's a circus, there's people. If you bring it, they will come. Anywhere on earth a circus tent pitches up, you get a crowd. Children come to look. Adults come to see what entertainment is on offer. City officials want in on it. And, of course, locals come… for work. There are always jobs on offer. It's happened at every single town we've ever worked. Since day one. Ain't no reason that won't continue overseas, you ask me."

Heavy felt strangely lifted by McCabe's speech. Privately, he had been deeply worried about selling tickets in Europe. It was all part of the gamble. But the 'circus effect' was a factor they were all banking on.

"Y'know, Jim, you've just put into words what we're all thinking. And hoping for."

McCabe seemed uninterested. "Say, is Kal coming down here? Before long, these men are gunna run out of work. We've shifted everything into place. What else needs doing around the camp?"

Heavy huffed. "Are you kidding? Right now, Kal is meeting his three aces – Shapiro, Olsen and Enqvist. Trying his darnedest to make them all get along. Again!"

McCabe snarled in disgust. "Jesus! I don't envy him, trying to talk sense into those three schmucks."

Heavy baulked. "They're national superstars, for Christ sakes!"

"Yeah, well, they look like morons. All dressed up in those ridiculous outfits. Prancing around like damn showgirls." He shook his head in contempt.

Heavy tongued the inside of his mouth. "Er, Jim… do you actually like it here? At all?"

McCabe finally cracked a smile. "I'm crazy about it," he said in a mock whisper. "Just keep the talent away from me. And leave the real work to me and my boys."

With that, he wandered across the gravel to the flatbed truck, joining his men.

Heavy could not help but chuckle as he watched him. "It's all a show," he mused to himself. "And the show hasn't even begun yet."

At that moment, Klondike was prowling around his office on the first floor of the pavilion, looking somewhat like a caged lion.

"Listen, guys. I need you three to set an example. To lead the way, if you like. The rest of the talent look up to you. I need you! I need you to get along, and inspire us all."

Seated in front of his desk in office chairs were Shapiro, Olsen and Enqvist. All looked at him earnestly, a little ill at ease though.

Klondike had eagerly anticipated this meeting with his three biggest-drawing stars. He had pencilled it in for as soon as he got back to camp. There would be no time for tensions and rivalries in his troupe, not on this tour. But how many times had he told himself that? he wondered.

Predictably, Shapiro spoke next. "You can count on me, chairman. The people, the roster, all can count on me. You trust me to lead the talent, Kal, and I am comfortable with this role."

Enqvist smirked. "He's not counting on you, flyer. He is trusting all of us to lead." He looked up at Klondike pleadingly. "Everything will be fine, Kal, if you just leave me and my boys to get on with it. And keep these… comic book characters out of our way."

Shapiro made to speak, but Klondike held up a hand angrily. "You see, that's just what I'm talking about, Tip. Why do you have to set people off? I don't want feuds and conflict. I want support, appreciation for each other's acts. A brotherhood."

Shapiro was eyeing the stunt rider shrewdly. "I say we all just do as he says, and stay out of his way. I'm happy with that."

Olsen merely ran a hand through his shiny blond hair, looking like he would rather be anywhere but here.

Klondike eyed the three men. It was hard to summarise his emotions at that moment. He felt so privileged to have them under his big top. And it was such a rarity to have them together like this, in one room. In many ways, it was a surreal experience.

There was Shapiro in his orange tracksuit, Olsen in a flowery hula shirt, and Enqvist in yellow coveralls. All looked up at him, waiting for a breakthrough.

Klondike thought for several moments, seeking inspiration. Finally, he spoke in a grand voice. "You remember Superstars and Stripes last summer, Gino? What you did for Roddy at the end? You held his arm aloft, in triumph. Let him have the applause. God damn it, that was one of the most beautiful moments I've seen in 20 years in the circus industry. Now, that… that is what I want to see more of."

Olsen, who hadn't said a word up to that point, nodded vigorously. "It was one of the happiest moments in my career. In my life."

Shapiro narrowed his gaze. "Si. It was a big moment. But… you want such acclaim, such a grand gesture, you have to earn it. Everybody has to earn it, amigo. That means you are at the top of your game every single night, in every single city."

Olsen shrugged. "You think the Europeans will like my… 'dolls' now?"

Shapiro was unrepentant. "I do not. The European audience is more intelligent, more cultured. Civilised. And I should know, dammit. I have played to enough of them."

Olsen rolled his eyes. He felt the anger rising. "Listen." He eyed Klondike now. "I have given it my all every single night for Klondike's Circus. Ever since that first, breakout show in Eureka. I was the ringmaster that night, remember? I have given 100 per cent for every single show since then. I've done it for the circus. And for the fans. Without them, I would be nothing."

Klondike nodded slowly. "Well said." He looked at each of them, sat before him like unruly pupils in the principal's office. "That is what we want. And respect. For each other. For the whole troupe. We are team-mates. The better we do individually, the better off we are collectively." He leant his palms on the desk. "Now, what I need from you three is teamwork. No nonsense, no feuds. Just support."

Shapiro pumped a fist. “You said it, chairman. Now, just get me on that boat!”

Olsen smiled thinly. “Whatever you say, Kal. I’m just happy to be here.”

Klondike nodded. “I know, kid. Thanks.”

All eyes turned to Enqvist, seated on the end. The Norwegian sat with his arms folded, looking strangely detached.

“What do you say, Tip?” Klondike probed.

“Listen,” he blurted, “as long as we have booze, broads and our bikes are kept in good condition, me and the boys will be fine. We ain’t looking for no trouble.”

“Good.” Klondike nodded enthusiastically, and settled down into his seat behind the desk. Subconsciously, he reached for his cigar box in the top drawer. “OK. Get back to practice, guys. I’ll see you later.”

He watched with interest as the trio all rose and hurried out, leaving in absolute silence.

Klondike leant back in his chair and thought deeply.

A breaking point. There is always a breaking point, he told himself. An event. A happening. A change in circumstance or personnel. Every season, it seemed to happen. That moment that turned his star names against each other. He almost knew it was coming. In one form or another. Right now, he could only speculate as to what it might be. But he couldn’t help trying to gauge the future. What might happen this season? There was always something. But with the tour being in another world, where customs were very different, it was hard to tell what this season’s breaking point would be.

After all, they came in many different guises.

Her name was Carla Selenzy.

As she walked into the saloon, a mighty hush descended over the barroom. It was followed by a series of excited whisperings, all appraising and singling out the new arrival.

She had spectacular, twirling black hair and a mischevous, almost comical expression, enhanced by ebony eyes and full lips. Dressed in a gold frock that would have been suitable for entry into a royal ball, she seemed to drift effortlessly through the air, her legs barely moving at all.

The San Tomarino Speakeasy in Venice was considered the height of contemporary chic in Italy at that time.

High-level politicians and city officials mixed with the cream of high society – stage stars, impresarios and nightclub performers.

Carla had her pick of them on this night. Every table she drifted past was full of admiring gazes, both male and female. After all, her face and her fame were known to all.

But it was a lone figure seated in a booth at the back of the bar that suddenly grabbed her full, undivided attention as she roamed around, exchanging pleasantries.

She smiled seductively at the older man in the bronze suit, who held a cane before him, a glass of red wine at his side. His face beamed as the woman approached his table.

"My Duce," she proclaimed in a light tone, "what a beautiful surprise."

She held out her hand.

Carmine Courtinio clasped it and kissed the knuckles softly.

"Carla," he breathed, "as always, a sincere delight."

She sat opposite him in the booth. A waiter appeared instantly.

"Espresso Martini," she said without looking.

Courtinio was grinning like a cheshire cat. "My darling. I swear, you are ageing in reverse. How can you look so angelic, so pure, even now? After all these years."

Carla removed a cigarette from a silver box and held it between her lips, waiting. With a nod, he lit it. "I live right," she said huskily.

Courtinio laughed. "You are like the wine, eh? You sweeten with age."

She threw him a haughty gaze. "Much like yourself!"

He clapped his hands in delight. "Alas, no more, sweet Carla. These days, I feel my age."

She looked around, uninterested, as the waiter brought her drink in a tall glass. "Alright," she said finally. "You came to me, Carmine. I presume you need me?" She took a long sip, savouring the taste. "The season is a month away still. Has there been… a change of plan, perhaps?"

Courtinio's smug smile dropped. The act slowly disintegrated. It had only been a matter of time, he told himself.

"For you, yes."

She rolled her eyes, dragging on the cigarette. "And so you came to snare me, Duce…"

He swatted a hand through the air, tiring of it all. "You are aware of the imminent arrival on our shores of the American touring company, Klondike's Circus?"

"Of course, it is big news, no?" she said quickly. Then, she smiled in understanding, nodding slightly. "Aha. Of course. Why, I should've known." She thought for a moment, as if trying to recite an old line. "The forbidden gate, right?"

Courtinio sneered. "Beauty and intelligence are such a rare and welcome combination, my dear. Intoxicating, in many ways." He nodded. "Yes, these Americans now think they can walk through the forbidden gate. Into our domain. And, what is more, they believe they can reign here."

Carla looked around the jazzy barroom. "And our Circo Grande cannot have that, right?"

"This is an invasion, in the name of God!"

"So, you're going to repel these, er, raiders? Like the Romans with the Vikings…"

"Nothing so bold, my dear." Courtinio produced a plain white handkerchief and dabbed at his mouth. "I am sending in my men. Tarz is going with them. They will make sure this Klondike turns around and withdraws his project. Before the tour reaches even Berlin."

She eyed him dourly. "How gallant."

"But," he continued irritably, "the beast may of course fail me. Which is why I have come to the beauty. The queen of Circo Grande. Darling Carla."

He smiled at her beautifully. She rolled her eyes again, impatient and restless. "And there it is…" she whispered dryly. "All the talk and pomp. The grandness. And yet it all comes down to this. The usual deal."

Suddenly, Courtinio frowned and leant forward. The charm and poise dropped instantly, replaced by the snarling manner of an underworld monster. “Need I remind you, sweet Carla, of our business understanding?”

She trembled slightly. “No, my Duce.” She shook it off. “Continue.”

Now, he looked her over with power, utter control. “Your orders are to infiltrate Klondike’s Circus. On my word. Create an audition, an opportunity, if you will. Showcase to his people your sublime circus skills. Seduce them with your trapeze, you will. Say you want in. Having an Italian national on board will no doubt prove appealing for the Americans.”

She stared at him in dismay. “You… you want me to work for the Americans?”

He smiled shrewdly. “Yes, at first. But then, you really go to work.” He laughed aloud, as she studied him curiously. He finally stopped chortling and lectured her in a smooth tone. “Everyone in the industry knows that Klondike is fully dependent on his two aces. The flyer Gino Shapiro, and the Puppet Master Roddy Olsen. Their rivalry has threatened to derail the whole outfit, that’s what they say. Jealousy. It is at the root of all of this. And so… we exploit it.”

Carla shrugged. “I’m afraid I don’t follow, Duce.”

“Come off it, Carla,” he said with contempt. Again, he patted his mouth and cheeks with the handkerchief. “You know what has to be done. This Shapiro is a notorious womaniser. A dog. He will pounce on you like a rowdy alleycat. Work him, work Olsen. And then…” again the slow, irksome laugh. “Sit back and watch what you have so skilfully created.”

Deflated, she glared at him. “What exactly am I creating?”

He stared back, his pointed features like stone. “An implosion.”

“A what?”

“A catastrophic crash that occurs from within. And then bleeds out. Until there is nothing left.”

Chilled by the deathly words, Carla decided to remain silent. She took a long pull on her Martini, gulping nervously. Then she reached for another cigarette, and lit it herself.

He eyed her speculatively. “You can… handle this, Carla?”

She blew smoke out towards the bar. “Of course, my Duce.”

There was silence for several moments.

Finally, Courtinio downed the rest of his wine and stood. Delicately draping a beige coat over his slight shoulders, he stepped around the table and hovered over her. Then, he knelt down on one knee and placed his hands over her ears, cradling her beautiful face. He whispered softly.

"I love you so much it is disgusting, sweet Carla."

Then, with a flourish, he was off, striding across the bar floor and out into the night.

CHAPTER SIX

Pablo's was a downtown bar and restaurant located on the main drag in Verndale, about 10 miles north of Napa.

The former farming community had become a major post-World War Two boomtown after a surge of new immigrant arrivals and a vast expansion of modern stores and business ventures.

Pablo's catered for many of the 'new wealth' residents, and scores of out of town visitors.

Jack Bannion sat at the bar, working his way through his third bottle of beer of the night.

As various well-dressed patrons sat around him in booths discussing business deals, the Englishman perched on a bar stool as if in a dream.

As he drank he reflected on the whirlwind few months he had experienced. It had only been last October when he'd been in a bar much like this one, only on the other side of the world, in the west end of London. The UK representative of Addison Incorporated had approached him with the offer of the consultancy role at Klondike. At the time, he was working as a promoter for Avalon Entertainment, a British circus firm planning a South Coast tour. Now, he was on board with one of the biggest promotions in the world, embarking on a tour of Europe.

Incredible, he mused. His life had been turned on its head. Again.

As he sat there pondering his good fortune, he became aware of a presence approaching him at the bar.

He looked up. And then shuddered with excitement.

A startlingly beautiful woman with long straight blonde hair, turquoise eyes and pale complexion took the barstool next to his. As she seated herself, she stared at him and smiled.

"What's good here?" she said softly. She wore a cream coloured dress that looked like it had just come off the shelf at Macy's.

Bannion grinned back. "I'm just having a beer."

She kept smiling. “Well, they say the Martinis here are the best in town."

She gave her order to an attentive young steward. Then she turned to Bannion again, eyes alive.

"Say... I know this sounds uncouth. But, don't I know you from somewhere?"

Bannion could not help but chuckle. In Verndale of all places. He had been recognised. Surely there was a mistake.

“Well, lady," he muttered. "Maybe. You ever been to Europe?"

She leant forward, her eyes sparkling. "I spent a year in England. When I was younger."

Bannion nodded. “Well, that may be it. I used to perform in a circus. Several circuses in fact." He moved a little closer and offered his hand. "The name is Bannion. Jack Bannion."

The woman froze and then seemed to gasp. "Union Jack Bannion!"

He stared at her in shock. "Er, yeah. That's the one. You know me?"

"But of course," she gushed. She composed herself as the Martini arrived. She was smiling coyly. "You're looking at a circus super fan. I know all the shows. All the stars. You were one of the greatest flyers in England. In Europe! I can't believe it! And now you're here in Verndale, California."

“Well, what are the chances? I'll drink to that..." he raised his beer. "Miss..."

"Carson. Julia Carson." She raised the Martini. They touched glasses. She laughed.

"It's really you," she exclaimed. Her eyes seemed to twinkle at him. "Oh my lord, that accent. I just love it. Like an old theatre actor."

He chuckled again, still a little off-balance. "Back home it's the voice of a commoner. Or so they all tell me.”

"Say," she blurted at him, sipping the Martini, "didn't I read somewhere that you're working for the Klondike promotion now?”

Yet again, he stared in shock. “Miss Carson,” he said in wonder, “you are incredibly well informed.”

She waved a hand through the air. “I told you, I follow all the shows… Jack. I know what goes on. Most seasons, I take in 10 or 12 shows. I have scrapbooks. Programmes. Mementoes.” She leant even closer. “I was very interested to read that Klondike’s Circus is going to Europe. That is huge!”

Bannion nodded absently. “Yeah. It sure is. Americans have been staying clear of Europe recently.” He had another swig, then studied the beautiful newcomer again. Her gaze was fixed on him, as if she were trying to communicate with her eyes. “You’re a fan of Klondike’s Circus?”

“Why, yes. Of course. It’s all so exciting. I saw the show in San Francisco last year. It is completely fantastic.”

He thought rapidly as they perched there at the bar, a sly grin forming at the ends of his lips. “If you’d like, I can arrange for you to have a VIP tour of the Klondike headquarters down at Rio Cristo. It will be just before we set off for New York. You can meet everyone. Take pictures. Get autographs. A free ticket for Frisco later this year.” He propped himself up on an elbow and smiled widely at her, their eyes locking again. “Now, what do you say about that… Julia?”

She ran a hand delicately through her hair. Then, she held his arm, softly near the wrist.

“Well, Jack, that all sounds very interesting. But…” a mischievous grin crossed her lips. “I’ve got to be honest, I’m more interested in you!”

Bannion almost laughed aloud at the words. They stared at each other. He winked. “The night is still young.”

Now, she laughed. “Let’s carry it on… elsewhere.”

“You know a place?”

“Sure. My hotel room. I’m staying at The Monarch. Across the road.”

Bannion could not stop smiling. Turning, he reached for a briefcase that had been lying on the floor next to his barstool.

“Julia,” he said with glee. “Has anyone ever told you… you say all the right things!”

She placed her arm through his and hoisted him up.

“Right this way, Union Jack.”

She opened her eyes. It was dawn. She had not been asleep. Just pretending.

Moving silently, methodically, she slipped out of the bed and crept to the dresser, pulling on a silk robe.

Still as silent as a hunting predator, she padded across the carpeting to the door. Then, she turned and looked back.

Bannion was fast asleep under the covers. Snug and away.

With a cold look, she left the room, pushed the door closed and paced silently across the lounge of her penthouse suite.

She headed into the bathroom, putting on the light.

There, on the cold marble tiles, she stood and stared at herself in the large mirror above the washbasin.

As she watched her reflection, the most extraordinary transformation seemed to occur. The lively smile, the full lips, sparkling eyes and excitable demeanour seemed to slowly fade away. As she stared back at herself, the turquoise eyes seemed to become darker, the lips paler and the face carried a look of unrest, of deep resentment and loathing. Suddenly, she had the look of a disturbed, twisted soul.

Her real name was Jenny Cross.

As she looked herself over, memories came flooding back to her like violent thunderclaps. Just like always.

She had been a flyer once. An apprentice to Gino Shapiro. And a lover of Kal Klondike. She had been the boss's girl. Practically royalty within that fast-rising circus promotion. Men pandered to her always. The troupe's women treated her like an untouchable deity. A fabulous life of fame and comfort had awaited her, after an upbringing of poverty and filth.

Then, everything had changed. Klondike broke off their relationship, citing an age old adage that management should never date talent. And sticking to the principle rigidly. Suddenly, she was just an apprentice again. Talked down to by managers and talent alike. And scorned by the only man she had ever truly loved.

The heartache and depression had quickly turned to anger, and then on to something else. A twisted, otherworldly feeling. One of cold, bleak malice. Jenny became obsessed with hurting Kal Klondike. And his beloved empire.

She had been coerced by a ruthless criminal madman, another figure who had a score to settle with Kal. Soon, she was being paid handsomely to destroy Klondike's Circus, from within. And then, what should have been her final, fatal act – causing Shapiro to fall from his trapeze ring to a gruesome death – had backfired. Then, all the world knew she was a saboteur. And a killer.

She had been arrested and then institutionalised. That had been three years ago. Three long, grim years.

Strangways Mental Hospital in Seattle had been a deep, dark abyss of horror. Her feelings and longings had spiralled out of control, as she struggled to balance a whole new range of emotions. Pain. Disbelief. Anxiety. Terrible, unspeakable thoughts, of suicide, of mass murder.

Jenny had been ritually humiliated and tormented at Strangways. By those who were supposed to help her. And all the while, dressed in those revolting lime green pyjamas, she had toed the line.

That had all changed when she was assigned a new therapist. Dr Howard Thornton. A vulnerable psychologist she had seduced and then used. And was still using. To get whatever she wanted.

He had secured her early release from Strangways last year. Set her up as his mistress, with her own apartment and trust fund. Just like that. Suddenly, Jenny was out again. Free. Purely because of one man's influence.

The game had begun. She coldly bled as much money as she could out of Thornton, opened up a fresh bank account, and then simply vanished – after casually robbing his home.

She moved away, some 3,000 miles, to New York. And a new life. Setting herself up with a wealthy new lover was simple. She didn't even have to try.

She was out. And she was free. To do whatever she wanted. And all she wanted now was the same thing she had desired for three years.

Vengeance.

Now, she looked herself over once more in the bathroom mirror. Her sheer beauty, presumptuous smile, shining blonde hair and natural allure were her chief weapons. She nodded to her reflection.

Jenny finally turned from the mirror and paced across the plush carpeting. At the dining table, she grabbed the briefcase Bannion had tossed aside when they had entered the suite several hours ago.

Sitting gently at the table, Jenny opened the case and was delighted to see a pile of papers and files.

With a deep breath, she began going through the documents methodically, picking up one page, skim reading through it, then placing it face down on the glass surface.

She had hit pay dirt. All the paperwork for the European tour was concealed within the raft of files. Invoices, cost projections, maps, some of the Tanner woman's press releases. There were even letters from various European firms confirming their involvement on the tour.

Jenny tried to remain calm. But her heart was pounding like a jackhammer. She could not believe her luck. The whole plan, everything, had come to glorious fruition. Closing her eyes, she reminded herself this was all merely an opening act.

With a raised eyebrow, she continued pulling out random files until she came to a selection of large black and white photographs. They all showed fields, fairgrounds, locations for the big top. Another picture showed a group of men in suits all standing arm in arm.

Finally, she reached the last photograph in the case. With a frown, she held the picture before her and studied it shrewdly.

She was looking at an ocean liner, possibly a freighter, she could not tell. It was painted plain white and looked like it was hosting a party when the shot was taken.

Her eyes took in a note written in felt tip at the top of the photograph.

The Floating Top.

She held the picture of the boat for several moments, her mind alive as her eyes twitched slightly.

Then, as if a switch had been pressed inside her mind, she suddenly began placing the items carefully back into the briefcase, in the exact order she had found them.

Moving fast, she slipped the case back atop the table and then frantically began getting dressed and gathering up her belongings.

All the while, she worked in total silence.

Rapidly piling her clothes into a carpetbag, she scanned the suite one last time, spotting a pair of shoes and quickly grabbing them.

Then, as if in a trance, she made for the main door and, just like that, she was gone.

"It's me. I have something for you."

"Well, it's about time. I was beginning to wonder if this plan of yours was all a thick ruse, Miss Cross."

"You couldn't be more wrong..." her voice was cold and monotonous, devoid of emotion and feeling. She stood in a callbox, watching people roam past during the morning rush hour. Dressed in an overlarge trench coat, she pulled the collar up over her face.

"You want to tell me more?" the voice on the other end of the line had a thick New York accent.

"Not here. I want to arrange a meeting. Can we say 10 days time? I'll come to you."

There was a slight pause. "Sure. It sounds like you've finally found something, Miss Cross?"

Her turquoise eyes were like stone as she watched a family – wife, husband and two kids – all walking down the sidewalk together. There was laughter, happiness.

"Yes..." she mused as she stared. "Yes. A breakthrough, you might say. Now, I know how this is all going to play out."

"Remember what I told you. This will get pretty expensive."

Finally, her face of stone evaporated. She slowly broke into a grin, an evil, twisted smile. Not of mirth, but of venom.

"Like I told you," she hissed, "money is not an issue here." She chose her next words carefully, as if playing a game with herself.

When she spoke, it was as if in triumph.

"Now, I can get anything that I want."

CHAPTER SEVEN

There was a carnival atmosphere at the Malloy Pier on New York's waterfront as a vibrant crowd of hundreds gathered at the harbour.

Scores of excited youngsters jostled for position among the thronging masses. A brass band played old patriotic numbers on an elevated gazebo on the water's edge.

And on a specially erected stage at the head of the harbour, a host of dignitaries were stood waving at the spectators. The stand was draped in Stars and Stripes flags and stewards stood by dressed as Uncle Sam.

Beyond the stage stood the grandest sight of all – the beautiful blue and white liner sat moored in the harbour.

The Floating Top had never appeared more majestic as it sat proudly next to the pier, tiny breakers lapping against its smooth sides. A huge banner sat pinned across its lines proclaiming, Klondike's Circus European Tour 1961.

Kal Klondike stood happily at the centre of the stage as the New York harbour master stood beside him, speaking into a microphone atop a lectern at the front of the elevated platform.

Behind him stood Shapiro, Olsen, Corky and Enqvist, all dressed in their circus costumes and waving at the fans all around.

A large ensemble of TV crews, cameramen, press photographers and reporters with recording devices all stood alert at the front of the gathering.

A cosmic energy seemed to pulse out from the excited crowd onto the stage, inspiring everyone.

Watching from a coffee stand to the side of the gathering, Lacey Tanner followed the proceedings with a sly grin. Publicity like this was dynamite, she mused, pure dynamite.

Beside her, Richie Plum stood transfixed, as if watching a political rally.

"I can't believe so many turned up here. Just to watch our ship depart!"

Lacey could not stop smiling. “It feels like a crusade, from days gone by. Americans embarking on a voyage into the unknown.”

The troupe had left Rio Cristo one week earlier for the three-day journey from California to New York. The circus train had done them proud, powering across the country in fine time on what was its longest single journey since its inception.

And now they were here, at the harbour, about to board the ship that would take them across to their new frontier. The departure press event had attracted more interest than anyone imagined.

Finally, up on the stage, the harbour master finished his welcome speech and introduced Klondike to the watching masses.

A mighty cheer erupted as the circus boss waded over to the lectern. He wore a tanned suit, his beloved fedora and carried his silver-topped cane, mainly for effect.

He held up a hand at the cheers, slightly taken aback by the hearty reception.

"Thank you everyone,” he drawled into the microphone, scanning the sea of faces before him. "What an honour it is to welcome you all here to Malloy Pier for our departure. It means a lot to us at Klondike’s Circus to see you all and we will take your heartfelt wishes and joy with us as we head across the Atlantic... and on to Europe!"

More applause broke out.

He smiled. "And I sure hope you all come back and see us on our return. And what's more when we come to New York in September for our show at Central Park. Our tour of the States this year will be real special. Spectacular! But, of course, first we are going to show all our friends across the pond just what an American circus is all about.”

He held up a hand as a series of whoops broke out. “And, I want you good people to know, we will never lose sight of the fact we are representing America abroad. And you can take that to the bank, folks. You have taken my circus to your heart over the years, embraced it, and I want you all to know… we love you all the more for that. So, god bless you all. And god bless America!”

A hearty cheer reverberated around the waterfront, as a cool sea breeze gently blew in.

"And now," Klondike continued, acknowledging the cheers, "I'm happy to take questions from you guys…" he waved a hand at the assorted press representatives at the front of the crowd before him.

A TV man holding a microphone shouted up first. "Do you really think European audiences will take to your show, Kal? Circuses are very different over there, they say."

Klondike nodded on stage. "It is hard to say, son. Tickets are selling well, so it seems there is an audience for what we do. I'm hoping to give them something different. Hopefully, it will be a success and we will come home all the better for it."

A female voice was next. "Have you ever been to Europe yourself?"

"Of course," Klondike said wearily. "During the war. I was posted across the continent for two years. But, alas, it was not a happy time, as I'm sure you will all appreciate."

Next, an oily-looking man holding a notebook spoke up. "And what do you make of accusations that you are walking through the forbidden gate, Klondike?"

He shrugged. "Well, I don't know about that. The circus is for everyone, people of all ages, races and nationalities. No matter where on earth they may be."

The same figure spoke again. "But some might say you are trespassing on others' patches, no?"

Klondike frowned. "Listen mister, the market is big enough for all of us to share, every circus in the world. No one has a claim over any specific territory. No one signed up to any treaty that says as much."

An eerie silence followed as boat horns blared in the distance.

"I have a question for Gino!" a woman carrying a giant camera called. "Gino, how does it feel to be returning to Europe?"

Shapiro, decked out in his trademark orange jumpsuit, held up his hands. "Thank you, thank you," he called out as he wandered up to the microphone stand. Everyone looked at him, bemused. "It is my honour, madam, to be returning to Europe, and in particular to the homeland of my father, Enrico Shapiro, who started out at the Azurri Circus when he was 12 years old. We will be playing at the Park Villa Borghese in Rome on this tour, where papa himself once appeared."

A polite applause followed. Then, another firm male voice called up from the press area. "And how about you, Mr Enqvist? Happy to be back in Europe?"

There was an awkward silence as everyone turned to the stunt rider. Looking like he was trying to outdo Shapiro in his yellow and black leather jumpsuit, Enqvist ambled over to the stand, looking once at Klondike, then speaking into the mic.

"Yes. The Daredevils are very happy. Although we are not visiting Norway on this tour, it will be, er, pleasant to see so many cities in mainland Europe again." He thought for a moment. "But, make no mistake friends, it is you – the American people – that have made us stars. Thank you, America!" He raised an arm in a kind of salute. A bemused smattering of claps followed.

Then, one of the reporters asked: "How about you, Roddy? What will Europe make of Rusty Fox and co?"

Olsen, in his trademark silver waistcoat, took his turn to walk to the podium. As he did, several females in the crowd screamed and gasped in delight. He grinned.

"The folks in England are going crazy for American rock n roll. But they have yet to see the biggest teen idol in the States… Rusty Fox, mister showbusiness himself. The crowds will go crazy, I just know it."

The teenaged section of the crowd laughed enthusiastically.

Another reporter cheerfully asked: "Anything new planned for the tour, Roddy?"

"Yeah," the youngster announced, "this!"

With that, he made a curious cupping gesture with his hands over his mouth. Then, a loud buzzing noise like a tannoy coming to life boomed out across the harbour front. It was followed by a feminine voice, the one that regularly makes announcements on the harbour PA system.

"Calling all passengers for the Floating Top departure for England. All aboard! All aboard!"

After a second of stunned silence, the crowd burst into rapturous applause. Olsen removed his hands from his mouth and smiled politely, waving to the fans.

Klondike grinned with glee at the reaction. The harbour master was gaping at Olsen open-mouthed. He glared at Klondike. "How the hell does the kid do that stuff?" he cried.

"Only he knows the answer to that," Klondike replied.

He looked out to the side of the assembled audience and caught sight of Lacey and Richie applauding by the coffee stand. He nodded at her. She waved wildly. That stunt from Olsen would make the six o'clock news bulletins. They both knew it.

Then, taking off his hat and waving it in the air, Klondike moved to the microphone stand one last time.

"Thank you very much, friends," he cried. "This is usually the moment when I say it's time to blow some trail dust. But, seeing as we are travelling over the ocean, all that's left for me to say is... let's blow some sea salt!"

The entire gathering stood and applauded, many crying out aloud and whooping.

Klondike waved again and, as if in finality, led his people towards the gangway that led down to their new home, the beautiful white and blue ocean liner bobbing just beyond them.

A half hour later, a screeching horn blared out across the waterfront, drowning out all conversation and commotion within a 100-yard radius.

The Floating Top was moving. Slowly at first, the great freighter, long ago transformed into a glitzy transporter, slipped away from the docks and inched into the New York harbour front.

Sticking to the official maximum speed of several knots as it crept away from the harbour traffic, the ship rolled lightly with the swells as it entered the traffic-ridden shipping lanes of the Atlantic.

Lurching quietly past oyster sculls, ferries, fishing craft, several yachts and a fleet of harbour patrol crafts, the Floating Top gradually picked up speed as it crept into open water.

Soon, the State of Liberty and Ellis Island were left in its wake as it exited the harbour and made for the deep blue beyond.

Most of the circus troupe – performers, staff, roustabouts – remained on deck throughout, clinging to the guardrail as they watched America disappear behind them.

It was an emotional moment, and one none of them would ever forget.

Their five-day voyage to Southampton, England, was finally under way. Before long, all anyone could see was the vast ocean. Nothing but a deep blue desert.

All around them. Forever.

Klondike and Heavy had stood, transfixed, at the deck rail as the ship had slowly floated away from the harbour.

Then, as they just about lost sight of land, both looked at one another. The deck bobbed up and down with the swells, and both men took a while to get used to the constant swaying.

"It's not quite the same as the train, is it?" Heavy whispered.

"No," said Klondike. "But, some things will remain the same, old buddy."

Heavy grinned. "Five card stud in your cabin?"

"You betcha!"

They both laughed and scuttled away from the crowd on the deck.

Heading down one of the liner's seemingly endless metal stairways down into the holds, they found themselves feeling giddy as they roamed across the ship.

The cabins were located on the next level down.

Klondike's cabin was small, sweet smelling and impossibly neat. A single bed, washroom, wardrobe and a round table with chairs. That was all the executive cabin consisted of.

They made themselves at home. Heavy shuffled the pack of cards sat idly on a sideboard, while Klondike pulled a bottle of scotch from a large suitcase and poured shots into two glasses.

They sat down and Heavy offered him the pack. Klondike smiled. It was another old season-opening tradition. One of them would cut the pack, and then make a prophecy for the year ahead based on the card. It had all started in their glorious, record-breaking 1958 season, when the cut card had been an ace.

Klondike said a silent prayer and reached for the pack. Pulling a card from the middle, he turned it and looked. Then, he frowned.

"How the hell did that get in there?"

Heavy frowned. "What is it?"

Klondike grimaced. "Must be a new pack. Or something…"

He flipped the card onto the table. They both gaped down at it in shock.

It was a joker.

The next morning was bright and breezy. The sea swells were smooth and the Floating Top bobbed gently as it cut a path across the Atlantic.

Many of the travellers had assembled on the open deck at the stern of the liner.

Most sat on deckchairs with books and newspapers, basking in the glorious, uninterrupted rays of sunshine.

Others slowly wandered about the ship, taking in the spacious canteen and bar area and the games room.

No one could resist the novelty of the ship, and many simply crept around the decks, gaping in astonishment at the endless ocean all around them.

Roddy Olsen was wandering about the gangways, offering brief greetings to the various staff members as he passed.

He came to an arched entryway that led to the sprawling open deck and looked out at the ship's wake beyond.

Leaning on the guardrail at the head of the deck, he froze as he noticed Lacey setting up a deckchair at the far side of the polished vinyl flooring.

Try as he might, he couldn't help staring at her.

She was wearing a beautiful yellow summer dress, with matching heels, and huge round sunglasses. Her deep red hair was loose and blew softly in the breeze.

Lacey eased herself into the deckchair, then pulled her handbag onto her lap. She pulled out a glossy magazine, then an exotic silver cigarette case. Fishing one out, she lit up and blew smoke leisurely into the sea air as she relaxed.

Olsen stood transfixed. He had never known anyone like her. Never knew such a woman existed. It seemed impossible.

He simply stood there dumbly, completely unaware of his surroundings.

"What's the matter, Olsen? Wanna jump ship with that dame?"

He turned suddenly at the sly voice from behind. Three men in lumberjack shirts and jeans were stood by the archway, sneering at him. Roustabouts.

Olsen shook his head. "Just taking it all in. I've never been on a ship before."

The lead roustabout sniggered. "Yeah, right. I saw what you was taking in, man. You and all the rest of us."

"What's that?"

The man grinned, showing a mouth full of yellow and brown teeth. "Miss Lacey." He cackled absently. "Go ahead, look son. We don't mind. Hell, we'll join you."

Olsen shook his head, looking the men over. "Hey, do me a favour would ya? Beat it!"

"Ah, come on," the first roustabout said. He looked around conspiringly. Then, he reached inside his shirt and pulled out a small bottle, three-quarters full. "Come on, Olsen. Why don't you join us? A little of daddy's juice will make you forget all about that dame. Will make the ship journey go a whole lot quicker!"

Olsen made to walk away, down the deck. One of the other three suddenly grabbed his arm. He looked down in shock.

"What's the matter, superstar?" the man rasped. He looked like a hobo, his breath reeking of stale whiskey. "We's not good enough drinking companions for you, eh?"

Olsen shook his arm free angrily. "I asked you to leave me alone!"

The three men slowly rounded on him. "Look at our superstar, boys," the first man said slowly. "Too high and mighty to drink with the help."

Suddenly, a new voice broke the tension.

"Why don't ya listen to the boy. He said beat it!"

They all turned back to the archway. An older man in sheepskin coat and stetson was walking down some steps leading to the upper deck platform. He leapt down and confronted the roustabouts.

"Now, get the hell out of here, dammit. Hell, if I told the boss three of his roughnecks were hassling his golden boy, he'd make you walk the plank. And swim back to New York!"

The trio all glared at the newcomer, who looked ready to throw himself at them in combat. "Hell, we's just playing," the lead man said.

"Well," said the newcomer in a steely tone, "no one wants to join in. Now, get outta here!"

"Come on," the man persisted. "I heard you like a drink as much as anyone…"

The stranger eyed him coldly. His voice was like a whipcrack. "Leave."

The trio all looked at Olsen, shook their heads, then ambled off, back down the gangway.

Olsen stared at the newcomer. "Thanks, friend," he blurted. "There was no telling how that was going to turn out."

The older man was watching them walk away. "Troublemakers. Every trip, every outfit, everywhere. Always troublemakers."

Olsen studied him. He had twinkling blue eyes, leathery tanned skin and grey hair under the white stetson.

"You're Williams, ain't ya?"

"That's right."

"It's a real pleasure, sir," Olsen said, offering his hand. "I was wondering when I'd meet you. The name's Olsen. Roddy Olsen."

Duster Williams laughed boisterously, accepting the hand. "Hell, son, you need no introduction. I know all about you. And, gee, your poster was on every wall in the camp back at Rio Cristo."

Olsen grinned. "I'm so glad you've joined us for the tour. Man, what a coup. The King of the Cowboys."

Williams rubbed at his jaw. "I told Kal he must be desperate, getting an old-timer like me on board."

They both laughed softly, leaning against the deck rail and gazing down at the placid ocean. The light sea breeze kissed their faces.

"Can I ask you a question, Mr Williams?" Olsen said.

"Duster. Shoot."

"OK, Duster. You've been to Europe before. What can we expect out there?"

Williams gazed out to sea, as if trying to find land. He squinted into the sun. "Well, son, it depends on how you look at it. For some, opportunity. For others, novelty. For others still, difficulty."

"And what about you, Duster?"

Williams closed his eyes to the sun. He tried to smile.

"Salvation."

Gino Shapiro waltzed into the barroom, dressed extravagantly as ever in a bright pink shirt and tight-fitting leather pants.

The area was essentially an extension of the main canteen, with an old-fashioned oak bar surrounded by tables and chairs in a semi-circle formation. The lighting was dim, and the polished mahogany tables seemed to gleam.

Shapiro offered pleasantries to several stewards and members of the Rocking Robins dance troupe, who were all seated at the far end by the door.

As he exchanged well wishes, he looked up at the bar and baulked slightly. Then, his face burst into an enormous smile.

There perched on a barstool, wearing a dazzling purple evening gown, sat Penny Fortune, his trapeze partner and carrier.

He approached the bar slowly, studying her. She had rich blonde hair and a California sun tan. After several months of having his advances emphatically rejected, he had given up on any ideas of romance and the two had developed a deep bond. This had only enhanced their trapeze act.

"Penny…" he breathed, grabbing her hand and kissing the knuckles. "Words fail me. As always. You look truly beautiful. Exceptional, my angel."

She shook her head and offered her usual reply. "As do you, Gino."

He took the barstool beside her and ordered a bottle of champagne from the youthful bartender. "How nice it is to finally spend some together… off the rings. Like this, in the bar, no?"

She was finishing off a cocktail and looked across as the barman popped the cork on the champagne bottle. "I guess I have been a little elusive since we got to Rio Cristo."

"You can say that again," Shapiro whispered, his giant brown eyes probing her deeply. "How I miss it, seeing you all dressed up, in all your beauty."

She rolled her eyes. "Alright, buster, that's enough. Don't make me storm off to my cabin."

He grinned mischeviously. "Only if I can come too, eh?"

Penny shook her head. It never seemed to end. She tried to change the subject. "Everyone seems to be enjoying this boat trip…"

Shapiro looked around the bar. The Range Rider cowboys were just entering, loudly laughing and making jokes.

"This is a real novelty for many, no? Setting sail like this."

The barman offered up two flutes. Shapiro passed one to Penny and held the other aloft. "To us," he said grandly.

They touched glasses. Then, he lightly grabbed at her hand.

"Listen, Penny. How are you? How are you holding up?"

She glared at him. "What? What do you mean?"

He waved his hand around, pointing to the sea beyond the bay windows. "On this ship? With the swells, the bobbing. No illness?"

She flushed. "No. Nothing like that. I've been on plenty of ships before."

"Good. This is good." He sipped his champagne. "You know, the seasickness, the stomach trouble… all of this. It can affect a flyer. Badly. That, how do you say, giddiness. It is bad, no?"

She shook her head, taking a long sip. "Think nothing of it, Gino."

He studied her, smiling hungrily. "You know, Penny… you truly are one of a kind. How blessed I am to have you as my carrier. The complete professional. Just promise me one thing…"

"What's that?"

He smiled beautifully at her. "Don't ever change, señora."

Out on deck, the sound of the waves gently lapping against the ship's sides were the only dominant sounds, aside from the gentle, constant hum of the engines.

It was a beautiful night, full of stars and a light mist. The Atlantic looked placid and serene under the starlight, like a blackened desert stretching to infinity.

Tip Enqvist breezed onto the topside gangway like a wraith in the night. Leaning against the superstructure, he fished a hip flask from the pocket of his windbreaker and took an almighty pull. Placing it back within his jacket, he then lit a cigarette and leant against the rigid metal cladding, enjoying the night.

Staring hypnotically at the endless ocean, he tried to remind himself he was embarking on a tour of Europe. His mind whirled as thoughts stabbed at him.

Just four years ago. He could remember it all so vividly. The Daredevils were performing at county fairs and motor racing circuits across Norway. Crowds of maybe 200 spectators would cheer happily.

Then, one day Enqvist had read about daredevil motorcycle riders making headlines in America. Performing outrageous jumps in Las Vegas and Atlantic City, to crowds of thousands. And, of course, appearing on television.

He had made his mind up then and there. Two months later, The Daredevils arrived in the USA. After just their third performance, at a carnival in Butte, Montana, he had been approached by Kal Klondike. And that had been the start of it all.

In the years since, they had performed on national television multiple times. They had starred in Las Vegas spectaculars and at major showgrounds and stadiums across the States. The group now had thousands of fans, many of whom dressed up in their yellow and black jumpsuits at the circus shows.

Enqvist smiled at the thought. After years of trying, he was finally famous. And fame was what he craved more than anything.

Suddenly, he was awoken from his reverie by an unpleasant spluttering sound to his right.

Frowning, he looked down the gangway. A figure was leaning over the railings and coughing over the side, perhaps even vomiting. He suspected the latter.

"Everything alright?" he asked as he approached the retching shape.

The figure stood slowly and faced him. Enqvist was surprised to see none other than Corky, minus the facepaint and bright suit. He looked terrible.

"Ugh, seasick. Again." Corky wiped a hand over his mouth.

Enqvist looked at him in near disgust. "That's too bad, clown. You, er, been this way the whole trip?"

"Pretty much. Since I could see the Statue of Liberty still." He made to take a step away from the rail, but swayed slightly. He grabbed the rail firmly. "I'm just not used to boats. Can't say I like em."

Enqvist nodded. "It's not for everybody, I guess." He thought for a moment. "I give you a tip, clown. Get yourself an apricot brandy at the bar. It's, er, good for the stomach, you know?"

Corky tried to smile. "Thanks, Tip. I'll do that. Anything to help."

Enqvist stared at him for a moment longer. Then, with a shrug, he simply wandered back inside.

Corky watched him go, somewhat bemused. He made to follow, but felt his head spinning. With a grunt, he swayed back against the railing and slowly slipped downwards, eventually sitting on the metal flooring.

He took some deep breaths, as he sat staring up at the moonlight.

"Roll on England," he whispered to himself.

Later that night, Richie Plum walked tentatively into the bar. It was a little more rowdy now, with most of the Range Riders, Rocking Robins, Daredevils and High Tops performers all seated, the laughter and storytelling in full flow.

As was usually the case, nobody seemed to notice Plum as he wandered in. He was dressed conservatively in a shirt and tie and attracted no well wishes or greetings of any sort.

Walking quietly to the bar, he ordered a cocktail and then looked around. Noticing Jack Bannion seated alone in the far corner, he made to join him, carrying his exotic-looking drink.

"Mind if I join you?"

Bannion, lost in his thoughts, looked up. "Not at all, Richie. Cheers!"

He raised the glass of beer he was nursing. Plum followed suit with his tall glass.

The financial whizz looked around at the crowded bar. "Feels like there's a party going on, but I wasn't invited." He looked at Bannion. "You seemed to be happy enough alone."

The Englishman smiled whimsically. "You could say that. These days, every time I drink I end up just sitting there, lost in my thoughts. Thinking about how my life has changed recently. All the wonderful moments I have been blessed with in America."

Plum tried to smile. "You enjoyed it? Being in the States?"

"Are you kidding? I love America. Everything about it. The culture. The people. The action. Not to mention the women…" he let the sentence hang as he swigged his beer. He half-smiled, lost in thought. "Even the ones that disappear."

"Oh," Plum said, trying to join in. He grinned. "That sounds like a tale, my friend."

"It is, Richie. But, alas, a sad tale. You meet the girl of your dreams. You hook up. Then, she vanishes without a trace." He shook his head with regret. "Oh, what kind of fool am I?"

Plum baulked. "Is everything ok, Jack?"

Bannion rolled his eyes. "Too many birds."

"What?"

"Girls. Too many girls." He ran a hand through his red hair. "They used to love old Union Jack. Back in the day. I had women queueing up to ask me out on a date. After every show. Paris, Monte Carlo, Barcelona… you name it."

Plum leaned in. "You were a superstar, Jack. That's… that's what happens to superstars."

Bannion sighed. "Well, that's all in the past." He raised his beer again. "Now, here's to the future. And what a future!"

Plum nodded. "I'll drink to that." Then, he said conversationally: "You're looking forward to returning to England?"

"I am," Bannion said slowly. He grinned across at Plum, slurping more of the beer. "It will be a glorious moment. Returning to my homeland… with the best damn circus in the world."

They both laughed.

"And the girl?" Plum said, eyebrows raised. "The one that vanished?"

Bannion drank some more. He stared into nothingness, looking lost. "Who knows? She's out there somewhere…"

A high-heeled boot stepped upon the old banner that had fallen from the stage.

Klondike's Circus European Tour 1961. The words were still visible, in bold red lettering, even though the banner was now muddied and ripped as it lay on the promenade, forgotten.

The stage was empty now. The bandstand vacant. Any semblance to the previous day's glorious scenes, when a huge crowd and media frenzy had witnessed the departure of the circus troupe, was long ago deceased.

Now, in the gloomy mist of the New York harbour, Malloy Pier was barren and devoid of life. Except for the two figures pacing slowly towards the water's edge, just beyond the stage that had yet to be removed. A man and a woman, slowly walking along the harbourside.

They were trying to picture the excitement and electricity from the previous day. It was impossible to even imagine such scenes now on the lonely waterfront.

Jenny Cross frowned as she walked over the fallen banner. Her boots scrunched over the fabric, walking over the painted letters.

She reached the edge of the promenade and stood just two feet from the harbour's end, where a short drop into the depths awaited. Gazing out into the sea mist, she looked straight ahead as she addressed her companion, who loitered just behind.

"So, you saw the whole thing, Zane. What do you think?"

The man joined her on the edge of the waterfront. He was a tall, well-built figure with dark hair and a beard.

"I saw a lot of things." His accent was pure New York, aggressive and snappy. "First circus boat I ever saw, I tells ya."

Jenny's icy gaze drifted from the sea to the man now beside her. "So? Can it be done?"

"Like I told you before. It's all gunna get real expensive for you, lady."

"Answer me, damn you! Can it be done?"

The man nodded. "Yes. It can be done."

She nodded slightly, her face emotionless and pale.

Jenny glared out at the ocean, as if some inner desire had now been satisfied. When she spoke, it was in a harsh, eerie tone.

"Then do it."

CHAPTER EIGHT

The Floating Top landed at Southampton three days later to a jovial welcoming reception.

Under a beautiful blue sky, the mighty liner docked and the circus troupe disembarked as a small crowd cheered happily and harbour stewards hastily directed everybody.

The dockyard seemed enormous, with liners and freighters everywhere, lined up like giant dominoes. The waterfront resembled a grey concrete jungle, full of shipping crates that seemed to be lying around for as far as anyone could see, in no apparent order.

But a small area had been reserved for the welcoming committee, with various officials and fans lined up, ready and waiting, then cheering as the circus folk began disembarking down the long steel gangplank.

Among the welcoming party was a group of local schoolchildren, who excitedly waved tiny Stars and Stripes flags at the new arrivals.

The enormous gangplank connected the ship to the dockyard, and once all personnel had walked down onto land, a mighty procession of vehicles soon dismounted.

Trucks, flatbed lorries and vans carried the equipment down to the dock, as the midway stalls, circus tent apparatus and various trailers of all shapes and sizes were unloaded.

Everything was directed towards a small enclosure at the end of the dockyard, where a branch line train stop appeared through the sea mist.

And there, waiting for everyone, was the old Imperial Circus train, ready for departure. It had all worked out as Bannion had promised.

The train looked old and slightly out of place, as if years had passed since it had last hit the rails. But it was adorned with Klondike's Circus posters and billboards and its vintage look actually seemed to fit in with its role as a pioneering circus transporter.

Like a giant conveyor belt, the trucks all unloaded the equipment into the great train's holding carriages.

Jim McCabe supervised everything. Like the rest of the troupe, he was enjoying the novelty of unloading his stalls and machinery from a great ship onto a train. And a new train none of them had ever seen before.

The Southampton dockworkers all happily joined in with the load up. Many of them tried chatting to the American performers, who all stopped and talked about the show, signing autographs and posing for photographs.

Klondike seemed to spend the whole time shaking hands with various dignitaries and harbour bosses, with a new figurehead approaching him every step of the way as he hurried from the gangplank to the train – a distance of barely 400 yards.

Behind him, Heavy followed, also shaking hands. After Heavy came Lacey, who rapidly handed out posters, flyers and programmes to just about everyone. She stopped by the cluster of schoolchildren, making sure each child got a poster of their own.

A great cheer went up as the Range Riders and their support staff led their team of horses off the ship and towards the branch line siding. To many, it was like a scene out of a Hollywood movie, seeing men dressed as cowboys holding horses by the reigns and leading them along to their next temporary home.

As the horses were housed in the train's stable blocks, the Range Riders joined the other performers in trying to locate their staterooms.

Before long, the immense loading operation was complete. Everybody was on the train, and every last piece of equipment safely housed.

As the assembled audience continued to watch the arrival of the American circus troupe, the spectacle was suddenly all over.

The dockworkers all left the hubbub of the train platform, doors were slammed shut up and down the great 34-carriage behemoth and then, as if to mark the next chapter of the journey, the deafening shriek of a train whistle rocketed through the sea air.

Every figure spread around the dock stopped what they were doing and watched as a great cloud of steam lifted into the air and the Imperial slowly inched forward, its great axled driving wheels stuttering into motion.

The train moved lightly down the siding and then, with another mighty toot of the whistle, it was gone. Disappearing in a cloud of steam and heat, the old express began chugging away towards the main line. And whatever lay beyond.

“Alright folks. It’s three hours to London. This is it!”

Klondike made the announcement as he stood at the head of his new stateroom, pointing to a series of maps and pictures pinned to a giant noticeboard behind his desk.

Heavy, Lacey and Plum all sat in wooden chairs before the desk at the far end of the room, while Jack Bannion – officially part of management for this tour – stood to the side, taking it all in.

The room was immaculately decorated, with fine carpeting, oak panels everywhere and even a crystal chandelier. Klondike again had to hand it to Bannion. As far as he could tell, the new on-loan train satisfied in every department.

Huge windows dominated the room’s perimeter, offering panoramic views of the English countryside as the train rolled along at a leisurely pace towards the capital.

Klondike used his cane to point at the largest picture on the board, which showed a huge green space on a map of London city.

“Hyde Park,” he drawled. “Almost two square miles of green parkland. We set up here…” he touched the end of the cane at a red circle drawn into the centre of the green area. “Near what is called Remington Crescent. Now, the park is a two-mile journey from Paddington Station. Once we pull in at the continental platform, we’ll disembark and everyone will assemble on a promenade we have reserved for the day. Then, the convoy of trucks will take everything, and everyone, down to the park. Me and Jack will ride in my jeep at the front. We’ll lead everyone down to the playing field.”

He eyed his principal lieutenants with a stern look. “Now, for Christ sakes, everyone keep in line. If there’s one thing you guys need to remember today, it’s this – make sure no one gets lost.”

"And," Bannion added, "drive on the left side of the road. We don't want a traffic accident on day one!"

"Right," Klondike said. He idly glanced out the window. All anyone had seen for 20 minutes were green fields, seemingly stretching into infinity. The train rolled along smoothly, hardly making a jolt at all.

"So," Heavy said, as if taking the baton from the boss, "we then have 48 hours to set up. Then, showtime." He thought for a moment. "I sure hope no one has travel sickness."

Lacey laughed in an airy fashion. "Ah, boys," she gushed, eyeing them all in turn. "It's all so exciting. London. England! We're here. After all that build-up. I can't wait to see the newspapers. Addison's man in London is meeting me at Hyde Park tonight. He's promised to bring all the English tabloids, with their circus previews. I can only wonder what they have printed."

Plum was a little more pensive. "I wish we knew how many tickets had sold."

Lacey nodded. "We'll know soon enough, Richie. The box office man will be waiting with his report."

Klondike was studying an official-looking document on his desk. It detailed the show's card for the evening.

"Medievel trumpeters heralding the start of the show. Gino wearing that king get-up, with his own fancy crown." He looked up at Bannion. "Jesus, Jack, I hope you're right about all this."

Bannion nodded coolly. "Like I said, Kal. The English crowd will love it. Americans acknowledging the British way… the royal family, the history. It is a proven formula. Like, er, paying homage."

Klondike nodded. "And putting the Range Riders on second to last? You still reckon the people will appreciate that?"

"On that, you're just going to have to trust me, Kal." Bannion paced across to the desk and studied the maps and pictures with Klondike. "Western movies and TV shows have exploded in Britain these last few years. Everyone loves them. I love them! Kids everywhere play cowboys and Indians. Actually seeing real-life cowboys, live and in the flesh, doing their thing on horses…" he shook his head. "It will be a dream come true for the paying spectators."

Lacey piped up. "Yes, yes. Our market research says as much."

Bannion nodded. "Throw old Duster into the mix, and you have a winning act. After all, he's one of the few performers we've got who has performed here in England."

Klondike watched the exchanges pensively. Then, he turned and went to the window. He watched with widened eyes as forests and meadows sped past outside. The sky was grey and irksome.

He whispered, just loudly enough for the others to hear.

"And so, on the other side of the world, our journey begins…"

The vintage Imperial express train rolled to a halt at a far platform within the sprawling Paddington Station complex in north-west London.

A giant cloud of steam seemed to settle over the carriages as the engines cooled and the commotion hushed.

Klondike opened up the door at the first combustible and looked out excitedly.

He was met by a seemingly endless parade of blank faces spread out all across the platforms and enclosures. Passengers, porters, ticket sellers, even the shoeshine boy on the corner... everyone was staring at the dazzlingly decorated behemoth.

Klondike nodded dumbly at the many onlookers. There was no applause, no band playing grandly, just endless blank faces.

He led the way down onto the platform, with Lacey, Heavy, Plum and Bannion all following. They were all slightly unnerved at the sight.

Then there was an almighty cracking sound as the holding carriages all opened up at once in a procession right down the length of the train.

McCabe appeared further down the platform and began directing operations. Soon trucks began pouring out of the holding stalls carrying the circus equipment.

Finally, an older man in stewards' clothing and a cap bounded over to Klondike, a huge grin dominating his features.

"Mr Klondike!" he barked in a rugged Cockney accent. "On behalf of National Rail, welcome to London, sir. It is an honour to have you here. Call me Grimes. Chief station foreman."

He extended a hand. Klondike shook it warmly. "Thank you, Mr Grimes. It is a sincere pleasure to be here. We have travelled across sea and land to get to England. It is a dream come true. Thank you for your welcome, my friend."

"That's alright, guv. Let my men help with the unloading."

"That's very kind. My thanks. We'll get our equipment outta your way as fast as we can."

He glanced again at the gallery of faces staring curiously at the train. Then he looked at Grimes. "This train will be parked here a few days. You think these guys will mind?"

Grimes bellowed with laughter. "Don't worry, Mr Klondike. Most of these people ain't never seen a circus train before. All we get up here are old steamers and inter-railers."

Klondike nodded blankly. With a glance at his lieutenants, who were slowly wandering around the station concourse, he nodded at the rail stewards, several of whom offered brief greetings. Then he fished an envelope out of an inside pocket and handed it to Grimes.

"Mr Grimes, please accept these passes for the show on Saturday night. With the compliments of all at Klondike's Circus. We thank you for your warm welcome and help."

Grimes snatched at the package. "Why thank you, guvnor. Wait till I tell the missus!"

The unloading operation was well under way, with McCabe barking orders at the roustabouts, who scattered about the platform like frenzied ants, everyone rushing.

Klondike signalled to Bannion and Heavy and they made their way to the carriage holding his jeep.

Lacey was walking slowly along the side of the train with Plum, both unnerved by the people all staring at them, as if they were aliens from another world.

"What ya think?" Plum asked quietly.

Lacey pulled her trenchcoat tighter around her. "Now I know how a zoo animal feels," she whispered.

"What gives with these guys?"

She laughed. "The magic of the circus train, my dear Richie. Most of these people have never seen anything like it. An express this size."

Plum looked about the concourse. Everything seemed dark, dank and gloomy.

"Lets get outta here."

She smiled. "Welcome to London, Richie. The most majestic city in the world."

He looked around. A station greengrocer in brown overalls was offering his wares to some of the roustabouts. They all argued.

He shook his head. “It sure doesn't feel like it."

Less than an hour later, Klondike led the convoy of trucks towards Hyde Park. Sat in his open jeep alongside Bannion and Heavy, he waved cheerfully at the scores of street dwellers who watched in wonder as the vehicles transported the midway stalls and trailers. It was a procession like no one had ever seen. This colourful convoy, from another world, carrying glitz, glamour and gaudy carnival attractions. The mass of trailers made the procession look like a line of caravans heading to a holiday park.

The circus vehicles dominated the roads.

It was barely two miles to Hyde Park, but the trip took forever. Traffic was heavy, and the convoy struggled to stay together.

Towards the back of the make-do caravan, the Range Riders rode their horses straight down the west London streets, attracting even more bemused glances.

Slightly ahead of them was a giant flatbed truck adorned with Daredevils signs and titles, carrying the famed stunt bikes and the Sphere of Death. At a cab in the back, Enqvist and his riders all rode along, standing and waving at the passersby.

Then, at the very back of the convoy, six beautiful custom-built Cadillac convertibles crawled along, looking as pristine as any motor the Londoners had ever seen. Each was painted a different colour, and carried the performers along, like astronauts on a parade after a triumphant mission in outer space.

Before long, gaggles of children flocked to the roadsides to watch. Many stared in rapt fascination and wonder.

The magic had started.

Up front, Heavy watched in awe as the giant whitestone buildings rolled by. He smiled as he spotted red telephone boxes, huge double-decker buses and helmeted policemen walking the beat.

He slapped Bannion on the back as they sat in the rear of the jeep.

"How does it feel to be back, Jack?" he wailed.

Bannion grinned. He felt like a medieval ruler at the head of a battalion of invading forces.

"Always a pleasure. Never a chore."

Before long, the jeep lurched onto a track that led to a huge gap between rows of trees, flanked by monolithic stone pillars. The three men all looked up with joy at a giant banner hanging over the entrance to Hyde Park.

It read: KLONDIKE'S CIRCUS – DIRECT FROM USA!

The jeep led the way into the park, which resembled an enormous field surrounded by overlooking apartment blocks, that soared above the trees making up the boundary.

As Klondike manoeuvred the vehicle down the track through the middle of the green, he marvelled at the natural beauty of the site. He could see a sparkling deep blue reservoir at the far end, and saw a collection of trucks and workmen all waiting for them nearby.

The convoy slowly rolled along the gravel tracks through the centre of the park.

Many of the excited spectators followed, all gathering at a fence near the main entranceway to watch as the many vans and lorries made their way through the park, followed by the horses and the eye-catching Cadillacs at the rear. It really was quite a sight.

As people of all ages and descriptions leant against the wooden fence to watch, a dandy-looking man with a jet black pompadour of hair and a light brown suit wandered casually to the fence, standing at the very end of the line of onlookers. He was joined by a bearded giant, wearing a fur-lined greatcoat.

"Quite the welcome," said Conrad Handel as he looked up and down the line of spectators. He removed a pair of beige leather gloves and fiddled with them. "It looks like our American friends have already generated a buzz, no?" He watched the trucks descending down the winding path, looking mesmerised. "They have come through the forbidden gate. And they hope to conquer. Just look at all this fancy equipment, Tarz."

The Hungarian giant was watching the commotion with a face of stone. "It's just like the boss said… all this razzmatazz. The dazzling colours, the cars, the cowboys." He shook his head. "These people… they are all drawn to it. Like flies to the jam."

Handel nodded absently as he watched. "One of those vans is carrying hot dog vendors. Another popcorn. And another one still brings machines that make their so-called cotton candy." He looked around worriedly. "Is this the future, Tarz? The future of our industry?"

Tarz was staring intently beyond the arriving convoy, where a grid of trailers was slowly being organised. Already, the far end of the field was resembling a caravan park.

"There's only one way to find out."

Handel nodded. "You know, you are absolutely right."

CHAPTER NINE

The team of roustabouts all began spreading the great blue and red fabric of the big top out before them, getting it in place for the mammoth task of the tent raising.

The tentpoles were assembled in place as the bizarre-looking contraption known as the groundhole punching machine, or simply 'Old Punchy', made large craters in the turf.

As the roustabouts worked, everyone else got settled into their trailers, a temporary home for the next few days.

Lacey was greeted by Addison's London representative, who delivered a great bundle of newspapers and magazines carrying previews and articles of interest.

Plum was met by another Addison Incorporated employee, who had overseen the local box office operation at the front of Hyde Park.

The man reported that 85 per cent of advance tickets had sold, with the rest for sale over the next two days at the temporary ticket booth by the entrance. As the representative explained, it shouldn't be an issue selling the remaining tickets if the excited crowd who had watched their arrival was anything to go by.

Klondike wandered about the camp, watching everything with interest. He stood with McCabe for a short while as his men prepared to raise the tent. Then, he checked in with all of his performers in their trailers, making sure everyone was comfortable and content.

Finally, he trudged back to his own trailer, which sat at the very edge of the park, close to the reservoir.

As he walked, Heavy fell into step alongside him.

"You spoke to Richie?" he said excitedly.

"I sure did. Looks like a sell-out. Addison's man thinks the rest of those tickets will sell in no time. Thanks to our grand arrival!"

Heavy chuckled as they waded among the trailers. "No doubt we have Lacey to thank for that. The papers have lapped up her press releases, just like back home."

Klondike nodded. "We'll go through the papers at our meeting tomorrow morning." They reached his trailer door. "Wanna a drink, Heav?"

"You bet!"

He led the way in and they both walked up the two steps and into the long, narrow enclosure. The trailer was separated into two berths, a bedroom/washroom and the main living room, with kitchenette. A lounge table in the centre was covered in paperwork.

Klondike reached for a bottle from the kitchen worktop and poured two glasses of scotch, handing one to his old friend. Then, with a sigh, he collapsed into the small couch.

Heavy perched on a tall stool, sipping his drink. "It's all happened so fast, Kal. Here we are, settled in at Hyde Park already. First the train to New York. Then the ship. Now, straight up to here."

Klondike sprawled in the couch, taking a cigar out of a small box on the table and sluggishly lighting up. Great wafts of purple smoke filled the small enclosure within seconds.

"You wait months for the big day… then suddenly it's upon you," he drawled. Cigar in mouth, he raised his shot glass in a toast. "To Europe! And the new frontier."

Heavy raised his glass. Then they both took a long drink. Heavy grabbed at the bottle, and brought it to the table for refills.

"Looks like Jim and the boys will be pulling the tent up any minute now," Heavy mused, looking out the window.

They were interrupted by a loud rapping at the door. It opened a foot, and an elderly man's head peered through. It was Marlon. He acted as a bartender and food server back at Rio Cristo, and took on roles as a general steward and camp watchman during circus tours.

"Sorry to interrupt, Kal," he called. "There's a gentleman here to see you. A Conrad Handel."

Klondike chewed on his cigar and looked across in confusion. "Handel? I know that name." He looked up at Heavy, who shrugged. "Thank you, Marlon. Please show him in."

The old man opened up the door and an extravagant-looking fellow climbed in, suited and wearing leather gloves. But it was his companion who caught the hosts' attention. The bearded giant could barely fit inside the cramped trailer, and stood by the doorway, as if guarding it.

"Kal Klondike!" the well-dressed newcomer boomed in his thick German accent. "What an honour it is to meet you. Handel. Conrad Handel."

He extended a hand. Klondike stood and shook it, before introducing Heavy.

Handel pointed to the giant behind him. "My associate, Tarz."

Klondike and Heavy stared in shock at the big man, both nodding slightly. Tarz folded his arms and stood perfectly still.

"Can I offer you boys a drink?" Klondike said in a tired voice.

"We are both fine, thank you." Handel looked out of the trailer window as the roustabouts began erecting the big top, pulling at the tent ropes.

"What an incredible sight," he gushed in an over-animated voice. He smiled broadly at Klondike. "My compliments on your circus operation, sir. Your successes have been transcendent."

Klondike nodded, sipping his scotch. "And, if memory serves me correct, you would know all too well." He paused, staring at the visitor. "Conrad Handel. You ran Wunder Welt, out of Munich, right? The show that launched Greta Strondheim, the juggling wire walker."

Handel clapped his hands together, laughing. "Remarkable. I applaud you, sir, your memory and information is immaculate."

Klondike smiled weakly. "I heard Wunder Welt was brought out a few years back…"

He motioned Handel to a desk chair. "Alas, it is true," the German exclaimed. "But we will always have the memories."

Heavy was staring at the giant in the doorway. "What brings you guys here?" he asked.

Handel nodded, removing his gloves. "Allow me to explain, gentlemen. I represent a network of entertainment firms operating across Europe. Our reach is far and wide. After my success with Wunder Welt, I act as an adviser and representative. A troubleshooter, if you will. My associates have taken a great interest in your circus. In your arrival here. And your proposed tour."

Klondike and Heavy immediately shot each other a look.

Handel continued smoothly, his voice soft and airy. "We consider you our brethren. And, as such, we felt it only right to deliver to you this… a warning!" He paused for effect.

Klondike had felt tired and weary when first entering the trailer. The German's words jolted him awake. He remained cool. "I'm sorry. I'm afraid I don't follow."

"It's ok," Handel said, as if addressing a child. "It has been many years since an American circus visited these shores. Randall's Circus. Out of New York. We all remember it well…" His eyes suddenly turned dark. "A true disaster. The people, particularly here in England, were disgusted. It's true, it's true. The fans even deserted the tent, during the damn show! By the end of their so-called tour of Europe, the circus was bankrupt. Finished!"

Klondike stared at him dumbly. It was Heavy who spoke, frowning at the surreal exchange. "What do you want?"

Handel looked at them, as if pained. He held his palms aloft. "OK, friends. There is no easy way to say this." He took a deep breath, looking riled. "You must leave!"

Klondike practically burst out of his chair. Heavy stood, alarmed.

"What?" cried Klondike. "What in the name of Sam Hill are you talking about?"

Handel remained calm. He held a hand out, palm flat. Like a remote controlled robot, Tarz stepped forward and deposited a large, fat manilla envelope into his hand. Then, the German slammed the package dramatically onto the table surface.

He stared at Klondike with wild eyes. "Ten thousand of your American dollars," he snapped. "It is all yours. Call it a good will payment. From my people. That will compensate your bookings for the tour. And bail you out for lost earnings. The only condition? You must leave. Now. Cancel this tour. And save yourself any further trouble."

He bowed, as if finishing a speech to an audience.

Klondike shook his head in dismay, then looked grimly at Heavy. "So that's it. A shakedown. Nuthin but a lousy shakedown! I thought we'd seen the last of this kind of behaviour." He stood and looked down at Handel with contempt. "Y'know, you got a lot of nerve waltzing in here like this and trying to buy us off." He leaned in close. "Now, who the hell are you? And who are these 'people' you claim to represent?"

Handel stood quickly and backed away. Towards the door. And Tarz.

"Easy," he hissed, the voice still soft and condescending. "Like I said, my people are trying to help you." He frowned, suddenly taking on a cold and predatory look. "There is a reason they call it the forbidden gate, you know."

Heavy took a step forward. "Your organisation… what is it called?"

Handel shook his head. "That, you will never know. But remember this… you cannot succeed here. My people have a deep reach. We have influence in every city on your schedule. I am trying to help you. Now, take the money. And avoid all of this. You will not regret it."

Klondike could not believe what he was hearing. "You… you're trying to buy us out…" He was glaring at the two newcomers. He nodded at Tarz. "You brought your heavy along. You actually think you can get away with it all. What the hell is this?"

Handel stood defiantly. "Take the money, Klondike. Nobody wants any trouble here."

Heavy had endured enough. "What kind of trouble you got in mind, mister?"

Finally, Tarz moved. He took a step forward, glaring at Heavy with murderous, hardened eyes. "All the trouble you will ever need, fat man."

Handel instantly nudged Tarz backwards. "Not here," he hissed. Then, he turned again to Klondike. "What do you say, eh?"

The whole episode felt like a surreal dream to Klondike. Then, suddenly, he grabbed the money packet and, with a snarl, hurled it at Handel. The package exploded into his chest like a football, making a queer thudding sound. Handel managed to catch it.

"You tell your people the forbidden gate hasn't just been opened, it's been destroyed, flattened…forever!" Klondike raged, shouting the words angrily. "And you tell them, my circus can't be bought out. Not by anybody! And... and you tell them to go to hell, whoever they are."

Handel had opened the trailer door and was already hustling Tarz outside. He looked at Klondike coldly. "You're making a big mistake, Klondike."

"You made the mistake, mister," Klondike snarled, "by coming here in the first place. Now... beat it!"

The confrontation was over.

Handel and Tarz retreated rapidly, sensing danger all around as more and more of the circus workers slowly descended on the trailer after hearing the shouting.

The two intruders walked briskly away from the clearing, and soon melted into the crowds beyond.

Klondike and Heavy stood in the doorway, watching them go.

Heavy shook his head. "Did that actually just happen?"

"It's hard to believe," Klondike murmured.

McCabe had followed his roustabouts across to the trailers, alarmed at how they had abandoned the tent and its many maintenance chores.

"What the hell was that all about?" he barked, reaching the boss's cabin.

Klondike shook his head. "It would appear some European big shots were ready for the arrival of us Americans. Battle lines have been drawn already. Hell, they're scared of us."

McCabe was astonished as he stood in the doorway. "What did they say?"

"They told us to get back on the ship and go home!"

"And what did you say?"

Klondike wandered back into the trailer's living room, and fished out his still lit cigar, ramming it into the corner of his mouth.

"Hell... I told em we've got a tour to complete." He grinned wildly, looking like a man possessed by some genial imp. "Now, we've got some European trail dust to whip up – and I don't care whose shirt it stains."

The great red and blue tent was up and running an hour later, raised to its full height and immense girth by the army of roustabouts.

The grandstands were quickly placed within and joined together on scaffold rigs, and before long the arena was complete.

Klondike had brought forward his executive staff meeting in light of the shock of his two unwanted visitors earlier.

There was no better place to hold the impromptu gathering than in the tent itself, he had decided.

"Who the hell were those guys?"

Richie Plum made the exclamation as the management team sat on the front two rows of bleachers at the tent's far end.

Klondike, Heavy, Lacey and Bannion all stared at him.

Klondike decided to stand and address his lieutenants.

"Trouble," he said. "Conrad Handel. Said he works for some kind of operation that runs circus shows across Europe. Or something like that. He basically offered us ten grand to turn around and set sail for New York again!"

They all stared at him in shock.

Bannion spoke first. "Handel? I remember him. Used to run Wunder Welt, German circus. Big in the UK."

Klondike nodded. "Right."

"They disappeared during the war, like everything else. Then they started doing shows again in Switzerland, Austria. Italy, maybe. But they fell off the map a few years back, as far as I'm aware."

"That seems to fit," Heavy piped in. "This guy seems to be an agent, or grease man, for something else now."

"Who was the big ape?" Bannion asked.

"Muscle," Klondike sighed. "Just another damn enforcer." He sighed, gazing around at his beloved big top. A few roustabouts were attending to minor duties, checking the grandstands and rigging. A sea of empty bleachers filled the tent. Even the sawdust was in place, covering the arena floor.

"No matter where we go," the circus boss was muttering, lost in thought, "no matter what we do... there is always someone. Always a new guy. Looking to intimidate us. Get us out. Or, of course, buy us out."

Lacey finally spoke, her face a mask of concern. "We have had this conversation before, boys. The price of success. Fame. It makes rivals jealous. Desperate. Keen to splash the cash. Just look at Eric Ribbeck and his behaviour over the years. It's shameful."

Plum looked aghast. "Did this Handel say where he came from? Who he's working for?"

Klondike shook his head. "No, dammit. No names. The whole thing was all over in minutes. I threw him and his grizzly bear of a pal out." He looked sick. "Looking back, we should've got more outta him."

Heavy nodded in understanding. "This was the first act. He'll come back. Whoever the hell he is."

"The forbidden gate..." Bannion mused.

They all looked at him.

Heavy was disgusted. "What the hell does this guy care where we came from? Who we are! We're a circus, dammit. Not a rival street gang. Why in hell do people get so intimidated by a travelling circus, for Christ's sake?"

Lacey rose and wandered to Klondike's side, looking up at the wall of empty seats all around.

"Again, Henry, it's because of who we are. What we are. One of the biggest troupes in the world. Stepping into someone else's turf. When you're as big as Klondike's Circus, people worry."

"It might be even more," said Bannion. "A fear of the Americans coming. The great invasion. I've heard talk about it at troupes all over England."

A grim silence filled the corner of the tent.

Finally, Plum asked the obvious question. "What do you think this Handel will do next?"

Klondike looked down at him. "Impossible to tell, Richie. But, one thing's for sure, we best be on our guard. Tell everyone to keep an eye out for troublemakers. Just tell them some Europeans aren't too keen on American invaders!"

Lacey shook her head. "This is the last thing we need."

With a huff, she pointed at a pile of newspapers she had brought to the meeting. "The UK press has skewered my releases into... well, something else entirely. I'm not sure if it's a stylistic issue or what. But some of these previews don't make any sense."

Heavy baulked, deflated. "You're kidding!"

She shrugged, walking to her seat and grabbing at one of the papers. "Just listen to this," she screeched. "From the Daily Herald." She cleared her throat and began to read aloud.

"Oh say can you see... a red, white and blue all-American circus extravaganza! First those crazy Yanks sent us their GIs and hamburgers, now they're sending over their top circus for a one-off show in Hyde Park.

"Yes, beloved readers, the Americans are coming! Klondike's Circus, in fact. No doubt hoping a gold rush will fill their pockets! As Brits soak up American rock n roll, sodas and movies, this all feels like yet another cash-in on our inevitable slide into Americanisation.

"Cotton candy, hot dogs and popcorn... it is all on the way. We can only imagine what a stars and stripes circus will bring us.

"Advertised are a gang of motorcycle stunt riders, a puppeteer, a team of cowboys - of course - and some gymnasts and acrobats. Oh, and there will be some traditional, actual circus acts, in the form of clowns and a trapeze artist.

"So, behold the razzmatazz and loudness of our Transatlantic friends. We will see just how their brand of entertainment goes down with seasoned fans of traditional big top fare..."

Lacey stopped, folding the newspaper.

They all stared at her, dumbfounded.

"What the hell was that?" Heavy cried.

"It doesn't even make sense," Plum added.

They turned to Klondike, who was staring at Lacey in shock. "Lacey, is that what Brits call a preview?"

She ran a hand through her hair. "I assure you, none of that was written by me. This... journalist, if we can call him that, has gleaned the details from my copy and... and come up with this condescending claptrap!"

Klondike shook his head. "I didn't even think an article like that was allowed. It's so rough!"

Lacey rummaged through her pile of newspapers. "British journalism is a different world entirely," she said weakly. "Their papers are full of opinion, comment, and the like." She looked around, seemingly ill at ease. None of the others could recall ever seeing her look quite so put out. "But, on the plus side," she said defiantly, "there is no such thing as bad publicity. It all does a job, one way or the other. Now, we have a gleam of notoriety. And that in itself can act as a firm hook."

Klondike stared at her, then out towards the flap entrance to the big top. "It looks like we've got a sell-out. Right now, that's the most important thing."

Lacey smiled at him beautifully. "It sure is, baby."

Klondike nodded in finality. "Good. Now, let's all be on our way. We have a big 48 hours ahead. Hell, I don't know about you guys, but I need some sleep. My head is spinning."

He wandered across the sawdust towards the flap, the others all slowly following in his wake.

The great circus tent was still, gentle yet foreboding, as they left its domain once more.

Suddenly, they could not wait for it to be filled to the rafters again with cheering spectators.

It wouldn't be long now.

Dusk had settled over Hyde Park, as a raft of street lights came on around the trees, illuminating the side roads and paths in a mystical gloom.

Beyond the park's entrance, the bright lights and booming glitz of central London beckoned.

Gino Shapiro walked idly down Park Lane with Penny at his side, both eyeing up the giant stores and swanky hotels in awe.

They had ventured as far as Oxford Street, with its massive shopping district, before looping back towards the park, enjoying the hazy spring evening.

As they neared the entrance to Hyde Park, both smiled at the sight of the great red and blue big top dominating the skyline at the far end of the green.

Shapiro stopped on the street corner opposite the gateway. On a fence surrounding a hotel garden complex were a raft of Klondike's Circus posters. They all sat there on display, side by side.

A picture of the tent dominated the poster, with Gino's photograph super-imposed over it, along with that of Roddy

Olsen, Corky, and the Daredevils. Gino studied the picture of himself, in his trademark orange fireball singlet. Then he looked around at the streets. Londoners shuffled along, passing him, not offering a second look.

Penny joined him, looking over the bank of circus posters. "Well, you can't say Klondike hasn't advertised."

Shapiro ignored her. "It's all so different…"

"What's that?"

"Look," he breathed, waving a hand at the pavement. "Nobody knows me here. There is nothing. We truly are in another world, Penny."

She smirked. "Don't tell me, champ… after tomorrow night, everybody will know you! Does that sound about right?"

He smiled. "That's the idea, mamacita." His dark eyes continued to study the poster. At the very bottom was a small picture of a man wearing a cowboy hat. The red text opposite read: FEATURING SPECIAL GUEST, THE KING OF THE COWBOYS – DUSTER WILLIAMS.

Shapiro frowned. "Only this man, this so-called king, Williams… only he is known here in England."

Penny looked at him. "That's the only reason he is here, as far as I can tell."

Shapiro thrust his hands in his pockets and walked along, stopping again. On the side of a newspaper stand straight ahead was another circus poster. This one just pictured Olsen, holding his puppets Rusty Fox, Napoleon and Tony Tan. The headline screamed: DON'T MISS THE PUPPETMASTER RODDY OLSEN! THE MAN WHO CAN MAKE ANYTHING TALK! DIRECT FROM HOLLYWOOD!

Penny rolled her eyes as she watched him. "Cute, huh?"

Shapiro sneered. "It seems everywhere I go, I see his face."

"I must've said it a thousand times," Penny exclaimed, "if only you two could just get along. Why, we'd have the greatest circus outfit on Earth. You could even perform together, on stage. Can you imagine?"

He merely stared back at the colourful poster. Then he eyed her, offering mock concern. "Let's see what the people say, huh?"

They kept on walking.

"Here's to you, kids! And a highly successful tour..."

Duster Williams held his glass of fruit juice high, smiling widely. "And for me," he added quietly, "here's to... well, to one more day in the sun."

Olsen and Suzi held their glasses high and joined the toast. They all said "cheers" and took a sip.

There were seated at an upstairs table in a Park Lane steakhouse, where they had dined on sirloins and the famous British chips. The restaurant was sparsely populated, and they were able to enjoy a quiet meal.

"Here's to you, Duster," Olsen was saying. "The greatest cowboy to cross the Atlantic!"

"Yee-hah!" Suzi gushed.

Williams chuckled. "Ah, you kids are too nice." He had another sip of his juice. Curious, he looked at the other two glasses. His companions had soda pops.

"So, neither of you drink either, huh?"

Suzi shook her head. "I can't stand the taste of alcohol."

He turned to Olsen. "What about you, Rod?"

The youngster looked downwards. He seemed to shudder. "I... I don't like what it does to you," he whispered.

Williams nodded. "Well, that makes two of us, son."

Suzi tried to change the subject. "You must be looking forward to the show, Duster."

"You bet," the old cowboy said. "Hell, it's been a while. And these Range Riders Kal has assembled are a top group. Make me yearn to be young again, they do!"

Olsen nodded happily. "We've got a great roster this year. A real nice mix of talents."

"Well, you're at the top of the bill, Rod," he wheezed. "Hell, these people out here in England... I'll bet the bank they ain't never seen nothing like what you do. You're gunna shake this city up, my boy."

Olsen and Suzi smiled politely. Then, the young singer got serious.

"Do you think we'll be a success here, Duster?"

Williams held his glass and looked at her solemnly. "Why sure," he mused. "But the success of a show is judged in several factors. Ticket sales. Commercialism. Audience reaction.

Critical praise. A lot of boxes to tick." He folded his hands across his stomach. "You want my opinion… I reckon the good people of London will be talking about Klondike's Circus for years to come."

His deep blue eyes took on a mesmerising, almost hypnotic look as he eyed the two youngsters whimsically. "But, then again, you just never know what will happen on any given Saturday night. Once those bright lights go on, the ringmaster blows his whistle, the crowd roars and we hit the sawdust."

He smiled at his own musings as the restaurant grew very quiet. "It's all so unpredictable. And that… that is why we love it."

CHAPTER TEN

"Ladies and gentlemen…"

Heavy Brown roared the traditional greeting into his microphone as he strode boldly onto the circus floor, resplendent in his scarlet blazer and black top hat.

As everyone had hoped and expected, the big top was filled to capacity. Every last ticket had been purchased at the temporary box office booth, and now the great tent was packed with excited Brits of all ages. Many waved Stars and Stripes mini-flags that were on sale at the merchandise stores outside.

The midway had already proved a big hit, as the thousands of visitors played happily at the shooting galleries, pitching stalls, ring toss and mini-bowling alleys. On top of that, the hordes of patrons had lapped up the cotton candy, hot dogs, popcorn, soda pops and toffee apples on offer at the food stalls.

Now, it was showtime.

As was his long-time custom, Klondike took his place at the flap, the main entrance and exit for all performers in the big top. Lacey and Plum stood with him. A team manager and his coaches, he thought idly as they took their places.

Klondike looked up and around at the thousands of fans seated in the stands. The wall of humanity that encircled his stage floor never ceased to amaze him, no matter where he was in the world.

Heavy's voice on the mic brought him back to the show as it boomed across the arena.

"Welcome to the greatest stage spectacular of them all. Welcome to Klondike's Circus – direct from America!"

Several stewards dressed in purple and white medieval costumes wandered onto the floor behind him, pretending to play trumpets as the sound of heralding bugles played on the tannoy. A neat trick.

The large man in the middle continued: "And now, to open our show, please put your hands together for the greatest acrobatic, gymnastic troupe on the planet. The fabulous, mysterious phenomenon known as…The Hightops!"

A pleasant applause followed as the female gymnasts, newcomers to the circus for this season, all trotted out, looking otherworldly in their wild gold and black leotards.

The Hightops went straight into their repertoire of unusual moves and motions, as dramatic classical music played over the sound system.

To begin, the 12-strong group formed a huge human dome, with members standing on each others' shoulders and joining hands to create the odd-looking apparition.

After disassembling themselves, six of the women then formed a circle of bodies by grabbing each others' ankles, which then became a wheel as it was pushed along by the others, with the females rolling round and round in a bizarre-looking creation.

Various painful-looking contortion moves followed as the women moved around the floor, performing in front of different sections of the crowd.

For their finale, the Hightops performed their customary "twin towers" speciality. Separating into two teams of six, the women defied gravity and, indeed, logic, by forming two human totem poles.

One climbed onto another's shoulders. Then a third came along and climbed up onto the second performer's shoulders. Then a fourth hauled herself up the pole. In mere moments, there were six women standing upon each other, two human poles, with hands clutching ankles and backs ramrod straight.

They held the twin towers for a full 60 seconds, before the descent began as the top mounted acrobat began climbing back down. Seconds later, all 12 were back on the sawdust, bowing and waving at the stunned, somewhat bemused applause.

"Let's hear it for the fabulous Hightops!" Heavy roared as the ladies began to jog back to the flap.

Klondike watched the audience apprehensively as the polite applause rang through the tent.

"Whatya think?" he whispered to Lacey beside him.

She looked mesmerised. "The applause… it seems different, tiger. Dignified. Casual. Almost forced."

Plum had heard them. "Maybe it's just the British way," he chimed in. "Elegant and restrained."

Klondike nodded absently as the Hightops raced past.

Next up were the Flying Batistas, a family of acrobats from Mexico who walked proudly onto the sawdust in their all-white gymnastics suits before performing a beguiling mixture of acrobatics and contortion acts.

The family's showpiece involved Maria Batista standing on her husband Raul's shoulders. Eldest son Tony then hauled himself up onto his mother's shoulders before, incredibly, Rodrigo scrambled up the three bodies until he stood aloft on Tony's shoulders.

Then, as the arena fell quiet with an almighty hush, Rodrigo executed a backward somersault to the ground, landing perfectly on his feet.

Seconds later, Tony performed the same move, landing squarely on his brother's shoulders.

And then, as the spectators watched in disbelief, fearless mother Maria turned on top of Raul before launching herself at her suspended son, landing in a sitting position on his shoulders. Once settled there, she held her arms aloft in celebration.

The performance drew more hearty applause.

The Flying Batistas all stood proudly, full of emotion, and waved their gratitude to the spectators.

The family then left the arena floor, to be replaced by dance act the Rocking Robins.

The eight women performed chorus line-style dances to old Broadway tunes played over the tannoy. Dressed immaculately in bright red skirts and leotard tops, their routine was a shot of traditional carnival entertainment.

They concluded their act with a showgirl-style dancehall piece, all linking arms together to form a long line and kicking their legs high in tandem. Every ankle almost hit its owner's head as the dancers showed off their athletic skills.

When their number was over and they bowed, more warm applause flooded the tent. The idea was that these three opening acts would form a gentle introduction to the show, before the audience was hit with the "big guns", as Bannion had put it. The construction of the show for this tour had almost entirely been planned by Klondike and Bannion.

As the Robins all bowed and waved at the clapping fans, Klondike turned to the flap behind him, where a small, fenced-off path led to the performers' trailers.

He grinned as he saw the clowns approach in their zany, multi-coloured outfits. Then, he saw Corky. And froze.

His star clown did not look right, despite the layer of white make-up covering his face. His eyes looked red, his head and neck somehow bloated.

Klondike stepped over to the open flap doorway and grabbed his arm as he entered.

"Corky!" he stammered. "Hell, you look terrible. What happened?"

"I'm ok, boss," the clown muttered, looking out at the crowds beyond the edge of the grandstands. "I guess I haven't adjusted to the English way of life yet."

"Are you sick?"

Corky watched as one of the other clowns slowly rolled his beloved eight-foot unicycle across. "I was seasick on the ship."

Klondike glared at him. "And?"

Corky grinned as the Rocking Robins all jogged across the floor in their direction, passing them with huge grins and dramatic waves.

"I found the perfect medicine."

"And what was that?"

Corky looked up and, finally in character, displayed a wild, zany grin. He spoke in a pitch perfect Cockney accent. "Why, fish and chips, guvnor!"

With that, he leapt up like a cat and mounted the unicycle, launching himself onto the seat as if climbing atop a barstool.

As the audience clapped politely, Heavy returned to the sawdust.

"And now, ladies and gentlemen, prepare to be dazzled and delighted by the world famous Klondike's Circus clown showcase, starring the world's fastest juggler, and a true institute in American entertainment, let's hear it for our very own… Corky the Clown!"

Again, the polite, somewhat gentle, applause broke out across the stands as Corky breezed into the arena on his unicycle, followed by four other clowns performing cartwheels and waving frantically at the spectators.

As frenetic piano music played on the tannoy, Corky began peddling furiously on the unicycle, doing laps of the arena floor, faster and faster as the other clowns attempted to run after him.

Then, the others took it in turns to throw juggling pins at the mounted figure in yellow and brown. Corky caught each pin and, slowing his pace, cycled expertly into the centre of the stage.

Then, after composing himself, he began juggling at seemingly supersonic speed, the pins becoming a blur as he sent them round at lightning pace. Applause began raining down from the stands.

Then, following his usual repertoire, he slowed down and performed the long juggle, sending each pin almost 20 feet into the air before catching them one at a time by pulling open the front of his pants.

Waves of laughter crashed down from the delighted fans as he continued cycling with the pins bulging out of his pants, before he duly hurled them one at a time to his clown assistants.

Then, he began cycling around the perimeter at high pace once more. His team had set up two small ramps in the centre of the floor, their tips 20 feet apart. Corky would ride up one, fly into thin air, perform a somersault, and land upon the second.

He watched as the clowns finished setting up the ramps, then turned from the edge of the floor and accelerated towards the centre, his eyes focused on lining up the ramp.

As he zoomed across the sawdust on the unicycle, his motion looked perfect.

Then, disaster struck.

As he neared the rim of the wooden ramp, Corky inexplicably fell from the cycle, his body slipping off the top like a rag doll off a swing. It looked like everything was happening in slow motion. His body plunged downwards, twisting, and then landing with a thud on the ground as the unicycle clattered into his frame and fell sideways.

Several screams emanated from the stunned audience. Then, the arena was deathly silent. Except, that is, for the comical frantic piano tune still blaring from the speakers.

Klondike did not even think. He raced across the sawdust in despair. A hundred deep, dark thoughts probed at his conscience as he sprinted towards the fallen clown, several roustabouts following in his wake.

The other clowns got to him first, gathering round in a circle.

Klondike ran straight into them seconds later. Everyone was looking down at Corky.

Thankfully, the veteran clown was pulling himself up into a sitting down position. Klondike knelt beside him.

"Corky!" he rasped. "You ok? What the hell happened?"

The clown looked stunned, his eyes wide in fright. "I… I feinted. I lost time."

"Are you hurt? Did you break anything?"

His eyes were full of horror, locked like stone into the comical white and red facepaint. "No. No, I'm ok. Just… just, er…" he shook his head.

Klondike looked up and around. The crowd was deathly silent. Thousands of faces staring right at him. A surreal, dream-like feeling.

He noticed Heavy, mic in hand, standing a few yards away from them. He nodded. Heavy nodded back, and addressed the audience.

"He's ok, folks!" Heavy roared, like a politician courting favour at a rally. "Everything's ok."

If he'd expected wild cheers of delight from a relieved arena full of concerned fans, he was wrong. The audience was dumbstruck. The terrible silence continued, everyone staring at the jumbled ensemble in the stage's centre.

Heavy baulked. This was a scenario he most certainly was not accustomed to. He looked aghast at the endless sea of faces all around, then back at Klondike.

"C'mon," Klondike whispered to Corky. "Let's get you outta here. Can you walk?"

Corky nodded and, standing as fast as he could, began walking stiffly towards the flap, Klondike and the roustabouts following in confusion.

The four other clowns, to their credit, attempted to entertain the patrons by performing cartwheels and pulling bouquets of flowers out of their sleeves. But this was a truly unprecedented moment.

Heavy tried to rouse the spectators again. "There he is folks, Corky the Clown. Now, on behalf of everyone at Klondike's Circus, we apologise for what you just witnessed. This is a live circus, after all, and we experience unfortunate moments from time to time." He thought rapidly, the mic at his lips. "But let's hear it folks for Corky! He's up, he's alright, he will be back, that's for sure. That's the world's fastest juggler, Corky the Clown!"

Finally, the audience responded with a mild ovation. But the stunned air of disbelief filled the arena. It felt toxic. Unnatural.

Klondike walked with Corky and the other clowns through the flap and outside to their trailer, where Corky threw himself onto the couch and placed his hands over his face.

He groaned inwardly, shaking slightly.

Klondike watched from the doorway. "You sure you're alright?"

"Twenty-two years, and never a fall… in a show!"

"Listen," Klondike barked, "never mind that." He glanced back anxiously towards the big top. "Are you gunna be alright, Corky?"

The clown was rubbing at his make-up. "I'm sorry, Kal," he whimpered.

Klondike turned to the four other clowns, who were now standing over Corky like hospital matrons. "Listen guys," he said. He suddenly, inexplicably realised he didn't know the other clowns at all, didn't even know their names. He shook his head curiously. "Look after him."

He ran back across the field, down the pathway and into the flap area again.

He reached the edge of the grandstands as Lacey and Plum approached. "Damn!" he snapped.

"Is he ok?" Lacey said quickly as she joined him.

"He's fine. Thank god. Just in shock. He feinted. Feinted! Up there on his cycle."

Plum nodded. "Must've been that seasickness. He had it pretty bad."

"God help us," Klondike said weakly. "That reaction from the fans. Jesus! It was awful."

Lacey put a supportive arm around him. "Let's hope they get it out of their system. And move on. If anyone can do that, it's these guys…"

She pointed to the floor, where the Showcase Revue were already assembled and beginning their routines.

Gargantua, Goliath and Rumpy Stiltskin all began performing their acrobatics and comedic routines to great effect, ably supported by the stewards in the medieval garb, who played fall guys to the clowning.

Heavy paced across to the flap nervously, his eyes bulging with worry. Klondike reassured him that Corky was uninjured, before commending him for his work on the mic after the emergency.

"God, he could have been killed," Heavy said quietly as he watched the Revue perform.

Klondike nodded grimly. "As you said, he'll be back."

They watched the Showcase Revue performers, still deeply unsettled.

The 400lb Gargantua flew across the floor, completing cartwheels, handstands and running leaps like a man one quarter of his size.

Goliath lifted the dressed-up stewards high above him, two at a time, before sitting on a stool and placing his right leg behind his neck in a bizarre-looking feat.

Then, Rumpy took centre stage, bouncing across the sawdust on his six-feet stilts. He threw a backward somersault, a forward one and then, as the applause finally returned, defied all logic by hopping along on one leg, or stilt, as he held the other stilt in his hands, nestled against his frame.

He left the arena in that fashion, followed by a cartwheeling Gargantua and a grinning Goliath, who carried a man on each shoulder.

Perhaps mercifully, the crowd applauded at the antics.

At the flap, Klondike watched with interest. Lacey was almost on top of him.

"Ok, tiger," she breathed into his ear. "The appreciation is building again. Just in time for the bikers."

With that, an ear-splitting roar reverberated around the tent, the unmistakable sound of motorbike engines revving.

"And now…" Heavy bellowed into the mic. "Prepare to be amazed by the greatest show of death defiance and stunt riding in the world today. Performing their world famous Globe of Death act, Klondike's Circus is proud to present… the wild riding motorcycle sensation, the Daredevils!"

The stunt riders raced onto the sawdust on their yellow and black motorcycles, dressed in leather jumpsuits of the same colours.

The team completed a lap of the floor, then set out performing a host of loops, wheelies and even a stunt where one team member ran on foot and leapfrogged over each rider as they zoomed toward him.

The noise was overpowering, as the sounds of motorcycle exhaust and wheels spinning filled the air.

Then, it was time for the Globe of Death.

The huge metal sphere, which resembled a circular cage, was wheeled out by a large team of roustabouts, and securely mounted on a mini-stage with a metal platform beneath it.

And then it began. The riders lined their bikes up in a queue. The first Daredevil mounted the ramp and drove slowly through a door into the cage. Once inside, the cage door was slammed shut and the biker began zooming round and round inside, eventually performing full 360-degree circles from top to bottom.

A second rider entered the Globe of Death, the door closed again and the man began executing his circles, the two riders storming round the cage and narrowly avoiding hitting each other.

Exactly one minute later, a third rider rode up the ramp and joined the melee, executing wild laps of the sphere with the other two.

The noise of the engines was overwhelming as the bikers spun round inside the cage.

But something was wrong.

Klondike sensed it more than anything. There was a reaction emanating from the stands. And it wasn't a good one.

He turned and moved to the front of the grandstand section next to him. Looking up, he was stunned at what he saw. But it hit him with an almost electrical ferocity.

Children were crying, whimpering uncontrollably. Women screamed, holding their hands over their eyes. People everywhere – old and young – seemed to have a strange look locked into their features. It was part fear, part alarm. An old man suddenly bolted from his seat into the aisle, as if in deep distress. Despite the overpowering noise from the machines, Klondike heard a woman scream at full pitch.

"Oh my god! Make it stop!" she wailed.

He turned away from the stand. Lacey was behind him, and saw the commotion. They both looked around the full circle of the stands. They could sense it everywhere. Fear. Panic. Almost delirium.

"What in hell is going on?" Klondike shouted at her.

She shook her head, glancing up at the sea of spectators in confusion. She locked eyes with a goggle of small children, all burying their heads into a woman's chest.

That was enough.

"Break it off!" she cried.

"What?"

"Look! People are up there having a fit!"

Klondike stared for a second, then looked across the sawdust at Heavy. The giant ringmaster was already staring at him in shock, as if awaiting a signal. Klondike waved his hand across his throat rapidly. Heavy nodded.

The fifth rider had just entered the Globe of Death. Tip Enqvist was now inching up the ramp, poised to join his team in their most celebrated stunt. He waited proudly at the door, oblivious to anything but the rhythm of the bikes.

"OK, folks," Heavy suddenly called on the mic, the noise diverting attention from the wail of the machines. "There you have it, the Daredevils! The greatest stunt riders on Earth. Please show your appreciation for their skills. Thank you very much."

Enqvist turned on his saddle at the top of the ramp, stunned. The Daredevils kept riding round the Globe, until they all slowly decelerated before coming to a halt on the bottom of the cage.

That in itself was unprecedented. Normally, they rode back out one at a time.

The five riders idled, all looking up at Enqvist. The leader of the troupe backed down the ramp again, pulling off his helmet. He glared at Heavy, possibly 20 yards away.

"What the hell, man? You just killed us!"

Heavy raced across the floor, stopping before Enqvist as the motorbike engines all idled gently.

"This is an emergency!" Heavy barked, looking incensed. "Don't make it any worse. Get off the floor!"

Enqvist looked ready to kill. "What are you talking about, man? You don't have the—"

That was as far as he got.

"Get off the floor, Tip. Now!" Heavy implored him with his eyes.

Finally, Enqvist shrugged, motioned to his team, and rode his bike slowly towards the flap, disconsolate. Finally, it dawned on him that there were no cheers, no screams of joy, and no applause. Just stunned bemusement. Everywhere. He rode slowly to the exit, looking up at the fans in shock. With a mild wave, he disappeared outside. The cage door opened, and his five team-mates all zoomed out of the tent as well.

And that was that.

Now that the almighty roar of the bikes had dissipated, Klondike could finally hear the reaction of the fans. It was a sensation that would stay with him for a long time.

He could hear crying, distress, anguish. Daring a look up into the stands again, he saw faces overridden with shock. It had to be said, a lot of the patrons looked relieved. He ducked back to his position by the flap, whipped off his hat and rubbed a hand wildly through his thick hair.

"Oh my god," he croaked, looking up at the heavens. "I've never seen anything like that before." He shook his head. "The Daredevils usually whip crowds into a frenzy. This crowd has been whipped into a… into a delirious mess."

Lacey hopped around him in desperation. "They weren't ready for this. Can't you see, Kal? No one has ever seen anything like it. They're frightened. They think all the riders will be killed!"

Plum was standing by the edge of the grandstand. "But this is a circus. Why would they think that? They're all performers. Professionals."

Lacey nodded weakly. "We know that, Richie. But remember, please, we are on the other side of the world. These people have no idea what is going on! They've probably never seen a stunt rider, much less the Globe of Death."

"Alright, alright," Klondike huffed. "We've still got plenty left for this crowd."

He smiled faintly as he looked outside. The Daredevils were all rolling slowly towards their trailers and holding stall. Then, from a separate trailer near the tent entrance, Roddy Olsen appeared.

In his silver waistcoat and purple pants, and carrying his large suitcase, the youngster looked like a Hollywood movie star approaching a film set. All tan, golden hair and white teeth.

Olsen walked casually into the big top.

"Go get em, kid," Klondike whispered. "Get these people happy and cheering."

Olsen smiled, his usual confident self. "Always, Mr Klondike."

"Good luck, Roddy," Lacey gasped. She looked him all over. "Time to conquer England!"

Olsen chuckled easily, and crept to the edge of the sawdust, awaiting his cue.

Heavy's announcement then boomed across the floor. "And now, ladies and gentlemen, behold at the talents of the modern sensation of the circus. Direct from Hollywood and Las Vegas. The wizard of ventriloquism… the Puppetmaster, Roddy Olsen!"

A warm, if somewhat muddled, applause sounded from the stands as Olsen walked out, waving happily to the fans.

He reached the mic stand in the centre of the floor, placed the case on the ground and addressed the audience.

"Thank you, thank you friends. Good evening. My name is Roddy Olsen and it is my sincere pleasure to perform for you this evening. Now, this is my first time in England and—"

"Woh, woh, woh, hold it!" a thick Brooklyn accent drawled, seemingly from out of nowhere. "Nobody cares, man. Tonight is all about my debut in England! Now… let me out!"

Olsen looked down at the suitcase. "Now, Rusty, I told you about this. I make the introduction first, and then—"

"LET ME OUT!"

"Very well." Olsen wandered to the case, opened it up, and put his head and arms inside.

"Hey," the voice cried. "Be careful now, Roddy. You know this hurts. Ouch!"

Then, Olsen stood again, this time holding Rusty Fox on his right arm. The small fox puppet was wearing his customary black leather jacket and jeans. A smattering of applause broke out as the puppet appeared.

"Ladies and gentlemen," Olsen cried into the mic. "Please allow me to introduce—"

"It's alright," Rusty interrupted. "I got this." He cleared his throat. "Rusty Fox. Rock n roll superstar. Teen idol. America's greatest export since spam." He held up a hand. "Thank you, thank you my fans. Finally, I am here. In England. First, we gave you guys Frank Sinatra. Then, Elvis. Now, the greatest entertainer in the States! Me!"

Olsen laughed, looking up at the subdued reaction from the stands. "Alright, Rusty, now behave yourself. We are in England now. The land of good manners."

"Say, Roddy, when are we going to go to a farm?"

"A farm? What are you talking about?"

"I want to see some British chicks. I hear they're real pretty. And tasty too!"

Olsen rolled his eyes. "Come on, Rust. Behave! Now, tell me, what do you know about England?"

The fox puppet shook excitedly. "Well, they tell me I oughta run for Parliament out here."

"And why's that?"

"Because it's full of dummies!"

Olsen chuckled, again noticing a lack of laughter all around. "What else do you think of England, Rusty?"

"I could be in the Royal Family!"

"What! How did you figure that one out?"

"Well, the royals all have people who speak for them… sounds like I have a lot in common with them!"

Olsen held up his spare hand. “Ok, Ok. Enough wisecracking, my little friend. Now, Rusty, are you going to sing for us or what?”

“I sure am, Roddy.”

“Yes,” Olsen was saying, “a nice slow number to soothe our beloved audience, right?”

“No,” Rusty blurted, “I was thinking of the Rock Island Line!”

Olsen gulped nervously. “That’s… that’s the fast one, right?”

Rusty’s face went right up to Olsen’s. “You bet,” he drawled. “We’re gunna sing Bobby Darin’s classic version. Just, er, don’t tell him. He’s still mad at me for eating his budgie!”

Then, a tune blared across the tannoy and Rusty began singing.

Suddenly, after two lines, another voice erupted, seemingly from the trunk.

"Attention! Stop that singing." This voice sounded like an old man, and was harsher.

"Uh-oh," said Olsen. He dipped into the suitcase and miraculously emerged with a second puppet on his free hand. Now he had a figure on each arm. This new model was a dummy version of a grey-haired old man in army fatigues. He scowled.

"Don't let that good for nothing punk kid sing! I've told him his singing days are over. No more juvenile delinquency. It's time for this kid to join the US Army. And that's an order!"

Olsen spoke next. "Ladies and gentleman, please meet my very dear friend, Napoleon.”

The new puppet saluted. "US Army. Retired.”

A faint clapping broke out from the audience. Olsen forced himself to look up. Something wasn’t right. He felt like he was performing in a crypt. The act continued seamlessly.

Rusty spoke next. "I'm not joining no army. I've got to conquer the music charts. And Hollywood. I'll be famous. Then I'll get all the chicks. To eat by myself!"

"You need to learn respect and discipline first, you slimy little maggot."

“I’m not a maggot, I’m a fox!”

Olsen spoke again. "There's only one solution, guys," he said, smiling. "We're all going to sing. Together. Come on, Napoleon, it'll be fun."

The army man puppet shook its head, but Rusty had already begun singing Rock Island Line, a track renowned for its speeded-up chorus.

Like a mini choir, Olsen and his two creations took it in turns to belt out the tune, a few lines each, getting faster and faster.

Round and round they went, as the song got quicker, and the lines came sharper. Olsen somehow held three voices, three personalities, two puppets and himself, as he maintained his super-fast singing.

The thousands of fans in the seats all stared at him, as if lost and confused. There was no wild applause, no whooping, and no screams of delight and uncontrollable laughter.

At the flap, Klondike was incredulous. Watching Olsen perform his most celebrated routine to virtual silence was as surreal as it was unwanted. He felt himself shrinking, caving into himself, like a dying plant.

"What the hell is going on?" he said in dire shock. He rubbed at his face, staring up at the audience in rapt fascination. "These people," he said weakly. "It's like they've been drugged. Like… like they don't want to be here."

Lacey looked at him, then back at Olsen in the centre of the floor. Subconsciously, she tugged at her hair.

The ventriloquist finished his Rock Island Line number, and bowed with his puppets. The applause was muted, almost forced. He was yet to hear a laugh or cheer since entering the big top.

He looked up, and his face was pale. The consummate professional, he continued wilfully.

Placing Rusty Fox back inside the case, he kept Napoleon on his arm.

"Ok, soldier boy, this one is for you," he said to the puppet.

A steward approached and handed him a tall glass of water. "Now, this is called the amazing water watch."

Napoleon frowned on his arm. "What is it, Olsen?"

"Well, Napoleon, you are going to sing Amazing Grace. Your favourite song. And I am going to drink this big glass of water. And all the people are going to… watch!"

With that, Olsen started Napoleon singing the classic hymn. Then, Olsen held aloft the glass and started downing the contents – while his puppet kept singing!

Olsen continued glugging until the water was finally all gone, as Napoleon reached the second verse.

He removed the glass from his lips as the puppet kept singing, without missing a single note.

The trick was a sensation, and Olsen had performed it several times on television and on stage in Las Vegas and Broadway. It never ceased to amaze onlookers, and its conclusion was always met with thunderous, startled applause.

But not this time.

As if to confirm that he wasn't over with this crowd, the "amazing water watch" skit was met with minimal applause, like all of his routines on this night. The only ovation was the sound of hands clapping, and not many of them at that.

Stunned, Olsen stared into the audience. He thought he saw looks of bemusement, almost annoyance. He shook internally, trying to remain cool. But inside, he felt a sensation he had never known, in all his years of performing. It felt something like failure.

Shaking slightly, he deposited Napoleon back into the case and withdrew his third puppet, Tony Tan, the Las Vegas cabaret singer.

Dressed in a tuxedo, with a deep golden tan and thick black hair and eyebrows, Tan was a Dean Martin clone, with a drunken persona to match.

"Ladies and gentlemen," Olsen said grandly, "please welcome our very special guest for this evening… direct from Las Vegas… the world's greatest lounge lizard, Tony Tan!"

As that strange clapping sound rang round the arena again, Olsen spoke to the new puppet.

"So, Tony, welcome to England. You must be pretty excited, huh?"

"Yeah," blurted Tan, acting drunk. "Man, I love it here. You can drink anywhere. In the park, in restaurants, in cinemas, the theatre, hell even in the street. God save the Queen!"

Olsen nodded. "It's all pretty different here, huh?"

“You got that right, Rod. And everyone keeps on calling me a Yankee. What the hell is that? Everybody knows I’m a Dodgers fan!”

The arena was silent as he waited for laughs. With a nervous gulp, Olsen continued. “Well, I understand you have a very special song for our hosts this evening, Tony?”

“That’s right.” He cleared his throat, coughing comically, as if struggling to breath. “Ladies and gentlemen, I would like to sing for you the national anthem of England. And Queenie, if you’re in the audience watching… well, I’m available for afternoon tea. As long as I can bring along my hip flask…”

With that, Olsen launched Tan into a rendition of God Save The Queen, riddled with comical errors throughout.

As he reached the climax, he held his spare arm aloft and made Tony’s arms spread out wide.

What followed was incomprehensible.

A bitter, death-like silence filled the big top. Olsen stood rigid, the puppet suspended on his right arm. Eyes wide in fright, he looked around dumbly. He had long endured nightmares involving this scenario. Even now, it felt like a dream. Never had he ever truly thought it would happen to him. But now was that time.

He remained stood there with Tony Tan, unsure entirely what was going on, not knowing what to do.

At the flap, Klondike, Lacey and Plum were beyond dumbstruck. Their mouths gaped in shock at what they were witnessing. It had actually happened. Olsen’s act had not caught on.

Klondike rested an arm against a scaffolding post to support himself. Lacey wandered around in a circle, then placed her head into his shoulder. He hugged her, eyes wide with dismay.

Plum just stood there, like an emotionless being.

Finally, after what felt like an age of terrible silence, Heavy’s voice returned to the sound system.

“There he is, folks, the Puppetmaster himself, Roddy Olsen! Star of Las Vegas, Hollywood, Broadway and US television. Let’s hear it for one of the stars of world circus. Roddy Olsen!”

As Olsen walked off with his case, waving absently to the fans, a tiny, embarrassing round of applause rolled quietly around the stands.

Olsen finally made it to the flap, looking about as crestfallen as anyone could possibly appear.

He looked pleadingly at Lacey. "What… what happened?"

Lacey embraced him in a mighty hug. "It's ok Roddy. It's alright. It's them, these people, not you. It's not you!" She held his face in her hands, looking him direct in the eyes. "Go back to your trailer. Just forget about this. We'll talk later. Don't you worry."

Klondike patted him lightly on the back as he lurched away, heading outside.

Then, he turned to Lacey again. "Tell me, please tell me, this is all a nightmare. We'll wake up in a minute ready for our show. For real."

She folded her arms, watching Olsen leave with motherly concern. "None of it feels real."

"What is going on here?" Plum croaked, still glaring up at the stands.

Lacey said: "It's the same thing again. The people… they are just not ready for anything like this. That kind of act. No one has ever seen anything like that out here. They can't—"

"Ah, come off it Lacey," Plum snapped uncharacteristically. "You can't keep using that excuse! This is insane! It's like someone put something into the sodas here! This crowd has been drugged!"

Klondike glared at them both. "We'll talk in our meeting tomorrow morning."

Heavy's next announcement brought them back to the show.

"Ladies and gentlemen, please give it up for our next attraction.

The wonders of the wild west, the kings among cowboys, please put your hands together for the fast-riding, hard-driving… Range Riders!"

This time, hearty applause bled down from around the big top as Heavy held his hat aloft and the team of 10 cowboys burst on to the floor on their immaculate-looking palomino horses.

"And for this tour," Heavy continued, bellowing into the mic, "Klondike's Circus is delighted to welcome one of the greatest cowboys of them all. You've seen him on TV, maybe even seen his show before... please give a warm English welcome to the king of the cattlemen, Mr Duster Williams."

The loudest cheer of the night so far emanated from the stands as Williams rode out on Goldie, moving into the centre of the floor as the other Riders continued racing around the perimeter in great laps.

Klondike and Lacey watched at the flap like a pair possessed, waiting for something dastardly to transpire again.

The applause for Williams was sustained though, and another cheer went up as the veteran star made Goldie stand on her hind legs for a full 30 seconds as he waved his hat to the crowds.

Then, he joined the rest of the team as the horses surged round the tent.

The riders performed their usual tricks as the mounts rode around the floor repeatedly. There were leapfrogs, saddle jumps and headstands, and all manner of stunts as the cowboys leapt from horse to horse, switching mounts as they raced round in a great circle. And the crowd responded with cheers. To the relief of just about everyone.

Williams had been following the Riders at the rear, keeping up with some of the saddle tricks but never leaving the back of Goldie.

Then, the veteran returned to the centre of the stage as the Riders continued bombing around the perimeter.

With the spotlight very much upon him, Williams slowly dismounted and then unhooked his lasso from his saddle bag.

In a second, he launched himself into his full repertoire of rope tricks. Creating a giant hoop with the inch-thick coil, he swirled it high above his head, then held it spinning alongside his frame. Then, to more cheers, he leapt delicately through the hoop several times, back and forth, maintaining the spin on the lasso.

He then expertly manouvered the hoop above him and let the rope loosen a bit, so that it began twirling over his entire frame, up and down, from foot to hat.

Letting the spinning rope hoop drop to his waist, he gave a mighty leap and was suddenly stood alongside the blurring lasso once more.

Then, with a flourish of his hands, he released his grip on the rope completely. It flew into the air, seemed to spin around on its own for several seconds, then the whole lot fell, landing in a perfect circle, with Williams in the middle, arms folded.

At this, the audience cheered and applauded mightily. Williams, the consummate professional, smiled happily and waved his hat in the air. One of the Riders then galloped towards him, and he hoisted himself up onto the back of the cowboy's saddle. The horse performed one more loop of the floor before racing towards the idle Goldie. As they approached, Williams launched himself off the back of his mount and landed on Goldie perfectly. Settled into his own saddle again, he roared out a "Yee-haw" before his beloved palomino performed another hind-leg salute.

Finally, the audience were on their feet, clapping and enthused by the cowboy performers. It was not an electrifying reception, but was warm and excited.

The Range Riders slowly rode back down the flap. Williams again stayed at the back of the group, waving his stetson happily at the cheers as he exited the arena.

As they passed the flap, Klondike slapped each rider on the leg. As Williams rode by, the circus boss reached up and shook his hand.

"Thank you, Duster," he cried, eyes wide as he looked up at the veteran. "They love you. Thank god!"

Williams just kept on smiling. "You bet," he murmured, before riding out into the park.

Klondike turned and looked at Lacey and Plum. "Of all the things," he gasped, still in shock, as he had been for most of this show. "Old Duster gets them on their feet."

Lacey was watching the old cowboy riding gently away outside the tent. "Keep the faith, tiger."

The sound of more medieval-style trumpeting blurted out from the tannoy.

Heavy then returned to the centre of the floor for his most well-known introduction.

"And now..." he roared into his mic, "ladies and gentlemen, prepare yourselves for the first wonder of the circus world... the most incredible act in America today... an extraordinary showcase of trapeze! On first ring, the queen of the skies... an angel from high above... the beautiful Penny Fortune! And, on centre ring, the world's greatest flyer. Cheer him, love him, never forget him. Klondike's Circus is proud to present the worldwide sensation... the debonair king of the air... Gino Shapiro!"

The audience all applauded as Shapiro and Penny slowly walked out onto the floor, dressed in their bright orange costumes. Both cast aside their extravagant, fur-lined cloaks. Penny wore a fireball leotard, while Shapiro wore his customary flaming orange singlet.

Both climbed their support ropes to the waiting rings high above.

The watching fans all followed with their eyes as the two orange-clad figures shot up the ropes towards the tent ceiling.

Once at the top, they settled on the rings and rubbed chalk into their hands. Neither looked down. There was no net. Just an ocean of sawdust. And the thousands of spectators staring upwards.

What followed was a showcase of classic trapeze techniques, as Shapiro whirled around from ring to ring, throwing and thrusting his body like a human dart. Penny acted as his catcher, twisting her legs behind her and hanging upside down off her ring seat, taking his hands and propelling him across to the next ring in line.

He performed three sets of vaults across the three main rings hanging from the trapeze rig at the summit. Back and forth he flew like a pristine tree-hopping animal.

Then, he showcased some traditional trapeze techniques. Shapiro performed all the customary moves – the double sault, the triple and the standing twirl. Each acrobatic somersault looked majestic and was performed with ease.

Then, Penny clasped his ankles and hurled him even higher. Shapiro hurtled towards the tent ceiling, before falling rapidly back down. A mighty "oooh" reverberated across the big top as he caught his ring and scrambled back into a sitting down position.

They repeated the move, and this time, as he shot towards the summit, Shapiro clasped his arms behind his thighs and produced five quickfire turtle somersaults, so fast they appeared merely a blur. As he fell back onto his ring again, the audience cheered loudly and applause broke out again.

Then, the duo performed a handstand perorate in unison, both standing on their hands upon their ring before swinging round in a 360 degree arc, releasing their hold and somersaulting in the air before defying gravity by landing on their hands again. Like synchronised swimmers at the Olympics, their timing was immaculate.

Next, both performers swung up some momentum and vaulted together across to a turret at the far side of the tent roof. Shapiro then descended to a wooden platform 20 metres off the ground that had been rapidly assembled while he flew high above.

From there, Shapiro would perform one of his specialities, the high wire. A thick plastic cord ran from the small platform to another erected on the far side of the tent.

The distance was a solid 40 metres, right across the arena.

After rubbing chalk into his stockinged feet, the great trapeze king held his arms high, and the big top fell deathly silent.

With a theatrical flourish, Shapiro effortlessly walked across the entire length of the wire, as the spectators looked up in shock and astonishment.

Arms out wide, he made it all the way across in under two minutes, walking at a slow, methodical pace, barely quivering at all.

As he neared the end of the wire walk, Shapiro produced a stunning cartwheel to push him onto the end platform.

This time, everyone in the crowd was on their feet, clapping and cheering.

Shapiro blew kisses to the audience, bowing endlessly at his station high above. Then, he grabbed at a nearby support rope and slowly scurried downwards to the floor. Penny followed suit at the opposite side of the tent.

On the ground again, Shapiro lifted his assistant with a mighty hug, before both bowed again, waved and jogged lightly to the exit.

A pleasant applause followed them, if not the usual frenzied cheers and exclamations they were used to.

"Tough crowd, chairman," Shapiro said as he reached the flap. As usual, he was draped in sweat, which poured off him as he moved.

"You don't know the half of it," Klondike blabbered. He looked up at the grandstands on either side. "But you've won them over, Gino. I knew I could count on you."

Shapiro led Penny to the exit. "Always, chairman, always."

Then, Heavy motored back out to the centre. "And there you have it, ladies and gentleman, boys and girls. The most incredible act in American circus."

He paused as the crowd went deathly silent again. "We hope you've enjoyed Klondike's Circus, friends. Here to sing us out is our resident songstress, the enchanting Suzi Dando."

Suzi smiled beautifully as she slowly crept onto the sawdust, taking the mic from Heavy as the familiar music began blaring out over the tannoy.

She wore a dazzling white and gold dress, and left no one in any doubt as to the power of her voice as she began belting out the circus's trademark anthem, Can You Feel The Magic Tonight?

The dramatic, climactic number was sung at the end of every performance as the grand finale of the circus, during which all of the performers would come out for a last ovation.

Suzi stood singing in the very centre of the floor.

Then, a succession of beautiful red Cadillac convertibles drove into the arena and completed a lap of the big top.

In the back of each car was each respective act, coming out one by one until all the performers were being chauffeured around in a beautiful automobile, waving at the audience as they paraded slowly round the floor in a big circle.

The Range Riders took it in turns to sit in their car, jumping on and off their horses as they went round on their mounts.

Duster Williams again followed slowly behind on Goldie, waving his hat at the cheering fans.

The Rocking Robins all stood in the back of their ride, blowing kisses and waving.

The Hightops performed another mini-human tower in the back of their Cadillac, standing on the seats and supporting their team-mates.

Roddy Olsen sat with Rusty Fox, Tony Tan and Napoleon all huddled up in the back seat. The puppets all waved.

The Flying Batistas, the Showcase Revue and Corky and his clowns all stood in the back of their respective Cadillacs.

Only Tip Enqvist of the Daredevils was actually seated in his team's allotted car, with the rest of the crew riding alongside on their bikes, engines revving.

The last Cadillac in the line held Shapiro and Penny, who stood tall, wearing their fancy capes again, and waving enthusiastically as the audience cheered them.

The procession of cars carrying the performers was another breathtaking sight. The audience responded in kind, applauding the majesty of the parade.

Suzi reached the operatic climax of the song, and the cars slowly headed on the last leg of their lap of honour towards the exit from whence they had come.

Suzi finished singing, and leapt onto the final car as it crept past, joining Shapiro and Penny, who helped her aboard.

Then Heavy returned for a final time to the arena floor.

"Ladies and gentlemen, we hope you have enjoyed the glamour, the razzmatazz and the sheer excitement of Klondike's Circus. And we hope you can feel the magic tonight. From all of us here, thank you so much for joining us and we hope to see you again. Until then, goodnight… and god save the Queen."

CHAPTER 11

STARS AND GRIPES! TOURING CIRCUS IS AN AMERICAN NIGHTMARE

By Godfrey Hargreaves, London Daily News

They came proudly from across the Atlantic, promising big-time attractions, sparkle and razzmatazz.

But last night, the so-called stars of Klondike's Circus were left scurrying out the back door in disgrace after a calamitous night of bizarre and unwanted "entertainment".

For decades, Hyde Park has played host to some of Europe's biggest and brightest circus troupes.

Last night, it was the turn of the Americans. Led by manager and promoter Kal Klondike (as if that is his real name), their pre-tour publicity had promised astonishing acts and a show that was out of this world.

Well, last night's offering was out of this world alright… but sadly belonged on another planet, in another solar system, far from where humans can see it.

We had the horrors of the Daredevils, a motorcycle stunt crew who seemingly tried to kill each other while locked, unable to escape, in a metal cage. This act was a frightening, maddening glimpse into near mass suicide. And NOT a form of entertainment.

Then there was Corky the Clown, who was way out of his league as he attempted an ultra-fast unicycle ride, only to fall from his saddle and run himself over. Again, the performer could have been killed, right there in front of the shocked, paying patrons.

But the final insult of the night came in the form of ventriloquist Roddy Olsen. This was no traditional puppeteer, but more a brash young man performing voice-throwing tricks, clearly with the help of hidden microphones and recording devices. His very American humour had no place here and, in a final insult, his disgraceful rendition of our national anthem using a drunken Dean Martin puppet was a very poor show. The silence that greeted it was a deserved riposte.

Throw in the Showcase Revue, a cruel performance that until a few years ago would have been labelled a freak show, and some repetitive gymnastics and acrobatic routines, and you have a very disappointing circus show.

However, the audience was saved by the night's final two acts. King of the cowboys Duster Williams, a veteran of European circus, performed his Wild West routine with some fellow cowboys and finally drew a standing ovation from the fed-up London crowd.

And, at the end of the show, trapeze artist Gino Shapiro also left the audience mesmerised by his high-flying antics, which included a daring high wire walk across the width of the circus tent summit.

It is most fortunate that these two final performances of the night gave the spectators something to cheer. Otherwise, there may well have been a riot, with patrons – quite rightly – demanding a refund.

Head back across the Atlantic please, Mr Klondike. And don't ever return. London has had enough Americana to last… well, several lifetimes.

The inquest had begun the following morning at breakfast.

Klondike had decided to gather everyone together – performers, management, roustabouts – into the big top for a full debriefing.

Makeshift wooden tables and chairs were brought inside and the chow line was moved from the kitchen trailer onto a temporary buffet station by the flap.

Now, everyone sat around inside the vast empty tent, drinking coffee and chewing sandwiches and oatmeal. The atmosphere was about as sombre as anyone had ever experienced, with everyone merely looking around, staring at one another, as if searching for answers.

Klondike was the only one not seated. Without his hat for once, he paced the sawdust floor slowly, trancelike, rubbing at his hair and jawline incessantly.

"What in Sam Hill was that?" he finally blurted, to no one in particular. "What we witnessed last night. What we went through. What…" he shook his head in anger. "Can someone please tell me what the hell is going on?"

He gazed around the tent, eyeing each table. He saw Corky and his clowns, now without their facepaint. Corky looked sick, pale and bloated.

He glared at the Daredevils, sat around a table at the far side of the gathering. They still looked incensed, Enqvist looking at him with cold eyes.

And Olsen, who was seated at a table with both Lacey and Suzi. The kid looked dumbstruck, an empty plate resting before him.

"These Brits had it in for us."

Of all people, it was Rumpy Stiltskin who spoke. Every head turned his way. Predictably, he was sat with Gargantua and Goliath at a tiny round table by the grandstands.

"You all saw that preview Miss Tanner read out," the stilt walker continued, angrily. "They had it in for us from the beginning. Before we even got here. All that condescending nonsense, putting us down, putting people off us, right from the start. It's like we were doomed from the beginning."

Klondike nodded absently as he paced across the sawdust.

Jack Bannion, who was sat with Heavy and Plum by the flap, spoke next. "There was some animosity, there's no doubt about that. A lot of folks wanted us to fail, it would seem."

"Come on, Jack," Heavy blurted next to him. "These are your countrymen. What the hell gives with these people?"

Bannion looked around blankly. "There are probably several elements, truth be told. Feelings of ill will towards the, er, 'brash Americans', as some people say. A lack of appreciation for American-style circus shows. A lack of respect."

Plum seemed to explode. "None of it makes any sense. They wanted us here. The public were wild for us. We sold out the tent before showday."

Bannion nodded. He felt every pair of eyes on him, as if only he held the answers. "I think," he said weakly, "I think what Lacey said is the main issue here. These people, many of them working class folk struggling to get by in life… well, their idea of a circus show is two clowns throwing custard pies at each other. Maybe a knife thrower and a magician pulling rabbits out of a top hat. They just weren't ready for something like this. Something so advanced. Americans have embraced our show. But the English… they were frightened and confused."

Everyone seemed to automatically look across at Lacey. The glamorous publicist rose from her seat, looking briefly at Klondike, before speaking in a firm voice.

"It's true. Nothing like our show has ever been seen in England. Never, ever. We shocked the crowd. Truly shocked them. Now, that can go one of two ways. Either you get acclaim and awe. Or… well, you get buried." She looked around the tables, taking in the performers, who all looked at her in disbelief. She could almost feel their hurt. "I'm sorry," she blurted. "That's honestly how I see it. For these Londoners last night, it must have felt like they were propelled into the future, watching a spectacle from another world. They didn't understand it. Couldn't comprehend it."

Enqvist snorted across the floor. "So, all this is the audience's fault eh?"

Lacey held up her hands. "They couldn't handle it."

She sat down heavily, and immediately lit a cigarette and took a long sip of coffee.

"Last night was a disaster," Enqvist was saying, "and we need to put it right. Fast! Because Paris is next. I'm not gunna be forced off my platform by anybody again."

"Your bikes are too damn loud," one of the Range Riders called across the floor. "They scared the hell out of everyone. That's why the people were screaming and crying."

Enqvist stared at the cowboy in disgust. "Stick to pitchforking horse manure, redneck!"

"I'm just saying it as it is," the man shot back.

Then, Suzi suddenly spoke, her high-pitched squealing making everyone shudder. "Why, the audience didn't even understand what poor Roddy was doing. One newspaper reporter said he was using hidden microphones and recording devices! They didn't even know it was his voice throwing."

Klondike looked at her, then Olsen. He held up a hand. "Alright, alright." He sighed heavily. "Listen, we will be putting some changes together before the next show. Subtle ones. But changes nonetheless. We can't have a repeat of last night. You'll each be notified of anything important."

He moved towards the flap and seemed to brighten. "Fortunately, we did have several saving graces last night. In the form of the Range Riders and Gino's act." He stood beside the table where Shapiro, dressed in a gold robe, and Penny sat, carefree and seemingly without concern. Klondike patted their shoulders. "You guys may have saved us… saved the whole circus."

Shapiro didn't even look up, sipping his coffee. "It was a pleasure, chairman. I have performed the world over. In stadiums, town halls, tents, palaces. You see every reaction. Shock, dismay, delight. Last night was another type of reaction. A kind of subtle pleasure, I call it. The English, no? So graceful and restrained."

Klondike looked down at him blankly, then nodded. "Right."

He looked to the next table, where the Range Riders all huddled eagerly. Williams was in the middle of it all, still smiling.

Klondike grinned at him. "And you, Duster. And all you boys. You did the seemingly impossible – got these people off their feet and cheering."

Williams cackled. "The English… they love their cowboys."

"They sure do." Klondike nodded at the Riders. Then, he looked up and locked eyes with Bannion. He nodded subtly, a show of thanks and support.

"Ok folks," the circus boss bellowed, suddenly storming off to the makeshift chow line. He grabbed a coffee pot. "Disassembly begins later this morning. The tent will be coming down by evening. Then, we're back to the station in the morning and off to the coast. From there, the rail ferry across the Channel. To a whole new country. A new language." He looked downwards. He had planned the speech in his head, but somehow it wasn't coming out as he had envisioned. It was no grand speech, more an audible murmuring. He finished it anyway. "A new world to conquer."

With that, everyone seemed to stand up and go their separate ways.

Most headed out of the tent – as fast as they could.

Olsen walked disconsolate across Hyde Park, hands shoved into the pockets of his green anorak as he strode slowly through the short grass. A gentle breeze added a slight chill to the morning's spring warmth.

He looked up as groups of children played in the green, flying kites and driving go-carts. Gangs of teens were stood in circles, smoking cigarettes and swapping magazines.

Olsen waded down a small dirt path, away from all the people, and joined another track that ran parallel to a large reservoir that dominated the west side of the park.

A large blue sign at the head of the water told him the sprawling lake was called The Serpentine.

Walking alongside the murky grey water for several moments, he stopped at a park bench and sat down. He stared at the ducks and geese playing out on the water, his crystalline blue eyes lost and devoid of emotion.

How he had longed to come to London. And now this. An experience he had only known in nightmares.

The previous night's performance repeated itself through his conscience again and again, gnawing at him like an unwanted old memory of a deathly conflict.

As often happened, his mind wandered, through the mists of time. All of the events he had experienced in this wild rollercoaster ride that was his life. The death of his parents in a drunken automobile wreck when he was a child. Being forced to live with his abusive and alcoholic Uncle Ray. Running away, living in boarding houses in Los Angeles. And, of course, performing. Stunning club managers and bookers with his skills. And then there was that unforgettable day when he had turned up at Klondike's Circus's winter camp, back in 1958. When he had met Kal Klondike and Lacey Tanner. Lacey, the most magnificent and beautiful woman in the whole wide world. Someone he never thought it possible could exist.

"Hey mister!"

His reverie was interrupted by the high-pitched childlike voice. He turned in shock. A small girl, no older than 12, was standing next to the bench, holding a large book. She had impish features and brown hair tied in pigtails. Olsen merely stared at her.

"Mister," she said again, frowning. "Can I sit on that bench too? I like coming here to read."

He tried to smile. "Why sure."

With an enthusiastic skip, the girl darted in front of him and jumped up onto the wooden seat, barely two feet away. Settling down and opening the book, she looked up at him cautiously.

"Say, what are you doing over here? I come to the lake every morning in the school holidays. I ain't never seen anyone just staring into the water like you are."

Olsen tried to smile. He found it hard. "Well, I guess you could say I'm reflecting. Thinking. Seemed a nice place to just sit and… and think."

She giggled. "You talk funny! You're American, aren't you?"

He managed a grin now. "That's right."

Her eyes enlarged. "Wow! What the heck are you doing here in London?" She seemed captivated.

"I'm with the circus. You've seen the signs and the posters? Our big top is back there, near the main gate."

"Boy, oh boy!" she wailed. "The circus! That's the most amazing thing I ever heard." She eyed him speculatively. "What are you? A clown? A fire-eater?"

This time Olsen laughed softly. "No, I'm a ventriloquist." He noted her blank look. "A puppeteer."

"Oh my goodness," the girl whispered. "How incredible. I ain't never met one of them. Are you any good?"

He sat back. "Well, I was. Once." He stared again at the water, frowning slightly as the ducks all scrambled across the surface, as if in a choreographed routine. "But last night… at the show. Well, something just went wrong. The people, the fans, they… I don't know. They didn't go for it. They didn't like me. No one cheered. No one at all."

She looked hurt and upset. "Oh. I'm so sorry. That's terrible."

His face seemed to drop. "Yeah. Yeah, it sure was. Just terrible."

The girl winced, and seemed to sum up a little extra courage. "What are you going to do about it, mister?"

He smiled again, studying her. "You know, for such a little girl, you ask some very grown-up questions."

She suddenly looked sad. "Well, I grew up fast. Had no choice."

He nodded. "I know what that's like."

"Well," she said quietly, "if that's true, you'll know exactly what to do."

Olsen studied her. "How's that?"

The youngster responded by holding her book aloft. It was an old hardback, with a green dust jacket. It hardly looked like a children's book.

"It's just like it says in my book," she explained forthrightly. "It's called The Ballad of Billy Joe. All about a man who goes to fight in the war. He gets shot and badly injured, but survives. Then, he tries to start a new life back home, as a guitar player and singer. But money is hard. Everybody he meets says to him, 'Hey Billy Joe, why do you do it?' And he tells him it's because he is doing what's important to him. And also, because it makes Miss Felicity happy. That's the woman he is in love with. A barmaid who loves to hear him sing."

Olsen was suddenly transfixed. "And what happens to Billy Joe and this Felicity?"

The little girl smiled smugly, making a mockery of her tender years. She tapped the book gently. "That is for me to find out, mister. I'm only halfway through. But I just know he is going to make it work."

Olsen nodded, as if in understanding. "Because he knows what is right for him. What's important in life."

"He really does."

Olsen stared again at the lake all around them. His sky blue eyes were alive now, as if reactivated. He nodded to himself.

Then, suddenly, he stood up. Looking down at the girl, he said: "What's your name, sweetheart?"

"Linda. Linda Robinson."

"Well, Linda, you don't know this, but you have just made my day."

Linda stared at him in shock and confusion. "I have?"

"Sure you have." He stepped away, eyeing the dirt path back to the main park area. He looked back at Linda. "You look after yourself now, Linda, ya hear? And, er, enjoy the rest of your book."

With that, he was gone, trudging up the path with a new-found zest in his steps.

Little Linda Robinson watched him go, briefly considering following him to see the circus tent in all its glory. But she discarded the idea, settled down on her beloved bench, and opened her book.

Lacey Tanner was sat on the couch in her trailer going through the newspaper reviews from last night's show.

It proved a depressing task, with paper after paper hammering their circus, the reviewers seemingly engaged in a private contest to see who could trigger the most offensive put-downs.

Outside, there was a whirlwind of activity as the roustabouts began pulling the circus tent down, the great canvas slowly falling in on itself like a great punctured balloon.

Lacey was finding it hard to concentrate. It wasn't just the incessant noise outside as the workers roamed around in their trucks. Last night's show had struck an unpleasant notion in her conscience. It had proven they were not, as she often proclaimed, "immortal".

With a huff, she rose from the couch and made for the kitchenette, pouring herself a glass of cognac and lighting a cigarette. She was wearing a black leather skirt and fashionable woolly purple cardigan as she lounged in her quarters, lost in her many thoughts.

A sharp rap sounded on the trailer door.

She leant back against a dresser. "Come in, Roddy."

The door sprung open and Olsen crept in, a look of shock on his face. "How did you know…"

"Sometimes, you just know," she said matter-of-factly.

He shut the door and looked at her, as if afraid. "I had to see you."

She dragged on the cigarette and exhaled slowly. "I know."

Olsen looked around the trailer lounge, his eyes catching the pile of morning newspapers. "Oh lord, don't read the reviews. They've killed us."

Lacey merely leant back, folding her arms and staring at him, her giant violet eyes boring into him. The look was overwhelming to the younger man, half motherly concern, half awe. She used the look on him many times. He was used to it.

Finally, she broke the awkward silence. “It’s alright, Roddy. Really, it’s alright.”

He looked at her. “What? Last night?”

“Of course. Why, I’ve seen performers go through nights like that, reactions like that, all the time. Several times a month. You’ve been riding a wave of success, critical praise, commercial acclaim, for three years now. You’ve been untouchable. The fastest rising star in America.” Her tone dropped as she looked at him mischeviously. “Now, you’re not going to let one lousy night in London get you down, are you kittycat?”

He smiled awkwardly. It was uncanny how she always knew what to say. “Hell, I guess not. It was just a shock, is all.”

She nodded, fiddling with her hair. “Of course. It was all a shock.” She downed the rest of her cognac and stubbed out her smoke. Then, she approached. “And you’re just so young, Roddy. So young, so pure, so beautiful. Of course, something like that will affect you.”

As she came to him, she took his hands in hers and jostled them slightly. “But I’m here to tell you, it’s alright. True talent always shines through. No matter what. No matter what some confused reviewer says.” They looked into each other’s eyes. As always, he found it overpowering. Her gaze was hypnotic, her eyes like a pair of crystal balls. She spoke quietly. “You’re the best, Roddy. The best. No one in circus history has risen to the top like you. No one ever will.” She thought rapidly. “The people love you, Roddy. Young and old, rich and poor. The country club elite and the rednecks in the backwoods. Last night was nothing. You are the greatest, Roddy. The star of the show.”

It was her way of rebuilding him. He knew it, but loved it all the same. Her voice was gentle and throaty and just being with her raised his spirits.

“And you’re part of that, Lacey. You’re like the architect. This has all happened because of you. I know it. You know it.”

They were still holding hands. She hesitated, shaking slightly and looking away. "I feel somehow responsible for you. After everything that has happened."

Olsen's gaze was unbreakable. "It's more than that, Lacey. Much more."

And then it happened.

He thrust himself at her and, gently grabbing her neck, kissed her long and hard on the mouth. She froze, allowing the lingering kiss. Her arms remained at her side, and she flapped slightly as he leant into her.

Then, in a swift and sudden movement, she pulled herself away and backed into the kitchenette in fright, as if she'd been attacked.

Her eyes were wide in shock, a hand at her chest, which was heaving wildly. "No!" she whimpered absently.

Olsen took a step toward her, and she took one back in response.

"Lacey," he whispered in alarm. "What's wrong?"

"No," she hissed again. She looked afraid, alarmed, like a cornered animal. She tried to regain some composure. "No. No, Roddy, no. I can't."

Olsen stood there staring at her. He could feel his heart sinking. But her look of alarm rocked him. "I'm sorry, Lacey. Truly sorry. But, well, I… I can't help it. I thought you… you wanted this."

Lacey ran her hands through her hair rapidly, suddenly looking dishevelled and off-balance. "I do," she whimpered, staring at him with tears in her eyes. "Or, a part of me does. But it's wrong, Roddy. Like I always try to tell you. It's all wrong. That's not our relationship. Our dynamic. That's not what we are. We've been through this." She was breathing frantically now. "Can't you see? Please! Please don't push me. Or push yourself on to me. We'll only regret it. Both of us will."

Olsen took a deep breath. He looked around the trailer, and shook his head. "I won't Lacey. Because…" he gulped heavily. "Because I'm in love with you. I always have been. Since that first day. When you got Kal to hire me." He chuckled, taking them both by surprise. "You were wearing that pink trouser suit. With the fur coat. Hell, I'd never seen anyone like you. You looked like a contessa from a European movie. I can still picture it." His dazzling blue eyes locked on to her. "You had me then, Lacey. Right from day one."

Lacey's breathing came in wild gasps as she tried to calm down. She lit a cigarette, poured another cognac, and downed it instantly.

"Oh Roddy," she muttered. "What we have is magic. Yes, I do know it."

He looked at her pleadingly. "So what's the problem?"

She looked up at him sternly. "OK. Just imagine we did begin a romance. With everything we've been through. And then it all goes sour. Can you imagine? The magic would be over, Roddy. It would die, right then. And then… then we would have nothing. And that… that one scenario is something I can't live with."

Now, it was like the Lacey of old had resurfaced as she strode slowly toward him in the trailer. Her eyes wide, she leant over to him. "Can you?"

Olsen quivered, helpless in her all-encompassing glare again. He felt feint. "I… I don't think I can live without you, Lacey."

Her eyes widened at the dramatic statement. She tried to cool the situation. "Well, there you have it."

Olsen stood there dumbly, feeling like a teen schoolboy at a dance. "I guess so."

Without warning, she raised a hand to his cheek. Her skin felt like silk, her long nails looked like pearls. "Roddy," she whispered, "I'm your guardian angel. Your manager, priestess, sister and mentor. It's a role I adore. Never, ever forget that. No matter where you go in life and what you achieve, I will always be there with you. In here…" she tapped his chest where his heart was.

Olsen just continued to stare at her, lost in her beauty and warmth. Finally, he laughed slightly. "Well, who could ask for more than that?"

Lacey also laughed. "I've never offered all that to anybody!"

He tried to smile some more. He looked at the door, back at her, and then fumbled with his hands. "I'm sorry, Lacey."

She patted his shoulder. "Come on. It's ok. I'm sorry. Sorry… sorry I'm so complex and emotional."

He looked at her, sad and somehow helpless. “You know what’s important. What’s important in life.”

Then, he moved slowly to the door, opening it up and stepping outside. With a last look into the narrow confines, he muttered one more line: “Thank you.” Then, he turned and wandered through the maze of trailers spread across the park.

Lacey stood in the doorway and watched him go. Then, she closed the door gently and stood against it, feeling herself shrinking.

As Olsen walked around disconsolate, he suddenly felt very lost.

“Roddy!”

He turned at the sudden shriek and saw Suzi racing across to him, dressed in a beige dungarees and a sunhat. Her face was a mask of concern as she hurried over.

“Roddy,” she cried, “what’s the matter? You look terrified! Like you just saw a ghost or something.”

As she reached him, Olsen uncharacteristically picked her up in a mighty hug. “Hey,” she squealed, laughing now, “what gives? Since when did you become a hugger?”

He looked down at her. “You’re a sight for sore eyes, dear girl. You know that?”

“And so are you, huggy!” She looked him over curiously, enjoying the attention. “Want to get hamburgers and shakes at the cafe?”

Olsen laughed, nervously. “More than anything.”

“Rock n roll songs. American pop songs. That’s the key to getting over in Europe, Rod. Trust me.”

Olsen stared at Bannion as the Englishman concluded his lecture. He felt desperate for advice and guidance, and the circus newcomer was shovelling it out.

“American pop music is huge in Europe right now,” Bannion was saying. “Elvis. Ricky Nelson. Eddie Cochrane. Johnny Cash. Frankie Avalon. All those chaps. So, my suggestion to you is… make your act song-based. No banter or jokes. Just do songs with the puppets. Popular, American songs. That will resonate with the crowds on the continent. They will recognise the material.

And, hopefully, will marvel at your talents, making the dummies sing their favourite hits."

Olsen sat back, deep in thought. They were in his trailer, having had a deep discussion about how to save Olsen's act after the disaster the night before. Klondike had sent Bannion over to go through a "new strategy". A veteran of European circus tours, Bannion's opinions were considered vital.

"American pop songs," Bannion repeated. "Let's try that in Paris on Saturday. What do you say, Rod?"

Olsen had just got out of the shower when Bannion had come knocking at his trailer. Now, he sat there in a white vest, pyjama bottoms and with a towel over his shoulders. Tired, emotionally drained and lacking in enthusiasm for just about anything, the youngster tried to think.

"So, I'll just stick to singing? Ditch the rest of my act…"

"Not exactly. Keep the whole routine where Napoleon interrupts you and Rusty. And when the three of you all sing together. That stuff is gold, mate."

Olsen grunted. "There was an arena full of people who would have given you an argument last night, Jack."

"The hell with them! I say it can work.Let's see what the French make of your skills."

Olsen rubbed at his eyes. "I'm willing to try anything. I was worried about the language barrier from day one, once we got into mainland Europe. Nobody listened to me."

"That's why the songs will be key," Bannion said mesmerically. "Everyone will know them." He thought for a moment, looking across the trailer's lounge at Olsen's famous leather suitcase, that contained his "guys". He nodded. "I'll tell you what. Do a few pop songs with Rusty and Napoleon. Then do a couple of Sinatra and Dean Martin numbers with Tony Tan. So, you'll do a mix of rock n roll and swing." He nodded again. "That oughta work."

Olsen suddenly seemed disinterested. He leant back on the couch and patted his face with the towel. "If you say so, man."

Bannion watched him, standing and hovering slightly. He took on a look of concern. "Listen, Roddy," he whispered, "I know last night was an unpleasant experience. Hell, I've been there. Back in the day. The single most important action for you now is to get back out there, on stage, under the big top. Where you belong. And then… then you can exorcise your demons. Banish that memory. Forever."

Olsen peeked up at him through the towel. "That sure sounds nice, Jack."

Bannion looked down at him knowingly. "Only you can make it happen, Rod."

He wandered slowly to the narrow doorway. Taking one look back as he turned the handle, he added: "I'll look in on you on the train tomorrow." He smiled, trying to perk the youngster up. "Now, keep your head in the game. Paris is the most romantic city in the world. Don't let the fancy buildings and high society get into your head, monsieur."

He laughed boisterously, and waved as he left the trailer.

Olsen stared at the closed door and muttered one word, in misery.

"Swell."

CHAPTER 12

The Imperial circus train hurtled past the meadows and pastureland of southern England, inching closer to the coast with each passing minute.

It was another grey, dreary day, a ceiling of thick cloud hanging over everything and smothering the sun's rays.

The faithful old train cruised over the ancient-looking railroad at a gentle, steady pace, with the line manoeuvring through a seemingly endless sea of luscious green fields, bordered by thick hedge growth, which seemed to be everywhere.

In his stateroom at the back of the train, Klondike watched the green ocean of grass roll by, fascinated by the openness all around. It was a nice distraction from the dilemma he and his team faced.

He finally turned back and faced everyone. Lacey, Heavy and Plum were all seated around the long table in the giant room's centre. Bannion stood, as he often did, against the window on the opposite side of the carriage.

"Alright," Klondike murmured, sipping absently at a white mug of coffee. "On we go. We hit Dover in 50 minutes. Then, this so-called ferry transporter takes us away, out of this country, and across the Channel into France." He thought it over. "We can only hope the French embrace our show in a more....um, enthusiastic manner. Hell, anything will be better than... than what we saw on Saturday night."

He gazed out the window again as the fields rolled past, as if somehow willing the great train towards the sea, and the next port of call.

Heavy was shaking his head mirthlessly. "All that time, we talked about playing London. The grandeur of it all. The wonder and tradition." He looked down. "And then... then the reality. Just look at what happened."

Lacey was smoking a cigarette coyly, arms folded. "I think we all agree our London performance was not what any of us ever expected, or dreamed of. Now, how many times do I have to say it… forget about it, boys. All of it. We move on. Another town, another show. Or, in our case, another land."

"Yeah," Heavy put in, "and, most important of all, we learn from it."

"Which brings us to you, Jack," Klondike said, suddenly looking all business again. "You've spoken to the talent, implemented those changes we talked about. What do you think?"

Bannion nodded slowly. "Yeah. Everyone was receptive, helpful. Almost as if they wanted advice." He cleared his throat. "So, Roddy's set will be song-based, singing American pop hits that European audiences will know and love. The Hightops have agreed to perform more dance-based routines, which are popular on the continent, particularly in shows across central Europe. They have loads of moves choreographed and ready to go. Same with the Rocking Robins. Their set will be more dance-based. Now…"

He rubbed at his face, as if about to make a sales pitch. "For Corky and the clowns, they are sticking to the juggling. Then the human cannonball, Corky's old speciality. Then, they are doing the fire house act."

Klondike raised his eyebrows. "The fire house?"

Bannion locked eyes with him. "It's a long-time circus winner out here, Kal. Clown troupes do the fire routine, putting the fire brigade hats on and putting out the blaze in the straw house. It's been going for as long as the circus itself in Europe. Same as the cannonball act. Trust me. It is a proven winner out here."

Lacey was staring at him as if hypnotised. "We trust you, Jack. With everything. It's, er, just been a while since Corky and his team pulled off that gaff."

Bannion nodded. "He said he is fine with it. They've got the set and props on board."

"Alright," Klondike said, draining the last of his coffee. "Smart ideas, Jack. But we still haven't broached the big one. The Daredevils. Now, how the hell do they change their act?"

The room was silent, except for the thumping of the tungsten wheels beneath the carriage. Bannion's lips formed a queer grin. "They don't."

Lacey was aghast. "Oh, come off it, Jack! You saw what happened in Hyde Park. It was pandemonium in there. We have to drop them, surely?"

"I say no," Bannion replied coolly. "Here, my friends, lies the difference between British crowds and continental audiences. Motorbike shows are huge in Europe. Italy, Germany… why, the Daredevils themselves started in Norway. Stunt riding is accepted and recognised in mainland Europe, if you ask me. Yet, for some unclear reason, us Brits have yet to catch on."

Lacey stubbed out her cigarette, her violet eyes boring into the Englishman. "Do you really believe that?"

"I do, Lacey. I've seen the differences between circus promotions across the world over the past 25 years. I've seen and identified trends and fashions. And, I sincerely believe, what the Daredevils do will go down a storm in France, Germany, Italy and the like." He looked down at four concerned, unreceptive facial expressions. They all eyed him with something close to suspicion.

"Alright," he said quickly, "why don't we just see how the act goes down in Paris? Huh? If the fans go into a mad panic, or anything like that, again… well, we will drop the Globe of Death. If… if that's what you want, Kal."

Klondike paced the room moodily. Idly, he reached into his breast pocket and removed a long, thin cigar. British, Bannion noted. He lit up, coughing slightly under the cloud of blue/grey smoke.

Then, he eyed Bannion sternly. "We are putting a lot of trust in you, Jack," he said slowly. "A helluva lot of trust. Hell, we're making big changes based on your judgement, your recommendations. We're practically putting ourselves in your hands, my man."

"That's why you brought me on board," he answered simply.

A grim silence engulfed the room. Before long, the hum of the metal wheels rolling beneath them sounded thunderous as the quiet atmosphere set in.

Finally, it was Plum who broke the eerie reverie. "It's just funny, isn't it? The Daredevils and their Globe of Death have been a massive part of our show these past few years. That act has been a major factor in our rise, our success. Fans go home talking about it, marvelling at it. And now… now, we are somehow even considering dropping the whole gig."

Lacey gently placed her hand on one of his at the table. "That nightmare in London changed everything. It… well, it made us realise we truly are a long way from home."

"Listen," Klondike spat out. "We have some of the hottest talent in the world, god damn it! The media know it, the people know it. That doesn't just evaporate overnight, after one crazy night out of a horror story. No, no, no. With a show like ours, we will be a success… anywhere in the world. Mark my words, people, we will prevail."

Plum spoke up again. "To be honest, Kal, London was a sellout." He glanced down at the usual pile of accounting books in front of him. "According to my projections, Paris could be a sellout too. Why, every show out here may well be a sellout for all we know. Capacity crowds. No matter what the press say. So, commercially at least, this tour could still be a big success for us."

"Yeah," Klondike sneered, returning to the window. "But that's not enough for me, Richie." He studied the view outside as houses finally began to appear, rolling by as the train slowed slightly. "I want to show folks out here, on the other side of the pond… I want to show everyone what us Americans are all about. What an American circus can really do. We're representing our nation on this trip. I've read too much condescending garbage in the papers out here. I want us to leave a mark. Plant a flag…"

He let the sentence hang as he studied the view approaching rapidly on the horizon. The train was cruising through a township now. Squinting, sensing something, he stared as if spellbound into the misty haze beyond. They were slowly coming down a hilltop. It was almost time. Gazing intently though the window, he finally spotted it, far in the distance. The deep blue sea. The English Channel. He smiled.

"Yeah," he growled, "we'll plant a flag alright. A giant, beautiful Stars and Stripes."

The voyage across the Channel to France was uneventful and surprisingly rapid.

Almost 30 miles of still, placid ocean separated the two nations, but the modern and surprisingly deluxe Normandy Line ferry transporter made it all seem so simple and straightforward.

The Imperial train was transported from the main line at Dover on to a specially-constructed siding that measured several hundred yards. Once the wheels were mounted onto the siding at the port, the train driver was able to simply manoeuvre the train gently along into a holding berth aboard the ship's deck.

From there, the train was essentially cut into three parts, separated at the appropriate interchanges, with each third placed into a different berth, manoeuvred into its spot by carriage pullers.

"Not exactly the Orient Express," was how Klondike succinctly put it.

But even the circus boss had to admit, the Channel operation ran smoother than anyone could have expected.

Once the whole vehicle was onboard, the mighty express represented something out of a breaker's yard, like three lines of old carriages lined up for scrap. Only these carts held trucks, tents, midway stalls, cotton candy makers and mobile grandstands. Not to mention a stable block full of neighing horses.

The ferry departed Shepherd's Hill and made a slow crawl across the Channel to Cap Gris-Nez, in northern France.

When it finally arrived in mainland Europe, the ferry crew essentially performed the same task as they had in Dover, only this time in reverse.

Incredibly, within one hour of landing in France, the Imperial train was back in one piece again and on its way, steaming down French rails, on its merry way to the romance capital of the world.

The Channel crossing could not have gone any better. And, like so many other issues relating to their tour, a lot of that was down to the forward planning and knowledge of Jack Bannion, who was quickly proving to be an ace in Klondike's pack.

And so the circus rolled on, heading to Paris, another whole new realm in this journey beyond the horizon.

COMING ON SATURDAY…DIRECT FROM THE USA!

AMERICA'S NUMBER ONE SHOW! IT'S… KLONDIKE'S CIRCUS!

The giant bill poster was plastered to the oak board with a sticky rolling brush covered in spirit water, an old man in work clothes operating the great roller, which resembled a mammoth broom.

Once he pulled the roller away, the bill stuck perfectly to the panel, and seemed to shine in the sunlight.

His work done, the old man wandered away, brush over one shoulder, on to the next board at the park's perimeter.

The Jacques Lemerre Memorial Field was a sprawling open space in central Paris, barely a mile from Gare de Nord, the city's main central station.

It was essentially a giant field surrounded by a tall wooden fence, full of forestry, an orchard, a small art museum and several ponds.

As the posters sprang up in and around the park, courtesy of the old-timer and his trusty rolling brush, curious passers-by began to gather around each billboard. Many were drawn by the jazzy stars and stripes decorations of the posters, which screamed Americana. The US flag emblems seemed to garner attention from everyone. Within minutes, a small crowd had gathered around the field.

As a gaggle of animated teenagers chatted excitedly while studying one of the posters, two unusual-looking men stood back, eyeing the bill with great interest.

"America's number one show. Very interesting…"

Conrad Handel smiled smugly as he watched the group in front of the billboard pointing excitedly, all chattering at once.

He was dressed in a beige trenchcoat, smoking a long, thin cigarillo. He somehow looked like he didn't belong.

The same could be said of Tarz alongside him. The giant strongman wore a denim dungarees, with a cream and brown fur gilet covering his hulking shoulders.

"It would appear," Handel was saying, "that Klondike's Circus is in the aftermath of a disaster." He laughed softly. "They come here, to Paris, seeking salvation." He looked up at Tarz coyly. "And so the killer blow is within our grasp."

Tarz grunted, annoyed. "It sounds like the circus will struggle out here, if those reviews in London are anything to go by."

Handel nodded. "Now, they realise they have bitten off more than they can chew. Like so many before them." He watched idly as the group of teens slowly drifted away. His face grew hard. "Now, we make our move. Our real move. They have seen this tour will be a struggle. Now, suddenly, our offer of financial compensation will appear a little more… how do they say? Appetising. No?"

Tarz looked angry. Restless and aggrieved. "I say we just hit them. The hell with offers and talking. Me and the boys can finish these jokers in no time." Now, Tarz smiled an evil grin. "And we'll enjoy it as well."

Handel laughed, an eerie, almost feminine sound. He placed an arm around his companion's hulking frame and steered him away as they began to walk.

"In time, dear boy. In time."

CHAPTER 13

The branch line from Gare du Nord ran right outside the Jacques Lemerre field, stopping at an old station house that looked like it had been standing since the days of Joan of Ark.

The journey from Nord had taken just minutes, the train rolling along at a gentle pace, as if gliding along the rails in the wind.

The passengers had all stood in their respective rooms and carriages, noses pressed against the glass windows as they took in the famous sights of central Paris, many marvelling at the breathtaking architecture.

The old Imperial train slowed to a stop at the station house, where scores of interested onlookers – the same folk who had earlier studied the posters by the park – rushed to the carriages as the train became stationary.

"This is more like it," Heavy muttered to Klondike as the duo pushed open an interchange door and stared at the crowd lining up alongside the great train.

Klondike nodded, smiling at the many astonished faces. "At least people here are interested in us."

Lacey suddenly joined them, dressed in a flowery blouse and sunhat. She seemed overjoyed. "Oh my, boys," she quivered. "Paris! Finally, after all these years, I get to see the romance capital of our world."

Klondike stepped onto the asphalt and helped her down with a grin. "Don't get any fancy ideas," he uttered dryly. "Five days. In and out. That's the schedule."

"Ah, tiger," she said sarcastically, "and isn't that just what every girl wants to hear. There I was expecting moonlight walks along the Reine, French cuisine al-fresco, wine and roses…"

Klondike half-smiled. "Hell, Lacey, I'm running a circus here, not a god damn escort service."

She rolled her eyes. "Alright, Casanova. I get the idea." She looked around at the crowds who had gathered to greet them. People suddenly seemed to be everywhere, staring at them excitedly. Inexplicably, a young man with shaggy hair approached her and produced a giant white rose.

"Mademoiselle," he said gallantly, bowing elegantly.

Lacey beamed as she accepted the flower. "Merci."

She turned and raised an eyebrow at Klondike and Heavy. "You see, boys. Romance. They live for it here."

She attached the rose to her sunhat. Several of the young men in the throng applauded. She waved, like a visiting dignitary. Then, she turned back to the train.

"I'll go and find our Paris rep. He is based on the other side of the park, so they tell me. I want to see how our press releases and ticket sales have fared out here." All business again, Lacey strode elegantly through the crowd, towards a footpath. Klondike and Heavy watched, as several men removed their hats and bowed to her as she walked by.

"Er, Kal," Heavy murmured as they watched. "What the hell gives with these people? What, they never seen a dame before?"

Klondike shook his head. "Not one like our Lacey, it would seem."

They ambled along the side of the train, shaking hands with several well-wishers, who blabbered excitedly at them in French.

When they approached the equipment carts, they saw Jim McCabe and his roustabouts clearing people away gently, so that they could begin the unloading operation.

The roustabouts, in their trademark brown cloth jackets, resembled an army, all seemingly identical, as they got to work.

Klondike looked beyond the welcoming committee, across a gravelled path, where the great field lay. A mass of green, several football fields worth. As he often did, Klondike imagined the site on show day. Before long the midway stalls would gradually start sprouting up, alongside the big top itself. Idly, he wondered what all of these local onlookers would make of it all.

"Well," Heavy said over his shoulder, "the public here all seem keen and curious. That's a start."

Klondike studied a group of teenagers excitedly pointing at a stars and stripes flag draped over a box the roustabouts were carrying from the train.

“The Americans are here,” he muttered. “Just like in the war. Only this time, we’re not here to fight and liberate. We’re here to entertain and enthral.”

Heavy grinned like a cherub. “They’re gunna love us, Kal.”

Klondike seemed to grimace. “Hell, old buddy. I sure hope you’re right.”

Before long, the enclosure surrounding the stationary train resembled an open-air, mobile warehouse as all manner of equipment was unloaded on to the gravel that ran alongside the Jacques Lemerre field.

A great pathway had been cleared through the woodland and hedgerows out to the green, where already midway stalls and booths were sprouting up, as well as the usual caravans and cabins.

The big top itself had also been transported across, and now sat sprawled on the turf like a great slain behemoth from ancient times. A mass of red and blue fabric, ready to be erected high above.

As the colourful midway stalls were set up and placed in formation, the excited public that had met the train earlier all bled out on to the field, eyes wide at the many carnival wonders now appearing before them.

At the heart of it all, Gino Shapiro wandered happily around the staging area, waving at just about everyone, posing for photographs and signing autographs.

Decked out in his orange fireball tracksuit, his name emblazoned on the back in midnight blue letters, he looked like a prince from another planet out there in the rapidly assembling circus midway.

He halted with joy as two women, barely in their 20s, raced over to him and hugged him together, almost crushing him in the middle.

“Oh, Gino!” one of them screeched in a heavy Gallic accent. “It’s really you.”

“Si, it is true, madam,” he said, grinning like a hyena. He placed his arms around both waists. “Your Gino is here.”

"It's been so long," the other wailed. "We saw you perform at the Trucadero. In Cannes. Back in '52. We both agreed it was the most incredible display of trapeze in Europe…"

"How we longed for your return, Gino," the other continued. "And you make us wait… er, almost ten years!" She pouted. "Bad Gino!"

He laughed playfully, loving every minute. "But now I am here, no madam? For the greatest show France will ever see!"

"We can't wait!" the second lady cried.

"Have you got your tickets, girls?" He held them close.

"Oh my, yes! And all the girls in our lacrosse club, too. It's like a pop star is coming! And from America!"

They all laughed.

Then, yet another female voice broke the joyous union.

"The debonair king of the air!"

They all turned, to find a tall woman wearing jeans and a riding top, running a hand through her long amber hair.

The newcomer smiled at him demurely. "Ten long years, for sure."

Shapiro stared at her, dumbstruck. Then, he came around and seemed to look to the heavens. "What a blessing this is. To have the company of three beautiful women. Why, hah! This could be the happiest day of my life."

The tall woman had a laser-like stare. "That's what you said last time."

They guessed she was German or Austrian, her accent soft but sounding vaguely American.

"Do we know each other?" said Shapiro.

"You don't remember me, eh king?"

He baulked, as the other two females stared at the newcomer. "I am sure I would remember a lady of such beauty and infinite grace, Miss…"

She huffed slightly, pacing towards him until they were inches apart. "I am Ingrid Shellman. From the International Herald Express. I interviewed you after your Amsterdam show on that last tour." She laughed slightly, eyeing him like a vengeful bobcat. "We had drinks, then went back to your hotel room, as I recall. Now, what happened the next morning? Oh yes, that's right… you left town!"

Shapiro gazed at her, lost in confusion and faded memories.

"Pah! Surely, you are mistaken, princess. I would have had to have been a madman to have entertained such lunacy." He eyed her with large, predatory eyes. "It has been a long while, eh Ingrid? But we have nothing but time now. To catch up. And, ah, maybe pick up where we left off, no?"

He laughed over-enthusiastically to himself. Then, ending his chortling, he looked at all three women, who stared at him as if he had gone mad. Suddenly, he felt somewhat trapped.

Gently, he eased his arms away from the waists and tried to appear gallant. "Why don't we all go get a drink? I know a place on the Seine…"

An awkward silence followed. The first two women seemed happy. Then Ingrid said: "I'll come. But… only if you give me the inside scoop on Saturday night's show. I want to know everything." She smiled. "Then, maybe, I will forgive you for leaving me all those years ago."

Shapiro nodded rapidly. "Ok. You got it, mamacita."

He made to herd them along the path when suddenly another figure emerged from behind a nearby trailer, stopping dead when he saw the commotion. Roddy Olsen.

Shapiro froze at the sight of the youngster. He eyed the three women, who detected his sudden unease. Then, he tried to smirk, turning on his charm persona yet again.

"Well, well, well," he purred. "Look who it is. The great crowd silencer!" He chuckled. "The darling of the dolls. It looks like you finally came unstuck, eh Olsen? That is what happens when you perform in front of a true circus crowd. One that has no time for your toy puppets."

He glanced at the exasperated trio next to him. Olsen stood there, trying to remain calm.

"Ladies," Shapiro exclaimed, walking between them again. "I would introduce you to our star puppeteer, but, well, how can I put it… he is no longer a star!"

"Alright Gino, that's enough," Olsen snapped. His hands were deep inside the pockets of his green anorak. "I was out walking after the train journey. I'm not looking for trouble."

"Take a good look around, amigo," Shapiro said, waving a hand about them at the stalls sprouting up all around. "Before long, this is where you will belong. The midway! Roaming! Showing your tricks to whoever is interested."

Olsen cocked his head, and actually smiled. "My, you must be loving this, Gino. My act goes down a disaster in London. And, suddenly, I'm a disgrace. Just like that…"

Shapiro snarled, as the three women backed away slightly, all spellbound, despite having no idea what was going on.

"That night was a long time coming, Olsen. You know it. I know it. The people… now they know. They see through your dumb little tricks. Your dolls. They are not entertained anymore. And that, amigo, that is the worst moment in the career of any circus performer."

Olsen gazed at him in shock and a kind of awe. Slowly, his mind flashed back to odd moments over the past three years where Shapiro had praised him, held his arm aloft in front of the circus's biggest TV audience ever. Even composed an offer for the two of them to go into business together, with a new show. He shook his head.

"Why do you do it?" He cried suddenly. "I have your respect. We both know the real truth. You have been in awe of me, you've said it yourself. Yet you persist with this crazy talk. All the damn time!" He eyed Shapiro squarely. "Your jealousy, your judgement, will kill this circus, Gino."

"Jealousy!" Shapiro cried. "What nonsense. The mouth of a clown." Then, he delicately manoeuvred himself among the women, placing his arms back around the two strangers, as Ingrid stood there, still bewildered by it all.

"Why is it, Olsen," the flyer said slowly. "That all the women, all the people… are with me, eh? Everybody wants their Gino, no?" He smiled with contempt at the younger man. "Everybody wants the star. Look at you. All alone. With nowhere to go. A boy, lost and alone now."

Olsen virtually ignored his ramblings. "So my act didn't work in England. I'm not the first. It's all a part of showbusiness." He cocked his head. "Besides, this tour has only just started. Then, of course, we will be back home afterwards. Las Vegas, Los Angeles, TV land. Lots of fans, Gino, lots of spots."

Shapiro chewed it over. He snorted. "All that matters, boy, is the next show. The next town, the next crowd. You know that."

Olsen struggled to stay cool. "How's that shoulder, Gino? I hope they have ice in Paris."

The flyer pumped out his chest, as if he had been inflated, and made a fist. Thinking better of it, he turned his back on the youngster. "This conversation is over, amigo. Like your career!"

Then, he once more tried to lead the females away from the midway stalls. "Come on, girls, let's get that drink. Gino is buying!"

Remarkably, all three backed off simultaneously, each making a vague excuse as they all retreated. Ingrid stared at Olsen for several moments, before idly wandering back into the hubbub of the midway. The other two seemed to disappear.

And then, like two old gunslingers facing off at a corral in the old west, Shapiro and Olsen were all alone amid the dust and haze.

Gino watched the females disappear mournfully, then glared at Olsen again, his dark eyes practically murderous.

"You have lousy timing, charro," he raged. "But, then again, losers usually do. I have had enough of you and your tricks, boy. Now, do me a favour, and stay out of my way."

He stormed off, heading back towards the crowd of fans pouring into the burgeoning midway.

Olsen eyed him, a bitter scorn forming in his youthful features. The beautiful, baby blue eyes had taken on a foreign, maddening look that was unknown to him. He could feel himself being slowly consumed by a queer, unfamiliar sensation.

He watched Shapiro disappear down the pathway and frowned.

"Why do you do it, Gino?"

Le Tarantula was a downtown bar off Gare du Nord, hidden away down one of the many dinghy backstreets that ran off the main drag by the Seine.

It was a cheap, dour-looking joint, its interior walls covered in wallpaper that depicted old front pages from Paris fashion magazines.

Tip Enqvist and two of his Daredevils, Bo and Justin, sat around a small, round table in the far corner opposite the bar. Each man wore a sullen, sour expression.

Enqvist looked around. He'd been in hundreds of bars across the world during his eventful life, but never a place like this.

Every patron seemed geriatric. Aside from the barmaid, there were no women. And, most curiously of all, everyone was drinking strange pink and green spirits in wide wine glasses.

Enqvist sipped at his beer, lighting a cigarette. He felt a long way from home. In every sense.

"Listen, we can't put this off any more." It was Justin, the tall and musclebound member of the stunt crew. He hadn't touched his tankard of ale at all, instead constantly looking about, nervously.

"Put what off?" Enqvist snapped. He inhaled deeply on his smoke.

"Come off it," Justin murmured, "Saturday night, man. What's going to happen out here in Frenchie land? Will it be a repeat of London? Was all that madness back there a one-off? What, man? What?"

"Alright, alright," Enqvist said quietly. He noticed several of the bar patrons had been eyeing them since their arrival.

"The truth is, I just don't know, boys. How can I? What happened in London was a first for all of us. An unwelcome, unwanted first. It changed our minds. That English fool Bannion put it down to the British crowd. I dunno know, though. There's word stunt riding hasn't caught on across western Europe yet. I had heard this before we left. I… I just didn't believe it. Couldn't believe it. You saw how the fans love us in the States. I couldn't comprehend the people not cheering us. Anywhere… in the whole wide world."

"It would appear," Bo said slowly, joining the conversation, "that we all underestimated the change in attitudes. In culture. The art of entertainment."

Enqvist grunted as he swigged at his beer. "The hell with it. Three months from now, who's gunna give a hog's ass about all this? About Europe? We'll be back in Los Angeles or San Fransisco, with the crowds singing our names."

Justin looked down. "We can't have a night like London again. Ever!"

"You think I don't know that!" Enqvist boomed. He calmed immediately, fiddling with his cigarette. "Hell, nothing will ever be as bad as that."

Bo studied his boss shrewdly. "You don't like it out here, do ya Tip?"

Enqvist visibly shuddered. "Let's just say if you offered me the chance to get back on that boat to the States tomorrow, I'd take it."

"But it wasn't meant to be like that," Bo said, strained. "We're all superstars, on a grand tour of Europe. Hell, there's so much to see out here!"

Enqvist looked around the bar morbidly. An old man was sat by the door, grinning at him maddeningly. A jukebox had just come to life playing an old jazz number. And the barmaid wandered by, carrying a tray of the odd-looking pink spirits.

He snorted. "I've seen enough."

An eerie spring mist settled over the circus camp that night.

The huge spattering of huts, caravans and midway stalls sat before the great tent, like a shanty town leading to the new world in ancient times.

The big top looked as majestic as ever, its electric red and blue design glowing in the twilight.

And the white trailers below were lit up by the red night sky, which looked burgundy as it was glimpsed through the mist.

There was still plenty of activity going on around the camp.

Roustabouts hustled cotton candy machines and hot dog vendors along the paths to their designated cabins. Several stewards wandered in and out of the tent, carrying equipment of all shapes and sizes.

Corky and his clowns were holding court at the midway gates, as was the long-standing custom. The group made balloon animals for curious passersby who stopped to gape at the circus site. Corky even handed out flowers to any females who walked by. Alongside them, the night man distributed circus flyers to anyone who showed an interest in the camp at this late hour.

Huddled among the trailers out back, Klondike ducked out of his quarters and lit one of his customary cigars, watching with glee as a giant cloud of purple smoke filled the nighttime air.

He closed his eyes. There were nerves, tensions running throughout his circus outfit. He could feel them, sense them. It was like a pulse. Beating away in the background. Coursing through everything.

He tried to phase it out as he enjoyed his cigar.

Meanwhile, in a trailer at the far end of the camp, next to the mobile horse stable block, nerves and worries were most certainly not on the agenda.

Duster Williams sat on his bed, dressed in a maroon robe, and sipped at a tall glass of milk. And he could not stop smiling.

He was staring at an old poster he had fixed to the wall, showing him in his youth, performing a hind-leg salute on Goldie the palomino. The poster was from his own smash hit country and western show from two decades earlier.

The words were etched in bright gold letters. DUSTER WILLIAMS…KING OF THE COWBOYS!

With a chuckle, Williams held the glass aloft and toasted his younger self.

"I'll be damned," he whispered to himself. "I'm back!"

That night, he slept like a winner.

CHAPTER 14

The big top was filled with a capacity crowd for the Klondike's Circus Paris spectacular.

The audience seemed to be made up largely of teenagers, with a number of elderly and middle-aged patrons thrown in. Many were once again waving the small stars and stripes flags, which seemed to be everywhere.

Standing in his customary spot at the tent flap, Klondike idly wondered where all those flags came from as he looked up at the packed grandstands all around him. A sea of faces filled the air, rising up to the summit high above, where the trapeze rig sat waiting.

Klondike felt that same queer, nagging feeling he had experienced in London. It was on show again here in Paris… the pensive, subdued atmosphere, the seeming lack of enthusiasm from the audience. He felt like he was in a football stadium between quarters, when all the fans talked among themselves idly. The pre-show electricity just wasn't evident.

Dressed in his instantly recognisable show outfit of brown leather jacket, black slacks, fedora and cane, Klondike prowled the entranceway like a caged lion. He looked out into the field outside beyond the flap, then paced back to the edge of the grandstands.

Lacey and Plum both stood like statues by the arena threshold. Bannion, yet again, stood leaning against something, this time the side of the stand.

Anticipation gripped the air as the clock wound down to 7pm.

Finally, it was time. The sound of trumpets blaring reverberated around the tent. The audience began a hearty applause.

And then, as if in slow motion, Heavy Brown began his ceremonial walk to the centre of the arena, microphone in hand.

"Ladies and gentlemen…"

In the end, it was to be another show of highs and lows, without the extreme disasters of London.

The Hightops' newly-choreographed routine involved an unusual blend of quick fire dancing with risky gymnastics moves and acrobatics, all to a catchy ragtime tune playing out on the tannoy.

As Bannion had predicted, the act went down well with an enthusiastic audience. The Hightops ended their routine with their standard show-stopper, the human totem pole.

The Rocking Robins followed up with another highly-charged dance act, as they strutted along to their usual Broadway songs and got the crowd clapping along happily.

The two acts were, as ever, a neat and gentle introduction to the circus itself.

Next up were the Flying Batistas, who managed to extract several exclamations of shock and awe from the patrons with their acrobatics... but, again, still not the wild ovations the Mexicans were used to in America.

As Corky and the team of clowns burst onto the sawdust next, everyone held their breath. Klondike shook hands with his beloved clown as he mounted his unicycle, and said a silent prayer.

To the immense relief of just about everyone connected to the circus, the clown revue went smoothly, and was met with applause... steady and sincere applause. But nothing more.

Corky's human cannonball stint got the biggest cheer, while the age-old firehouse sketch – where several clowns fool around in a wooden hut with fire sticks, before the firemen clowns douse everything in water – was also warmly received.

The Showcase Revue was met with a distinctly reserved reaction, almost as if the paying patrons somehow felt such revelry was beneath them. Even the sight of Rumpy Stiltskin performing a full somersault while wearing six-foot stilts failed to generate much energy from the bleachers.

Next up was the Daredevils. If they were nervous after London, the riders did not show it. They looked strong and professional as they donned their helmets at the flap and rode into the arena.

The reaction to the Globe of Death this time was equally foreign to the circus team – but for different reasons.

The Parisian crowd were truly stunned by the Daredevils' performance. But they were so flabbergasted, they didn't know how to react. This time, it was the Daredevils' turn to be greeted by a deathly silence.

As the bikes spun round and round inside the great metal sphere, an almighty, cumulative gasp seemed to reverberate around the big top.

Klondike, curious, stood at the front of the nearest grandstand and looked up at the audience.

He saw thousands of hands covering mouths, a whole stand of people stiffened in shock and awe. The whole spectacle just supported Bannion's theory, and Lacey's intuition, that Europe was not ready for an act so "otherworldly".

As the Daredevils finally exited the Globe of Death, they were met with a polite, delicate applause. But even that felt strange and surreal, like failure. The clapping was slow, not wild and riotous.

Klondike could not put his finger on it. Were these people really so shocked and staggered by the Daredevils that they simply did not know how to react? Or did they just not care for such entertainment?

The questions swirled through his mind as the stunt riders raced off, out of a subdued and withdrawn arena crowd.

For Klondike, there was little time to analyse it all as Roddy Olsen strode out onto the sawdust. As the youngster in the silver waistcoat began his own freshly adjusted act, Klondike felt Lacey grab at his arm. She seemed to cower.

Olsen made a brief introduction with Rusty Fox, then burst straight into a repertoire of songs.

He performed a duet with the fox puppet, a medley of several Elvis hits. Then, Napoleon joined him for Amazing Grace.

After that, he pulled out Tony Tan and performed a Sinatra number and ended it with a Pat Saunders country folk song that had been popular in France the year previous.

The audience applauded respectfully at the conclusion of each song and clapped politely at the end of the act. But, again, it was all a long way from what the wunderkind Roddy Olsen was used to back home.

The consummate professional, Olsen bowed and waved to the fans, even indulging in a group bow with all three puppets. He felt like he had just performed a gentle warm-up for the star attraction. It was all very different to his usual acclaim and adulation. Still, he acted with grace and continued to wave at the audience as he walked off stage.

As in London, the crowd finally kick-started into life when Duster Williams and the Range Riders burst onto the stage, racing in circles on their shiny mounts around the sawdust and performing their customary saddle tricks.

This time, the applause was constant, and there were finally cheers and exclamations of delight from those watching.

Williams' solo spot was met with a large cheer, and as the cowboys rode off for their final lap, some of the patrons actually gave a standing ovation.

To Klondike, it felt irksome being so happy at seeing one or two fans stand up and cheer. In their US tour last year, the entire crowd would be on their feet at the conclusion of every act. The atmosphere would be electric, overpowering.

Now, as he stood watching the Range Riders gallop to the flap on their pristine horses, he frowned at the cheers as they quickly evaporated again.

A similar reaction greeted Gino Shapiro and Penny Fortune as they walked proudly out on to the sawdust.

Once again, Shapiro's high-risk trapeze skills and daring maneouvers drew hearty applause. Several fans yelped and whooped as he flew through the air high above. There was just something missing…the ecstatic, high energy adoration of a circus audience.

Shapiro's renowned high wire walk finale also failed to draw its customary wild reception, with the usual screams and shrieks replaced by the now familiar, monotone-like applause.

Several women screamed and cried out his name as the trapeze ace left the arena, but that was as good as it got.

When Suzi Dando came out to sing Can You Feel The Magic Tonight, and the dazzling Cadillacs emerged carrying all the stars of the show, the crowds in the stands just sat there patiently, as if waiting to be allowed to leave.

At the song's conclusion, as the last car disappeared down the exit way, a final round of applause rang out.

After Heavy delivered his customary closing announcement, the bleachers quickly became deserted. Everyone just shot up and left, as if someone had rung a dinner bell.

Down on the sawdust, Klondike watched the people. All were shuffling rapidly to the exits, heads down, like a procession. There was little joy or scenes of unbridled glee and happiness. The patrons heading to the exits looked unimpressed. Confused. And distinctly underwhelmed.

Klondike continued to watch. Rooted to the spot, he looked up at the bleachers. The empty seats. He wanted to scream at the departing crowds. Demand to know what their problem was. He felt so helpless.

He became aware of Lacey alongside him. She too looked up at the last few remaining spectators, her eyes locked in dismay.

"What the hell is happening to us?" Klondike whispered.

Lacey looked at him, concern clouding her beautiful features. "I just don't know, tiger. But, whatever it is, it seems to be catching."

He pulled off his hat and ran a hand roughly through his thick hair. "This is insane! These people don't give a damn about us. They don't give a damn about anything."

Lacey turned back to the bleachers, watching the last few spectators head out of the exit doors. The big top was suddenly silent once again. Barely two minutes after the show had ended.

"It's almost like they've been paid not to cheer," she whispered.

Klondike stiffened. His dark eyes took on a deep, queer look. "Paid off," he said dryly.

Lacey faced him. "What's that, Kal?"

He seemed to nod to himself. "Paid off. Not the people. But the press. The negative publicity. All this nonsense printed about us in London and god only knows where. It's planted a seed in the public's minds. Steering them against the so-called 'brash, big shot Americans.'"

She glared at him. “But why are they still coming to watch us? If they really are against us, why pay their money and come to the show?”

Klondike laughed mirthlessly. “People paid a fortune to go and see John Merrick. The same can be said for Santiago the Ape Man back home. You pay your money, knowing you’re going to be repulsed. All because the seed has been planted in your head…by publicists and the media.”

Lacey’s giant violet eyes were wide in wonder. They stared at each other, their noses just inches apart. “Kal… what are you saying?”

“I’m not saying anything…yet!” he snapped. “But it’s like I always say, Lacey. Someone’s out to get us.”

She nodded. “There’s always someone, right?”

“Damn straight.” He looked around at the empty bleachers, the barren sawdust stage floor. “And, dammit all to hell, I think we all know who it is!”

With that, he stormed off down the exit way, through the flap, and out into the night-time gloom of the Jacques Lemerre field.

Flushed, Lacey thought for a moment and then trotted off after him.

A bad feeling consumed her. Another one.

“And so, as these flashy, expensive motors all rolled off the circus floor, at last, the paying customers left in a bewildered exodus, many vowing never to return…”

Lacey frowned as she read from the sheet of paper, partly through trying to decipher the handwriting inked down, but more due to her shock and disgust at the words printed.

“There’s more,” she murmured dourly. She read from the sheet again. “And all that’s left is for this reviewer, a devout disciple of European circus for decades, to declare this…the American circus is dead! If it were ever alive on these shores at all, that is. So, please, Mr Klondike, or whatever your name is, be gone… back to your land of stars and stripes, of glitz and glamour. And, my word, please take those rotten hot dogs with you. Au revoir!”

Lacey calmly folded the sheet and placed it on a desk. The words had been translated by a French steward, having been printed in that morning's Paris Nouvelle, the city's leading tabloid.

She looked at the sea of blank faces all around her. Klondike, Heavy, Plum and Bannion were all sat around in her trailer, holding untouched mugs of coffee as they went through the morning debriefing.

It had not been one of their most celebrated meetings.

Outside the trailer, the unmistakable sound of the work crews pulling down the tent and transporting the equipment back to the train filled the morning air.

"What I tell ya?" Klondike finally broke the grim silence. He sipped the coffee. "They're out to nail us. Again! It's just like last season all over again."

"I don't know, Kal," Bannion said quickly. "The crowds all came. Again! The voices of a few lousy reporters haven't changed the box office receipts."

"Yeah," Heavy blurted. "Who cares what these schmucks think? The press can't sway the public that much." He looked at the others rapidly. "You ask me, these people are stunned by our show. But stunned beyond comprehension. Stunned into silence!"

"Look at the faces in the stands," Lacey said quietly. "They can't believe what they are witnessing. The Globe of Death is like a mad science fiction movie come to life for these people. Roddy's ventriloquism… they don't understand it. With Gino, they've never seen a flyer up there, whizzing around, without a damn net underneath. Because of that, they don't know what to think. Or how to react."

Klondike grunted angrily. "I dunno about that, Lacey. I say you're clutching at straws."

"I think there might be something in it." It was Plum who finally spoke, his high-pitched tone making them all stare down at him.

"Would you care to expand on that, Richie?" prompted Lacey, sitting back on the couch and hugging at her coffee cup.

"Well," the little man said nervously, "I know a little about psychology. Human inner workings. And the mind reacts to different sights and actions in different ways. Shock, awe, horror, disbelief. That's what our crowds may have experienced. And all of those emotions can result in sheer silence."

The others silently chewed it over. Finally, Klondike rose angrily. "Argh, the hell with it. I still say that German sucker is out to nail us." He thought for a moment. "Whoever the hell he is."

He made for the narrow doorway.

"Where are you going, tiger?" Lacey said casually.

Klondike turned. "Where's this so-called Paris rep of Daryl's based?"

She frowned. "He's working out of an office next to the art gallery, on the other side of the park. Why?"

Klondike took on a knowing look. "He's handled our press releases and advanced publicity. Ticket sales. Promotions. If anyone has seen something out of the ordinary recently, it would be him."

Heavy nodded. "I'll come with you, Kal." He shot up.

Plum seemed to panic. "I still need to draw up our figures from last night. Ticket sales, merchandise, midway take, the usual. It's bound to be a profit. Why not wait for that?"

Klondike sniggered as he and Heavy left the trailer.

"Because I smell a rat," the circus boss muttered.

Klondike and Heavy strode across the green wearily.

As they left behind the noise and commotion of the circus decamping operation and made for the other side of the Jacques Lemerre field, they were struck by how tranquil and sparsely populated the rest of the park was at this early hour.

Couples walked along gently, enjoying the woodland, while morning joggers motored by in tracksuits.

Finally, the duo arrived at the art gallery on the park's far side. Several small office buildings flanked the old gallery on either side.

They looked like log cabins, with modern glass windows and tiled roofs.

Klondike and Heavy examined marker cards placed on boards by the door of each outer office before determining which one was their correct destination.

Klondike rapped on the door several times, before grabbing the doorknob and pushing his way in.

Inside was one large room, full of filing cabinets, cupboards and other office furniture.

At the opposite end to the door was a large mahogany desk, behind which sat a figure with its back facing them.

Klondike frowned at the sight of the seated figure at the desk. He was facing the outer wall and seemed to be reading something. All they could really see was a head of thick black hair and an amber blazer.

"Good morning," Klondike called out as they waded inside. "I understand you're my company's representative in Paris. Klondike's Circus. I'm Klondike."

The figure finally spun around in his chair.

Klondike and Heavy froze. They were staring at Conrad Handel, the man who had surprised them at their camp back in London. The German sat there grinning up at them, calm and assured, as if he owned the park.

"I've been expecting you," he said in his strange, almost feminine voice. "I figured this would be your next port of call. How satisfying to be proved right. Again!"

Klondike stared at him in shock. "You!"

Heavy took a step forward. "What the hell are you doing here? This is a private office."

Handel laughed, a slow, gargled sound. "I'm just, ah, filling in for your 'rep' while he goes and gets his breakfast." He made a show of going through some of the morning newspapers spread across the desk. "It seems the ladies and gentlemen of the press are not in favour of your beloved circus, my friends. These reviews are unwholesome. Savage, in many ways."

Klondike sneered at him. "And you wouldn't know anything about that, right?"

"But, of course!" Handel looked up at him, seemingly concerned. "I tried to help you, Klondike. I warned you. Said us Europeans would not take to your venture. Your acts. I was there in London, my friends. The people were appalled by your

American so-called razzmatazz. The silence… it spoke volumes, no?" He shook his head sadly as the other two gaped at him, still stunned. "And then last night. The Parisians, who love their circus traditions. They were not much impressed either, it would seem, no?"

Heavy grew tired of it all. "Alright, the hell with all this nonsense. What do you want, Handel?"

The German held up his hands. "What I wanted back in Hyde Park. To help. To give you poor people a way out. Before it is too late."

Klondike marched to the desk, until he was standing over the seated man. "What in hell are you talking about, god damn it? Spit it out!"

Handel glared at him. "You are two shows in to a six-show tour. You know yourself…already, it is a disaster. If London and Paris don't like you, the others will despise you! I should know. I've been running circuses on the continent for 15 years. It isn't going to work, Klondike. I can promise you that." He reached down into a drawer and hauled up a bulky leather pouch, placing it on the desktop. "Now, my employer is a very generous man. He has designated me as your saviour. And today is your lucky day…"

"Who the hell is your employer?" Klondike raged.

Handel shrugged. "Again, this is unimportant. For you. What is vital, though, is that, this time, you accept his help. And move out. Out of here. Away from Europe. And back to America." He pushed the bulky pouch across the desk towards Klondike. "And take this. Your compensation. And our blessing. We, ah, wish you well with your future endeavours."

Klondike placed his hands on the desktop. His knuckles were white. "For the last time, sucker… who's we? Who are you people?"

Handel leant back, sure of himself. "That doesn't concern you, Klondike. We are helping you get out. We are saving you."

"You're paying off the press, aren't you? Making them bring our show down? All across Europe!"

Handel shrugged yet again. "We are doing what is necessary…"

"You want us out of Europe? But why?"

"Our reasons are our own!" Now, Handel was agitated, his face flushed. "And, like I said, we are compensating you. So, do as I ask, and take the pay-off. Do it now!"

Klondike was ready to hurl himself across the desk. "Who are you working for, dammit? I want a name!"

Suddenly, Handel surprised them both by leaning back in his chair, looking sad and bemused. He said something loudly in German.

Then, as if a signal had gone off, Klondike and Heavy heard footsteps charging up the path and a handful of men burst into the cabin, flanking Handel on either side of the desk. There were six in all. All were dressed in black fatigues as if this was some kind of combat mission. They were hard-looking men, tough and cold. All stared at the two circus men.

Klondike looked about warily. "What the hell is this? A goon squad?"

Handel laughed again. "Something like that. I was hoping it wasn't going to come to this. But, well, you two are proving to be very tiresome."

Heavy seemed unimpressed by the newcomers. "Where's your big ape this time? Didn't fancy it, eh?"

Handel glared at him. "Tarz is being restrained. He wants nothing more than to break Shapiro's legs. Break Olsen's hands. Break your clown's face up. And eat those fancy horses for breakfast! Now, please… I beg you, don't let it come to that."

Klondike stared into the cold, crystal green eyes of Conrad Handel. An enemy. From a new, foreign world. A foe who had stalked and targeted him. He frowned deeply and spoke in a murderous, rasping tone. "You've come after the wrong outfit, Handel. We ain't quitters. We're winners. Conquerors. Tell your boss that."

Handel shook his head, almost sadly. "It would appear… he is already aware of this."

Klondike's eyes widened. "What?"

Suddenly, there was another commotion behind them, as the door swung open again with a whack.

They turned, and saw the burly figure of Jim McCabe wade in, followed by four of his roustabouts, dressed in their standard uniform of lumberjack shirts, jeans and brown sack jackets.

“Jim…” Klondike breathed with relief.

The foreman was decked in sweat, his faithful porkpie hat sat at a jaunty angle on his balding scalp. “One of the boys saw these bums all dressed in black, all heading over here. We thought there was trouble. Hell, we smelled trouble.” His hardened gaze took in the men surrounding Handel in the cabin. “Looks like we was right.”

Heavy moved next to him. “Jim, you’re always in the right place at the right time.” Then, he turned back to the desk. “So, what’ya say now, Mister Money Man?”

Handel was smirking at them, trying to maintain his position of power while hiding his disappointment. Then, he leapt out of the chair and moved slowly around the desk, grabbing angrily at the pouch. The men in black seemed to surround him, forming a shield of sorts.

They all inched slowly towards the door. The circus men watched, backing away slightly as the strange-looking ensemble approached.

Handel addressed Klondike. “This changes nothing. You will leave Europe, Klondike. Mark my words. Between the fans hating your show, the press ripping you to pieces and, well, your talent giving up on you…there will be nothing left for you here.” He held the pouch aloft. “We offered you a way out. You should’ve taken the money. Now, the offer has been rescinded. You are on your own, Americans.”

That did it. Klondike made to lurch at him, but the strong arms of Heavy and McCabe held him in place with a vice-like grip. With those two holding him, he was going nowhere.

The two groups eyeballed each other in a final stand-off. No one moved. Every body seemed to tense, and inflate slightly.

“You’re not a man, Handel,” Klondike said in a fierce tone, “you’re garbage. All garbage.”

Yet again, the German laughed. He led his team of men out of the cabin in one fluid movement. Suddenly, the weird confrontation was ending, before anyone had even thought about throwing a punch or defending a blow.

Handel called back into the cabin. “You’ll be hearing from us again, my friends. Only next time, it won’t be a social call. Far from it.”

The group began walking casually down the pathway, away from it all. Klondike and his team moved outside, all staring at the unusual figures in wonder.

McCabe turned to Klondike, confused and bemused. "What the hell was that all about, Kal?"

Klondike squinted into the morning sun as he watched their visitors walking away. They looked like a group of tourists on a nature walk now. Then, they were gone.

"Hell," Klondike said quietly. "It looks like it's OK Corral time. There's a new set of gunslingers in town. And the old guard don't like it."

Later that day, the vintage Imperial circus train departed the park, gliding silently for the few miles of track that led back to Gare de Nord in central Paris and then connecting on to the main line heading north.

Then, after a few mighty toots of its horn in farewell to the city, the train was chugging through the French countryside.

The Belgian border was several hours away, and from there it was barely 100 miles on to Antwerp.

In his stateroom, Klondike poured four glasses of scotch and handed them to Heavy, Lacey and Bannion, who all sat around the coffee table, watching him with trepidation.

The atmosphere was tense, the sound of the rapidly accelerating steel wheels underneath them the only sounds for several moments.

"Who the hell are these guys?"

Klondike repeated the question for the umpteenth time since London. He sipped his drink, seemingly in disgust.

"Like I said," Bannion mused. "I'll make the enquiries. I have some contacts in Germany and Austria. But… well, Handel is a freelance man these days, so I'm told. He could be working for anyone."

"Or maybe he's part of a syndicate," Heavy said in awe, eyes wide. "All these big European outfits clubbing together, to take us down!"

"I doubt that, Henry," Lacey said gently. She seemed to shiver as she held her glass before her. "If what you and Kal said is accurate, and the truth, he is some kind of representative. For someone else."

Heavy leant towards her. "Or something else…"

Klondike watched them all. He turned to Bannion. "Just do what you can, Jack."

The Englishman nodded.

"There's something else," Heavy muttered. "Do we tell the guys? The whole team? That someone is out to get us…yet again?"

Klondike sighed. "Well, they know about that little visit in London. They know there's trouble in the air. Everyone does. But let's just leave it at that, folks. There is enough going on in this tour, with the crowds and these damn reporters. All the negativity. Any more bad news could tip some of the guys over the edge." He stared across at Lacey. "Don't you think?"

"Absolutely, Kalvin," she breathed. "Everyone is struggling to comprehend what is happening out here. Uncertainty and apprehension is everywhere. Let the performers perform. And we'll do the rest."

Klondike nodded slowly as he moved to the giant window at the edge of the carriage. Staring out solemnly, he studied the reddish-green pasture land that seemed to be everywhere, rolling past as the train sped north through France.

"It's all so hard to comprehend," he whispered, almost to himself. "We waited so long for this moment. For Europe. All the planning, the briefings. And now we're here… it all seems so god damn confusing."

Bannion joined him by the window. "It can all change, Kal. With just one show."

Lacey joined in. "The next town, the next crowd. Just like always."

Klondike returned his gaze to the fields whizzing by outside. He caught sight of an old farmhouse with a French tricolour flag hanging proudly from a pole outside. He shook his head.

"Roll on Antwerp."

CHAPTER 15

The Antwerp show would prove to be an almost exact re-run of Paris. With one notable and worrying exception. The grandstands were far from full, with the tent about half-filled to capacity. In all, barely three thousand fans turned out for the Klondike's Circus Antwerp spectacular.

The ovations were once again the same as what the troupe had come to expect. Polite and almost forced, with no wild cheers or jubilant ecstasy. A seemingly disinterested Belgian crowd, as unimpressed with the cotton candy and popcorn as they were with the performances.

For this show, there were no stars and stripes flags being waved by excited youngsters, and no lines of patrons queuing up at the midway for the shooting galleries and games of chance.

It felt more like an audience at a community theatre production, as Lacey so aptly put it afterwards.

Duster Williams and the Range Riders had been the undoubted stars of the tour up to this point, but even the cowboys could not force the fans out of their seats, with an underwhelming round of applause greeting the end of Williams' solo spot.

It was the same for Gino Shapiro's high-flying trapeze and wire walk. The crowd reacted as if they did not care.

Earlier in the night, the Daredevils had garnered almost the exact same reception as they had received in Paris, a mixture of shock, disdain and disbelief bleeding down from the bleachers as everyone seemed to treat their act as a loud, raging avalanche. An unwanted mess.

Roddy Olsen had received a vaguely cheerful round of applause after each of his songs, as his new musical gig style continued.

And the same reaction greeted Corky and his clowns. Nothing seemed to excite the paying customers. It was as simple as that.

But, for Klondike and his staff, the main, and very real, concern to emerge from the night was the low turnout – something none of them were used to having played to a sellout crowd for almost every show in the past three years.

This was unchartered territory, and an unwanted development. Its reach and ripple were felt throughout the entire circus operation, like a dark cloud hanging over a beach resort.

For as painful and surreal the sight of their circus stars struggling to garner cheers from a disinterested audience was, the lines of empty seats dominating the arena was even more horrific.

AMERICAN DREAM IS HERE…BUT IT'S OUR WORST NIGHTMARE!

By Alain Dacroise, International Herald Express

Eighty years ago, PT Barnum's legendary travelling circus came to Europe for a thrilling tour of the continent's grandest cities.

The three-hour spectacular was hailed a glorious success, and Belgians, Germans and Britons all longed for the return of Circus Americana to our circuits.

Last night, that return finally happened. And now, alas, we wish we had not spent all these years longing for it.

Klondike's Circus appeared at Antwerp's legendary Diamond Pavilion Grounds, and many of the city's circus-goers chose to avoid it.

The show came on the back of performances in London and Paris that were critically panned, and that had left audiences largely dumbstruck. The poor reviews had no doubt been read by many in Belgium, who chose to stay away and wait for the more traditional Rizzo's Circus, out of Lucerne, and the many other domestic brands due to tour this summer.

Indeed, the Klondike big top was barely half-full for what its managers had proudly proclaimed to be, "One of Europe's most spectacular circus shows of all time".

Instead, the tent was full of alcoholic tramps, juvenile delinquents with nothing better to do and seemingly misguided pensioners, who all endured this bizarre, mish-mash of a show.

There was no narrative, no showmanship, no animals – beside some horses ridden by brash cowboys – and quite simply no sparkle.

Instead, the Antwerp faithful were "treated" to a bunch of ballet dancers, a shameful freak show of carnival creatures, a hyperactive clown who performed no magic, a noisy motorcycle gang who had everyone holding their ears, and a child puppeteer who sang a load of rock n roll songs. Then we had the cowboys, with some alleged Hollywood star among them, and a trapeze pair who seemed to think they were royalty.

It was obvious to your correspondent, and all present last night, that this show was pure American hogwash. Las Vegas glamour and glitz served up on a cotton candy stick. Each star wore a costume that shined to the heavens. And each was introduced by the overly loud ringmaster as if they were some kind of international superstar.

The American-style circus is a long, long way removed from what Belgian audiences are accustomed to. They don't want it, and won't tolerate it again.

The whole thing was a loud, bright, shining mess of a circus, that only re-enforced what most of us already think about our American friends. That they are just too much.

Klondike's Circus, based out of California, will surely never return to Belgium after last night.

Let's hope it is another 80 years until the next American circus returns. And, when it does, that it is more Barnum than Klondike…

Carmine Courtinio laughed aloud as he looked up from his copy of the International Herald Express.

Letting the newspaper fall lightly to his desk, he clapped his hands with delight, beaming away as he let the review sink in.

He was seated high above the sprawling metropolis of central Rome, safe from the outside world in his luxurious office at the summit of his industrial tower.

His massive ivory desk was covered in Continental newspapers and magazines, and he had spent the morning going through them all. But the Herald's scathing review of Klondike's Circus in Antwerp was the one article he had savoured.

Now, Courtinio looked across his desk at Lucia, his secretary, who stared back at him in shock.

She seemed to read his mind. "So, the Americans are struggling, no?"

The older man laughed again. "Indeed, my dear. They performed their third show of the tour last night and, my god, the reviews are terrible! Just as we said..."

Lucia cocked an eyebrow. "Our newspaper people did their job, no?"

"They did. The press may be righteous guardians of virtue and honour...but they are struggling like every other middle earner in post-war Europe. I offer them too much. I pay too well. Nobody says no. Nobody."

She smiled, as if excited. "It is incredible, Duce. How you make people bend to your will."

Courtinio offered a smug smile. "Circus people across Europe... whether they succeed or fail, it is all down to me. And whether or not I like them. I buy any act I choose. And I shoot down anyone who won't conform." His face became a smirk as he picked up the morning's Herald again. "These Americans... they are learning a very important lesson, Lucia. You don't invade a foreign superpower. You don't just come over here with your big shot show and presume success. Oh no! If they had come to me first, I could have offered them a business deal. A partnership. Now, they are slowly dying. And the killer blows are yet to come."

Lucia was entranced as she looked across the desk at her boss. "Why didn't they just take the money and run?"

"Pride," Courtinio spat out. "Dumb, American pride. It will be the death of them."

She glanced at the newspaper article as it sat sprawled over the desk. "They've still got a few dates left. Do you think they will make it here to Rome, Duce?"

He sat back, stroking the soft flesh around his chin. "There are a few surprises for them yet, my dear. Beauty and the beast, you might say." He laughed again, lost in his inner thoughts.

Lucia still did not understand his merriment. "But they will be here soon, in barely a fortnight. They'll be right here, in Rome!"

Courtinio nodded, smiling like a wisened jackal. "Indeed they will. And I will be right there, in the big top, watching. Watching as the death knell finally sounds for Klondike's Circus. It will be their final act…and the finest hour for Circo Grande."

With that, he rolled his head back and laughed uncontrollably for several moments, a strange, somewhat bewildering spectacle.

The hideous laughter floated out of the office window and bled down to the endless traffic and commotion of the busy streets far below.

Some 5,000 miles away from the bustling streets of central Rome, it was the dead of night in Central Park, New York.

A lonesome figure walked slowly down a gravelled pathway that ran alongside a reservoir. The woman wore a long green trench coat, its collar pulled up high over her cheekbones. Her long, straight blonde hair blew in the slight breeze, offering a glimpse of her pale features and seagram blue eyes. The face seemed to shine in the faint moonlight.

She made her way to a park bench that sat at the far edge of the reservoir, near an old bike stand. She looked around for several moments, happy that there was not a soul in sight. Finally, she sat. And waited.

A full five minutes passed. Then, she sensed rather than saw some movement. A darkened figure emerged from a line of trees across from the path, opposite the water.

The shadow moved along quickly, like a wraith in the night, finally slumping down on the bench next to her.

It was a man, dressed all in black. He was well-built, with curly dark hair and a beard.

"You're late," she snapped.

"One can't be too cautious," the newcomer replied. He had a thick New York accent. "No one can know I am here. Or, for that matter, that you are here, Miss Cross."

"Don't get cute with me," she hissed. She looked around. All was quiet in the moonlight. "Just tell me what I want to know, Zane. Now!"

The man looked across at her. "Haven't you got something for me first?"

She sighed and pulled a large manilla envelope from her handbag. She handed it to him, and he immediately ripped it open and peered inside. "It's all there," she whispered irritably.

Satisfied, Zane placed the package next to him on the bench. He seemed amused. "Where do you get all this cash, Miss Cross?"

She shook her head, the anger rising. "I told you. I have set myself up with a wealthy man. A very wealthy man. He suspects nothing." She smiled to herself now. "He actually thinks I love him."

Zane spoke quietly. "And he is not the first, is he?"

Jenny Cross froze all over.

Her worst fear had just been realised. This man was tracking her. Investigating her. He knew. Somehow, he knew. And that meant he could expose her. Ruin everything. All she had worked for. After all this time.

"What…" she began with a quiver.

"It's all right, Miss Cross," the man said calmly. "Your secrets are safe with me. I promise." He looked at her in surprise. "Come on… a man like me… I have to do my research. I can't go to work for anyone, just like that. I have to know what I am getting myself into."

"But how could you possibly know-"

"Relax," he said soothingly. "Forget it. Right now."

She sat there, shaking slightly. She made to speak, then stopped, putting a hand over her mouth.

Zane took the initiative instead. "You want to know if I am ready? That's it, right?" He eyed her. She remained still. "Well…yes, Miss Cross. I am ready. Me and my men have acquired the necessary… er, equipment. I have made all the arrangements you asked for. And our deal is on." He studied her again. She seemed suddenly terrified. "That is… if we are still on?"

"Yes!" She gasped, looking straight ahead. She tried to snap out of her sudden fear. "We must go ahead with it. Oh god, we must…"

Zane stared at her. "Miss Cross, is everything alright?"

"Everything is fine," she snapped, suddenly rising and moving away from him. She backed away down the path, her eyes wide in fright. "Just remember what I told you when I first made contact. Goodnight!"

She turned and sped away, her trench coat flapping in the breeze, and her long hair blowing up in the night air.

Zane sat there alone, trying to remember. He recalled a phrase she had uttered on the telephone, all those weeks ago. Frowning to himself, he whispered aloud in the night as he shrugged on the bench.

"This is my destiny."

CHAPTER 16

The Imperial circus train had rolled into Berlin at nightfall, its multi-coloured carriages lighting up a grim, foggy evening that was still and quiet.

The journey across West Germany had provided the travelling circus folk with some spectacular sights, with the Rhine and the various Bavarian mountains and hillsides ensuring everyone gathered by the train's windows to admire the scenery.

The train had chugged along ageing railroads that dipped and fell across the rolling countryside.

But the picturesque surroundings had given way somewhat to the industrialisation and commercialism rife in west Berlin as the train neared its destination.

As the great behemoth began to slow, it glided down a narrow, ancient-looking track into the city itself. Factories and food processing plants seemed to line the railroad for the final few miles of the journey. Unsurprisingly, the enchanted train occupants gradually moved away from the windows as the giant, brown stone constructions obscured any kind of view.

Since the end of the war, a seemingly endless rebuilding project had gripped Berlin and its proud occupants. New industries and business ventures had been at the core of the rebuild job, and much of the endeavour and workmanship of the city's saviours was on show now.

For Kal Klondike, sat alone at his desk in his luxurious stateroom, the entry into Berlin represented yet another surreal episode on this odyssey of endless extremities.

He had last been in Berlin in 1945, when the streets were little more than charred, stacked debris, the inhabitants dust-covered survivors of a destructive nightmare. The top brass had called it Operation Clean Up. It had been his last assignment as a US Army soldier. And that was enough. He had resigned his commission on his return to the States.

Now, he watched with queer fascination as the train rolled along the rails into the sprawling, modern metropolis. As he had told many of his staff during this tour, the last time he had entered

Berlin, he had been in the back of a tank. Now, he was riding in a train bearing his name.

Klondike looked down at the papers on his desk. The European tour had been a critical, if not entirely commercial, disaster up to this point. Now, with Berlin, there came a moment of potential salvation. At least he hoped that was what lay ahead.

The circus was playing at the US Air Force Base in Haddenhacht, west Berlin. It was the only venue where Bannion had been able to secure a licence.

The show was open to all US military staff and officials, as well as neighbouring British troops and German members of the public.

Klondike hoped the American spectators would make up a large number of the audience. Some of them might be familiar with his star performers. And most of them would probably appreciate their brand of entertainment. Though it was impossible to predict how many American patrons would be there compared to German citizens.

He watched as the train slowly left the main line and joined the branch track that would lead to the air base. Travelling at barely 20mph, it lurched round the angular rail track and passed through a complex of airfields and rows of grey hangars.

Watching the murky scenery, Klondike said a silent prayer.

The circus company formed its usual encampment on arrival at the air base.

Equipment and loading vehicles covered a swathe of ground outside the still train, while a small settlement of trailers and midway stalls and booths spread out across the base grounds.

Beyond the main air force headquarters building, a strange-looking array of tentpoles, ground maintenance machines and ropes sat in a mess all over the grounds, ready to raise the big top at first light.

Roddy Olsen wandered aimlessly among the stalls and attractions, lost and confused. It was late now, and he wore a black tracksuit in the cool night air.

The silent response he had received in London two weeks ago still haunted him. The barely audible reactions in Paris and

Antwerp had hardly pacified his angst. The whole experience had left him withdrawn, and something more. A deep, dark feeling he had never experienced.

As an orphan who had spent his teenage years in boarding houses in California, the grim sphere of loneliness had never been far away. He had accepted it when it was apparent. In many ways, it had helped him perfect his act.

But this was different. Rejection of an alternative nature.

As he stumbled along, lost in his thoughts, Olsen turned around the back of a large supplies trailer and found three of the circus's roustabouts all sat around the small stairwell, seemingly oblivious to everything. Each held a bottle.

Squinting in the moonlight, Olsen recognised them. They were the same group that had harassed him on the ship in the middle of the Atlantic.

The trio were all conversing in low tones, but stopped as the youngster emerged from the shadows.

"Well, look who it is, boys," one of them snarled, looking up with a grin. "The superstar." He was leaning against the side of the old trailer, holding his bottle casually. "What's the matter, boy? Got lost?"

Olsen shrugged. He looked down at the group. "Just walking."

The lead roustabout studied him as the other two each took a pull.

"We offered you a drink once before, superstar. Back on that ship. You didn't want any part of us." He grunted. "How about now, eh?"

Olsen looked around the camp. There seemed to be general clutter everywhere. "I didn't mean to interrupt. Just leave me alone." He made to turn.

"Ah, come on," the speaker said, wheezing slightly. He held the bottle above his head and motioned for the newcomer to join them.

Olsen studied the bottle and saw there was no label.

"Moonshine," the roustabout whispered with a wink. "We got us our own still. Keep it in the bunkhouse on the train. Even managed to keep it going out here." He sniggered. "Just don't tell Mr McCabe."

All three laughed aloud.

Olsen looked at each of them, then at the bottle.

"Come on, boy," the leader said, slightly more aggressive now. "Drink! It'll do ya good. Believe me."

Olsen hesitated, looking around the camp. He thought of things that had not entered his head in a long time. Forgotten memories, the scars of life. Somehow, for reasons he could not comprehend, none of that seemed to matter now.

With a sigh, he sat down with the roustabouts. They seemed to cheer his decision.

The speaker handed him the bottle, and he took a slow, unsteady sip. The red-hot trickle seemed to burn his throat and inflame his stomach. But something in there hit the spot.

He took a longer sip, then nodded his thanks at the lead man.

The roustabout lit a cigarette. He nodded knowingly. "There's a big difference between wanting a drink and needing one, son." He eyed Olsen. "I reckon you needed one. Real bad."

Olsen looked at him in the moonlight as they sat on the ground. He nodded dumbly. Then, he took another drink.

Lacey pulled open her trailer door in a panic. She had been lying in bed, and had pulled on a pink robe after hearing the frantic knocking.

"Roddy!" She shrieked. "What's the matter? It's so late."

She glared at him as he stood in the doorway. He looked tired and beat.

"I'm sorry, Lacey. I know what time it is and all. I just...well, it's just that... that I needed to see you."

She eyed him skeptically. Something was off. "Come in," she whispered.

He lurched inside and, without invitation, sprawled on to the small couch. She watched him coyly, unsure what to say.

An awkward silence followed. Lacey stood there studying him as he shifted restlessly. "Roddy, you look terrible. What happened?"

He rubbed at his eyes. She thought she saw tears. "I'm so sorry, Lacey. Really I am." He looked up at her. In that moment, he could have passed for a 16-year-old boy, afraid, alone and confused. “It’s just this feeling I got. This god awful feeling. It feels like… like failure. Like defeat.” He rubbed at his face angrily now. “It feels like I’m through.”

Lacey stammered, reeling from the revelations. Then, she rushed to his side and placed a comforting arm around his wiry frame.

“Now, Roddy, stop that talk this instant. We’ve been through all this. My word, how many times have we been through it all? It’s the crowds out here. The European crowds. They don’t like you, but they don’t like any of us. Gino, the Daredevils, Corky… the whole show. Look at what happened in Antwerp! Now, please, don’t just think you’re being singled out by the people out here.”

She looked him over, lingering on his soft, sky blue eyes. They looked innocent, tender and fearful. He locked eyes with her. Both seemed to hesitate, and shake ever so slightly.

“You’ve got to snap put of this, Roddy,” she whispered, holding his hand in both of hers. She squeezed. “You can’t let these audiences get to you like this. You’re a superstar. You’re the greatest. You know that!”

“I can’t help it,” he wailed suddenly. He threw himself back into the couch. “I’ve never been through this before. The fans turning like that. The press saying all those things about me. I mean…what the hell is happening to me?”

She pulled at the hand. “For the last time, Roddy. It isn’t you. It is us! All of us! We are all going through it, this madness.”

He closed his eyes. “I said this was going to happen, Lacey. Back at Rio Cristo. In your cabin. That day before we all left. You remember?”

“Of course I remember. I said back then, none of us knew what to expect out here.”

He shook his head. “I can’t take this anymore, Lacey. I want to go home. Back to Vegas and LA. Where we belong.”

She paused suddenly, frowning. “Roddy!” she said harshly. “Oh my god! Have you been drinking?”

He seemed to tremble. “I can’t help it, Lacey. I’m afraid. I’m alone. I can’t think straight. And I don’t know what to do.” He leant over towards her. They locked eyes again. “That’s why I came to you, Lacey. Because you always know what to do. And I…I'll always listen to you. I need you…"

His vulnerability and isolation was overwhelming. Lacey stared into his impossibly vibrant eyes again. Now, they seemed to shine once more. Just like that, the teen idol was back. It was a remarkable transformation. And it had all been down to her.

She moved her head closer to him, still grasping his hand. He closed his eyes.

Then, she kissed him. Softly on the lips. They held it for several moments.

Suddenly, she pulled away. She wiped at her mouth and then stood, recoiling slightly. He looked up at her, as if in a daydream.

"Oh god!" she gasped, shaking slightly. "I'm sorry, Roddy. Oh…I shouldn't have done that! Forgive me."

He looked up at her in shock. "What's the matter?"

"You know what!" she snapped uncharacteristically. She tried to soften. "Again, we've been through this as well."

"Been through what?"

"Us! The fact there can be no us! Remember what we discussed back in London. And every other time. Please, Roddy!"

Olsen sat there looking hurt. "We both want it."

Lacey was beyond flustered. She hugged at herself, pulling the robe, and paced in front of the couch, fiddling with her hair. He had never seen her quite like this.

"Be that as it may," she whispered sternly, "we both know, we both agreed, that getting involved with each other is wrong. All wrong. The results could be catastrophic. I am committed – beyond committed – to your career. To your success. We all are."

With those final few words, an ugly frown formed on Olsen's brow. He suddenly looked mad. He leant forward, gazing up at her.

"It's him, isn't it?"

She baulked, taking a step back in the trailer. "What? Who? What are you talking about?"

Olsen nodded to himself, rising up off the couch. "It's him. Kal. Of course. Everybody suspects it."

Now Lacey frowned. "What? For god's sake, Roddy…"

“It’s true,” he said, as if possessed. His eyes were wide as he stood up. “You’re in love with Kal Klondike.”

She winced, shrugging uncontrollably. “That is nonsense, Roddy.”

“Say it ain’t so!” He suddenly cried. “Say you’re not in love with Kal. With the boss man. You and him… the dream team. Of course. The connection you two have… nothing can ever match that. It is like electricity. That bond you have.”

She was desperately trying to remain calm as tensions rose wildly in the trailer. “Roddy,” she pleaded softly. “You’re upset. I understand. I shouldn’t have kissed you. Especially after what I said back in London. But, well, it’s just that…that…”

He nodded emphatically. “That you’re in love with another man.”

“That’s not true. Kal and I are partners. Like you and I, in a way. And like with you, Roddy, Kal and I have a special relationship. We understand each other. We have a deep, mutual respect for one another that is very rare in this industry. In any industry.”

He gazed at her with his mesmerising blue eyes. “You’ve got feelings for me, Lacey. I know it. You want more from me. You hear all those girls screaming my name back home, and all the while you know that you are the one! And it makes you feel special and superior and-“

“Stop it!” she suddenly screamed. Her hands went to her face and she glared at him in horror. “Roddy! What the hell has happened to you? You’ve gone crazy, or something.” She studied him. “You shouldn’t have been drinking. I thought you never touched alcohol. Look, just look at what it’s done to you.”

That seemed to have an effect. He put his head down and seemed to lurch away from her, back towards the door. “You may be right,” he blurted, turning away. “Or maybe this god foresaken tour has changed me. Put a whole new perspective on life.”

They stared at each other. She seemed to hug herself, but soon looked away from him.

Olsen put his fingers around the door handle. “All that I truly know,” he mumbled, “is that I am in love with you, Lacey.”

Then, he was gone. Out of the door and into the still of the night.

Lacey felt like she was going to collapse. She rushed into the kitchenette, pulled a bottle of cognac from a cupboard and poured herself a tall glass.

With a shaking hand, she downed the lot in a series of rapid gulps.

She wandered about the narrow trailer in a daze, absently carrying the empty glass. Fishing in her handbag, she pulled out a pack of cigarettes and lit one quickly. She stood in the far corner of the lounging area, arms folded and holding the smoke before her.

She thought of them both. She couldn't help it. Klondike and Olsen. Why, oh why, had they both fallen into her life like this? She told herself that it didn't matter. She had a job to do. And her role was as vital to the success of the circus as anyone's.

She told herself that. But, deep inside her soul, the dilemma raged through her like a tornado.

Outside in the cool night, Olsen wandered slowly back to his trailer. He felt sick all over, and so very tired.

Reaching the door, he collapsed awkwardly onto the mini-stairwell that led to the glass door.

Sitting on the top step, back to the door, he placed his head in his hands and sat there stiffly.

"Roddy?"

He looked up suddenly at the soft feminine voice. Something inside him seemed to brighten.

"Suzi…" he whispered, gazing at her as she stood over him in the dark, one hand on the side of the trailer.

Her childlike, almost angelic features were like a beacon of light and hope as she looked him over with concern. She was in her pyjamas, but came and sat on the steps next to him, grabbing at his arm.

"I was awake next door and heard you wandering around. It's nearly midnight! What happened?"

Olsen stared at her. "Was a bit upset, I guess. About everything that's been happening out here."

She rubbed his arm. "Tell me about it. I feel like I'm singing to an empty tent half the time." She looked around solemnly. "Let's hope the good people of Berlin take to us…"

Hearing her voice had an extraordinary effect on him.

"Come here."

With that, he grabbed her tiny frame and pulled her close to him in a mighty bearhug. He held her close, and she gladly held him back.

And they just sat there, embracing on the stairs under the stars.

On the other side of the air base in the main headquarters building, the officers' barroom was virtually empty at that hour.

A handful of men in blue air force uniforms hunched over tables, as an elderly swamper absently mopped the floor in the corner.

Klondike sat alone at the polished oak bar, nursing a beer and chomping on an all-but dead cigar stub.

A middle-aged man in full uniform waded in, smiling when he saw the circus boss at the bar. He approached and took a barstool next to him.

"Hey, Kal. I figured you might be here."

Klondike looked up and smiled at Sergeant Bennington, their liaison officer for the show. He had introduced himself out on the airfield earlier, explaining how he was friends with Klondike's old commanding officer from the war. Incredibly, the old colonel was still in service.

"Good evening, Sarge," he muttered. "What can I get ya?"

"Whiskey Mac, please."

Klondike motioned to the youthful bartender. Then, he said: "Thanks for all your help with everything. Did you find much out today?"

Bennington leaned in. "Well, I got good news, old buddy. Your tickets have been selling just fine. Old Gus at the front office reckons three-quarters of the seats have gone already. You still got tomorrow and then the show day to sell plenty more. As far as that other thing you asked me… well, it's hard to say how many Americans will be there. Plenty of German natives work at the base and in the stores. They've been getting tickets for their families, friends, you get the idea…"

"Sure," Klondike drawled, sipping at his beer. The whiskey arrived in a small glass. Bennington downed half of it in one.

"Ah, that's the stuff," he said with glee.

Klondike looked at him. "I want to thank you and your men for all you've done for us, Sergeant. You've really gone all out for us here, and we appreciate it."

"Hell, we're all real excited," Bennington exclaimed. "We ain't never had no circus out here before. It's a huge moment in our history."

Klondike smiled. "So… your people are happy? Ready to be entertained?"

"You bet." Bennington finished his drink, then seemed to read Klondike's mind. "Listen, Kal. I know this tour hasn't gone as you planned. I've seen the reviews. Heard from people on the grapevine, y'know?" He removed his cap and ran a hand through his thinning red hair. "It's tough being away from home. I've been stationed here three years. I know how it is dealing with foreigners. The cultural differences are huge. But…" he eyed Klondike shrewdly now. "I want you to know I think you're doing the right thing."

Klondike frowned. "What do you mean?"

"Well, your circus has brought joy and happiness to thousands of people in the States. And everyone should have the chance to experience that."

He nodded slowly. "That's a good way of putting it, Sarge. I thank you."

The last group of airmen left the barroom behind them, all cackling and name-calling good-naturedly as they stumbled back to their barracks.

"Listen," Klondike murmured, changing the subject. "Have you ever heard of a Conrad Handel?"

Bennington shook his head. "Handel? Like the composer? No, I'm afraid not, old buddy. Who is he?"

Klondike waved a hand gently through the air. "Just a sucker we've come across on the trail."

"I'll let you know if I hear anything, Kal." With that, the airman hopped off his stool and rubbed his hands down his uniform. “Well, I’ll say goodnight. Hell, you oughta get some sleep. From the looks of all that equipment lying around outside on the airfield, you got yourself a big day tomorrow.”

They said their goodbyes. Klondike continued to sit there in silence, relighting his cigar and watching in awe as a deep cloud of purple smoke seemed to envelope his frame.

Then, barely a minute after Bennington left, his seat was taken by another. Again, Klondike looked up to see who had joined him. This time, he found himself looking into the freckled face and green eyes of Jack Bannion.

“Bannion,” he drawled, suddenly feeling very tired.

“Hi Kal. Richie told me I’d probably find you up here.”

“Yeah. Just reacquainting an old love affair… with this incredible German ale. You want one?”

“No thanks,” the Englishman replied. “I’m just reporting in.”

“What did you find out?”

Bannion looked around the bar absently. “No pay dirt. Otto Klannheim, my man in Berlin, said Handel left his circus outfit, Wunder Welt, about three years ago. Before the war, as a young man, he had enjoyed much success across central Europe. He had been a booker and promoter for the show. They were number one in Germany and Austria for several years. It seems they struggled to recapture the glory days after the war, like so many entertainment firms. It appears they may have folded some time in the 50s. Then, well, Handel apparently disappeared.”

Klondike nodded. “When people supposedly ‘disappear’, it is never good.”

Bannion licked his lips. “Well, an old reporter friend of mine from the Berlin Bugel said he thinks Handel has been working freelance for various troupes across Europe. Booking acts, bringing in top talent.”

“So,” Klondike mused, holding his cigar before him, “maybe our boy Handel has hooked up with an outfit that sees us as a threat. Say… another circus, from these shores, that is also conducting a tour across the continent. They want to ensure we fail, while they get the glory…”

“What if it isn’t that at all, though? What if someone is out to get us for reasons we haven’t even considered?”

Klondike stayed impassive. “Let’s stick to what we know, Jack. Handel and whoever controls him have been paying off reporters to write negative reviews – right across Europe. Now, does this reporter contact of yours know of anyone who’s been paid off lately?”

Bannion shook his head, almost in sympathy. “Kal… this is post-war Germany. The country may never recover from 1945, economically and emotionally. Everyone in the press is taking pay-offs. They’ve got no choice. They have to in order to survive.”

Klondike thought it over. “And so people will exploit them…”

Bannion tried to sound positive. “Maybe Handel and his goons won’t try anything at all. They’ll leave it with the negative reviews, and be happy with the result.”

“No,” Klondike blurted, taking another sip from the tankard. “I saw the look on that son of a bitch’s face. When he was trying to taunt me. He’s enjoying it. It’s like a game to him. I’ve seen that look before… in others who have tried to ruin us. He’s toying with us.”

Bannion shook his head. “But why? Why go to all this trouble? Just to try and make us leave.”

Klondike downed the remains of his tankard and grunted as he slammed it back down on the bar top. “Why?” He roared. “I’ll tell ya why, Jack. Cos we’re the best. The best god damn circus in the world. And, when you’re at the top, everybody wants to bring you down.” He glared at the Englishman’s bemused expression.

“But this tour will be our finest venture. And, mark my words, we will return to America in glory!”

With that, he snatched up his hat and cane and strode proudly out of the barroom.

CHAPTER 17

The following morning brought beautiful sunshine and a light, refreshing breeze across the air base.

The circus set-up operation was in full swing by 9am, with roustabouts roaming the massive air field and transporting equipment across from the train, sat idle at the base's station house.

Workers seemed to be scattered everywhere, with many preparing for the gargantuan task of erecting the big top. A further army of men were setting up the midway, which would lie ahead of the tent like a shanty town before the gateway to a city.

Performers and staff all busied themselves about their trailers in the morning sun; the circus outfit having seemingly taken over the air base for now.

Gino Shapiro strode gallantly around his trailer at the edge of the accommodation blocks. As usual, it was hard to miss him in his bright orange tracksuit, his name emblazoned across the back in black and gold letters.

His warm-up equipment, consisting of a high bar mounted on a steel post, and a mini-tightrope frame suspended eight feet off the ground, was neatly laid out on the turf.

After performing a few stretches, Shapiro leapt up to the bar and pulled himself over. He performed a handstand on the smooth iron bar, holding it for 60 seconds, before propelling himself round in a circle several times, building momentum, and completing several lightning-fast swirls. For his dismount, he suddenly let go in mid-swing and flew high into the air, completing a turtle somersault, before landing smoothly on his feet. He held the pose. Then, he relaxed, smiling slightly. Massaging his ever-troublesome right shoulder several times, he wandered slowly to the wire apparatus.

Walking the eight steps that led to the top of the first platform, he stood tall, not even looking at the wire. Instead, he surveyed his surroundings, taking in the grey, grim-looking airplanes that surrounded the edge of the base. A platoon of soldiers were marching across a bank to his right.

As he looked about idly, he suddenly froze, a queer look spreading across his face.

There, about 100 yards in front of him in what looked like a small parking lot for air force personnel, a woman was performing what appeared to be a rhythmic gymnastics routine.

Shapiro frowned. Of all the places, of all the sights, he thought in dismay.

The figure wore a sparkling stars and stripes leotard and had a perfect action as she leapt across the concrete, apparently to music only she could hear.

Then, the woman spotted the man watching her on the elevated platform. He saw her smile, almost mischievously.

Suddenly, she raced across the lot, before launching herself into a cartwheel, followed by several more. Soon, she became a blur as she turned herself into a human wheel, propelling herself across the ground at lighting speed. The cartwheels then became backward somersaults and she flew, hands and feet skimming the concrete like a skipping stone as she moved acrobatically through the air. It was an electrifying display.

She finally came to a stop, just in front of the watching Shapiro.

Gobsmacked, the trapeze artist offered a small round of applause.

The mystery woman raised a hand in acknowledgement. Then, chest heaving, she walked slowly over to his practice area.

Shapiro was rooted to the spot, watching as the newcomer approached, his mind trying to make sense of it all.

He studied her. She had beautiful, twirling black hair, fiery ebony eyes and full lips, like a movie starlet. She pranced across, pacing before her spectator.

"Thank you," she gushed, eyes alive and sparkling. "It's always nice to play to an audience. Even if it is just one, no?" Her accent was heavily Italian, husky and bright.

Shapiro smiled, enchanted and bewitched in equal measure. "That was quite a display, Madam. Breathtaking, actually. And out here… at the air base! I really have seen it all now."

"That's not true," she said haughtily, smiling up at him. "There is so much more to come."

He laughed, clapping his hands. "I don't doubt it." He realised her eyes were locked on him, and frowned slightly. "Have we met, madam?"

"Well..." she whispered, "I feel like I know you, mister king of the air."

"Alright," he said quickly, shaking his head. He finally moved, dismounting the wire walk platform and jumping down next to her.

"What in heaven's name are you doing here? Doing all those fancy twirls out here... in the middle of a United States Air Force base?"

Still, she smiled a dazzling smile. Her white teeth seemed to shine. Even Shapiro was overwhelmed.

"Call it an audition," she purred.

"What?" Despite her undoubted beauty and charisma, Shapiro was a little unsettled. The whole encounter felt surreal. He looked her over yet again. "Do you have a name, sweetheart?"

She held an arm aloft in a haughty pose. "Carla Selenzy. The empress of acrobatics." She laughed aloud. "Maybe you have seen my act, no? I have performed all over Europe. In Italy, I am always at the top of the bill. It is expected... demanded by my fans."

"Selenzy..." he said slowly. "Hey, I have heard of you! Elanzo's Express, right? You were the flyer for old man Elanzo, out of Milan I believe? I have heard much of your act, angel. Even in America."

She nodded, grinning like a hyena. "You are quite correct." She walked forward like a performing tiger, circling around Shapiro as if interrogating him. "And you, the great Gino Shapiro. Much I have heard about your exploits. Oh so much, no? Las Vegas. Hollywood. The Superstars and Stripes show. And of course... the devil drop!"

He chuckled, still somewhat bewildered. "What on earth are you doing here, angel? At the air base? How did you get in? This place is like Fort Knox."

"Ah," she sighed, swatting a hand through the air. Her eyes still had not left him. "Me and a few showgirls from Italy, we do a show for all the forces. You know the type… entertaining the troops, that kind of deal. Me and the piano man, Al, arrived a little early for our show tonight in the mess hall. We do a few songs, dance, then a comedian tells jokes. It's a regular gig. They all know me here."

Shapiro nodded. "The troops here get all kinds of entertainment, it would seem."

"Yes, it would," she purred, looking across to the far side of the airfield where the tent was slowly rising on its poles. "A circus, no less." Her eyes seemed to twinkle. "Now, that's where the real action is."

"Why, the guys here must love you, Miss Selenzy."

"Of course," she said boldly. "They all scream my name when I dance. They all want a piece of Carla." She moved in a little closer, brushing a hand through her hair. "But I long for something else. When you know fame, adoration, you want something more, no? I need a man like me. A superstar? A… king!"

Shapiro's eyes were bulging, despite his unease. "What else do you want, Miss Selenzy?"

"Oh, I don't know," she whispered mischeviously. "A spot in your circus, maybe…"

Shapiro laughed aloud. "Now, why would you want that?"

Carla moved very close to him now. "Because it would mean we can perform together, Gino. As one. Can you imagine? The electricity, the excitement. Our, yes, our names on the billboards. I can hardly-"

"I think you will find that role is already taken!"

They both turned in fright at the shrill voice from behind.

Penny Fortune stood there, arms folded, a bemused expression locked on her face. She had just walked over from her trailer, dressed like Gino in an orange tracksuit.

Carla's face dropped instantly, as if someone had pressed a switch. Her eyes seemed to inflame, her mouth turning into a sneer.

Shapiro seemed to snap to attention. "Carla, allow me to introduce Miss-"

"I know who she is!" Carla snapped, her voice an angry snarl now. She looked at Penny with pity. "And I have no ambition to be a mere catcher like you, Miss Fortune. Puh!"

Penny frowned, on her haunches. "Actually, I do a whole lot more than that. Me and Gino have-"

"It is not important!" Carla snapped. She turned to Gino, her back to Penny. "Yes! It is no secret, Gino. I hope to join your circus. Why wouldn't I? It sounds like you need me, no? My name is known across Europe. And beyond! This sounds to me like a good bit of business for you, Gino."

Penny was irate. "Now, wait just one minute, whoever the hell you are! You don't just breeze in here, out of nowhere, making demands and asking for a spot." She turned angrily to Shapiro. "What the hell is this?"

Shapiro looked from Penny to Carla and shrugged. "I'm sorry, mamacita. I am not really sure."

Suddenly, a new voice broke the drama.

"What the hell is going on out here?"

They all turned. Klondike and Heavy were walking briskly across to the trailer area. The raised voices had seemingly attracted their attention.

Shapiro shrugged again, feeling lost. Carla performed a curtsy and giggled like a schoolgirl. "Oh my! Kal Klondike himself! Is it really you?"

Klondike stopped before the three of them, a tired and bemused look on his craggy features. Heavy stayed behind him, equally confused. Both stared at the beautiful dame in the colourful leotard.

"Alright," Klondike drawled. "Let's have it."

"Chairman," Shapiro said in an airy tone. "May I introduce Carla Selenzy. They call her the empress of the, er, acrobatics. A big, big star in European circus."

Carla walked forward and extended a hand, much like a countess from high society. Klondike took it and gave a firm handshake. "Miss Selenzy."

"What an honour," the newcomer squealed. She looked around impishly. Then, she stared at Klondike and tilted her head seductively. "Are you here for my audition?"

"What?" Klondike glared at her, then at Shapiro. "Gino! What in hell is happening here?"

"Chairman," Shapiro said weakly. He pointed to the parking lot. "Miss Selenzy here was performing by herself out there, by the trucks. She does a regular show here for the troops, she tells me. She was doing her gymnastics. Then, er, we talk. And, of all things in heaven, she wants a place in our show!" He tried to laugh. "I don't know how else to explain it all, my chairman."

Klondike listened intently, raising an inquisitive eyebrow as Shapiro filled him in. He looked Carla over. "You say you're a big star out here, Miss Selenzy?"

She pouted at him. "The shows are big," she hissed. "I am enormous!"

"Oh, for goodness sake!" Penny cried from behind. "Please! This is ridiculous. How much more of this nonsense must we listen to? Now, Gino, we have our routines to practice." She walked up to Carla and glared at her. "That is if Miss Little Leotard here has no more objections!"

The two women eyed each other like prize-fighters before the bell.

"Alright," Klondike said, holding up a hand. He could not stop looking at Carla. There was something about her. The way she carried herself. Like a star. When she spoke, he felt like he was watching a scene from a movie. It was a strange, eerie phenomenon.

Carla seemed to sense his feelings. "OK, Mr Klondike," she suddenly said. "How about a deal? Put me in your show… for Saturday night. I am a star around here. It will help sell tickets. If you like what I do, up there on the trapeze, I'll stay with you for the rest of your tour. If you don't like… ah, I will head my own way with my troupe. There will be no hard feelings."

"You cannot be serious!" Penny raged.

Heavy moved next to Klondike. "Is this actually happening, Kal?" He whispered.

Shapiro held up his hands. "You talk rich, sweetheart. But, alas, there is no place for you in our show. I am sorry, si. But me and Penny are a well-oiled unit. Nothing can break our bond up there on the rings. We cannot bring in a newcomer, just like that."

"You misunderstand me, King Gino," she said matter-of-factly. "I have no desire to fly with you and your catcher. I perform solo. My own act. Just me, the rings and the wire." With that, she pranced across like a ballerina to where the mini-tightrope was and rubbed her hand gently along the plastic cord.

They all stared at her in shock.

Klondike quickly came back on track. "Er, Miss Selenzy… I want to thank you for coming out here, and for your interest in our circus here. We are honoured. Truly. But, well, it's like this. We have a tried and tested formula here, in our show. Integrating a new act, especially a solo trapeze piece… well, that is a big deal. It can take weeks, months even, to introduce a new spot. And, even then, that is after we have scouted the performer… watched them dozens of times, helped train them, got to know them. Our show is perfected."

Carla seemed to snarl. "Your show is a disaster!" They all recoiled at the statement. She ran a hand through her hair again. "I'm sorry. I didn't mean to be so, ah, blunt. But, come on. I have seen your reviews. I have heard the talk. You are losing sales. Losing face, even."

It was Heavy who spoke, angrily. "That is none of your concern, miss."

Penny turned and walked away, back towards her trailer. "This is all crazy. Come and get me Gino when you're done with this… this princess!"

Carla watched her go happily. "It's…empress," she whispered, eyeing each of the three men now before her.

Shapiro looked disjointed. "Listen… Carla. Just because we don't get to perform together doesn't mean we can't, y'know, get to know each other a little, eh?"

She nodded delicately, before turning back to Klondike. She moved her hands along the two-inch thick plastic wire again, and seemed to brace herself.

"Alright," she cried, suddenly poised as if on stage. "You can turn me down, gentlemen. But, tell me, have you ever seen anyone do this?"

With that, Carla gripped the wire and jumped, effortlessly heaving herself up, up and into a handstand, her hands gripping the wire with brute force. She held herself vertically, upside down, on the wire, her grip faultless as it supported her entire frame. Then, she half-turned her body and moved a hand forward on the wire, followed by the next, her body straight as an arrow as she balanced herself there.

Incredibly, she was walking across the high wire… on her hands!

Her biceps and forearms were taut and looked rock-hard as she moved along, arm following arm as she manoeuvred herself across the 10-yard long wire.

It was a breathtaking sight. Impossible! Klondike, Heavy and Shapiro stood there, transfixed by the bizarre scene. None of them had ever seen what could only be described as an upside-down wire walk. Shapiro had a queer look on his face, and tilted his head as he watched, as if trying to understand it all.

Finally, Carla reached the end of the tightrope. Once there, she shimmied her hands, changing the grip so she was now facing outwards again. Holding herself upright, she loosened the grip, letting her body swing round. The momentum was staggering. She went round three times in a blur, then released the hold in mid-turn. Her frame flew into the air, where she threw a textbook backflip before landing flat on her soles, one arm aloft. The haughty smile was still there.

The three men all applauded on the spot.

Shapiro was beside himself. "Miss Carla," he panted, mesmerised. "That was staggering. Like nothing any show has ever seen. You are… you are blessimo!"

Klondike wandered slowly over to her, smiling in disbelief. "That certainly was something. In all my years of scouting circus talent, I've never seen anything quite like that. Walking on your hands on a wire. Wow! Just saying it takes an effort." He pointed at the rapidly ascending circus tent out in the distance. "Can you do that in there? Up high? With everyone watching?"

Carla laughed yet again, throwing her head back. "Of course, chairman! How do you think I got my reputation?"

Klondike nodded. He looked at Heavy, who shrugged. Then, he stared at Gino. It was all too much.

"Well? Maybe now you want the empress in your show, no?" She was still laughing to herself, seemingly feeling no pressure or fear.

Klondike tried to smile. He looked back at the big top. His mind was racing. "Well," he drawled. "It looks like we've got a decision to make."

And that was the truth.

"Carla Selenzy. My, that takes me back. She was like royalty in Italy back in the day. My god, what a beautiful woman. Everyone loved her. Like a circus version of Sophia Loren."

Bannion appeared misty-eyed as he spoke softly.

"Yeah, that's her," Klondike mused. "She sure is something else."

He had gathered together his management team in his trailer to discuss what had happened out in the practice enclosure.

Now, he stood leaning against his minibar, looking down at Heavy and Lacey on the couch, and Bannion, who stood in the kitchenette.

"And, let me get this straight," Lacey said slowly, a cigarette in her hand as she leant forward. "This Carla, the so-called empress of acrobatics, just appeared out of nowhere? Asking for a chance? An audition?" She looked up at Klondike pleadingly. "This is all a bit odd, don't you think?"

"The whole thing is crazy," Klondike rasped. "But, somehow, that seems in keeping with this whole damn tour. I feel like we're living in some kind of soap opera out here. Nothing makes any damn sense!"

Heavy was nodding wildly. "Something happened out there. Gino… he was under her spell. It was like he'd been hypnotised."

"Oh, please!" Lacey spat out. "Come on, Henry. Gino. A beautiful woman like that. We all know what will play out."

"This was different."

Lacey raised an eyebrow. "Well, maybe she is the first star name flyer he has ever flirted with."

Bannion seemed intrigued. "And she wants a solo spot? On the trapeze?"

"That's right," Klondike barked. He poured himself some more scotch and took a sip from his tall glass. "Now, look, what it all boils down to is this… do we want her in our show? I've thought it all over in the past few hours, ever since she bamboozled her way in." He looked at them each in turn. "The positives are she is famous out here. People love her. Not just in Germany, but at this here air base. She does regular shows at the mess hall, on their stage. I've checked out her story. She plays here once a month with a dancing troupe, piano man and some Italian comedian."

"Yeah," Heavy blurted, "but the main positive is what she can do! What she brings to the show. Her hand walking act was unreal."

Lacey nodded thoughtfully. "Of course, we need a bit of due diligence here, boys. We need to check out her story, star or not."

"I'm on it," Bannion said quickly. "But I myself can vouch for her. She was a superstar for many years."

Lacey sat back. "What happened to her?"

"That I need to check," the Englishman replied. "But I imagine she is now a freelance performer. It's a good way to get big bucks. Big, one-off pay days. No contract. No obligations. But a demand from all over."

Lacey shrugged. "Dancing in a mess hall? You call that a big gig?"

"It's like I keep telling Kal. Post-war Europe is a desperate place. No matter who you are."

Klondike began pacing the room, nodding thoughtfully. "Now, what are the negatives? Anybody…"

Lacey looked up. "Apart from signing up an unknown into our show, just like that, for Saturday night?" She rolled her eyes. "It's a gamble, Kalvin. This is a big move, for all of us."

Heavy leant forward. "You think we should let her go, Lacey?"

The ace publicist sighed, then smiled thinly. "Actually, boys, I do not." They all looked at her in stunned silence. She inhaled on her cigarette deeply, blowing the smoke out in a long, hazy cloud. "To be honest, after London, Paris and Antwerp, we may have experienced our lowest ebb. I'm sorry, I know it sounds painful, but we all know these three shows were something none of us could ever have imagined. My point is… I don't think things can get much worse. There are few incidents in our industry that will out-trump an audience that doesn't cheer, a troupe of performers left shell-shocked." She looked up at

Klondike, her giant, violet eyes wide in fright. "And a sea of empty seats."

Klondike glared down at her. "You're saying it doesn't matter what we do now? Anything will be a bonus after Antwerp?"

She shrugged. "All I'm saying is, why not? And if she manages to get some of the fans excited… well, let her loose, I say."

Heavy pumped his fist. "Well said, Lacey!"

Klondike's mind was throbbing. "Bold words, I'll give you that."

She shook her hair. "Why, thank you, boys." She smiled deliciously. "Giving big speeches is something I've had a lot of practice doing, ever since I first rolled into Klondike's Circus."

Heavy smiled whimsically. "In that fancy motor. With your Park Avenue glad rags on…"

"I think what Heavy is trying to say…" Klondike interspersed, "is that your opinion is as important to us now as it has ever been."

She nodded, dragging on the smoke. "So…as for our empress, Miss Selenzy. Is she joining us on Saturday night?"

Klondike looked at Heavy, then smiled down at her. "I think it's unanimous."

The others grinned happily, excited.

Bannion spoke next. "OK. I'll get to work on the, er, due diligence, as it were."

Klondike wedged one of his giant cigars into the corner of his mouth. "You do that, Jack." He looked out of the trailer window at the now fully assembled circus tent outside. "We've got to start spreading the word to the good people of Berlin. Come Saturday, we're gunna have a real spectacle under our big top. A king and an empress! In one god damn show!"

It was like a scene from an old western movie.

The air force flyers all stood and watched in awe as the beautiful golden palomino rode elegantly across the field, its rider decked out in full rawhide gear.

The mount completed several laps of the green before tottering across towards the grass to the makeshift stable block aligned by the circus trailers. The servicemen had all assembled, resplendent in their blue uniforms, many of them still captivated by the prospect of the big top.

As the cowboy rode over upon his horse, they all applauded heartily. Many of them had never seen such a sight in person, only when they could manage a night at the movies.

"Thank you," Duster Williams cried as he manoeuvred Goldie across to the stables. Once on the asphalt, he dismounted and led the horse across to its berth, at the far end of the block. The other horses were all resting in their individual stalls.

He let Goldie in, where she made a beeline for the water trough at the far end. Williams latched the gate door as the great beast wandered inside.

In his buckskin straps and jacket and white stetson, he cut quite a figure.

The airmen all tried to talk to him at once.

"Hey, Mr Williams, sir, that sure was something, seeing you ride old Goldie… out here! In our airfield!"

"It's great you're here, Duster. I used to watch your movies at the old picture house when I was growing up in Detroit."

"Hey, I caught your show one time out in Oregon…"

Williams smiled politely, nodding at the greetings as he made his way around the stables and across to a small hangar, which was serving as a base camp for the circus people for the week.

"Thank you, boys," he mused happily, removing his leather gloves as he walked. They all followed, like children.

"It is a sincere pleasure to be here, performing for you all. Out here, in Berlin." He looked at the eager young faces all staring at him as he turned. "Bet you don't get many cowboys out here, eh?"

They all laughed. "I can't believe you're still performing…" one of the air men exclaimed.

Williams nodded as he moved through the giant hangar door. "You and me both, young man."

Another cried: "I hear it's going to be a sell-out!"

"Great!" said the cowboy. "That's what we want to hear." He smiled again at the servicemen, who were positively enchanted. "It will be wonderful to have some Americans in our audience again. Trust me!" He laughed to himself.

Then, as he walked up to a desk holding a jug of water and glasses, he paused, his eyes drifting to the wall opposite. There, a collection of Klondike's Circus posters covered the plaster. They were the individual star posters Miss Tanner had brought over. Each one had a giant picture of each of the show's top performers, with a picture of the glorious big top underneath. Each name was written in dazzling gold letters.

The glossy posters had been stuck up seemingly everywhere on this tour, wherever they played. Someone had gone to town in this hangar, he thought idly, with the posters all stuck up together to form a wall of colour.

One of the air men walked over to it and smiled excitedly. "It's going to be one world class spectacular. Just look at all these star names."

As he threw his hand aloft, Williams gazed at the portraits. There was Shapiro in his orange singlet. Olsen in his silver waistcoat. The Daredevils in those yellow and black jumpsuits. Corky in the classic red and yellow clown get-up. And then there was him, Duster Williams, in his buckskins, clutching a lasso.

He smiled at the picture of himself. Deep inside, he was truly thankful for being given this second chance. In life, not just show business. "You're right, son," he muttered. "They are star names. I'm honoured to be among them." He turned to the assembled group. "You boys are in for one hell of a show!"

They all cheered again.

"And that's not all," one of the youngsters exclaimed excitedly. "I heard that Carla Selenzy is joining you guys. As a special guest. How about that!"

They all whistled, each man grinning like a juvenile.

Williams gazed at the poster of Shapiro before him, then back at the air men. He chuckled.

"I'm sure she will make quite the impact."

At that moment, Shapiro and Carla were strolling gently through Littzmann Parken, a sprawling woodland a few miles from the airbase.

After Shapiro had talked her through the show, and briefed her on when she would take the stage, she had suggested they continue the conversation at the park, away from all the hubbub of the trailers and midway.

Carla's bandleader had driven them through the city, and they had embarked on a walk through the luscious trees and greenery of one of Berlin's most popular spots.

Penny had happily stayed behind, having witnessed such a scene many times before. Just not with a fellow trapeze flyer.

"I often come out here before a show," Carla was saying softly as they strolled in the sun. "You know, to get away from the people. The prying eyes."

They had walked down a pathway between some forestland and were now at a clearing, which led to a stream rolling across grey rocks. The water seemed to sparkle in the sunlight.

"Si, it is a nice spot," Shapiro murmured. He looked at her. "You are sure you're alright, angel? This has all happened very fast, no? We've only just met, out on an airfield. And now…"

She smiled mischievously. "And now I'm a part of your show."

"Indeed. I can't help but feel all this is not purely down to chance."

Carla laughed lightly, suddenly taking his arm. "Oh, Gino! Of course not. Everyone who knows me understands I want to be in a big show again. A circus! Sure, I have done the Italian circuits. Europe, and the UK. But this… a touring American company! With you, the great Gino…" she seemed to shake, as if electrocuted. "This is just so absolutely fantastic. A dream for me."

Shapiro nodded, trying to remain calm despite the dazzling Carla hanging on his every word. "Well, it may be that you help us, dear. The people seem to love you out here. Maybe this will help the audience enjoy the show even more."

She waved a hand through the air haughtily. "I'll do my best."

"I'm sure." He rubbed gently at her hands as she clung to him. "You made quite the impression back by my trailer. Even making the Chairman stand back. Now, that is something…"

They reached the edge of the stream, the noise of the water rushing past a pleasant distraction. Suddenly, she grabbed at his arms and turned to face him dramatically.

"Fate brought us together, Gino!" she rasped in a husky voice. "And at some point in time, we were destined to be together. In a show. In our lives. You and I. We both know it. The king and queen of trapeze." She pushed a hand through her hair, as if overcome by it all. "My god, the electricity there is between us. Even as we talk. Imagine… just imagine what it will be like, performing together!"

He smiled. "I am through imagining. Now, I want it!"

"Oh Gino!"

With that, she threw herself into him and they kissed passionately. Holding the embrace, his feet almost slipped into the water.

As their lips finally parted, he held her head, staring into her beautiful ebony eyes. "Mamacita…"

She giggled. "I knew it."

He frowned. She looked shocked suddenly, her face dropping. He noticed it. It was like a switch had been flipped, the way her expression changed like that.

"What was that?" he whispered.

Carla looked frantic for a second. Then, the confident, self-assured look returned, the eyes cool and twinkling. "I said I knew it. I knew… knew we would be together. You know, like this…" she planted a tiny, quick kiss on his lips. "Like I said, fate."

That made him grin again. "In the stars, perhaps…"

She brushed a hand across his jawline. Her skin felt like a silk thread. "I've dreamed of this moment, Gino."

He held her tight, his eyes locked on her mesmeric gaze.

"I feel like I'm dreaming right now."

They kissed again.

CHAPTER 18

To the immense relief of Klondike, his staff, performers and just about everyone involved with the circus, the Berlin show at the US Air Force Base in Haddenhacht was met with a vibrant, raucous audience.

The heavy mix of serving Americans, German locals, excited children who lived near the base and assorted local dignitaries made for a jovial crowd, who were enchanted by the visiting performers.

To Klondike, it almost felt like being home.

The Hightops, Rocking Robins and Flying Batistas were all welcomed and applauded with their loudest ovations on the tour so far.

The Showcase Revue brought the house down with their unforgettable antics. The shock and awe on the faces of the younger patrons as they glimpsed the monstrous forms of Gargantua and Goliath was a sight to behold for all.

When Corky and his clown troupe entered the tent, the laughter from the children was overpowering. Corky drew maximum enthusiasm from the stands by engaging with the spectators, offering animal balloons and his seemingly never-ending supply of flowers, all magically emerging from his suit sleeves.

Corky's human cannonball act drew mighty cheers, with hundreds of fans screaming as the cannon fired and the clown flew across the arena floor into the great net at the far side.

Corky and his clowns all waved with delight, and a great deal of relief, as they jogged off the sawdust.

The veteran performer approached Klondike as he left the floor, a twinkle in his eye again. "Looks like we've finally found some friends again, Kal."

Klondike patted him heavily on the back as he passed, heading for the flap exit. "You said it, Corky. This is more like it!"

The boss grinned as the clowns all slowly came off, their zany theme music booming from the tannoy. He was visibly more relaxed than he had been at the top of the show, and was finally alive and enthused. He looked across at Heavy, Lacey and Plum, stood as always just behind him at the flap, in the shadow of a grandstand. For this show, Bannion was seated in the bleachers with the press pool, in an attempt to see if anyone had been paid off or coerced into writing a negative review.

Klondike prowled the flap area as Heavy made his way out for the next introduction. Lacey, arms folded, rested her head momentarily on his shoulder.

"Thank goodness. Applause! It's working."

Klondike finally laughed. "A good crowd. A lot of our countrymen up there, though."

She gazed at him mischievously. "Hell, I'll take anything tonight. It's beginning to look a good idea, picking this air base for our venue."

He nodded as Heavy roared out the introduction for the Daredevils, which was followed as always by the electrifying sound of the motorbike engines revving up wildly. They turned as the gleaming bikes approached from the field outside, rolling through the flap and hitting the entranceway. The last rider rolled towards them.

As Enqvist rode past slowly, holding his helmet still, he grinned up at Klondike. "I hear cheers! At last!" He rammed the yellow helmet on. "Now watch, chief, as we give these guys the spectacle of their lives!"

With that, he zoomed off to join the others. The Daredevils raced round the tent floor several times, to rapturous applause. Their initial stunts, the leapfrogs and wheelies, drew cheers from all sections of the stands.

Then, as the famous Globe of Death was wheeled out on its flatbed truck and secured to the iron platform in the arena's centre, the audience – not to mention Klondike and Lacey – all held a collective breath.

The riders all entered the great caged sphere, one every minute, and raced around in their circles. The multiple loops began.

And the crowd loved it.

The cheers were what everyone had remembered about the death-defying act. A mixture of ecstasy, shock and adulation.

When Enqvist finally drove his motorcycle up the small ramp towards the Globe's entrance door, he performed his trademark pose, removing his helmet, holding it aloft and pumping the air for several moments before preparing to enter the madness.

But this time, Enqvist pumped the air for a full minute. It was part relief, part sheer joy. He had missed this. Klondike could almost feel the adrenaline pouring off the rider as he held that arm aloft.

Then, he was inside, roaming round and round the sphere in a straight, direct 360-degree arc, as a steward hurriedly closed the door.

Watching the Daredevils perform this fearless act, Klondike felt a surge of pride once again. Signing up the Norwegian troupe to his circus had been one of his shrewdest moves, and nothing had changed his view on that. Not London, Paris or Antwerp.

When the Globe door opened again two minutes later, the riders all emerged one at a time and performed their customary lap of honour.

The audience were all on their feet, applauding wildly. If anyone had objected to the stunt with cries or shrieks, nobody noticed.

Klondike, Lacey and Plum all stepped to the edge of the arena floor and glanced up at the cheering patrons. It was a beautiful sight, especially after what they had experienced of late.

Plum grinned like a cherub. "We're back."

Klondike nodded, almost laughing at one over-excited female spectator who was screaming at the riders as they flew past.

"Let's hope it continues, pal."

As the Daredevils all headed for the exit, the noise of their engines filling the air, the applause continued.

And it hardly paused at all as the show continued.

With a jovial air filling the big top, Roddy Olsen walked out on to the sawdust, carrying his suitcase.

Reaching the mic, he placed a hand on the stand and introduced himself.

"Good evening friends. My name is Roddy Olsen and, tonight, it is my pleasure to perform some of America's greatest rock n roll and swing hits for you."

The opening notes of a Chip Franklin song boomed out from the tannoy. Olsen began to sing. Then, suddenly, another voice emanated from somewhere.

"Hey! Stop that singing! And let me out! Let me out!"

The laughter that rained down was the sound of a knowing audience. Again, Klondike smiled in relief. Many of the fans were familiar with Olsen and his act. That would be a blessing.

Olsen performed one of his usual skits, as he struggled to remove Rusty Fox from the suitcase.

"Yow! Don't put your hand there! What are you doing!"

Then, Olsen stood up again, with the fox puppet on his arm.

Another cheer came from the stands.

"Hey, man," the puppet snarled. "If there is singing going on here, I am the one doing it. I'm a rock n roll star, remember?"

"Of course," Olsen said to his puppet. Then, he addressed the audience: "Ladies and gentlemen, may I present my very good friend, Rusty Fox."

"That's Rusty Fox, teen idol. Heart-throb. Popular with all the chicks. Even the ones I try to eat!"

Another roar of laughter reverberated around the floor.

Klondike and Heavy had instructed Olsen to perform more of his customary sketches and comedy for this performance, instead of just doing songs, as he had done for Paris and Antwerp.

With the high number of Americans expected in the crowd, and the general westernisation of many of the locals, as a result of the US presence, Klondike had a feeling the usual ventriloquist act would be a hit. Olsen was slightly reluctant, but it was no secret he wished to return to his usual repertoire.

"OK Rusty. So, you're a singer? What else can you do?"

"Impressions."

"Oh yeah?"

"Sure. Look, here's my impression of Elvis…" with that, the small fox puppet began shaking uncontrollably as if having a fit, while Olsen sang the opening lines of Heartbreak Hotel in a perfect Elvis voice.

"And here's President Kennedy…" Rusty put on a cocky pose, before giving a speech in a Kennedy accent, complimenting all the females in the crowd and telling them where he would be that night.

"Alright, alright," Olsen said. "Come on and sing then, Rust. I'll let you do the next song, but only if we make it a duet."

"You got it."

They both began the hit rock song, Darling Of Mine, taking it turns to sing a line each, the crowd mesmerised by Olsen's voice manipulation as he traversed from his voice to his puppet's.

Afterwards, Olsen introduced Napoleon from the suitcase and held a puppet on each arm. After introducing the army veteran, it was time for his oldest and most celebrated gig as he performed the ultra-fast track Rock Island Line, alternating each line between himself, Rusty and Napoleon.

The sketch had been a perennial crowd pleaser since day one, and hearing the audience roaring their approval was as beautiful a sound as Klondike could recall ever hearing.

At the flap, a strangely emotional Lacey held his arm as Olsen performed. She looked proud, and somehow afraid.

Klondike frowned. Lacey and Olsen had endured a complex relationship, he knew that.

"You alright?" he whispered.

She nodded. "I'm just so happy for Roddy. He was so upset after London. Really. I'd never seen him like that. It's so… so wonderful to see this. What we are used to."

He frowned slightly as she blurted the words out. "This will do Rod a world of good."

After Rock Island Line, Olsen placed Rusty Fox and Napoleon back in the trunk and removed Tony Tan. Another customary number was finishing his set, with a swing song from the crooner puppet.

After Tan gave his usual drunken, backwards introduction, Olsen launched him into his traditional finale, the Sinatra classic High Hopes.

The beautiful rendition was met by another loud ovation.

Olsen, the consummate professional, remained as cool as ever at the conclusion. He produced all three puppets in his arms and bowed with them as one. Then, returning his 'guys' to the suitcase, he waved happily to the stands as he jogged off the stage. No fist pumps. No signs of ecstatic relief. Just his usual exit.

As he approached the flap, Klondike wrapped an arm around his shoulders as he passed.

"You did it, Roddy. Well done. They love you!"

Olsen remained cool, grinning slightly. "Thanks, Kal. I was beginning to wonder if I'd ever get screaming fans again!"

Then, Lacey embraced him. Pulling him away, she held his face and said: "You see, Roddy. These people loved you. Every audience is different, just like we said."

The youngster looked at her awkwardly, like a gangly teen eyeing a housewife he was sweet on. "I couldn't have done it without you, Lacey."

Then, he was gone, out the flap and into the field.

The crowd were soon cheering wildly again as Duster Williams and the Range Riders stormed into the tent on their horses.

The cheers were constant as the cowboys performed their riding repertoire of tricks and stunts, with several doffing their stetsons to the applauding fans and acknowledging the response.

When Williams performed his solo spot, a sudden silence engulfed the big top.

The veteran star had Goldie perform several hind leg salutes. He then dismounted by standing on the saddle and leaping onto the ground.

With a flourish of his hands, he removed his lasso from the saddle horn and began his roping. The full range of tricks followed as he span the rope into a large hoop and began jumping through the spinning circle, continuing the leaps as the hoop got smaller and smaller through his adjustments.

After completing the falling hoop trick, when the lasso is thrown high into the air before falling neatly into a perfect circle around his feet, he turned to Goldie again. It was time for an old favourite as a treat for the air base crowd.

Holding his hand towards his trusted horse, he said loudly: "Put it there, partner."

Goldie stood erect and offered a front leg, with Williams shaking the hoof as if the two had agreed on a deal.

Delighted laughter echoed down from the bleachers.

With a grin, Williams ran his arm round in a corkscrew motion and Goldie set off at a trot. He sprinted after her, expertly pulling himself on to the saddle and remounting the horse as she took off on another lap of the arena floor.

The rest of the Range Riders then joined in and, suddenly, the entire team were racing around in a giant loop again, with the cowboys performing saddle handstands and riding backwards as the act continued.

As the cowboys departed the tent to hearty applause and whooping, they all waved their hats in thanks to the watching masses.

Williams rode at the back of the procession, and got an almighty cheer as he made his exit. A few yards from the flap, he had Goldie complete another hind-leg stand, and raised his hat aloft once more.

As he guided his mount to the exit, he high-fived the outstretched hands of Klondike and Plum.

"Nice handshake!" A delighted Plum exclaimed.

Williams chuckled, looking back at the raucous crowd. "Folks always used to like that trick." He rode out into the air field beyond.

"And now," Heavy's voice brought everyone's attention back to the centre of the floor. "As a special treat to the good people of Berlin, it is the pleasure of Klondike's Circus to introduce our very special guest for this performance. You all know her well. One of the golden girls of European circus for over a decade. Ladies and gentlemen, please give it up for the empress of acrobatics… Miss Carla Selenzy!"

The ovation was half surprise, half excitement. In many ways, just what Klondike had expected.

And then, Carla came racing out on to the sawdust, like a princess from another planet.

She wore a giant gold and purple cloak, which she discarded once she reached the centre, revealing an outrageous leotard designed to mimic the German flag. The black, red and yellow all meshed together in a startling look. And the audience loved it.

Carla's act was like nothing Klondike and his team had ever witnessed.

First, pop music began blaring out from the tannoy and she threw herself into what looked like a rhythmic gymnastics display from an Olympic medallist. The energetic moves were incredible, as she thrust her body through the air. She ended it by throwing herself into a series of lightning fast cartwheels, which then became backward somersaults as she turned over and over until she reached the far side of the floor.

The audience mesmerised, Carla then began running back towards the centre, before leaping through the air and pirouetting like a figure skater.

Just as everyone wondered how she would land, the dazzling flyer never came back down again, instead clinging to a hanging trapeze support rope like a sloth.

Barely pausing for breath, Carla pulled herself up, slithering along the line at a rapid pace. She was, of course, heading for the high wire, placed about 25 yards off the ground, almost halfway towards the tent roof.

Klondike folded his arms and smiled smugly. He had been unable to get Carla's extraordinary hand walk out of his head these past two days. Seeing it up there, on the circus wire, here in his tent, would be an unrivalled treat. He caught Heavy looking at him to his left, and the two exchanged a nod.

Then, it began. Dumping a generous helping of chalk on her palms, Carla executed a handstand on the thick plastic wire and then, inexplicably, turned her body to face the far platform, opposite where she was now poised.

One hand reached past the next, over and over, as she slowly hauled herself across the high wire. Her tiny frame remained straight and firm, barely quivering at all, as she guided herself across.

The tent was filled with shocked, awe-struck silence. Mouths gaped, hands hit foreheads. Astonishment gripped the grandstands.

Then, finally, Carla was at the other end of the line, her legs sloping forward like a contortionist until they rested on the far platform, before the rest of her body followed in a bizarre-looking, slick movement.

As the crowd erupted into wild applause, the dazzling Carla stood there, one hand on her hip, the other running through her hair, as if nothing out of the ordinary had occurred.

Then, she waved with both hands, blowing kisses to the stands. She dived smoothly to the nearest support rope, a good six yards away, and slid down effortlessly.

Heavy strode out on to the sawdust as she reached the ground. "Have you ever seen anything quite like it, ladies and gentlemen?" He roared into the mic. "How about that? The legendary Carla Selenzy, your empress of acrobatics! Let's hear it for Europe's own queen Carla!"

The applause continued as she jogged around the perimeter of the arena, waving happily, apparently allowing herself her own lap of honour.

Klondike watched with a wry smile. "She really is a piece of work, that one."

Lacey was watching coyly, arms folded. "Full of talent, yes. But perhaps a little full of herself."

Plum laughed next to her. "Who cares? These people are crazy for her!"

Klondike watched her as she approached the flap. "And she chose us. As wonderful as it is, it just doesn't quite add up."

"Correction, tiger," Lacey murmured. "She chose Gino!"

Carla gave one last wave to the arena as she entered the enclosure by the flap. She stopped by Klondike and his team, as if posing for a photograph. Her smile looked strangely hypnotic.

Klondike stammered under her gaze. "Miss Selenzy, thank you so much for joining us. That was truly spectacular. We are indebted to you."

She seemed to prowl before them, like a model on a catwalk. "The people," she panted, "they love their Carla."

They all stared at her, almost in shock. "Thank you, Carla," Lacey said formally.

With that, the Italian turned to the flap, where Shapiro and Penny were just coming into the tent, adorned in their pristine fur cloaks.

"Ah," Carla gushed. "And now, our royal court is complete. We have our king!" She moved up to Gino and kissed him heavily on the cheek. Shapiro was usually unflappable as he entered the big top, but smiled awkwardly as Carla grabbed at him.

"If you don't mind," Penny hissed, "we have a show to put on!"

"Is ok," Shapiro mumbled, gently easing Carla away. He looked at Klondike and Lacey, clearly embarrassed.

Klondike patted him on the back. "Blow them away, Gino. Just like always."

"Si, chairman."

On the sawdust, Heavy was just finishing his grand introduction to the enchanted, screaming fans. No one in the stands had gotten their breath since the last act.

"…so cheer him, love him, never forget him. Klondike's Circus is proud to present the one and only debonair king of the air… Gino Shapiro!"

Another electrifying ovation poured down from the bleachers all around as Shapiro and Penny strode out, waving as if they were royalty.

As they walked confidently to their ropes, Carla jumped out several yards on to the arena floor, and enthusiastically began encouraging the crowd to cheer louder, raising her hands upwards and whipping everyone into more of a frenzy.

Klondike watched her curiously. She worked the audience like a natural. Everyone seemed to roar with excitement. It was deafening in the tent.

"What is she doing?" Lacey cried.

"Look at how they all respond to her," Klondike exclaimed.

Carla returned to the flap, grinning like a wisened bobcat.

Then, as the dramatic circus music began playing all around, Shapiro and Penny threw down their capes and hauled themselves up their ropes.

Carla watched over Klondike's shoulder, her chin almost touching his back. "See how the people love their king, chairman."

Klondike half-smiled as he craned his neck to watch the action high above. "They seemed to like you encouraging them."

"Of course." She smiled mischievously. "I know these people. What to do. You see now, eh… your tour changes direction today. No one will forget this show tonight."

As bewildered as he was, Klondike had to admit it – the dazzling, self-proclaimed empress was saying everything he wanted to hear. And it all seemed to be true.

Up in the tent's summit, Shapiro was performing his trademark array of leaps and jumps. There was the double and triple roll, the helicopter spin, the turtle somersault, the standing fall and the long dive. Each jump followed the last in a seamless blend of human aerobatics.

The great Gino flew effortlessly back and forth across the rig under the tent's ceiling, a blur of fireball orange as he went back and forth, propelled at a rapid pace by Penny, who hung upside down on her ring in the very centre.

For this performance, Shapiro and Penny were to perform their chair balancing act, which they hadn't brought out in a while. It seemed like a good idea for a hot circus crowd like Berlin.

Two wooden desk chairs were attached to the tall ropes at the ground by stewards, and Shapiro and Penny hauled them up to the trapeze rig in no time, pulling the ropes vigorously at their ends.

Then, both artists placed the front two legs of each chair on their respective ring seats, tilted precariously, before audaciously standing on the backs of the chairs and balancing perfectly, hands away from the ring ropes.

The crowd cheered wildly again. As Penny remained hovering, Shapiro lowered his hands to the top of his chair, pushed down and then inexplicably raised his legs until he was performing an inverted handstand – on a chair, that balanced tentatively on his ring seat, high above the watching thousands. Then, as a drumroll sounded on the tannoy, he lifted one hand off the chair and held his position for a full 10 seconds.

That did it. The spectators were on their feet, screaming his name and applauding with all their might.

Shapiro and Penny both slowly returned to a standing position upon their ring seats.

They retied the chairs to the support ropes, let them drop, and then climbed down slowly.

While Penny dropped to the floor, Shapiro halted at the high wire platform. He still had to perform his traditional show-closer.

Barely pausing for breath, the master trapeze ace held his arms out wide and walked simply across the wire, as if he was popping out for a stroll.

Carla's earlier hand walk may have made the wire stunt look somewhat basic now, but Shapiro's trademark cartwheel at the end of the wire to reach the far platform was still a joy to behold for all who witnessed it.

As he waved to the cheering patrons and then descended on a tall rope again, the crowd saluted his brilliance with rapturous applause.

The old familiar chant of "Gino, Gino, Gino", filled the tent once more, as it had done so many times before.

As Shapiro waved with both hands and jogged to the flap, he was met with a mighty group hug as Klondike, Lacey, Plum and Penny all embraced him as one. The relief was palpable. They could practically taste it.

Klondike was not entirely sure how it had all transpired… but the Berlin show was a monster hit.

Carla seemed to elbow them all out of the way, before throwing herself unashamedly at Shapiro. They kissed. In full view of the others. Penny looked like she was about to explode. But, somehow, everyone held it together. The almost surreal atmosphere was having a strange effect on everyone.

The crowds were cheering frantically all around. It looked like some fans wanted to jump down on to the sawdust themselves, like a pitch invasion in a sports match.

Klondike looked at Carla and Gino embracing, then back to the grandstands, and found himself almost laughing.

And then, as everyone was reaching a feeling of near-euphoria, out came Suzi Dando and the finale was on.

The gleaming Cadillac convertibles began lurching past the over-excited group at the flap. Klondike tried to pat or high-five each group as the parade cars floated by, and found himself almost falling over himself.

Suzi's song echoed all around, as many in the audience began swaying, holding their hands aloft in joy.

Shapiro, Penny and Carla had no time to freshen up or find their discarded capes. The final, orange Cadillac was motoring through the tent flap and into the arena. The three flyers simply had to jump into the back, stand in the gulley and wave frantically as the parade reached its full circle.

As the Cadillacs drove round in their customary final lap for the finale, Klondike realised it felt like an eternity since he had enjoyed watching the parade. Usually one of his favourite sights in life, as the stars soaked up the applause one last time in the grand closing of the show, the events of London, Paris and Antwerp had extinguished his enthusiasm.

But now, he leant against the side of the aluminium grandstand and joined in the applause. Lacey, Plum and Heavy, who had joined them temporarily before his final address, all clapped heartily.

Then, after that great final lap of honour, the Cadillacs slowly carried the parading stars out of the big top. Suzi finished her song on a dramatic high note, and suddenly it was all over.

As the mighty applause finally died down, Heavy made his closing statement.

"Ladies and gentlemen, we hope you have enjoyed the glamour, the razzmatazz and the sheer excitement of Klondike's Circus. And we hope you can feel the magic tonight. From all of us here, thank you so much for joining us and we hope to see you again. Until then, goodnight... and god bless the beautiful country of Germany."

Outside in the airfield, the Cadillacs all rumbled on almost silently towards the car port at the side of the trailers in the circus encampment.

Wire fencing separated this enclosure from the rest of the field, where the thousands of spectators were now exiting the tent, excitement and laughter gripping the night air.

The bright floodlights employed by the air force all around the base made it feel almost like daytime, as waves of patrons headed for the parking lot at the site entrance.

As the Cadillacs all began to idle by the huge steel trailer that housed them, Shapiro leapt out of the final car and clapped his hands in delight.

Penny and Carla also jumped out, almost in a continuation of their flying acts.

"Just like old times," Shapiro cried, as he eyed the fans all flocking past in the distance. Many still screamed and cried aloud as they left.

Penny looked up at the big top one last time and smiled. "Well done, Gino. That was just what we needed. Everyone! All of us."

"Thank you, Penny. You were terrific. As always."

A sudden mass of roustabouts, dancers and clowns all seemed to flood past at once. Everyone seemed excited. The performers were all milling around outside the trailers, as if a party was about to break out.

Carla prowled around as if she owned the place. Penny watched her, ill at ease.

"I'll say goodnight, folks," she said quietly, sloping off towards her trailer.

"Goodnight Penny," Shapiro called out. "And remember. We're back!"

Carla came over and hugged him yet again. He smiled at her smugly, holding her tiny frame close to him. Their eyes locked.

"I told you," she gushed. "You are the greatest, King Gino. The people… they all love you."

Shapiro could not stop grinning. "Mamacita! I feel so alive. So captivated. What a night!"

She kissed him quickly. Then, she pulled her head back. "This calls for a celebration."

"Damn right!" He looked down at her, suddenly concerned. "So… you will stay for the tour, Carla? Surely after tonight, you will stay?"

She purred like a cat, rolling her eyes. "Well, if your chairman will have me… of course, I would love to stay on. After all, there is so much to look forward to, no? I have much to do still. So much to put on… people to enchant…"

As she said it, she looked over Shapiro's shoulder towards the trailers, where everyone seemed to be standing around, relieved and excited.

Like a master marksman, she locked her stare onto the handsome young man with thick blond hair and seagram blue eyes, dressed in the extravagant silver waistcoat and purple pants.

Roddy Olsen.

He was just standing there, as if in shock, looking up at the great red and blue big top.

Finally, he realised she was staring straight at him and looked at her curiously, as Shapiro held her close. Olsen studied her, somewhat taken aback as she eyed him unashamedly.

She smiled at him, the distance between them suddenly seeming like nothing. Olsen smiled back, confused but still on a high from the show. Her glare was mesmerising, like a spotlight. He felt like he could barely move.

"What is it, dear heart?" Shapiro whispered, as he held her hand and made to lead her away.

"Oh, nothing, darling," she said, stammering slightly. She clung to his arm as they walked.

"I was just thinking about all the forthcoming attractions. There is much to look forward to, no?"

CHAPTER 19

It was with a great air of belief and a reanimated longing that the men and women of Klondike's Circus set out on the next leg of their European tour.

The great circus train departed Berlin with welcome fanfare, and headed south for the long voyage to the Switzerland border.

The journey was to be the most spectacular of the tour so far, as the Imperial express train chugged over the mountainous railway that ascended through the Alps.

Every passenger on board was glued to the windows for the most part, staring in wonder and awe at the crisp, glistening summits and beautiful lakes and forestland that seemed to spread out into eternity. The track hugged the edge of the mountainside in some parts, offering spectacular Alpine views.

After passing through Nuremberg and Stuttgart, the train had breezed over the border into Switzerland. Several hours passed, and the circus troupe travelled through Zurich and Berne.

Finally, after a memorable trip full of sightseeing for all involved, the train arrived in the southern city of Geneva.

The carriages were transferred via an old freight line from Geneva Central Station to an abandoned rail yard, their somewhat unusual headquarters for the next few days. The site had been chosen months before by Bannion as it was close in proximity to the sprawling Parc Giresse, their performance venue.

As the train finally pulled in to the vintage works yard, many passengers gazed out at the park and noticed a funfair was already set up at the far end of the main field.

The circus operation would occupy the rest of the parkland, giving visitors a whole entertainment complex to explore.

The rail yard, essentially a warehouse with a railroad running into it, looked barren and in need of refurbishment.

As everyone slowly disembarked after the long journey, many stared in shock at the rusted iron walls and dusty concrete below.

However, Parc Giresse was barely 100 yards away from the site, meaning much of the set-up operation could be completed on foot.

Due to the train's immense length, half of the carriages were able to be housed inside the warehouse itself, with the other half open to the elements and streaming out of the giant hangar-like factory doors. It was an odd-looking set-up, with the train half in and half out of the huge construction.

As the performers and roustabouts all decamped from the train and began wandering around the yard towards the park, Jack Bannion made his way across to Jim McCabe, who was inspecting the premises with his team.

The Englishman stood next to the foreman, both studying the ugly old yard.

"Whatya think, Jim? It was the best option, believe me. Getting everything across from the main station would have been tricky, especially with the short roads they have here in Switzerland."

"I hear that," McCabe murmured. He looked from the yard and across to Parc Giresse. "No, this is perfect. All things considered. Being so close to the show ground is a dream come true for me and the boys. Why, we can carry a lot of the equipment over by hand."

Bannion nodded. "Great. Let's hope we get another sell-out and more big crowds."

McCabe grunted, lighting a cigarette. "What can possibly go wrong?"

Later that evening, Klondike and Heavy headed downtown to sample the local Geneva nightlife.

Both were still enamoured and in a state of bemused wonder after the high point of Berlin. Now, for the first real time on this tour, they had agreed to find a bar and engage in a poker marathon… almost as if they were back home.

The Alpenhorn was a traditional, old-fashioned saloon pub, with tables decked out in green and red cloths and everything looking as if it had just come out of a woodwork class. Various Alpine horns and paraphernalia hung on the walls as decor.

Klondike and Heavy had found a small table in a far corner and quickly went about sampling the local wheat ale, along with several glasses of cognac.

As for the poker, Heavy had never seen his old friend enjoy quite such a momentous winning streak. Klondike won 12 hands in a row, seemingly with minimal effort. And he displayed a deep repertoire of skill and tactical nous, triumphing with a busted flush, several full houses, a two and a three of a kind and even a deadman's bluff.

As the circus boss raked in his latest collection of winning chips, chosen from the Las Vegas collection gifted to him by an old casino boss buddy, he chuckled good-naturedly.

"Hell, you had enough Heav? You're gunna be out of chips any time soon!"

Heavy looked down with mock concern at his rapidly diminishing pile of counters. "I'll quit alright… just as soon as I actually win a hand."

He watched ruefully as Klondike carefully erected fresh piles of chips on his side of the table. Then, he gathered up the cards and began to shuffle.

"Why, oh why, didn't you ever try to make it as a pro? Out on the gaming circuit? Hell, you could've made a fortune. Maybe even won the world series out in Vegas."

Klondike took a long pull on his giant steinglass of beer. "You know why, old buddy."

Heavy grinned. "Sure. The lure of the circus world. Nothing could ever keep us away from that, eh Kal?"

"Ain't nothing like it in the world. Never has been. Never will be. Just look at that grand finale in Berlin. The electricity of the audience. The cheers and the joy." He squinted over at his oldest friend in the world. "Magic time."

Heavy nodded as he made to deal the fresh hand. "That certainly made this whole trip seem like a good idea. Hell, I was beginning to wonder."

As he dealt the cards, a shadow crept over their table and both men looked up. A handsome, middle-aged man in a black suit had approached, smiling widely.

"You must be the circus people," he said emphatically.

Klondike looked up and smiled. "That's right," he said. "Klondike's Circus. I'm Klondike. We're pitching up at Parc Giresse across town. Are you coming for the show, sir?"

"Oh yes," the man said in accented English. "I am very excited to see an American touring company, here in my home city." He extended a hand. "Christian Lago. Pleased to make your acquaintance. Welcome to Geneva, my friends."

They both shook his hand and offered their thanks.

"Care to join us, Mr Lago?" Heavy asked casually, motioning to a spare chair. "Poker is the game, but the man opposite me is in formidable form."

Lago laughed enthusiastically. "My thanks, but no. I just wanted to come over and say hello. You see, I am a long-time circus fan, since childhood. I have watched many top acts from across Europe down the years. But this… an American production. Out here! Well, this is historic."

"Thank you for the kind words," Klondike said. "We will do you and your countrymen proud, Mr Lago."

"You have excellent English," Heavy interjected.

"Oh yes," said Lago. "It is practically the national language out here, my friend. We all speak English at my public house. At home. And how we all love and admire your American movies, eh? John Wayne. Gary Cooper. I can't get enough, personally."

Klondike and Heavy both glanced at each other. That would only help with the language barrier issues, both thought. An imperceptible nod, an understanding, passed between them.

"I'm glad," Klondike finally uttered. "You'll enjoy the show all the more."

"I can't wait, friends." He seemed to giggle to himself as he studied Heavy with an odd gaze. "You are the ringmaster, no?"

Heavy smiled. "That's right."

"I bet you have a, er, mighty roar! I can almost hear it now."

"You'll hear it from this bar come Saturday night," Klondike jibed.

They all laughed.

Then, Lago turned to leave. "I wish you all the best for the show, my friends. I have seats for the mid rows. Enjoy your stay in our city."

They all shook hands again, and Lago slipped away into the throng of local patrons gathered at the bar. He seemed to be among friends, clearly a regular.

Klondike watched him as another customer handed him a giant stein glass overflowing with a heavy-headed beer.

"Good to know the fan base is here and dear," he quipped.

Heavy was fiddling with the cards. "It just goes to show. Geneva was a good choice. They don't get many big tops out here. And, it would seem, there is a fair bit of Americanisation already."

Klondike nodded. "Let's just hope for more of the same, old buddy. Hell, this tour is just getting started."

They both raised their glasses in a silent toast.

Two hours later, Klondike and Heavy stumbled out of The Alpenhorn, worse for wear after several beers and cognacs.

Disorientated, they had left via the rear exit and now found themselves in the parking lot, a dingy, gloomy square surrounded by the walls of neighbouring buildings. Garbage dumpsters and several dustbins were scattered around idly.

The duo looked grimly at the surroundings.

"Ah, the glamour of circus life," Heavy wheezed as they strolled through the lot towards an alley leading to the main drag beyond. Once on the high road, it was a short walk back to the train and their trailers.

"Trust me, it's a short cut," Klondike muttered.

"Ah, it was good to be out on the town again," Heavy said as they walked. "We'll do it again in Rome. I need to win some hands. My confidence is shattered now!"

Klondike chuckled. "There will be plenty of chances, old buddy. Hell, I think our luck has finally changed out here. Something happened back in Berlin. Now, I reckon we're on a roll again. It will be just like when -"

"Hey, boys!"

The loud call from behind broke their gentle chit-chat. They both turned curiously, and immediately panicked.

Klondike froze on the spot. It looked like they were being charged by a buffalo. An enormous figure was racing straight at them, now possibly three yards away, his two giant arms spread out wide like a massive clothesline. It looked like the shadow of some prehistoric beast closing upon them, and Klondike felt like he was standing on a railroad as a train ran him down.

"What the…" he blurted.

The onrushing figure bulldozed into them like a wrecking ball.

The outstretched arms caught both men at the throat, almost crushing each voice box. The overall impact was shattering.

Klondike and Heavy flew to the ground like rag dolls, shocked and confused.

The giant raider huffed and puffed like an animal.

Klondike rolled over and tried to stand, rubbing his head. Suddenly, two giant hands clamped around his neck in a death grip. He gasped uncontrollably. Then, he looked up into his attacker's face and froze.

Thick brown hair was matched by a wild, shaggy beard on a huge, square, anvil-like head. The eyes were filled with a maniacal anger. It was Tarz, the giant who had visited them in London. The face and bulk were unmistakeable.

Klondike grabbed at the attacker's wrists, futilely trying to lessen the vice-like grip. It was a pathetic attempt. The hands were almost the size of his head.

Then, Tarz stood to his full height, effortlessly lifting Klondike with him and holding him aloft in a stranglehold, leaving his feet dangling a yard off the ground.

The effect of the hold was startling. Klondike felt himself passing out, his vision fading badly as he wrestled with the mighty bear-like arms.

Then, he saw Heavy approach with a steel garbage can, which he smashed into the monster's back.

Tarz released Klondike, who fell in a heap on the asphalt, struggling for breath.

As the giant turned, Heavy made to throw a punch, then his eyes widened. "You!" he blurted.

Tarz snorted in disgust. "We told you to leave Europe! You should have taken the money, Americans. Now, you are going to pay!"

With remarkable agility for a man his immense size, Tarz swung up his right leg and booted Heavy in the chest in one swift movement, the sole of his leather shoe slamming into the breastplate.

Heavy stumbled backwards but remained standing. Then, he moved into a boxing stance and seemed to square up to his aggressor.

A brawny tough guy standing well over six feet, even Heavy looked small compared to Tarz. It was a match-up he was not used to.

He threw a lightning cross at the monster's head, but Tarz easily caught the blow with his left hand. He then held on to the fist and squeezed, making Heavy wince involuntarily. He could not believe the man's strength.

When the Hungarian strong man began to twist the wrist, Heavy cried aloud and dropped to his knees.

Tarz smiled mercilessly. Then, with calculated poise, he threw a punishing kick into Heavy's face, the leather boot smashing into the fallen man's jaw.

Still clutching the hand, Tarz prepared for another deadly blow.

But, suddenly, Klondike was up and launched himself on to the big man's back, his arms encircling the neck in a rear choke hold. He wrapped an arm clean around the throat, then clasped the elbow of his other arm, which grabbed the skull. He squeezed with all his might.

It was like wrestling an elephant. Tarz released Heavy's wrist, and seemed to stumble slightly. His meaty hands immediately latched onto Klondike's arms and tugged frantically.

Klondike hung on grimly, trying to encircle his legs around the giant's frame for leverage. Something was working, as Tarz swayed slightly and made a gurgling noise.

Then, as if sensing he needed to change tactics, Tarz moved his hands away and instead grabbed ahold of each of Klondike's legs, which clung to his sides. He gargled loudly, before suddenly running backwards at full steam, with Klondike stuck to his spine.

The circus boss suddenly realised what was about to happen, but simply could not move. As they sped backwards, he jabbed an elbow wildly into Tarz's cranium, but it was futile. The outside wall of The Alpenhorn was rapidly approaching.

With an almighty whack, Tarz backed into the stone wall. Klondike felt like he had been crushed between two boulders in a landslide. His ribs screamed and his spine felt like it had shattered. He slipped feebly to the ground after the impact and groped around aimlessly, his vision hazy.

Tarz shook himself slightly, then glared down at Klondike. With one hand, he hauled the circus boss to his feet, then held him by his jacket collar. Their faces were inches apart.

"You don't listen, do ya?" the giant roared. He slapped Klondike across the face viciously. "Leave Europe! Now! You understand me, Klondike?"

Klondike tired to focus on the terrifying face before him. He felt in pain all over, as if his body had been crushed. But he snarled up at the beast clutching him. "Go screw yourself, you overgrown son of a bitch!"

Tarz roared and threw Klondike back against the wall as if he were an infant.

He was preparing his next blow when a loud hail stopped him.

"Hey! What is going on out here? What the hell are you doing?"

They both turned at the new voice. It was Christian Lago, who was pacing frantically out of the bar's rear exit, followed by three fellow drinkers, all of whom looked menacing and aggrieved. They marched towards the melee.

Tarz snarled like an enraged beast. His face looked murderous. Without a further thought, he approached one of the green garbage dumpsters just behind them and grabbed it by the side holdings.

Then, in an unbelievable show of strength, he lifted the skip towards himself and spun around in a circle, dragging the entire dumpster with him.

As he spun around a second time, he released his hold on the dumpster. It was like a bizarre-looking human slingshot. The huge plastic crate flew 10 yards through the air and landed with a mighty crash directly in front of the approaching group, sending them sprawling. A huge cloud of dust seemed to explode into the night air as the contraption crashed down.

Klondike, on his hands and knees and trying to stand, watched in a strange kind of awe at the incredible feat of strength. Never in his life had he seen such brute force. He looked on as Lago and his comrades slowly rose to their feet, covered in dust and litter shards.

They all turned to look at the super-strong intruder.

But Tarz was gone. The slingshot of the garbage dumpster had not only thrown off his agitators, it had also been the ideal cover for a fast getaway.

Within seconds, Lago and the others raced over to Klondike, who held his ribs in agony, cuts and bruises all over his hands and face.

"Get after him," he rasped, pointing to the alleyway Tarz must have fled down. One of the men ran in that direction.

Lago threw Klondike's arm over his shoulder and helped him stand.

"Are you alright, my friend?"

"I'm ok, buddy. Thanks to you and your boys. That was a timely intervention, man."

Lago looked him over with concern. "We heard a bang. Like the wall was going to collapse."

"It nearly did," Klondike muttered, rubbing himself all over.

Then, he looked across at Heavy, who was wandering towards him, holding on to one of their saviour's shoulders.

Both men stumbled towards each other in the dusty parking lot, each assisted by a helper. They faced each other and nodded.

"The big ape is back," Heavy mumbled through a swollen mouth.

"Never thought I'd fight King Kong," Klondike replied, rubbing his jaw vigorously. "I guess Handel and his friends have had enough of offering pay-offs. Now, they're gunna try and throw us out. Literally!"

Heavy nodded. "Well, he did warn us back in France. I just never thought he'd set his war dog loose like that."

Klondike squinted at his old friend. "You alright?"

"The son of a bitch hit me with a couple of real suckers. But nothing is broken. Maybe a tooth or two. You?"

"I'm fine. But we need to tell everyone at the camp. Tell em all to be on the lookout for intruders, attacks. Nobody leaves the site on their own. This… this could just be the start."

Lago and his companion stared at the two men in shock and awe. They could not believe the Americans were so casual after such a frightening assault.

"We need to get you two to a hospital, right now," Lago blurted.

"We're fine," Klondike rasped. He reached into his breast pocket, removing a crumpled, battered cigar. Lago watched incredulously as he lit up. "If you can just give us a ride across town, we'd be obliged."

"But… but you need medical attention, my friends."

"We've got all we need on our train," Klondike breathed as he clamped the cigar into the corner of his mouth.

Everyone looked up at the sound of rapid footsteps. It was the other bar patron, who had raced down the alleyway after Tarz.

"No sign of the big guy anywhere," the man reported as he joined them. "What a monster."

The Swiss men all looked dumbly at the two Americans, as if trying to solve some form of puzzle.

The newcomer stepped forward. "That was no mugging. Why on earth would anyone want to harm you people? Circus men? I don't get it."

Klondike looked to the heavens, as if preparing a speech.

"Well boys, there's something in our industry called the forbidden gate. And we haven't just walked through it. We've smashed it down!"

CHAPTER 20

The next morning, there was a full staff meeting in the newly-erected circus tent.

Klondike had spread the word after returning from The Alpenhorn, battered and bruised and completely dumbstruck. Everyone needed to be there to hear his warning about potential attacks and disturbances.

Management, staff, performers, stewards and roustabouts. All made their way to the tent. Such meetings were rare, but it was impossible to tell how far the situation could escalate.

The big top sat at the near side of Parc Giresse, with the train, parked half in and half out of the rail works building, barely 200 yards away.

Already, the midway stalls and attractions were assembled. The main entrance to the park sat just behind, on the other side of the big top.

With everyone gathered inside, it was left to Marlon, the elderly caretaker and watchman, to remain in charge of the train and trailers. A handful of roustabouts also stayed around to continue the set-up operation. Two men were currently unloading the ticketing booth for the circus's box office.

Inside the great tent, Klondike and Heavy stood in front of one of the hastily assembled grandstands, which was packed with just about everyone who had come on the tour.

Both men had cuts and bruises on their faces, and were still a little stiff after their ordeal.

Lacey was stood to the side of the front row of bleachers, arms folded in anger, but her face full of concern.

Klondike had explained the attack and its implications to her in her stateroom last night as she patched him and Heavy up.

Now, it was time to explain what had happened to everyone.

Once he had told the grim story, Klondike opened up the floor to questions.

To everyone's surprise, one of the roustabouts opened the discourse. "So, what you're saying, Mr Klondike, is that we all have to be on the lookout… watching out for thugs trying to nail us?"

"That's right, Bud," Klondike snapped. He looked at the assembled crowd, all staring down at him from the stand. "Anyone see anything suspicious, hear anything… well, you just let me or Heavy know. Immediately."

"Sounds like we've been here before," one of the Range Rider cowboys called down. "This sounds like that Paul Agostino mob business last year."

Klondike nodded. "Same story. Someone wants a piece. Only this time, instead of buying us out, these suckers want to chase us out of town."

"So much violence, all over a circus," said Suzi Dando near the front.

"Well," Heavy blurted angrily, "it's just like we always say. We are a successful outfit. People, rivals, they get jealous, angry, confused maybe. And that leads to this kind of business. Attacks, rage, madness."

Tip Enqvist spoke up. "This giant, Tarz, he must be crazy, man."

"Maybe," Klondike answered from the front. "As I am sure you can all see, he tried to kill me and Heavy last night. If anyone sees him, anywhere in this city, you let us know."

Goliath, the circus's own giant, grunted from the back. "I'd like to meet this so-called strong man."

Heavy smirked. "We'd all like that, Gol."

Klondike nodded at the exchanges. He eyed the front row of the ensemble. Shapiro and Carla were huddled together, gazing at each other instead of listening. Penny sat just behind, arms folded and staring at the ceiling. Corky was in the middle, looking pale and as if he was struggling to concentrate. Enqvist sat there angrily in his leather jacket, seemingly ready to start a fight of his own.

And then there was Olsen, perched on the end of the bench, looking withdrawn and lost. Suzi sat beside him, and Lacey was standing on his other side on the sawdust. He looked at neither though.

Klondike watched them all curiously. There was still a queer, ill feeling hanging over his troupe. Like a black cloud that would not shift. Despite the frenzied success of the Berlin show, the overall uneasiness of being so far from home seemed to grip the collective consciousness.

Klondike shook it off and spoke again.

"OK. So, anyone got anything else they want to get off their chest?"

Back at the rail yard, Marlon was pacing up and down the length of the train like a centurion from days gone by.

At 34 carriages in length, it took more than 10 minutes to walk from front to back. Marlon looked in on various carts as he wandered past.

The back 14 carriages were lying out in the open air, as the train bled out the giant warehouse doors. These carts housed all of the staterooms and communal areas, including the kitchen. Then there was the bunkhouse, where the roustabouts all roomed.

It never ceased to amaze him how the entire circus world, a home to all who worked within it, could be accommodated on wheels like this.

He turned as he heard several roustabouts wheeling the ticketing booth down a ramp from a train cart onto the tarmac. He watched as the men, in their 'uniform' of brown sack jackets and jeans, led the large wooden booth across the yard on a pulley towards the park.

Marlon finally reached the end of the train, and stopped to look around idly. The vast, snake-like hulk of the express spread out before him, like a never-ending stream of machinery.

As the ticketing booth was transported across the yard, he noticed several more brown jackets delicately pulling confectionary stalls out from another carriage nearby.

Then, more movement suddenly caught his eye to the left of the train. Several roustabouts in their brown jackets were moving hastily around the trailers that were spread out beside the warehouse. The accommodation blocks had not been removed from the train for this stop due to the close proximity of the show ground. But the stable blocks for the horses, the Daredevils' garage and several other shacks had been assembled alongside the Imperial express.

Marlon was not aware of how many roustabouts had been left on the train, and how many were in the tent. He approached the trailers.

As he neared, he saw several men in the brown sack jackets carrying pieces of machinery across the yard. Another held a clipboard and seemed to be watching the others.

The men seemed to be engrossed in their work. One of the roustabouts jumped out from behind a trailer and greeted Marlon as he approached.

"Howdy. Anything we can do for you?" He had an unusual accent, like he was trying to imitate John Wayne or Robert Mitchum.

"No, sir," Marlon replied. "Just checking everything is in order out here."

"Yeah, we're doing just fine," the man said in his peculiar tone. "Well ahead of schedule."

Marlon smiled. "Good. Mr McCabe will be glad to hear that."

The roustabout stared at him blankly. "Right."

Marlon watched the other hands just behind the speaker, all working without looking up. He offered a slight wave as he turned.

"So long."

The speaker waved. "You all take care now."

Marlon slowly wandered back down the side of the train.

The roustabout watched him, with suspicious eyes. Then he spoke in a loud whisper.

"He's gone."

The others all stopped what they were doing and stood behind a trailer, just beside the speaker. One of them spoke to him.

"That was good, Klaus. The accent worked. My compliments."

The one called Klaus watched a little longer as Marlon gradually disappeared in the distance. Then, he turned and walked behind the trailer to join his comrades. There were five of them in all. But one man, clearly the leader, strode forward, eyeing the surroundings as if about to make a decision. The others all seemed to wait for him.

The leader turned. With his thick, styled black hair and reddish, almost feminine complexion, he looked strangely ill at ease dressed in a roustabout's jacket with jeans.

Conrad Handel smiled devilishly. "The accent worked. And the jackets worked. OK, let's move."

In a flash, the group went their separate ways about the trailers like a well-drilled military unit.

A dastardly operation was under way.

One of the men headed straight into the horses' stable block. As he entered, he removed a large plastic bottle from an inside jacket pocket and stood beside a water trough at the head of the horses' berths. He delicately began pouring a mysterious green liquid into the trough, and then repeated the move with the other water blocks in the stable. None of the animals seemed to notice him. Within 60 seconds, he was out in the yard again.

Two of the men had entered the bike garage, where one produced a tool belt from a pack he had been carrying. The duo bent down beside the stunt bikes and went to work.

Within a minute, caps had been busted open, spools ripped apart and wires snapped.

Another of the infiltrators headed for the giant steel car port towards the back of the enclosure. Once inside, he looked over the gleaming array of Cadillacs within. Then, he propped open the hood of the first car and produced a large pair of pliers from the inside of his jacket.

Outside, Handel kept watch at the front of the enclosure, smoking a cigarette as if on a break. Marlon had not returned and he could see no one else. He was aware of the team of roustabouts on the other side of the train – barely 15 yards away from him – but they didn't concern him. They were completely immersed in their unloading, and would know nothing of the infiltrators on the other side of the track.

As the first man emerged from the stable blocks and walked over to him, Handel motioned towards a small, portable wooden hut close to the train.

"That cabin is full of electrics and sound equipment. Go in there with your cutters. Destroy every cable in sight."

The man made for the hut like a robot under command, and quickly produced some pliers.

Silence engulfed the enclosure, despite the eerie destruction all around.

As if bored, Handel wandered idly among the trailers and cabins. He spotted a Klondike's Circus poster pasted on to the side of a wooden storage hut. With a grin, he stubbed out his cigarette into the poster, the end smouldering into the picture of the circus tent. It left a grubby black mark.

Then, his men all joined him as one, like a commando unit returning to base camp.

Handel eyed them. "Anything?"

Klaus stood to attention. "No. Nothing. No one is here."

A faint hubbub of noise could be heard in the distance, on the other side of the train. Voices, commotion. The meeting was over, and the circus people were exiting the tent.

Handel nodded towards the side road beside the yard enclosure, where a large black van was parked next to an iron shed.

"Let's go, let's go," he murmured.

The men in the brown sack jackets jogged to the van. Handel walked briskly behind them, pausing at the passenger door at the front of the vehicle.

He looked over the circus encampment, the train and the giant rail works building. A sinister smile ruined his soft, angelic features. He whispered to himself as he gazed.

"Try putting on a show now, Americans!"

Then, the van began to inch away from the kerb and quickly disappeared behind the sprawling complex.

Inside the big top, Klondike idly watched as his audience slowly left through the flap. Everyone seemed enlivened, as if his warning had set off a sense of danger and excitement. Roustabouts mixed with performers as they all exited the empty arena, everyone chatting among themselves.

He turned and strode over to the bleachers, where Lacey, Heavy, Plum and Bannion had all remained, sitting in contemplative mood.

"They were right, y'know," Heavy muttered. "This is just like that Agostino business all over again. I'll be damned!"

"Except for some changes," Klondike said dryly. "This time we are in a strange and foreign land, and we have no idea what the next crowd is going to make of our show. Plus... we still haven't got the foggiest idea who the hell we are really dealing with!"

Heavy glanced at Bannion. "Still nothing on Handel, Jack?"

The Englishman folded his arms and shrugged. "It's a weird one, chaps. Everyone has heard of him, remembers him. No one seems to know what he's up to now. Or, rather, who he's working for."

Lacey lit a cigarette, flourishing the match in the theatrical manner she seemed to bring to just about everything. "Alright, boys. Well, like we always say, we can only control what we know. We have just enjoyed a triumphant return in Berlin. Now, we must build on it here."

Klondike nodded eagerly. He glanced down at Plum. "What is the latest from the box office, Richie? Looking like a good turnout?"

Plum had his head buried in a file, as he often did, but looked up hopefully. "So far, as of last night, some 74 per cent of tickets had sold. That's good for this point in time. Now, if we were to project a mean average profit take of ten thousand Francs, that's about 12 thousand dollars in the current exchange rate, well, I'd say we're looking at-"

"Ok, Richie," Klondike said, holding up a hand, "it's alright. We all trust you implicitly with the figures. The fact we're close to a capacity crowd right now is what we want to hear."

Plum looked somewhat put out then, glancing at Lacey, smiled happily and nodded.

"So," Heavy murmured, "build on Berlin, eh?" He looked at the others knowingly. "I think we all know that means one thing. Giving our own newcomer, a certain empress, some prime time on the sawdust. Am I wrong?"

Lacey blew out a long cloud of smoke and smiled awkwardly. "I have to admit, Heavy is right." She shot up from her seat, exited the grandstand and paced across the tent floor, closer to Klondike. "You all saw what happened when Carla came out. The place erupted. And then, well, after that...that exhibition she produced. That hand... thing..."

"The hand walk," Heavy put in.

"Yes, that. Well, I don't think I'm alone in saying I have never seen anything like that in my life. And probably never will. A woman who walks on her hands… on a damn tightrope, for Christ sakes." She shook off her dismay and strode over to Klondike. "She was a sensation, Kal. You know it. I know it." She hardly sounded delighted.

Klondike nodded. "There's no doubt anymore. That woman is a phenomenon. Up there!" He shook his head, as if trying to figure out a puzzle. "But she brings something more. Her bravado. Her aura. The way she talks…"

"I agree entirely," Lacey purred, walking in a circle around him. "It's almost as if she's an actress. Playing a part. A role. Making us all fall in love with her. Her manner… it's almost like she's delivering lines."

"Yes, that's it!" Klondike said. "She is like a movie character. Right here with us."

Heavy looked from one to the other. He rubbed his jawline. "So, what are you guys saying?"

A queer silence engulfed the front of the grandstand, the light chatter from the folks outside drifting in through the flap beside them.

Lacey took a step forward. "I guess what we're saying is… Carla has undoubted star quality, even if her presence here is somewhat strange and bewildering. Despite whatever each of us may think of her, she deserves more show time. Am I right, Kal?"

"You're damn right," Klondike breathed. He seemed lost in thought. Absently, he reached for his cane, which had remained idle on a seat in the front row. He spun it playfully in his hands.

"Hell," he muttered, "that dame is a loose cannon. A wildcat, alright." He looked towards the flap, and the parkland outside.

"I wonder what she will do next?"

At that moment, Carla Selenzy was walking slowly through the funfair at the opposite end of the park.

At this early hour, all the rides were empty. Scattered children ran around carelessly, pointing at the ferris wheels, dodgems, ghost train, razzle dazzler and other attractions that they would visit later that day. Aside from that, porters and stewards roamed around, cleaning the stalls and checking the machinery.

Dressed in a flamboyant, skintight purple trouser suit, Carla could not have looked more out of place as she breezed past the funfair staff. The workers, nearly all young men from impoverished backgrounds, stared at her in shock.

She soaked up the admiring glances that followed her as she trotted along the central pathway of the fair, looking about her as if lost.

Then, finally, she saw him. Straight ahead, at the very edge of Parc Giresse, leaning against some railings, watching an elderly woman feeding some ducks at a lake just beyond.

Carla stopped, straightened her outfit, and ran hands slowly through her hair. She looked strangely distraught. Then, after a deep breath, she approached.

Roddy Olsen watched the hungry ducks wade around their breakfast saviour, an elderly bag woman, as they flapped and chirped with relish.

He was dressed in his green anorak, and pulled the collar tight around his neck as a breeze rolled in across the park.

Hands in pockets, he leant there running the events of the past few weeks through his mind. Again and again.

His late night encounters with Lacey. Everything he had said. Everything she had said. It was like one big, surreal nightmare.

He thought of Suzi, his best friend and sometime counsellor. And all of his friends at Klondike's Circus. It was crazy, he thought. All these people in his life who cared about him. Who he cared about deeply. Yet just a few years previous, there had been practically no one.

He lived to perform, to entertain. Yet the reactions to his act in Europe had been ridiculous. Up to Berlin, which had been rapturous. Like back in the States. Home, where success and adoration seemed to be everywhere. Present in every town he performed in. Where fans waited at each stop for the train to arrive, and for a glimpse of their idol.

How could something so abundantly evident at home be completely absent in a foreign country?

The many notions whirled around in his over-animated mind.

"Finally, I find you."

Olsen turned in shock at the soft, overtly feminine tone behind him.

He spun around and almost gasped in awe.

There stood Carla Selenzy, hands on hips, as if posing for a studio photoshoot. She was wearing an outfit like nothing he had ever seen, even in Lacey's glamorous wardrobe.

She smiled longingly, and seemed to smell the air with relish.

"There you are, Roddy," she gushed, walking over to him like a model on a catwalk. She acted like she was on stage, he thought.

"Miss Carla," he stammered. "I was, er, just taking a walk and, er, I, well, it's…"

"I was looking for you," she said directly. Her beautiful ebony eyes locked onto his baby blues like a magnet. It was an overwhelming sensation for the young man. "I just had to see you, Roddy."

Olsen broke away from the mesmerising, almost hypnotic stare. He looked down. "You were? Me?"

"Oh my," she whispered as she joined him at the railings. She held his arm lightly. "Do you have any idea what you did back in Berlin? The effect you had on the fans? My god, Roddy. You owned them! Your act is extraordinary, something of sheer beauty." She eyed him coyly, pouting slightly. "I have been performing in the circus in Germany for many years. And never have I seen such a reaction. You were the star of the show, Roddy. Believe me. I saw the faces on the fans up there. The joy, the wonder."

Olsen baulked, looking around slightly. He finally looked at her again, the eyes swallowing him up. "You didn't do too badly yourself, Miss Carla. Your skills are incredible. And everybody sure loves you!"

She batted a hand through the air. "Maybe. But your talent… what you do with your voice, those adorable puppets. This is spectacular. Original. Beautiful. You heard the audience applauding."

He tried to grin. "Well, that wasn't exactly the case at our other stops on this tour."

"The hell with that," she snapped. She gripped his arm tighter. He stared at the hand upon him in shock. "You are il genio. I saw your act and it made me shake all over. My heart was pounding, Roddy. You are a phenomenon." She eyed him in awe now. "No wonder all the big TV people in America want a piece of you."

Olsen wanted to shake her off, but was strangely overwhelmed and excited, like he had been drugged. The whole exchange was bizarre.

"Well, your boyfriend may beg to differ, Miss Carla. He hates me and my puppets."

She took on a strange look of disgust. "Gino? Pah! He knows nothing beyond the trapeze. Your talent terrifies him, no?"

Olsen tried to smile. "A lot of folks seem to think that."

Carla's gaze had not shifted. Still, she eyed him hungrily, like a predator. "They tell me you like the coffee, no? Good, continental coffee?"

He stared at her. "Er, well, yes. Sure, I like coffee."

With that, she clung to him, looping her arm through his and practically heaving him along on to the path, back towards the deserted funfair.

"Come, Roddy. I have the best Italian coffee on the train. I never travel without it. We will have a cup. And toast your success."

He didn't argue.

Carla's newly appointed stateroom was near the centre of the train, previously one of several guest rooms maintained on board for various occasions.

However, the empress of acrobatics had decorated the small space to perfectly match her excessive tastes. Oriental rugs, Victorian lanterns and glossy silk throws seemed to be everywhere, covering the small couch and table.

The Italian laughed aloud with glee as she stood by the washbasin fiddling with an antique percolator, which was filled with pure black liquid.

"Where, oh where, did you learn your voice skills, Roddy?"

Olsen sat on the couch awkwardly, somewhat bemused. He tried to relax. He couldn't help but feel daunted around Carla

Selenzy. She was overwhelmingly beautiful and acted like a movie star on location, right down to the tiniest mannerisms.

"When I was a boy," he said quietly. "It all started after I saw a famous American ventriloquist on stage. Edgar Bergen. I was so mesmerised. So entranced. I knew I could do that and… and I knew right then that's what I wanted to do. I practised all the time. Bought my puppets at a place in Los Angeles and, well, started doing shows. I began at colleges, caravan parks, saloons, you get the idea. And it all grew from there."

Carla looked sharply at the clock on the wall. She seemed to tense. Then, she continued with the coffee. She turned a small wheel at the top of the percolator and moved to the window sill, pouring the boiling hot brew into two china cups.

"Cream or sugar?"

"No thanks."

She allowed herself a dollop of cream from a small jug and then walked slowly across the carriage to the couch, handing Olsen his cup and sitting next to him on the small, comfy seat.

Olsen took a sip and murmured his approval.

She leant towards him slowly, holding her cup before her with both hands.

"I have heard…" she gushed in a strange, breathless tone, "how the casinos in Las Vegas, they all want you, Roddy. To appear in their shows. The TV executives in Hollywood. You have all the offers, no?"

Olsen tried to remain cool. "Well, I guess. Almost as many as your boy Gino."

Her eyes went wild. "Gino is insanely jealous of you! Everybody knows this. He has his fans, but I hear the fans in America… I hear they scream your name! The teenagers, the young people. They all go crazy for you. More than for Gino! It is true, Roddy."

Despite every instinct in his being telling him this was madness, Olsen could not help take a surreal delight in Carla's praise.

Especially considering all the hardship Shapiro had subjected him to down the years. After seeing them together, now hearing Carla like this…

"Tell me, Roddy," she whispered delicately. She moved even closer to him on the tiny couch, so their faces were now inches apart. He was lost in her eyes again. "Tell me about all the girls..."

He shook his head. "Wha...what? What girls?"

She laughed airily, as an adult would at a confused child. "Oh, come on. The girls. Who all call your name when you're on stage. Who all want you! Every one of them. Oh my..." she wiped a hand across her brow, as if she might faint. "It must be so completely overpowering. Having all those hundreds of women... wanting you, dreaming of you. Idolising you."

Then, she stared again at the clock on the wall. Olsen noticed it, her strange hypnosis suddenly broken.

Carla made a mental calculation. Any minute now, she thought to herself.

Olsen studied her. "Is everything-"

"Oh Roddy!" she gasped, leaving her reverie. "I can't withhold it anymore. You are a beautiful, beautiful man. You should be in the movies, you know. With those eyes! Your hair, your skin. I... I can't stand it anymore."

With that, she flung herself at him, moving her head sideways as her lips surged at his mouth and kissed him passionately.

She grabbed his head from behind and seemed to hold him in place, pushing his skull towards her as she stuck to him on the couch.

Olsen was stunned and found he could barely move. As Carla had seduced him, he had felt trapped, like a besotted child mesmerised by an older woman. He knew he had fallen into her spell, yet was happy to be taken. This whole experience was a new avenue for him completely.

Carla moaned with pleasure as she continued to kiss the youngster. She moved her left arm behind his neck, and placed the other hand on his chest. Subconsciously, Olsen slipped his hands around her waist.

All was silent.

Then, the dreamlike scene was mercilessly shattered as the room door opened slowly and a mighty roar erupted from the corridor.

"Santamaria!"

Olsen froze. Carla stopped her kiss abruptly. She looked at the doorway with wild, crazy eyes, while curiously still clinging to Olsen. He was conscious that she would not let him shrug her off. Both looked up at the enraged figure hovering over them.

Gino Shapiro was stood there in shock, like a man facing armageddon. Fists clenched, nostrils flaring, he appeared like a demonic apparition, on his haunches and ready to pounce.

"Gino!" Carla screeched in a theatrical tone. She still clung to Olsen, before he gently brushed her hands away.

"Gino!" she cried again. "This is not what it seems, Gino! I can explain, I promise!"

Shapiro's chest heaved as he breathed wildly. He looked from Carla to Olsen. "What is the meaning of this?" he snarled. He focused on Olsen. "This is how you get back at me, eh dollmaker? Like this! With my angel!"

Olsen was trying to remain calm. He eyed Carla, who was panting insanely as she stared up at Shapiro. Something very odd was going on, but he didn't have time to process it. He put a hand up.

"Easy, Gino," he said soothingly. "It's not like that at all." He looked across at Carla. "I think Miss Selenzy has something to tell you. Carla?"

On the edge of the couch, Carla put her hands over her face and squealed. "Oh my god! Oh my god!"

Olsen made to stand, staring at her. "What the-"

Then, in a flash, Shapiro lurched forward and pushed him heavily in the chest, knocking him slightly off-balance.

"I know what you are doing, Olsen," he screamed. His jet black eyes were wild with alarm. "Finally, you turn, no? All this madness in Europe has got to you. So you try to bring me down with you, eh? You can see I am crazy about Carla, and still you… you…"

Olsen raised a hand. "Gino, listen to me, that's not what happened here."

Shapiro was unrepentant. "You cry because Miss Lacey has no interest in a boy like you. Only a man like Kal. And so you try with my Carla!"

Olsen gazed at him. "What did you say?"

"I said go to hell!"

With that, Shapiro launched a quickfire right cross at Olsen, the closed fist smashing into his jaw with lightning fast speed and accuracy, knocking the younger man clean off his feet.

Olsen could not believe the power of the punch. He flew through midair and went straight into the couch, slamming into its backrest like a car in a demolition derby.

Carla screamed and leapt up, racing out of the room with a shriek.

Pandemonium reigned. Shapiro threw himself at the now seated Olsen. His upper body slammed into the prone form, the momentum as he charged into him sending the small couch tumbling clean over backwards.

Shapiro rolled straight over, then used his acrobatic skills to flip straight onto his feet again. Olsen sprawled on the floor, dazed and rubbing his jawline.

Then, in a flash, Shapiro was on him. He sat on his chest and grabbed him by his long blond hair, slamming the back of his head viciously into the wooden floorboards.

The trapeze artist looked like a man possessed, all rage and no conscience. Olsen was struggling to see, as the blow sent him into semi-consciousness.

"Alright, dollmaker," Shapiro panted as he pinned him to the floor. "You think you are better than me. Show me!" He slapped Olsen wickedly across the face.

Olsen was desperately reaching for an object on his right side. Manoeuvring his arm free from Shapiro's body, he stretched and grabbed ahold of an item he had made out with his failing vision. Finally touching it, he realised it was a small tin bucket used for ice. That would do.

He brought his arm up fast, the bucket smashing into Shapiro's skull and denting as it impacted.

The flyer looked like he was about to pass out, wobbling atop the youngster. He fell to his side, and crawled to the couch, pulling himself up groggily.

Olsen rose even slower, rubbing at his face and the back of his head. He watched Shapiro struggling to stand before him. "Gino…" he whispered.

Suddenly, Shapiro turned in anger, his eyes murderous. He screamed insanely and threw a vicious backhand blow at Olsen's neck. The youngster just about managed to put his hands up to cushion the wild blow, but realised the intention. Shapiro had targeted his voice box, either willingly or by chance. In Olsen's mind, that was an act of pure sin. Such a blow could put him out of business.

Now, the youngster cried aloud. "You son of a bitch!"

He charged at Shapiro and slammed himself into the wiry veteran, sending him backwards as he pushed until he slammed his quarry into the far wall of the stateroom. Shapiro let out a grunt of agony.

They wrestled wildly. Olsen now grabbed at his rival's throat, trying to choke him. Shapiro grabbed at his arms and tried to break the hold, before firing a jab into Olsen's ribs. It didn't break the hold.

The two men snarled at each other as they grappled in an ugly melee.

Then, footsteps were heard racing into the stateroom and a shocked cry thundered into the confines.

"Gino! Roddy! What the hell!"

Klondike charged in like a rampaging bull. His worst fear suddenly realised, he launched himself into the fight in pure desperation.

With a snarl of alarm, the circus boss grabbed ahold of Olsen in a mighty bearhug and quickly pulled him clear of Shapiro, who slowly sank down the wall, holding his throat.

Klondike's arms encircled Olsen as he backed him away. Olsen tried to push him off. With a two-step run-up, Klondike released him and pushed the youngster across towards the doorway.

Olsen kept his balance and faced Klondike.

"Cut it out, god damn it!" Klondike was raging. "What in hell is going on here?"

Olsen seemed to explode. He glared up at him. "You're the problem, Kal Klondike! It's you. You… you are the one!"

Without warning, Olsen threw a wild right hook.

Klondike, standing before him, was not expecting anything of the sort and reacted far too late. The blow struck him clean on the cheek, sending him sprawling into the fallen couch in shock.

A deathly silence suddenly filled the stateroom.

Olsen was as stunned as anyone. He looked down at his fist, then at the figure of Klondike on his back. He felt his chest heaving uncontrollably.

Then, a soft voice emanated from the train corridor behind him.

"Oh, Roddy! What have you done?"

Olsen turned slowly, his heart sinking.

Lacey was stood there, her hands over her mouth, her eyes wide in fright. Her body shook with tiny sobs.

Then, she hurtled past him to where Klondike had risen to a sitting position. Rubbing his cheekbone, he glared up at Olsen in confusion. Lacey was on him immediately, holding his shoulders and rubbing his back. They both looked up at the young man at the door.

Olsen was horrified by what he saw. Klondike and Lacey. The two people to whom he felt he owed everything. His guardians and trusted mentors. Both on the floor, unable to comprehend what had just transpired.

"What is happening to you?" Lacey screeched.

Olsen just looked at them dumbly. He could feel tears forming. His mind was whirling, his senses blurred and over-stimulated.

Then, with a shake of his head, he fled, charging down the train corridor and then out into the daylight.

And away. Away from it all.

CHAPTER 21

The stateroom was eerily quiet for several moments. Dust seemed to be floating in the air throughout the entire living space. Furniture sat around, broken and trampled.

Lacey held Klondike's face in her hands. She was crying.

"Are… are you alright, Kal?"

Klondike looked shocked and bewildered. He ran a hand over his eyes and grabbed for his hat. "Fine," he barked. He stared across the floor at Shapiro, who was also struggling to his feet.

"Gino. Gino! Are you hurt? Gino! Answer me, god damn it!"

Shapiro leant against a bookcase, rubbing at his throat. "Si, chairman. I am alright. Is all ok." He looked down, seemingly embarrassed. "I am sorry you had to witness that, chairman."

"The hell with that," Klondike cried, sitting up. "What in the name of Sam Hill was that all about? You were fighting like a pack of dogs, for Christ sakes. What happened?"

The flyer shook his head, in regret. "It was Carla…"

Klondike was incredulous. "Jesus Christ!" he growled. He rose to his feet. Lacey helped him, placing an arm around his mighty frame, but he gently moved her away. "You mean all this was over her?"

Shapiro moved across to them, still rubbing at his throat. A mighty bruise was forming on his forehead. "I caught them. Together. Kissing. Right here!" He looked like he might pass out, swaying slightly. "My Carla! And that treacherous dog Olsen!"

Lacey was staring at him in bewilderment. "Roddy did that! I…I don't believe it. Can't believe it!"

Shapiro snorted, wagging a finger at her. "Ah yes, madam publicist. Your golden boy is not an innocent child. Not any more! He went after my woman. He made to hurt me…to hurt my mind."

Klondike looked from one to the other. "What the hell! Where is Carla? Where did she go?"

Shapiro shrugged. "She run when we fight. She had asked me here, to her room, for coffee. At 11am. I open the door, and find them in an embrace. I ask you, what the hell is that?"

Klondike and Lacey shared a knowing look. An unspoken communication passed between them. A solution to a puzzle seemed to be appearing. Lacey nodded in understanding.

"So that's her game."

Shapiro froze. "What's that?"

Klondike shook his head wearily. "Gino…" he said weakly. "I, er, don't think our Carla is quite… well, what she appears to be."

Now Shapiro got it. "You are actually saying this? To me, Kal?"

The circus boss frowned as he studied his old friend. "Surely, you can see it? Now, you must see it?"

Lacey was pacing the room. "She is working for him. For Handel. For Handel's organisation. Oh my god! We let her live here, with us, in our train!"

"Are you crazy?" Shapiro snapped. It was an uncharacteristic turn for the flamboyant showman. "You think she is an enemy? After her star turn in Berlin! My god, she saved us back there."

"Or," Lacey whispered in fright, "that was her play to get on the inside. A hook. Then, her real work begins."

Klondike nodded. "Like a damn Trojan horse. She got on board, then set out to destroy us."

"How?" Shapiro snapped.

Klondike was angry now. "How? By turning our two greatest stars against one another, that's how. God damn it! And we fell for her razzmatazz and grandeur. Her showmanship. We all fell into the trap!"

Shapiro made to protest, but Klondike stopped him, placing a hand firmly on his chest. "Leave it, Gino. You need to cool off. Get some ice on that bruise. Clean yourself up. And, for Christ sakes, think! Think about everything that woman did after showing up at the airbase that day. Then, you will understand."

With that, he grabbed Lacey by the arm and hustled her out of the room and into the corridor. They walked rapidly together, leaving a confused Shapiro in the smashed-up stateroom.

When they reached the interchange vestibule, he opened the carriage door and they climbed out, into the morning sunshine.

Klondike hailed a passing roustabout. "Johnny! Find me Carla Selenzy right now. She's here somewhere. Just find her, right now!"

The youngster in the brown sack jacket practically saluted. "Yes sir, Mr Klondike." He took off towards the big top at a sprint.

Klondike looked up at the great tent before them, then back to the train. He took off his fedora and ran a hand through his thick black hair.

"Why, oh why didn't we follow our instincts on that dame?" he snarled.

Lacey nodded helplessly. She looked around. "We need to find Roddy too."

Klondike looked at her. "What did he mean back there? That he's jealous of me? You and me? Our relationship?"

She quivered. "I don't know what to think anymore."

Just then, they both jumped at an alarmed call from further down the train, from the part under cover in the rail yard.

"Kal, you've got to see this!"

It was Jim McCabe, jogging towards them, his usually disinterested look now one of shock.

"Not a great time, Jim," Klondike called back.

"We got trouble, Kal. Real trouble."

That got his attention. Klondike stared at him. He felt great clouds of fear and dread forming in his mind.

"Tell me, Jim… please tell me it isn't serious?"

McCabe finally reached them. He was drenched in sweat, his fleshy face reddened in anger.

"We've been raided!"

"What!"

"Someone… someone has been into our camp and… and messed everything up. All the Daredevils' bikes, they've been busted up and worked over. Same with the Caddys. And the sound and lighting equipment… everything is cut open and vandalised. And the horses…"

Lacey's hand covered her mouth. Klondike froze all over. "What about the horses?"

McCabe looked genuinely distraught. "Well, it looks like they've been drugged. They're all lying down in the stables, barely able to stand. I never saw anything like it, Kal. And their water… it's gone a green colour."

Klondike felt like his head was spinning. McCabe's voice suddenly sounded like it was 100 yards away. His words echoed through him, throbbing at his conscience. He looked around wildly, as if expecting a sudden attack from somewhere.

Lacey held him as he swayed. Her face was a mask of concern.

"Kal!" she squealed, tugging at his arm. "Kalvin! Are you alright?"

He rubbed at his eyes. Then, he patted Lacey gently on the arm and glared at McCabe.

"Show me! Now!"

"Steady there, old girl. I got ya. You're still with us, old buddy."

Duster Williams gently massaged his beloved Goldie's mane as the stricken horse led on its front, its entire head resting on its front right leg in a highly unusual pose. The great beast looked like it had been struck a mortal wound, its eyes like slits as it soaked up its master's attention.

Williams continued to rub the horse's neck and head. He glanced at the man next to him. Dr Lamatz was a veterinary surgeon from Geneva, who had been called over immediately once the poisoning had been detected. McCabe had even driven to his surgery in a circus jeep to fetch him.

The specialist had examined all eight horses, provided each with an injected tranquiliser and antibodies, and had compelled the Range Riders to try and feed them fresh water, as much as possible.

Lamatz watched Williams nurture Goldie. He half-smiled, then turned from the stable blocks and headed to the doorway, where Klondike, Lacey and Heavy were all watching. The Range Rider cowboys were all busying themselves around the block, changing the fibre feeds and straw supplies. Lacey felt moved to tears, again, as she watched old Duster tending to his mount, the care and devotion truly a sight to behold.

Lamatz, rubbing his hands down his white doctor's jacket, came and stood next to them in the stable block doorway, watching the cowboys tend to the animals.

"Hard to believe anyone could do such a thing," the Swiss said quietly. "Poisoning such fine beasts. And for what?"

Klondike seemed to break. "Alright," he stammered, "just what in the hell happened here, Doc?"

Lamatz was strangely calm. "We used to call it spatzlick. I believe the western term is botulinum. A dangerous toxin, derived from an ancient bacteria, found in rivers and streams. Even soil. If digested, it can cause this severe drowsiness, spasms, organ shutdown." He looked at the horses sadly. "Even death."

"Alright, alright," Klondike said, shaking his head. He felt himself imploding. "Are they going to be ok? Will they make it?"

The doctor looked up at him. "You are lucky. The signs were spotted early on. Very fast. With the antibodies I have provided, and constant fresh water, they should be ok. In time."

They all breathed a steady sigh of relief. "Thanks Doc," Klondike said. He put an arm around him. "My associate Henry here will get your fee and get you a ride back into town. We sure appreciate you coming out so fast."

Lamatz nodded gravely. "I came when I heard there were horses in distress."

Then, Heavy led him away. Klondike and Lacey ducked into the stable block and watched helplessly as the cowboys all tended to their mounts. Each horse was lying down in its straw. The whole scene looked abnormal and unsettling.

They approached Williams, who was sat cradling Goldie.

"I sure am sorry this happened, Duster," Klondike whispered, placing a hand on the older man's shoulder.

Williams looked up and nodded. His hand did not stop massaging the animal's mane.

"Thanks, Kal. But it's not your fault. Or anybody here's. Who was to know these people – whoever they are – would try such a thing. Trying to poison our beautiful, innocent babies."

Klondike and Lacey exchanged a glance. She was struggling, he could see that. He patted Williams's shoulder and shook him reassuringly.

"Anything you want, Duster, anything at all. You just let me know."

He nodded. "Appreciate it, Kal. I'm obliged."

They silently left him, slipping out into daylight again.

With a deep breath, Klondike now headed across the concrete to the motoring pool. Lacey struggled to keep up.

A similar sight greeted them inside. The Daredevils were all stood around, lost in thought, their motorbikes all on their sides, spread across the aluminium floor, as if ready for the scrap heap.

The riders were just staring at the bikes, in utter dismay.

Tip Enqvist slowly wandered over to them. He was dressed in a grease-streaked white vest and jeans, a hip flask in his hand.

"Come to see the carnage, Kal? Eh? The new freak show."

Klondike held up a hand as they entered. "Tip, boys, I'm so sorry about all this. This destruction. I, we, had no idea anyone was going to come into our camp and do all this."

He looked at the bike closest to him. Chunks of metal were hanging off the engine as if it had been mangled in a cement mixer.

"Listen," he continued, "we're doing all we can. A specialist mechanic is on the way from the other side of the city. Specialises in fixing bikes up. He may want to ship them off to his garage but, hell, we need to fix all this. We need to make sure-"

"We need to make sure the show doesn't suffer, right chief?" Enqvist snarled. He took a sip from his flask. The others all stared at him, no one challenging him or even attempting to speak.

Enqvist reached Klondike and eyed him menacingly. "These bikes are our life, Klondike. We ride every single day. They have been with us for five years. They are our livelihood. Now…" he took a step closer and stared at Klondike with angry eyes. "You tell me now, who the hell did this to our bikes? Who? We want names, dammit!"

"Alright," Klondike said, holding up a hand. "I told you, we don't know for sure. It's my fault. I let my guard down, allowed this to happen. I don't know how, but it's on me. But… I will get you your bikes fixed, Tip. I promise."

"We have a show on Saturday, dammit!" Enqvist raged.

Klondike shook his head. "That show has taken a dramatic turn and is being completely redrawn. Just as soon as I get a spare five minutes to actually sit down and process just what the hell is going on here!"

Enqvist pushed him angrily in the chest with the hand holding the flask. "They're trying to make you quit, Klondike. Why don't you just go ahead and do it? Quit! End this tour, and put us all out of our misery."

With that, Klondike grabbed at the flask, ripped it out of the rider's hand and hurled it wildly against the metal wall. Brown liquid sprayed across the floor.

"Now you listen to me," Klondike growled savagely at Enqvist, the pair of them nose to nose. "The day I quit will be the day this circus dies! And this circus will never die so long as I'm running it. You understand me, Enqvist?"

They squared up to each other, both chests heaving.

Klondike seemed to calm slightly. "Now, I told you we are doing everything we can to fix your bikes. To get you back out there again. I can do no more. Just try…" he kept his eyes locked on Enqvist's. The Daredevils all stared at them both. Lacey stayed back. It was all too much for her.

"Just try not to cause any trouble, Tip. Leave the bikes to me. Leave the show to me. You got that?"

Enqvist looked at him curiously for several moments, then backed off. "OK, Kal. If that's how it is. All I'm saying is… ain't no one gunna bust up our bikes and get away with it. Not like this. We want to know who it is, dammit."

Klondike exhaled slowly. "I know. I know. I'll get to the bottom of it." He looked around at the other riders. "Just look after your boys. The bike man should be here soon."

Then, he stormed out of the improvised garage, Lacey at his heel.

The duo wandered aimlessly around the circus encampment for several moments. They watched as roustabouts raced around, from the trailers to the train, and out to the field. The brown sack jackets were everywhere.

Heavy joined them, shaking his head as he moved through the camp. He caught the look on his old friend's face and froze.

"What is it, Kal?"

Klondike was watching the roustabouts. Those brown jackets. Everywhere. He seemed to nod. "Marlon."

Lacey looked up at him. "What about him?"

"It was Marlon," Klondike whispered. "We left him on watch during the meeting earlier. Remember? Everyone was in the tent. Roustabouts, stewards, all the crew. Everyone! Save a few hands out here. That's when the raiders came…"

"And Marlon didn't see anything?" Lacey asked.

"He wouldn't have known. Why would he have challenged anyone? Handel's team crept into the camp when no one was here. Just a couple of roustabouts, nothing more."

"Why, that old buzzard," Heavy snapped.

"It's not his fault, Heav. It's mine. Why didn't I think? We're under attack. Under surveillance. These people chose the perfect time to invade the camp. We never even considered that. And why the hell would we? Nothing like this has ever happened… to anybody!"

Their debriefing was shattered as McCabe suddenly waded over, by now looking more exasperated than ever. He approached, weary and confused.

"She's gone," he said helplessly.

"What!" Lacey shrieked.

"The Selenzy woman." McCabe removed his porkpie hat and rubbed at his receding hairline. "She has left the camp. The last anyone saw of her, she was running as fast as she could towards the road. One of my boys said it was the damndest thing he ever saw…. a dame in that fancy purple outfit, outta a Broadway show or something, sprinting like a greyhound outta here."

"She's gone?" Heavy blurted.

Lacey was shaking her head furiously. "So, she has jumped ship? Her belongings, her costumes, her personal effects… all just left behind? Just like that?"

McCabe looked around helplessly. He held his hat in his hands. "It would appear so, Miss Lacey."

She frowned, eyeing Klondike next to her. "So there it is. A hatchet job. She has caused chaos, planted her bomb and then, whoosh, she has fled. Job done." She looked back at the train and shook slightly. "And look at the damage she has caused."

"I don't believe it," Heavy said.

Lacey was pained. "We all fell for it. We said it was as if she was acting in a movie, or something. She had a mission. And boy did she succeed. Wowing us all with her act, her performance. It made us overlook her true role – trying to destroy Gino and Roddy."

Heavy looked crestfallen. "My god. What is going on here?"

Klondike seemed to be possessed by some unseen demon as he walked slowly across the concrete in the direction of the big top. After a few paces, he crouched down and went into a squatting position. He pointed a fist up at the heavens, then slammed it angrily into the ground with a whack. He looked downwards, his eyes squinting at nothingness.

Lacey approached cautiously. "Kal…"

When he spoke, his voice was a cold, hoarse whisper. But his words were unforgettable.

"Just when I thought we were back on top… we've gone and hit rock bottom."

CHAPTER 22

The basement bar just off the Geneva city main drag was dark, dank and gloomy.

Several patrons sat gathered around tables on the cracked, ash-filled floorboards, with several drunks slumped at the bar.

At the very end of the old mahogany bar top sat a young man, fair and handsome, who truly looked like he belonged someplace else, far from this dump.

Roddy Olsen sat on his stool, slouched over the bar. Several empty beer and shot glasses sat before him, and he reached for a short glass of whiskey. Gazing in the bar mirror opposite, he barely recognised himself. His skin looked redder, the eyes like hollows and the blond hair wild and unkept. His green jacket needed a wash.

Olsen sat there relaying the many strange events of the European tour through his over-activated mind.

Try as he might, he could not recall the one precise moment everything had turned upside down.

He glanced down at the brown liquid in the glass he held. Alcohol. A menace he had spent his youth in despair of. After all it had done to him, the havoc it had wreaked. His parents had been killed in a car accident while drunk at the wheel, after a lifetime of drunken failures. Then there was his Uncle Ray, who had cared for him after the tragedy, taken him in when he was 14. Another drunk, who had beaten and humiliated him.

It all seemed to come back to alcohol. And now here he was. At a bar so very far from home. Drinking. It seemed the only solution to his troubles. He was beginning to understand why so many turned to the bottle to help them through life.

As the many notions whirled through his mind, a gentle, familiar voice awoke him from his reverie.

"Roddy… are you alright?"

He turned and saw a middle-aged man stood at the bar beside him. With greying hair and lined, haggard skin, his true identity would have been a shock to many. Corky the Clown was now simply John Lone, a native of Cleveland, Ohio. A veteran entertainer who had worked the circus trails his entire life.

"I'm alright," Olsen blurted. "Just, er, trying to make sense of a few things."

Corky glanced in shock at the empty glasses. "And you found a little help along the way?"

Olsen seemed to deflate on his barstool. "Yeah. Never thought it possible. But the drink seems to make the pain go away."

Corky mounted a stool next to him and leaned over the youngster in concern. "No," he said. "It just masks it. Like paper over a crack." He watched gloomily as Olsen sipped the whiskey. "This isn't the path to go down, Rod. Believe me, I know. More than most."

Olsen put the glass down and stared at him. "What is happening out here, Corky?"

The veteran sighed, shaking his head. "This tour has done something to all of us. Affected each performer in a different way. Being so far from home has made us think… real hard. About life, about every aspect of it. And that isn't always a good thing."

Olsen held his head low. "Back there at camp… I did something terrible, Corky. Hell, I owe Kal and Lacey everything. But I, well, I…"

"I know, kid. I heard. There's a lot of strange stuff going on back there. You don't even know the half of it." He eyed the young man over again. "I heard you split from the camp. No one knew where you went. So I came out into town to try and find you. One of those roustabouts said they'd given you a drink a few times, so… well, I figured I'd look in on some bars." He placed a hand on Olsen's shoulder and forcefully turned him on the stool.

"But, dammit son, I didn't expect to find you in one."

Olsen sat there, swaying slightly. There were tears in his eyes.

"I messed up, Corky. Real bad. I… I just don't know what's happening to me out here. Why, oh why, can't we just go home? Back where we belong. Where people love us."

Corky remained impassive. "Is that the whole thing?"

Olsen rubbed his eyes. "Aw, hell. It's Lacey! I'm in love with her!"

The older man nodded thoughtfully. If he was shocked, he didn't show it.

"That isn't love," he suddenly declared. He leant in, holding Olsen's arm. "Sure, you find her attractive. But it's awe, admiration, respect. Hell, you and her would never work. You yourself can see that! She's your manager, you're an act to her, man. It's just that... it's just that, well, the bond you two have had, ever since you first rolled into camp, is unique and well-layered. Special."

Olsen looked down gloomily. "That's what she said."

"Don't let it get you down, man." Corky patted him gently on the back. "You're a beloved figure in this circus. For so many."

"Well, it sure doesn't feel that way right now..."

Corky turned and stared at the door, making a gesture to an unseen figure behind them. "Oh, I beg to differ, son."

Olsen just picked up the shot glass and stared at the dark liquid.

"Oh, Roddy!"

He turned in alarm at the sobbing whimper that came from behind.

There stood Suzi Dando, crying into a handkerchief as she stood in shock, wearing a grey trenchcoat several sizes too big for her.

That did it. Olsen cried out in anguish, rubbing furiously at his face. Then, he was on to her, hugging her tightly, a wild rush of emotions flooding him – hurt, shame, confusion and then, overwhelmingly, relief.

"Suzi!" he breathed as they embraced like long lost siblings reunited. "Oh Suzi. I'm so sorry. What a fool I have been."

She wept uncontrollably, burying her head into his shoulder.

"Roddy, what... what has happened to you?" She glared at the bar top in horror. "You're drinking! Whiskey! I don't understand. This goes against everything you've ever told me. Your life, everything!"

He groaned. "I don't know. I don't know what's happening. All I know is I want it to end. Right now!"

Still they held each other, as the bar patrons watched in muted shock. Corky quietly stepped away.

"I've done some stupid things, Suzi," Olsen was blabbering, as if in shock. "It feels like everyone's wanted a piece of me. And what with all the negative publicity and audience reactions, being out here in Europe… I feel like I'm losing my mind."

"It's alright," she said soothingly, her maternal manner belying her tender years as she stroked his back. Finally, they relinquished their hold and sat at the bar together. "It's alright. Everything will be fine, now." She gave him a mock expression. "Looks like I've let you out of my sight for too long!"

Olsen laughed, spluttering. He looked terrible, she thought.

"You know, you're right," Olsen mumbled, his eyes starting to brighten. "I think… I think we need to hang out more, like before. Like when we are back home."

Suzi smiled sweetly, looking like a child offered a treat. "There is nothing I would like more, Roddy." She frowned. "This tour has been awful lonely, so far."

He shook his head. "And I haven't even asked. I've been too wrapped up in myself." He grabbed her hand. "Please forgive me, Suzi girl."

She looked around in disgust at the surroundings. "Can we get out of here? Please!"

He mumbled a reply and made to climb off his bar stool. Instead, he stumbled as he tried to stand, with Suzi grabbing his slight frame to stop him plummeting head first to the floorboards. Corky quickly reappeared to help her.

"Whoa there, son. Good job some helping hands arrived, eh? Let's get you out of here in one piece."

But Olsen had passed out.

Grabbing an arm each, Corky and Suzi began hauling him out of the bar.

The mood in Klondike's stateroom on the train was distinctly downbeat.

Everyone just sat there, staring at each other in turn, various looks of beguilement and angst creating a dire atmosphere. Everyone had a drink on the go.

Klondike was at the desk, a cigar clamped into the side of his mouth and a large scotch beside his right hand.

Heavy and Plum sat on the couch, both nursing a cognac. Lacey was perched on the armchair opposite, with a cognac of her own in a tall glass.

For once, Bannion too was sat down, on a desk chair by the window. He held a bottle of Swiss beer.

They had been discussing the wave of misfortune that had hit the circus over the past 24 hours – but the conversation was leading nowhere, just further and further into an abyss.

"Bottom line," Klondike finally barked, slumped behind the desk in his leather chair. "We have a show tomorrow night. Tomorrow, god damn it! And we need to come up with a plan or, help me god, we are finished."

It was Bannion who responded first. "I just don't see how we can do it, Kal. Look at the roster. The Daredevils are out. The Range Riders and Duster are out. The sound is out. The parade is out. My lord, Roddy is out – and could be out forever for all we know." He swigged his beer. "What kind of show can we possibly put on?"

Lacey held her head high. "We can't cancel."

"Absolutely not," Klondike rasped. "We've got eight thousand people coming out to see our show. And, dammit all to hell, we're going to give them a show. No matter what."

Heavy nodded slowly. "We'll give em a show. It just won't feature our advertised attractions."

Bannion shook his head. "Now, that is a problem. It's letting the fans down. You know that, Kal."

Klondike sat there chewing his cigar. He thought of the screaming crowd back in Berlin. Then he thought of all those he had met in Switzerland. He remembered Christian Lago.

"We'll do our best," he finally blurted. He rubbed at his eyes and seemed to wince.

The others all looked him over. The circus boss's face was a battered mess. He had cuts and bruises from his fight with Tarz in the bar parking lot, plus a new bump in his cheekbone courtesy of Olsen.

Lacey lit a cigarette and seemed to come to life. The others knew this was a sign that she was thinking of a plan.

"Alright boys," she said airily. "Here's what we do." She cleared her throat. "Klondike's Circus proudly presents a new kind of show. One where the worlds of dance, acrobatics and carnival all come together in a one-of-a-kind extravaganza."

If she was expecting a rousing round of applause, she was sadly mistaken. The others stared at her in confusion.

Undeterred, Lacey stood, cigarette in hand, and walked theatrically around the stateroom, trying to rouse some enthusiasm.

"This new show will see the Hightops, Rocking Robins and the clowns all do their sets one after the other, and then again simultaneously. Then, in a big change, they will all stay on stage and continue their, er, antics as the Showcase Revue guys come out for an extended set, like they did in that practice show we all watched back in March at the camp. And then, the Revue will join the others on the ground as Gino and Penny perform their trapeze act. Then, Suzi comes out and sings not one but several songs, and the parade is performed… on foot. Walking and waving, like in old times."

She had ended up walking towards the door at the far end, and now turned triumphantly, as if on stage.

But the others still looked unimpressed. Heavy nodded vaguely. "I get it. Try and drag out what we have to make it a two-hour show. And make up for the lost talent with more from the other guys."

Klondike tried to smile. "Lacey, if marketing was an Olympic sport you would be a gold medallist." He looked at her with a kind of awe locked in his vision. "The day you don't have a plan will be the day I pack this gig in."

She laughed slightly. "We have to make the best out of what we've got. Or what is it you boys say in poker?"

Heavy grinned. "Make your hand spin."

"Right. How sublime. So, that is what I propose. A new format, where the acts all blend into one. An ensemble production, if you will." She stood by the window and eyed the great big top out there in the field, illuminated now by the light of the moon. "I can't see what else we can do, boys."

Plum finally spoke. He had been deeply affected by the events of the past day. "And what about Roddy? Where the hell is he? The people will want to see him."

Lacey looked down. She shuddered. "I… I just don't know, Richie."

Klondike studied her. "We'll find him."

"And then there's Gino," Plum continued in alarm. "Is he even fit to go up on the trapeze after all this with Carla? She got in his head. What if he has an accident up there?"

"These are all good points," Bannion opined from the corner. He stifled a yawn. "And this, er, change of show… the talent that won't be performing. This has to be conveyed to the paying fans before the show starts, somehow."

"I'll relay it to the audience during my introduction," Heavy said.

"With what? We don't have any sound!"

"I'll use a megaphone for it. It's not ideal, but people will hear me."

Bannion glared over at Klondike. "This is all sounding like a desperate gamble, Kal. A song and dance show with clowns and carnival acts, and then a struggling Gino out at the end to save it all. Think of the reviews, the fans, the word on the circuit."

"I don't give a damn about the circuit," Klondike raged, suddenly angry. He stood up, tired and stiff, looking like a geriatric. He glared at the Englishman and tried to cool off. "Listen Jack, I know this sounds crazy. But what the hell are we supposed to do? I'm not cancelling. Especially at the 11th hour." He thought for a moment. "This 'circuit' you speak of, the circus folk out here… they are the ones who have done this to us. Crippled us." He eyed each of his confederates soberly. "And I'm not going to let them win."

"So, we go with Lacey's idea then?" said Plum quietly.

"We've got no god damn choice," Klondike replied.

Lacey nodded furiously. "We'll start tomorrow morning in the tent. Briefing everybody. We need to go through the acts, what is expected from all of them. Some kind of rehearsal, in what time we have. It will be a race against time and we-"

She cut off abruptly as the door flew open and everyone stared at the end of the stateroom.

Corky stuck his head into the confines and made a simple announcement.

"We got him back!"

Olsen led peacefully on the bed in his stateroom, still dressed in his clothes but with a warm blanket covering him.

Suzi sat over him like a protective nurse, dutifully dabbing a wet flannel across his forehead.

The room was half-lit by an old-fashioned lantern in the far corner, giving the confines a hazy, dream-like feel.

Corky had led everyone down the carriages to the talent staterooms, and now held the door open for them to peek inside. They all stayed in the corridor.

Lacey manoeuvred her way to the front of the group and looked down sadly at Olsen. She felt herself shrinking inside but maintained her composure. The corners of her lips were tucking downwards, an involuntary response. He looked different – haggard and broken, not the super-confident youngster they had all grown to adore.

Her gaze shifted to Suzi, who was staring at her.

"Thank you Suzi," Lacey whispered in the strange, surreal atmosphere.

The youngster nodded. "It's alright, Miss Lacey. I'll take good care of him."

"I know."

They eyed each other for several seconds. Then, Lacey patted Corky on the chest. "Well done. We all owe you, Corky."

She moved away from the door and backed down the corridor, wiping a hand over her mouth.

Klondike looked into the room. "What the hell happened to the kid?" he whispered.

Corky remained at the door. "He'd been drinking all day. Probably a good thing I found him when I did."

Klondike shook his head. "After all he has been through, all the problems caused by alcoholics in his life… he still hit the bottle."

Heavy was on his shoulder as they all gazed inside. "That whole episode must have hit him real hard."

Klondike looked down. "It did, Heav. It really did." Then, he eyed Suzi. "Roddy is lucky… we are all lucky… to have you, Suzi. Thank you."

She smiled up at him from the bed. She seemed prepared to stay there forever. "It's alright, Mr Klondike. Roddy's just a little upset. He'll be fine."

The visitors all moved away from the door, and Corky pulled it closed, leaving Suzi to it.

They walked down the corridor in dismay, no one knowing what to say or do.

"Thank god he's back," Plum muttered.

Klondike nodded. "He's back, but he's not going on tomorrow. Not like that. After all that happened."

Bannion spoke up. "His face is adorning posters all across the city."

"I don't give a damn, Jack. He can't go on. I won't have it."

The group stopped as they reached the vestibule. Corky put an arm around Lacey, who was visibly upset.

"It's alright Lacey," he said warmly. "Our boy took quite a hit. But he will come back stronger."

"Just never seen him like that," she whispered.

Klondike opened the side door and led the way off the train and out into the night. Then, he addressed his team one more time as they stood outside by the rail yard.

"Alright people," he barked. "This has been one hell of a day, there's no denying it. But tomorrow, we roll. It's showtime, and you know what that means. We'll get everyone together in the tent for the briefing. The show plan will be laid out. And then, help me god, I'm going to put my head into the lion's mouth…"

They all stared at him. "Excuse me?" Plum uttered.

Klondike sighed. "I've got to get Gino and Roddy together. One on one. With me in the middle. Before this whole god damn circus gets blown apart!"

CHAPTER 23

The Mannheim Hotel, a beautiful white sandstone building on the opposite side of Parc Giresse to the big top, was the setting for the crunch showdown.

It was 11am, and the hotel bar was deserted, which perfectly suited the occasion. It was a typical central European affair, all brown oak and beige wallpaper.

Klondike had arrived first, and now stood at the far end of the long bar, lighting a cigar and waiting. A whiskey mac sat beside his right hand on the bar top. He was nervous, pensive.

Deep down, he always knew such a moment would arrive at some point or another. A confrontation between his two crown jewels. A head to head. He just never imagined it would happen out here, in the middle of Switzerland, in a strange and unknown land. And all because of a woman. A con woman, at that.

Now, he waited. He had passed instructions for Olsen to arrive first, then Shapiro 10 minutes after. It had to be that way.

Klondike watched coolly as a figure emerged at the far end of the room, half-hidden by sunlight gleaming through the tall windows.

Roddy Olsen walked over slowly, dressed in his jeans, shirt and green jacket.

The youngster stopped five yards from the circus boss. Both men eyed each other, almost in fear. The stand-off lasted possibly 30 seconds. Then, Olsen seemed to crack.

"Aww, Kal," he moaned. He looked pained and sick. Real sick. "I'm sorry about what happened. About everything, man. I…I don't know what's happening to me out here. I just ain't felt right. Not since we left. London, Paris, out here, everywhere on this tour. I can't think. I can't sleep. It's killing me."

Klondike nodded. "I know, kid. I can see it. This little expedition of ours has been a wild ride. Like nothing I imagined."

Olsen wiped at his mouth. Klondike looked at him. He seemed to have aged years in such a few weeks. His beautiful, tanned skin looked calloused, his eyes forlorn.

He reached behind him at the bar. "Here, drink this." He handed Olsen a tall glass of what looked like water, with a strange cloudy solution in it.

Olsen took it. "What is this?"

"Just drink it, kid."

"But, what-"

"Drink!"

As he gulped it down, Klondike watched him. "Belso water. A hangover cure I discovered out here in the war." He squinted as he watched his young star down the murky liquid. "Alcohol. I never thought I'd see you touch a drop, Rod. Not after all that happened to your folks. Your uncle. Seeing you become a drinker…it's awful."

Olsen placed the empty glass on the bar top. "That's what this tour has done to me, Kal. It's driven me to it."

He looked the rugged boss man over, frowning at the bumps and bruises that now dominated his face.

Klondike sighed. "I've been running a circus for over 10 years now, kid. In all that time, ain't no one, and I mean no one, ever had a swing at me."

Olsen baulked. "I didn't mean it, Kal. You can see that. That… that wasn't me back there."

"You can see now, I hope, that she set you up. You and Gino. It was all a ruse. A scheme. To turn you two against each other… even more. A way to finally rip my circus apart. For good."

Olsen nodded vaguely. "Yeah, I guess. I, er, I still don't know what happened. It was all so fast. So insane. Like a dream."

"You fell under her spell, Rod. Gino too. You ain't the first, I imagine, and sure as hell won't be the last."

"Oh god," the youngster blurted. "We tried to kill each other."

"I saw that," Klondike muttered dryly. "That's why we're all gunna straighten things out right now." Then, he frowned. "Just before you slugged me… what did you mean, Rod, those words you said?"

"Huh?"

"You said that I was the problem, that I was 'the one…'"

Olsen shook convulsively and swatted a hand through the air. "Ah, hell, I dunno, Kal. I was hysterical. I was lost."

Klondike frowned. "It's something to do with Lacey, isn't it? It's no secret the way you feel about her, kid. That, er, special relationship she has with you. But you're not...not jealous of me?"

Olsen rubbed at his eyes aggressively. "Ah, man. I don't even know anymore, Kal." Then, he looked at him directly, a solemn gaze. "I owe you and Lacey everything. My life, my world, everything. And, hell, I'm just so truly sorry that I acted the way I did, Kal. The last thing I want to do is let you both down."

Klondike nodded. "Ok, good. Now..."

He was about to continue when a loud voice cut him off.

"Well, well, isn't this cosy, eh? And now the circle is complete... I am here!"

Klondike and Olsen stared as Shapiro breezed across to them, dressed in an extravagant pink shirt and short fur coat. He ordered a sarsaparilla from the elderly bartender standing in the corner, then paced anxiously before the other two.

"So, here we all are," he said, almost joyfully. "Ready for a desperate pep talk ahead of the latest show, eh?"

Olsen spoke. "Gino, I-"

"I have heard enough from you, dollmaker!" he snapped savagely, pointing a finger at Olsen. "You are lucky I don't strike you again now, boy, after what you did to me."

Klondike finally stepped forward. "Gino, for Christ's sake, the whole thing was a set-up. Carla used you. Used Roddy too. She didn't have any feelings for you. It was a ploy to turn you both against one another. To create this, damn it! Can't you see that?"

"Oh, I can see it, chairman," Shapiro whispered, a queer smile on his lips. "I see it now, si. And, yes, I hold up my hands. In regret. I fell for her game. I fell for her. Truly, I did." Then, he looked sad and bitter, taking the glass offered him by the barman and gazing out of the window. "I have loved maybe 10 women, truly, in my life. And Carla... sweet Carla, she was five of them."

Klondike raged. "She wasn't sweet, god damn it. She's a con artist. Sent here by whoever is trying to wreck us. Conrad Handel, or whoever he is working for. Someone controls her."

Shapiro looked downwards. "It would appear so. She tricked me. Humiliated me. And after one of the greatest shows of my life, back in Berlin. What a tragedy this is."

Klondike and Olsen exchanged bemused glances. "So," Klondike said, almost pleadingly, "it would seem the best thing to do is put this all behind us, right?"

Now, Shapiro glared again at Olsen. "You knew!"

"What?" the youngster blurted.

"Carla and me were in a relationship. Even if it was a flawed one. And yet still, dollman, you come to her room, you kiss her, and who knows what else, eh? Even though you knew she was my woman. Why? To get at me! The only way you can. This is your way of getting back at Gino, no? For being in my shadow, being my competition in every town we play."

"Gino, for the love of god!" Olsen cried. "That is all nonsense. I don't think like that. How many times do I have to tell you? I don't hate you, I admire you. You know that! You have admitted your respect for me too, for what I do. What happened back in Carla's stateroom was something…something I can't explain. My mind hasn't been right since we hit Europe. Carla knew that and she… she…"

"She exploited it," Klondike finished. "She preyed on you, using her skills." He addressed Shapiro directly. "Now, listen Gino. You have to get all of this madness out of your head now. You hear me? Now! None of us are leaving this place until the two of you shake hands."

Shapiro appraised him, his dark eyes suddenly gleaming. "Such drama, chairman. A scenario you could surely never have imagined."

Klondike backed down, then leant back against the bar. His mood seemed to change. He was now melancholy.

"You're right," he said slowly. "In all my years under a big top, never could I have imagined anything like this. To be so lucky, for one thing. To have two such talented performers in my tent. You two. Like nothing else I ever saw. Two men who have made me proud beyond all expectations. And two performers the people love, adore. And yet, the two of you, so very different."

Lost in thought, he paced in front of them. Both watched, transfixed. He pointed at Shapiro. "The great Gino. King of the trapeze. Born into circus royalty. Son of Enrico Shapiro, one of Italy's greatest flyers and a promoter of multiple circuses across the world. You have your diamonds, your girls, your friends in Hollywood, and an invite to any party that's worth going to."

Klondike's gaze shifted to Olsen. "And then we have Roddy. Born into poverty. Parents killed when he was 12. Raised by an abusive uncle. On the street at 15, living in boarding houses. Just another ham and egger. But instilled within him, an overwhelming desire to be a performer. A talent that was born in his head and his heart, and a talent so unique that no one can quite believe it is real."

Klondike shook his head sadly, looking from one to the other. "How many times do I have to say it? If you two could just get along, this troupe would be the most beautiful circus organisation in existence."

Shapiro and Olsen were both strangely silent. Neither looked at the other. Olsen quivered, still looking sick.

Klondike said: "We have a show tonight. And a tour to conclude. But none of us will see any of that…cos we ain't going anywhere until the two of you shake hands."

A deathly silence filled the barroom.

Olsen turned and faced his rival, awkwardly. He finally offered his hand. Strong and straight.

Shapiro eyed Klondike, shook his head, then groaned. He took a look at the hand.

Then, finally, in a fast move, he slapped his palm against Olsen's, never once making eye contact.

"OK," he said, turning and walking towards the exit, "let's get this show on the road."

Klondike and Olsen slowly followed.

"Kal, I don't think I can…I can't…"

"It's alright, kid," Klondike said gently. "You're not going out there tonight. Not like this. We're having a few, ah, changes in tonight's show."

They walked behind Shapiro, who was heading through the foyer towards the hotel's main revolving doors at reception.

Olsen was glum. "I can't stand letting everyone down. You, your staff and… and most of all the fans."

Klondike grunted as they walked. "We've been busted open. Our whole operation. These people… they've ripped a hole right though my circus. It's a raid. And Carla was up to her neck in it."

"There's a lot I need to put right," Olsen muttered as they passed the reception desk.

Klondike turned. "Not anymore. Now, there's just Lacey. You need to make peace with her, kid." He seemed to growl as they went through the revolving door and faced Parc Giresse, the big top sat before them like a great monolithic temple.

"She's worried sick."

He found her standing idly next to the confectionary booth, watching as a roustabout put the cotton candy whirler together.

The newly-constructed midway was a hive of noise and activity, as workers raced around performing last-minute tasks. As usual, the mass of stalls and booths felt like a miniature village, all of its own.

"Hello, Lacey," Olsen said from behind.

She didn't move to begin with, then turned slowly. She wore a stylish white and pink cardigan and arty green slacks. A coffee in a disposable cardboard cup was in her hand.

"Roddy…" she breathed. Her violet eyes seemed to enlarge and lighten. "You're… alright?"

He shrugged. "I'm getting there."

Lacey shook slightly. "My god, I've never seen you like that. In the train, that fight with Gino, and then passed out… drunk!"

He held up a hand. "I know. And there's something I want to say to you, Lacey. Need to say." He took a deep breath. "I'm sorry. For all these late night games I've subjected you to on this tour. For allowing myself to fall for Carla's schemes. For the fight on the train. For getting drunk." Then, he moved towards her, so close he could smell her eucalyptus-scented perfume. "But, most of all, I'm sorry for letting you down. In every way I have."

Lacey looked at him with that trademark, overwhelming gaze, the eyes boring into him. "Roddy, my dear, sweet boy. This tour, everything that has happened out here, has had a bad effect on you. Everyone can see it." She gazed out at the field beyond. "Maybe I should have done more to help…"

"No. It was me. All me."

She slitted her eyes and pouted at him. "I didn't think you'd try to find the answer in a bottle."

He shrugged helplessly. "What can I tell you? I'm a mess."

Then, as if a seal had suddenly been broken, she placed her cup on the wooden fence and surged over to him, hugging him tightly. "It's ok, Roddy. It's ok. We've all got you here. We're your family. Never forget that."

Olsen seemed to explode with relief. "I sure am glad to hear that."

She held him for a moment, then inexplicably grabbed his hand and hauled him towards the tent. He paced rapidly to keep up as she pulled him along.

"Now," Lacey cried as they moved, "you may not be performing tonight, but there is still work to be done. Poor, dear Suzi is having to sing through a megaphone of all things tonight. Can you imagine?"

They walked up to the circus tent, into the tunnel way and through the flap into the arena. Grandstands were being fastened together by an army of roustabouts and local workmen. The sound of clanging and metallic thudding filled the tent air.

And there on the sawdust, looking somewhat befuddled as she swayed around, holding that big red megaphone, was Suzi.

Lacey gently prodded Olsen towards her in the centre of the stage.

"She could use a little reassurance. From her main man."

With that, the publicity ace scuttled out.

Olsen watched her go, then jogged over to Suzi, the two embracing in a joyous hug.

At the top of the tent, three rows from the very back of the stands, high up above Olsen and Suzi on the sawdust, the boss and the ringmaster sat in the bleachers, watching everything.

Two men. Sat in a sea of empty seats, six hours before showtime.

Klondike nodded to himself as he watched Lacey leave and Olsen join Suzi. "The kid will be alright. Thank god."

Heavy, already dressed in his scarlet announcer's jacket, leant forward as he gazed at the figures below.

"Well, that's one problem solved. But we've still got one hell of a mess on our hands. And two shows left. Here and Rome."

Klondike looked around at the thousands of seats that encircled the stage like a great bowl of dormant energy. It was always a strange, mesmerising sight to see the empty grandstands. Especially from up here.

"We're still no closer to the truth," he growled. "Who is doing this to us? Who is Handel? Who does he represent? Who, dammit!"

Heavy smirked. "And why go to all this trouble? Infiltrating our troupe, paying off newsmen, trying to buy us off."

"Well," Klondike mused, "we may never know. Once Rome is done, we are finished. The Floating Top picks us up at Naples and then we are outta here… for good! Our European tour will be over." He looked down ruefully. "My god. This isn't how I pictured things. I thought this trip would be our finest hour, a crowning glory."

Heavy tried to sound positive. "It still might be, Kal. We've got here and Rome still. As we have seen out here, anything can happen."

"Yeah," Klondike rasped. "But it feels like instead of embracing these last two shows, we are trying to survive them."

Heavy nodded wisely. "All those plans. All that optimism when we left New York, out on that waterfront. And now this…this emptiness."

"All because someone didn't want us over here," Klondike whispered. He smiled mirthlessly as he surveyed the movements of his staff far below. "And we'll never get to pay them back."

CHAPTER 24

Once again, the big top was filled to a capacity crowd for the Klondike's Circus Geneva spectacular.

This time, the audience seemed to be made up largely of older citizens and pensioners, with a number of families and teenagers thrown in. Many were dressed conservatively in suits, and everyone appeared serious and alert, as if attending a business conference.

Standing in his customary spot at the tent flap, Klondike idly wondered about the many cultural differences they had experienced in Europe as he gazed up at the packed grandstands all around him.

He had felt a queer, nagging feeling before every show of the tour so far. Now, he felt exasperated, almost like he was on his last legs.

There was little atmosphere in the tent, hardly any excitement and electricity bled down from the bleachers, despite all the fans. Sadly, this was the norm out here – he expected and accepted it.

Holding his cane with an iron grip, Klondike paced around the flap enclosure, glancing out at the field outside and the performers' trailers, then wandering back to the edge of the stands.

Lacey and Plum both stood silently by the arena threshold. Waiting. Bannion hovered around, dipping in and out of the tent.

Klondike glanced up at the grandstand beside him, the sea of faces looking down in anticipation. He finally spotted Olsen, sat in the 10th row, looking forlorn and strangely ill at ease up there, so very far from the action.

Then, it was 7pm. Time. The traditional sound of trumpets blaring was absent without the sound equipment. There was no way of letting everyone know the show was starting. Nothing at all.

Klondike winced as he watched Heavy Brown wade out on to the arena floor, bawling at the top of his voice into that old red megaphone. The whole spectacle made for a bizarre sight.

It suddenly hit him that this was a bad idea. Why hadn't he stopped it? Listened to Bannion? And called the whole thing off. He could see it now, and foresaw what would unfold. But it was too late.

The show had begun… yet the spectators barely knew it.

Klondike was 20 yards from Heavy, the ringmaster shouting out his introduction. And yet even he couldn't hear a word the man in red was saying.

That inauspicious opening to the Geneva show unfortunately set the tone for a night of disaster.

Nobody in the audience outside of the front three rows could hear a word of Heavy's introductions. And this planted an immediate seed of confusion for the whole show, with most of the crowd unable to understand what was going on – and know who they were watching.

The circus followed Lacey's rapidly-conceived show plan.

The Hightops, Rocking Robins and Flying Batistas all performed one after another, as usual, and then completed an extra, extended set together on stage.

However, having the three groups all doing their acts at the same time, in their own little teams, looked messy and disjointed out there on the big night. Klondike struggled to understand why the spectacle did not look appealing. He decided there was simply no connection there, like trying to watch three ball games at once.

The fact the dance team had no music to dance to killed their whole act, an irreversible error.

As Klondike watched, he wished he had allowed the time to think it all through. He found himself involuntarily backing further and further away from the sawdust, right to the tent's edge. Lacey and Plum simply followed.

In the end, the acts all joined together in the centre. The Hightops performed a human dome, covering the Robins, who performed their Rockette-style high kicking routine. The Batistas executed their human totem pole on the edge of the dome.

The audience responded with muted applause, unimpressed and underwhelmed. Many still seemed unsure of what was happening before them.

Then, after another indistinguishable introduction from Heavy, out came the Showcase Revue.

For their extended set, Gargantua unleashed a seemingly endless array of acrobatics. Cartwheels, flying leaps, somersaults, handstands and gymnastic patterns greeted the watching patrons, who could not help applaud the tireless big man.

By the end, Gargantua was soaking wet in sweat, and barely able to stand. As he acknowledged the hearty applause, the Hightops and Robins continued dancing and performing acrobatics at the arena's perimeter, which actually proved distracting.

Goliath then came out, waving enthusiastically despite a lack of cheers. For his segment, he picked up members of the Batistas and Hightops and placed them on top of each other, as if building a wall. Two of the Hightops crew took it in turns to leap on to his shoulders, before being deposited back on to a different team member. The whole escapade went on and on as Goliath made it his mission to seemingly hoist up everyone on the stage floor. The giant's movements grew slower and slower as he carried on lifting, over and over again.

Rumpy Stiltskin came next, bouncing in and out of the mass of bodies dominating the sawdust on his giant stilt legs. But nobody in the grandstands seemed to notice him, there was just too much going on across the floor.

Klondike realised this, as he watched the vacuum of activity spaced out before him. It was difficult to truly focus on anything in particular. The fact Heavy could not explain and herald each act just made the whole thing even more regrettable.

Lacey moved up to him and placed her forehead on his shoulder.

"I'm sorry, Kal," she whispered. "I was wrong. This isn't pleasing on the eye at all. It isn't working."

"No one knows what the hell is going on," Klondike breathed. He grimaced. "Why the hell didn't we try out that megaphone properly? Poor Heavy. That thing is killing us."

"How could we do a practice run?" Lacey said. "We would have needed thousands of people to test it. It seemed fine earlier."

"We should've thought of that. No one even questioned using that thing instead of a mic. We all just presumed it would be fine. And now look!"

"There was just no time," Lacey said weakly.

Klondike shook his head and watched as a group of brightly dressed figures on unicycles all whizzed past.

Corky led his troupe of clowns through the flap and out on to the sawdust, blaring their horns.

Klondike almost wanted to try and stop them, haul them back in. It was too late. The circus floor represented a wild can of worms, everybody racing around this way and that. And now in came a group of clowns on cycles.

The clowns all sped round the floor in ever-widening circles, slamming custard pies into the faces of the performers and handing flowers to others.

Then, as the clown team joined the other acts around the perimeter, all cheering and waving, Corky performed his solo stints.

The unicycle leap, his various juggling acts – including the fire sticks – and some bewildering hand magic all followed. The clowns then assisted him with the legendary human cannonball act. Only this time, instead of flying across the arena floor and landing in a safety net, Corky was caught by the Hightops, who had created a human net, of sorts.

This act drew the largest cheers of the night so far, though many of the patrons looked somewhat bemused.

Then, as all the assembled circus performers gathered on the sawdust, Heavy began his most famous introduction of all.

But, yet again, almost everyone watching was none the wiser over what was happening.

Gino Shapiro and Penny Fortune appeared through the flap in their extravagant, fur-lined cloaks, hands aloft. Unfortunately, just as they emerged, the applause for the human cannonball feat was just finishing.

Shapiro could not remember ever entering an arena to virtual silence. Indeed, many in the stands did not seem to realise he had entered at all. Gino quickly realised what a huge, unforeseen problem the wrecked sound system was. He could see Heavy screaming into the megaphone – and it was making no difference.

Ever the consummate professional, the trapeze artist removed his cape and hauled himself up to his rigging and completed his set. Penny caught his eye several times, drawing his attention to the apparent lack of interest in their act.

After landing back on his ring after a triple roll, she shouted over to him from her perch: "Do they even know we are up here?"

Shapiro ignored her. He looked down at the thousands of fans all around him. Some craned their necks to look up at what he was doing. Many were still looking on at the antics of the range of performers on the floor.

In truth, no one really seemed to know what to look at.

Shapiro dutifully completed his vaults across the tent's summit, then descended his tall rope.

He performed his high wire walk with zero fuss or fanfare, just striding across rapidly and executing his cartwheel at the far end of the wire without gusto. He bowed, waved and climbed down from the wire platform.

Penny joined him on the sawdust and they both waved at the audience.

There was vague applause, but many of the faces that looked down at them were confused and joyless.

Penny turned around in a circle, staring at the crowd in horror. "What is happening?" she shrieked.

Shapiro shook his head, and made to join the line of performers all now clapping and dancing around the edge of the floor. He and Penny merely stood with the others.

"This should never have happened," Shapiro said bitterly.

At the flap, Klondike watched in agony at the tangle of bodies spread all across the floor. Everyone waved at the stands, and no one seemed to know what to do. The enormity of all the last-minute changes hit him again and again, mercilessly prodding at his conscience.

Then, he froze all over as Suzi Dando made her way through the flap, looking beautiful and angelic in her white silk dress.

"Suzi!" he gasped, suddenly grabbing her arm.

She looked up in shock. “Mr Klondike!”

“I’m sorry,” he released his grip. “You can’t go out there, Suzi. That damn megaphone ain’t working. No one can hear a thing. We’re gunna have to skip your act tonight. I’m sorry, sweetheart.”

She looked agonised. “But I’m down to do four songs tonight! All that new material we discussed.”

“That was before I realised that thing can’t project a voice like we all thought. I’m sorry, Suzi. You can’t go out there. It will kill you.”

She glanced out at the arena floor, up at the bleachers above.

“I know Mr Brown’s voice isn’t getting heard, but I figured with my singing, I can-“

“It’s not gunna happen.” Klondike said it with finality.

He looked out at the mayhem on the floor. Then, he saw Heavy staring at him, awaiting instruction. Klondike had no choice. He raised his hand and made a circling gesture.

But Lacey’s idea to perform the finale parade by having everyone walk around the perimeter, a lap of honour, never took off. No one knew what to do. Suzi was due on. Her gig had been cancelled on the spot. And now Heavy could not communicate that it was time for the finale.

The ringmaster grew ever more exasperated. In the end, in a final, futile gesture, he walked up to Shapiro and Penny and looked at the line of performers spread out before him. He cried out as loud as he could: “Everybody just hold hands and bow. This is the finale!”

The word filtered through and, within a minute, all of the performers managed to form a line cutting straight though the diameter of the circus floor. All held hands and bowed several times in unison.

There was no lap of honour. No one within the group thought of trying to instigate the act. Some had forgotten that was the plan. Others simply wore a mask of confusion. Several wanted to flee.

Yet again, the audience responded in shock and disbelief, as if unable to comprehend that this was the end of the show. Indeed, many were still unable to fathom what was going on.

Klondike, Lacey, Plum, Bannion and a tearful Suzi all just stood there in stunned silence.

The brief applause died out almost instantly, leaving a big top filled with eeriness.

Klondike and Heavy made eye contact again. They both nodded.

Then, Heavy simply said to the others: "Let's go!"

He led the way off the sawdust, followed quickly by Shapiro and Penny. The rest duly followed, everyone in a rush to get away from the shocked and confused faces that appeared everywhere, no matter where they looked.

And then it happened.

As if given a green light by an official starter, the assembled thousands all started booing. It started in an instant, and came like a hideous pollutant that destroyed the very air within the big top.

It was a truly sickening noise, the sound of anger and disgust, a devastating and ugly sensation. And it poured down from the stands and into the hearts and souls of everyone associated with Klondike's Circus.

Klondike felt sick all over, unable to comprehend what was going on. He led Lacey and Suzi outside and they all practically sprinted to the trailers.

The others, all of the performers, were right behind them. Nobody wanted to be a part of the harsh wave of misery thundering under the big top.

As the Hightops, who were bringing up the rear, exited the tent, many fans hurled soda cups and popcorn boxes down from their seats, showing their disgust at what they had witnessed.

Before long, the arena floor – scene of some of America's greatest ever circus moments – was covered in plastic beakers and discarded garbage.

Lost among the disgruntled patrons, Olsen sat there in shock, a grim expression locked into his features.

After what seemed like an age, the thousands of spectators finally began to leave the big top.

It was left to Jim McCabe and his army of roustabouts to direct and police the people as they left, ensuring everyone went via the designated exits.

The paying public seemed to storm out, as if keen to put as much distance between themselves and this accursed circus tent as possible.

Before long, the sea of humanity was filing out across Parc Giresse. The nightmare was almost over.

Cooped up in Suzi's performance trailer, Klondike watched them leave through a side window. He could not remember ever feeling so pathetic. His heart sank, further and further.

Finally, he turned from the window and crumpled to the floor. The others all watched him in shock.

"First time in more than 10 years, we got booed off stage," Heavy said quietly.

Bannion collapsed into the couch. "We should never have gone ahead with it."

Suzi was beyond fraught. "Who could have known that would happen?"

Lacey was staring at Klondike, who sat on the floor, his back against the trailer wall. "Kal..." she whimpered. "What are we going to do?"

Klondike looked up at her, his face a wall of desperation. But there was anger in his eyes. His nostrils flared.

"What? I'll tell you what," he snarled. "We get the hell out of here!"

NIGHT OF SHAME AT THE CIRCUS!

By Klaus Augenmacht, Continental Review

It had been billed as a night of stars. Major, American stars, gracing Switzerland for the first time ever.

Instead, what transpired last night at Parc Giresse, Geneva, was a night of scandal.

Klondike's Circus was in town, its huge red and blue tent attracting thousands of fans for a sell-out crowd. Unfortunately, those present witnessed nothing more than a shambles of a show, in every respect.

The entire production, if you can call it that, was a mess from start to finish.

There was no music, no announcements and no structure to any of it. A traditional ringmaster in a red blazer and top hat was out there, but seemed to be trying to address the giant audience with a megaphone, of all things.

Dancers in fancy leotards came out and danced...to no music. Acrobats and gymnasts all threw themselves around wildly, for what purpose I have no idea.

They were joined by two giants - one obese and the other very tall - who performed various tricks for far too long, as the others carried on prancing around alongside them.

Then, a bunch of ridiculously dressed clowns came hurtling out on unicycles. Their leader performed a big leap, lots and lots of juggling, and a human cannonball act. But it was hard to see what was happening, due to the sheer mass of bodies all over the place. Indeed, trying to focus on one performer in a human hornets' nest was impossible, and the whole thing looked like nothing more than an awful lot of clowning around.

With all these acrobatics, dance moves, gymnastics and tomfoolery going on everywhere, the show descended into chaos.

Suddenly, someone pointed out two trapeze artists high above, vaulting through the air.

So, this was the great Gino Shapiro. His moves were faultless, but it is a shame most of the audience barely noticed him. By the time he performed the high wire, everyone seemed to have realised he was out there. But the walk itself was performed with zero gusto and flamboyance, almost as if he didn't want to be out there.

This is not what anyone expected from the king of the air, who had been advertised as one of the most charismatic figures in world circus.

After that, the whole slew of performers merely held hands in a long line, bowed, and exited the tent in double quick time, to the shock and despair of everyone in the stands.

Quite rightly, a loud chorus of boos erupted from all sides. Rubbish was thrown on to the stage. No one could believe this ungodly mess was what they had bought tickets for, had waited weeks to glimpse.

Among the many major sins Klondike's Circus committed last night was the non-appearance of so many advertised performers.

Where was the puppetmaster Roddy Olsen, whose face adorns posters all over the city? Where were the Daredevils, supposedly the most incredible components of death defiance in the world? And where was the king of the cowboys Duster Williams, who so many children sat waiting for in the big top... only to be left disappointed and upset. Simply unforgivable.

I would like to learn just how the ridiculously named Mr Kal Klondike intends to justify these seemingly last-minute changes to his card.

Shame on him, and shame on his people. For leaving this Geneva crowd without all those advertised stars, with no explanation or announcement at all, is the worst sin of all. And there were a great many sins committed on this night of horror.

Circus fans across Switzerland will this morning be wondering why they wasted their time attending this nonsense. Surely, most will avoid going to a big top ever again.

But none of this will bother Mr Kal Klondike. After a sell-out crowd, I am sure he will be tucked away in a caravan somewhere, counting his money.

I have but one thing to say to you, American. Don't ever come back!

CHAPTER 25

The Primo Nazionale Country Club on the outskirts of Rome was a rich man's paradise.

Tucked away in rolling green hills, the beautiful Navajo white mansion sat among the fields like a palace in a fairy tale of old.

A large marble courtyard held varnished oak tables and chairs, where the great and good of society mingled freely.

To the side of the great house, a large swimming pool was full of youthful socialites. Bronzed men wandered around in swim trunks, and women sunbathed in their costumes. Laughter seemed to fill the air everywhere.

Into this gleaming upper class utopia entered two men. The tanned, well-groomed man in front wore a peach-coloured suit and fit in easily with the inhabitants. But behind him strode a giant with wild black hair and beard, dressed in a denim dungarees. Many stopped to stare at the monster, but many more knew better and avoided a glance.

Conrad Handel exchanged pleasantries with various passersby as he wandered across the huge courtyard. Tarz merely followed, eyeing the decadence all around him with muted disgust.

At the far corner of the patio, under an awning, sat a large oblong table, which showcased a mighty feast.

A whole Pacific lobster sat as the grand centrepiece, surrounded by plates of freshly cut hams and cheeses, salads, rolls, dumplings and oysters. The spread was fit for a multi-generational family get-together, but just one man sat at the head of the table.

Carmine Courtinio looked immaculate in a white silk shirt and soft pink cravat as he looked over some papers in the morning sun.

He looked up and smiled as Handel and Tarz approached.

"Gentlemen," he said, "welcome to the top table."

They exchanged pleasantries, before Courtinio indicated for them to sit. Both ordered coffee from a passing busboy, before Tarz hungrily began loading a plate.

"First of all, my compliments," Courtinio was saying. He held aloft the morning's Continental Review with relish. Passing it across to Handel, he continued: "That review is the latest in a summer of terrible reports for Klondike's Circus. But this is surely the final hammer blow for the Americans. And, bueno, it perfectly allows me to see the damage you have caused, Conrad."

He raised a small glass of pink liquid. "Congratulations, my friend. It would appear you have succeeded, and killed off these unsavoury invaders. For good." He drank, savouring the strange-looking drink.

Handel smiled as he read the review. "What a disaster," he muttered. "I heard about the booing. The disgust. They say Klondike and his team ran away. Actually ran! Away from the tent and into their trailers, desperate to hide."

Courtinio smiled thinly. "Maybe now our foreign friends realise this whole European tour was not such a good idea."

Tarz grunted from the other end of the table as he put together a ham sandwich. "They run home! With their tails between their legs."

"You have done well," Courtinio said.

"It was easy, really," Handel replied, as his coffee arrived. He took a sip. "Once Klondike refused the pay-off, we just went to work. Hit the boss, then hit his equipment. Reading this review, it seems that smashing up their sound equipment was a shrewd move. I'm glad me and the men found it."

"A masterstroke."

Handel squinted over his coffee cup. "Speaking of masterstrokes, it would seem Carla Selenzy played her part to perfection. From what I hear, Shapiro and Olsen came to blows over her. All like you said, my Duce."

Courtinio sat back and smiled, tapping his stomach. "It is all as I foretold. Carla has never failed me. She is the best at what she does."

Tarz looked up. "Where is the Selenzy woman now?"

"She is rejoining the Circo Grande camp now, ready for our new season. I believe she is making a few appearances at an old friend's circus in the north first. We will see her for the rollout next month. No doubt she will enjoy her bonus."

Handel looked over the feast before him. It was like a banquet from medieval times. "And what of Klondike? His last show is in six days. Here, in Rome of course."

Now, Courtinio laughed. A soft, queer sound. "And there, my dear Conrad, lies the true beauty of all this. We will attend his last show of the tour. Oh yes. And we will witness first hand the destruction of an empire. I intend to confront Klondike face to face. I want to see the defeat in his eyes. Want him to know that I am his superior. That it was me who killed his tour, his dream. And then he will know, will understand, that Circo Grande is the world's greatest circus. And that he is nothing."

Handel nodded obediently. Then, he sat back, hugging his cup. "You know," he said speculatively. "Klondike has a lot of staff. Performers. That beautiful circus train. All those fancy midway stalls and booths. Not to mention that tent. Trailers, machinery, equipment. All in his name. Not to mention Shapiro, whose name is known everywhere here." He eyed Courtinio like a wisened old wolf hound. "A lot of stock. All right here."

Courtinio caught on immediately. He nodded. "It would be a shame to see it all disappear, off our shores." He clapped his hands. "Excellent, Conrad, excellent. But what if our dear Mr Klondike intends to take everything with him, back on that godforsaken boat to his homeland."

Handel looked across at Tarz, who was fiddling with an oyster. The giant smiled an evil, sinister smile. "We can be very persuasive", he uttered.

Courtinio raised his glass again. "A toast, dear friends. To the death of Klondike's Circus."

They all laughed merrily.

There was laughter elsewhere too.

Some 5,000 miles away, on the east coast of the United States.

The Atlantic City boardwalks were alive with colourful funfairs, markets and confectionary stands, dominating the wooden piers that jutted out into the ocean.

At the far end of one of the central promenades sat a giant pavilion, designed and built with an Arabian Nights theme in mind. An old-fashioned sign atop the main double doors at the entrance read: RIBBECK'S WORLD CIRCUS, EST 1922.

In a spacious first floor office, seated in a throne-like leather chair behind his cavernous desk, an elderly man cackled endlessly, pumping the air above him with his airmailed copy of that morning's Continental Review, which he held as if it was a coveted sports trophy.

Eric Ribbeck was in his early 70s, tall, lean and wiry with leathery, caramel skin and a magnificent pompadour of snow white hair. Dressed in his favourite burgundy smoking jacket, and with a briar wood pipe hanging from his mouth, he looked every inch the tycoon he had become.

Opposite him sat Veronica Hunslett, his executive assistant, a plain-looking woman in dark blouse with tied-back blonde hair, as well as Luca Marconi, his bodyguard and errand boy. Marconi, a known hard case with greased-back ebony hair, wore his usual black leather jacket. Both waited patiently for their employer's unnerving laughter to cease. The large office was like a circus museum, with framed show posters and flyers from yesteryear covering the walls, while old pieces of trapeze rigging sat in a glass display case in the corner.

"Well," Ribbeck was saying, clutching the newspaper, "it looks like our boy Klondike bit off more than he could chew with this European tour nonsense." More cackling. "Have you read this report? By god, they have crucified the double-dealing son of a bitch! Just like I said they would." He placed the copy of the Continental Review gently on the desktop. "Why, that boy's gunna be lucky to get his troupe out of Europe alive. Sounds like a posse of outraged fans are after his blood!"

Veronica carefully took the paper, and scanned the page of the review. "That's as nasty a review as I've ever seen." She looked up at Ribbeck. "It's hard to see where Klondike and co go from here."

Ribbeck chortled yet again, wiping at his cold, emerald green eyes. "I love it," he rasped. "It's about time that glorified camp gopher got his comeuppance. He lived off my name all those years, off of Gino's too. Then, he survived my every attempt to nail him for good, as well as god knows how many other bids to put his circus out of business. He's riled more men up and down the country than J. Edgar Hoover! But now…" he pointed at the newspaper again and grinned wickedly. "Now, it's all over. Now, maybe he understands that if you ride the rails up and down the states, putting me and my people over in a bad light… well, eventually, your luck will run out. Somebody, somewhere, will nail you!"

Veronica glanced up. "You think that's what happened? Another promoter tried to bury him?"

Ribbeck tapped the mouthpiece of his pipe against his teeth, a long-time habit. "Got to be. Those boys out in Europe are very protective of their circuses. Anyone who tries to get in on their action is marked for trouble. They call it… the forbidden gate."

"Cute," Veronica replied dryly. "By the sounds of it, Klondike is in a pretty bad way. Talent missing. Equipment not working. And fans booing."

"Hell," Ribbeck said acidly. "If I knew who was behind it, I'd send them a god damn hog roast on a silver platter."

Marconi, who had watched the whole exchange while idly fiddling with a deck of cards, finally spoke: "So, maybe now, boss, the time is right for you to make your move? To get Shapiro and Olsen to join us."

The old man sat back, as if suddenly pained. "Those two golden boys," he whispered, as if in awe. He looked glassy-eyed at Marconi. "You are right, Luca. Maybe now, there will be a time. I've always said they will never join me…old Kal will never sign them over. But… if they have no god damn choice… if there is no Klondike's Circus! Then, they will come to our show. All the circus barons will want them… but I'll be the highest bidder. Maybe, just maybe, we can finally have them."

Veronica huffed. "They may be keen to jump ship after this tour. All of Klondike's talent may wish to quit."

Ribbeck settled back in his great leather chair, again tapping the pipe on his whitened teeth. "How many stops have they got left on this godforsaken tour?"

"Only one," said Veronica, eyeing him. "In Rome. This Saturday."

Ribbeck laughed mirthlessly. "Well, there ain't gunna be no Colosseum and conquests for that yahoo Klondike. Ha! More like a massacre, but with reporters instead of gladiators."

Marconi leant forward, strangely excited. "What are ya thinking, boss?"

Ribbeck dragged at his pipe, allowing a long cloud of brownish grey smoke to engulf the desk. When he finally answered, his voice was a croak, the sound unnerving.

"I'm thinking I'm gunna enjoy it, boy. These past few years of him getting one over me... well, it's gunna be different this time. If his troupe even makes it back to California, I'm going to enjoy it. Picking over the remains of his outfit, like a vulture feasting on dead flesh."

The cackle returned. Veronica and Marconi simply stared at the old man as he concluded his verse.

"Nothing will make me happier. Nothing."

Dazzlingly beautiful, a picture of sheer elegance, the woman strode quickly down the Park Avenue sidewalk in Upper Manhattan.

She was dressed in a long, Arctic silver fur coat, and clutched a shiny Macy's store bag in each hand.

As she approached the imposing revolving doors of a giant apartment block halfway down the street, an elderly concierge in red and brown uniform and cap practically fell over himself rushing down the few short steps to welcome her.

"Good evening, Miss Cross," he beamed, holding the swinging door still.

She ignored him and rushed inside, catching the elevator to the 19th floor. A short walk down a plush beige carpet brought her to door 1202. Fishing out her key, she stood perfectly still and took a deep breath, exhaling slowly.

Then, she entered.

"Darling, I'm home," Jenny Cross called cheerfully. She strode through a hallway into a huge, plush penthouse suite. There was a massive lounging room full of leather couches, coffee tables and featuring an antique piano in a far corner. Beyond that was a porch way leading out to a sumptuous balcony. A long and narrow kitchen sat to one side, with doors leading to the bedrooms. Everything reeked of opulence.

Jenny nodded once again at the surroundings with sheer satisfaction. She casually dumped the Macy's bags on an oak dining table and removed her coat and gloves, revealing a designer Fifth Avenue dress.

Then, he appeared.

"Darling! You're home!" Lloyd Griffiths. One of the city's leading art dealers. Middle-aged, portly, with a thick shock of salt and pepper hair. Dressed as always in a suited waistcoat and slacks.

"Oh man, I missed you," the older man exclaimed, rushing to her.

They embraced, and he kissed her passionately. She stared at him, transfixed, as if in awe.

"I missed you too, darling. Three days is just too long!"

"The nights were the hardest."

"They were for me too." Jenny looked around sharply. "Whatever have you been up to?"

Griffiths looked at her, confident and smug. "Sold another two Rembrandts yesterday. To the guys from LA. Oh man, they love it. Can't seem to get enough."

"My, my," she said, trying to sound interested. "My baby is just so talented."

He moved away from her to the Macy's bags. "And how about you, Jen? Been busy?"

She walked over to a drinks cabinet and poured herself a tall glass of vodka. The vodka went all the way to the top of the glass. "Frocks for the yachting season. Hats for the racing. Cocktail dresses for all these gala luncheons you have lined up for us. And so many other delights."

Griffiths grinned, his mind racing. "You'll be the belle of the ball."

She smiled demurely. "Of course, darling."

"Was there enough in the expense account? I put plenty away in there for you."

"Yes. But, well, it's practically empty now, of course."

"Not a problem. I'll transfer more in the morning."

She kissed him on the cheek. "You're just too much, Lloyd."

Jenny carried her drink and wandered over to a small side table containing newspapers and magazines from the week. She pored over them absently as Griffiths began twittering away behind her.

"Well, you've got one message babe. A Mr Zane. Said he has some modelling work for you. Down at the waterfront. Asked you to call him back when you return."

Jenny froze all over, almost dropping her glass. Eyes wide, she gulped heavily. "Did he say anything else?" she called, recovering.

"Er, no. Just wants you to call him. How abut that, eh? Modelling! Looks like those fancy portraits we commissioned are bearing fruit, no?"

She didn't face him. The act could not be maintained. "It looks like it."

Moving hastily across the living room, she made for the door. "What do you know," she said quietly. "I forgot to get my smokes. Be back in 10 minutes."

"That's ok, babe," he called as she fled. "I got a couple of packs right here."

She opened the front door. "Not my brand."

Then she was gone.

"Are you out of your god damn mind! Calling me at home! What were you thinking? And how in the hell did you get the number?"

She stood in the callbox, eyes wide in terror, clutching the receiver with trembling hands. It had started raining and Manhattan suddenly looked grey and foreboding.

Finally, the deep voice, with a crisp New York accent, replied.

"Why, Miss Cross, it's almost like you've got something to hide. Such paranoia. I told you. There is nothing to fear. Your secrets are safe with me."

Jenny shuddered convulsively. How could he know? "What secrets?" she blurted down the line. "What do you know, damn you?"

A slow, bloodcurdling laugh flowed into her ear. "Enough."

She stared in shock at the wet street, as endless yellow sunshine cabs cruised by. "How did you get my home number?"

"We both know that is not your home, Miss Cross."

This time, she yelled out loud down the phone. "Why are you doing this, Zane? I hired you! To do a job. Not to spy on me."

"Like I told you that first time, I like to know who I'm in business with. I like to know everything. Also…I need you to understand that I'm not a man to be messed with."

She rolled her eyes, staring back and forth, up and down the street, a woman in a fur coat, helpless in a callbox.

"Alright, alright," she stammered. "What do you want? From the cryptic message you left with Lloyd, I take it this is good news?"

There was a pause. "Oh yes. It's very simple, Miss Cross. We are good to go."

Jenny was visibly stunned. She put a hand on the telephone stand, reeling slightly. "What? Are you serious? You mean… everything?"

"Like I said, we are good to go."

She brushed hair away from her face. "Oh my god, Zane. That is incredible. But… how, what, did you…"

"Relax, Miss Cross," the gruff voice replied tersely. "It's what I do. Remember what we discussed? I had to do a lot of work to make it all possible… test the waters, if you will. But now, I am satisfied. We are all set."

"And so…" she breathed, in a dreamlike voice.

There was a pause. "And so… what exactly?"

Jenny finally smiled. "And so it begins."

CHAPTER 26

The atmosphere within the big top was disconsolate, downhearted and full of sorrow, akin to a memorial service.

Figures were assembled within, still and quiet on the garbage-ridden sawdust, like mourning warriors looking over a battlefield the day after a heavy defeat.

As usual, the talent were all seated in a grandstand, covering the front few rows of one tier.

Before them, on the floor, stood Klondike, with Heavy just behind, arms folded.

A sea of pale, depressed faces seemed to stare across at the circus boss. He sensed no optimism, defiance or passion from his troupe, just despair. It was the morning after a night of horror. There was nothing left to feel, it seemed.

Klondike looked down at Lacey and Plum, sat on the front row on the very end. Then, he held up his cane as if to call for order, though there was clearly no need. The tent was as quiet as a crypt.

"Alright," he said in his rasping tone. "Let's not beat about the bush, people. We've all had nightmares about something like this. Stinking the place out. Well, last night it finally happened. Yes, most of the problems were out of our control but… dammit, I let you all down. Yes, that's right. It was my call and I accept responsibility. That show should never have gone ahead. We were ill-prepared, ill-suited and there were too many components out of place. I… I can see that now."

Klondike removed his hat and ran a hand through his thick, wavy hair. The hand lingered by his face as he massaged his tired eyes, the scars covering his forehead.

The others simply stared. None of the team could recall ever seeing the boss like this, so visibly pained. An eerie silence engulfed the big top. The screams of joy and endless applause so often heard within its confines belonged in another realm right now.

"Y'know, it's hard to understand," Klondike continued at the front, staring at the gathering helplessly. "What exactly has happened to us out here. The events we have fallen victim to. But, in the days before that show last night, it all got out of hand. With the attacks, the issues going on right here, within the camp… hell, everything. It seemed to reach a crescendo. And, well, I guess I just tried to get through it. Like we always do. Adapt, survive… and put our beloved show on for the people. Maybe… maybe if I'd taken a step back, and really thought it out… well, maybe I could have saved us from that disaster."

He realised it was the most uninspiring speech he had ever given, completely out of character. He seemed to crumble on the spot as he stood there before the bleachers.

Lacey finally stood and moved herself alongside him, as she often did during these moments.

"What Kalvin is trying to say is we pushed ahead with the show because of the fans. Because we never, ever let the people down. No matter what."

"Those same fans who booed us and threw their garbage at us!" It was Enqvist, seemingly drunk, shouting down from the fifth row.

"It's alright for you, Tip, you weren't out there being slaughtered," said Rumpy Stiltskin.

"Hardly any of us were out there," cried one of the Range Riders angrily. "Those fans were given half a show. No wonder they were appalled."

Lacey stepped forward, angry herself now. "Surely you can all see this was beyond our control!"

Heavy joined her. "We were nailed, folks. Targeted and taken down by criminals. Now, we did our best. But somebody, somewhere, is determined to cripple us. Jesus Christ, look at what has happened to us out here!"

Shapiro, seated with Penny at the centre of the front row, finally spoke. "What happened to her? Carla? Do we know where she is?"

Klondike looked at him weakly. "Disappeared. Back to her bosses, I imagine." He glanced at Bannion, stood to the side of the stand. "Jack?"

The Englishman shook his head. "I've asked a few contacts about her, sent telegrams. Nothing so far. As she's freelance, it may well be that nobody knows who she is working for."

Shapiro shook his head in disgust. Penny patted his knee. "She did her job, alright," she murmured.

Everyone seemed to mumble incomprehensibly for several moments. Then, Corky spoke from the centre of the gathering.

"I think the big question, Kal, is where do we go from here?"

Klondike took a deep breath at the front. "Rome. We have one more show to honour. Maybe another sell-out. There are people there waiting to see us." He noticed a sea of astonished faces gaping at him.

He continued. "Now, this time there will be no surprises. No attacks. No nonsense. We are all going to be on our watch. And the roustabouts will run security details around the train all day and night. In the meantime, once in Italy, we are going to try our damndest to fix everything. Everything! So, that means curing the horses, fixing the motorbikes, mending the equipment and, in the name of heaven, getting a new sound system. I want the same show format we put on in Berlin... that's the goal, people. Now, we got us six days. Six days to get back to full strength. That... that is the challenge for all of us."

If he had expected cheers and fist pumps, he was sadly mistaken. The gloomy faces all stared back at him. The atmosphere remained sombre. Klondike felt his shoulders sag again.

"I sure appreciate your enthusiasm, Mr Klondike." Everyone turned and stared at the very back of the ensemble, where Duster Williams sat in the top corner, holding his saddle like a gunslinger from days gone by. "And there's nothing I'd like to do more than get back out there and perform, in front of these wonderful people." He placed the saddle on the seat beside him. "Unfortunately, fact of the matter is... these horses are sick. Real sick. Poor Goldie can only stand for a few minutes at a time. I... I just don't know what I can do for her."

He bowed his head, and a fellow Range Rider consoled him with an arm around the shoulders.

"Once again, Duster, I'm real sorry about the horses," Klondike drawled, looking to the back of the group. "Whoever did all this needs to pay for it. I want payback more than anyone. These people have gutted my circus, wrecked my outfit."

Suddenly, a chorus of voices rained down from the grandstand.

"This is ridiculous! How can we perform in these circumstances?" cried one of the Rockin Robins, aghast.

"We're finished Klondike! Why don't you just admit it?" yelled an irate Enqvist.

"I don't think going to Italy now is a good idea," Goliath piped in.

Then, a furious, high-pitched voice broke the erupting discord with finality. "We have to cancel the show! This cannot go on."

Everyone stared at the front row in shock. It was Richie Plum, seemingly cracking as the debate raged wildly on.

Klondike, Heavy and Lacey glared at him, stunned.

"Richie!" Lacey hissed. "I can't believe we're hearing this from you. You… an inspiration to everyone here."

Plum held up a hand. "I know, I know. It seems an extreme reaction but, for Christ's sake, look around you folks. Someone has planted a bug into the guts of this operation and it is eating us apart. Piece by piece. Day by day. And, yes, it has all gotten out of hand."

He wandered to the front, standing between Klondike and Lacey, pleading with them. "Look what we've become. It's like we're dying out here. But no one seems to realise it." He backed down suddenly, looking set to burst into tears. He faced Klondike. "I'm sorry, Kal. I don't mean to say such things. It's just that, well, riding with your circus has given me the happiest days of my life and, well, I can't… I can't…"

"It's alright, Richie," Klondike said softly. "I think we all feel it." He put a hand on the little man's shoulder. Then, with a nod to Heavy, he addressed his people again.

"Listen, folks," he bellowed, "all we can do right now is pack up and head to the next town. Like we always do. Only this time, the next town is Rome, and the final date of our tour. I say let's get over there, set up, and then see where we are at. Take stock. Then, by Thursday, we will have an idea of what we are going to give the good people of Rome. Hell, there's not much else we can do."

Again, the awful silence. He noticed Enqvist, a hip flask in his hand, staring at him incredulously. “So you actually want to go ahead with this?”

Klondike felt drained. “It’s the only option. Now, let’s move.”

The meeting was over. The talent all stood and slowly made their way across the aisles and down the metal stairs of the grandstand. Klondike watched Enqvist and his Daredevils arguing with each other as they left. He caught sight of Olsen and Suzi near the back, both shell-shocked.

The others all left their seats like zombies, stumbling aimlessly.

Klondike simply stood and watched, with Lacey, Heavy and Plum all close by. He studied his troupe as they sloped off, seemingly directionless. The roustabouts all wandered into the tent as the talent all exited. Everybody moved like a machine, without emotion.

“It didn’t use to be like this,” Heavy said quietly as they stood there in the sawdust.

Lacey was watching Klondike, distraught at his defeated demeanour. She slowly slipped her arm through his and tried to guide him gently to the flap.

“Come on, tiger. We can do this. We’ve survived a lot worse.”

Klondike allowed himself to be guided out of the tent. He studied his many performers as they walked, disconsolate, back to the train.

“Never seen a rollout like it,” he wheezed.

Lacey made it her mission to perk him up. “Well, we should keep it as normal as possible. Imagine we are back home, in the States.”

Klondike nodded absently. He looked up at the tent as they left it behind, back at the roustabouts busy dissembling everything inside. Then, he eyed the train, the men loading the midway stalls back into the holding carriages.

He remembered his rallying call from the olden days. He used to roar it out loud from the roof of his train, like a revivalist leading a congregation into the new age. Now, when he said it, the words came out in a tired, haggard voice, more of a whisper than a roar.

"Hell, it's time to blow some trail dust."

"All aboard!"

The mighty roar from the driver was followed by an ear-splitting whistle from the cab as the great tungsten wheels began to roll and the old Imperial lurched into motion.

Finally, after what had felt like an eternity, the circus train was on the move, slowly veering away from the old Parc Giresse rail yard, where so much had transpired over the past week.

Picking up a steady cruising speed as it rolled through industrial areas and the outer suburbs of Geneva, the train was soon back on the main line and on its way to Alpine territory. The snow-capped silver/grey mountains seemed to hover over them, without ever getting any closer.

Gino Shapiro stood staring at the pristine countryside as it rolled past the window of the lounging area of his enormous stateroom.

He idly poured himself a glass of cognac, knocking it back in one.

The great trapeze king looked a sorry sight right now, standing in brown slacks and a white vest, a giant icepack locked in place around his right shoulder thanks to a special leather strap. He poured another shot, frowning as the train passed a nature reserve, where elderly hikers all ambled along in their green alpine hats.

"What, no sarsaparilla?"

He turned and saw Penny wander in, dressed in a robe, her wet hair clinging to her skull.

Shapiro huffed. "I need a real drink. To forget."

Penny slowly walked through the suite, joining him at the window, momentarily gasping at the stunning, luscious scenery. She eyed her trapeze partner.

"There isn't a soul in this company who isn't glad to see the back of Geneva."

"Santamaria," Shapiro breathed. His eyes were dark, withdrawn. Finally, he eyed, her, nodding solemnly. "I owe you an apology, Penny girl."

She shook her head. "It's alright, Gino."

"No. I was sucked in. Taken in. Humiliated. All by that… that strange woman. My god, how she played me. She made a big fool of Gino."

Penny gritted her teeth, angry now. "There are plenty of women like that out there. But, I have to admit, she was good. Too damn good. Like a damn actress, or something." She glanced at Shapiro, noting his lack of venom. "Gino… please tell me you are over her? Yes, she had a hold over you. But now?"

He shook his head. "Si. I am over all of it."

"And Rome? Are you, er, alright to go out there again? To perform?"

"But of course!" He manoeuvred the ice pack on his shoulder. "I remain, as always, the consummate professional."

Penny probed further, rubbing at her wet hair with a white towel. "In Italy… the land of your father?"

Shapiro turned back to the window, as the train barrelled through a rocky canyon. The stone looked a purple colour. "Si, it is true. The Shapiros were once like royalty out there. How proud he would be to know I was finally performing in his homeland. I… I only wish it were under brighter circumstances."

Penny had genuinely begun to care for Gino over the past year. Having started out as a wide-eyed apprentice, constantly brushing off his romantic overtures, she had grown into a loving confidante over time on the road together. However, she had never seen him quite like this.

"Don't worry," she whispered, a hand on his shoulder. "We'll do the old man proud, Gino."

They stood together for some time at the window, admiring the Alpine scenery. It looked cold outside, but the feeling within the stateroom was one of pure warmth.

Four carriages up, towards the train's centre, another angst-ridden meeting was commencing in Klondike's quarters.

His principal lieutenants were all there, gathered around his desk and sprawled on the couch by the coffee table. Lacey, Heavy, Plum and Bannion all looked exasperated, beaten. Klondike had tried to rally everyone, before slumping behind his desk, while Lacey was still somehow clinging to optimistic snatches of hope.

"The fact of the matter is," Heavy was saying, "we need a miracle in Rome. Horses healthy again, bikes all fixed up, sound system, equipment repaired. Everybody singing from the same song sheet. And…" he rolled his eyes. "Fans that actually cheer us."

"Italy," Klondike whispered. "It's a circus country, in every respect. In ordinary circumstances, it would be perfect. And a great homecoming for Gino."

Plum spoke up from the couch, where he was slumped next to Lacey. "I think the big question is… if we can't fix all those problems, what are we going to do? We can't run with that same show again."

"We are working on that, Richie," Lacey replied calmly. She fished out a cigarette, lit up and seemed to sink into the soft sofa. "This show needs more of Gino, we all know that. And he himself wants it. That is a strong foundation."

Heavy piped in. "And Suzi singing opera is another plus. I can't believe she is going ahead with that!"

"The darling girl has been practising since yesterday," Lacey replied.

"Them's all good points," Klondike drawled from the desk. "But as soon as we land in Rome, the number one priority has got to be fixing everything up. I've wired ahead, let Addison's tour man in Rome know what we need. We'll head over to the rep office pronto, and, well, just go from there, I guess."

Bannion, as he often did, stood by the window, watching the countryside roll past. He seemed to enjoy pacing around Klondike's office rather than relaxing within it. Finally, he spoke.

"I must object," he said, almost sadly. He looked at each of his comrades in turn, noting the startled faces. "Listen, that show in Geneva was a travesty. We can all see that now. And the most important element here and now is to never, ever allow anything like that to happen again." He took a breath, sipping his whiskey. "If we go ahead with this show in Rome on Saturday night, we are opening ourselves up for a killer blow." He eyed Klondike squarely. “And one that could have ripples far and wide, even in America.”

A hush descended over the carriage. The only sound for several moments was the clatter of the mighty wheels beneath them.

Klondike sat back in his leather chair, pulling a cigar from his customary green tin. He eyed the Englishman straight back.

“Just what exactly are you saying, Jack?”

Bannion was unrepentant. “We’ve got to call the show off, Kal.”

The others stared at him in shock.

Klondike was impassive, fiddling with the cigar. “You don’t think we can pull it off, Jack?”

“It’s not that, it’s just that… come off it, Kal. We’re teetering on the brink of disaster. This is our careers we are talking about, people.”

“You want to quit?” Klondike suddenly roared, glaring up at him.

Bannion stood there helplessly, uncomfortable in the sudden spotlight. He held out his hands. “Listen, I’m signed up for the whole tour, whatever happens and wherever we end up.”

Klondike lit up his cigar. “Glad to hear it.”

“But I don’t see what good can come of this, Kal. The word will have spread to Italy by Saturday. There may be folks there wanting our blood. We just don’t know what’s waiting for us out there!”

Klondike stood and faced him directly, his lean figure engulfed in a hazy cloud of smoke. “First of all, we’ve got us five days. Five full days to get ready – show-ready. And second, something very important that seems to get forgotten about these days.” He paused for effect. “My word. I gave my word to the people in Rome that Klondike’s Circus will be there, putting on a show, for all the fans. The people there are expecting us, the officials at the show ground are preparing for our arrival. Fans have bought tickets, seen our posters. So, dammit all to hell, we will play there.” He looked around at the others thoughtfully. “You give a man your word, by hell you stick to it. I gave my word six months back. Before any of us knew anything about Europe and what we might find. Well, now, we’re sticking to it.

That's how I operate, Jack. How I will always operate, so help me god."

Bannion looked exasperated, crestfallen. Then, as he looked at Klondike queerly, he seemed to brighten. "Well," he muttered, "who can argue with that?" Everybody laughed slightly. The Englishman moved to the drinks cabinet and refilled his glass. "OK, let's do this. Bloody hell. I'm a long, long way from Dorset."

He held his glass up to Klondike. The circus boss looked about his desk, found his scotch, and clinked glasses. "Attaboy. We're all a long way from home, Jack. But… we're all in this together."

Everyone seemed to mumble in agreement.

Then, Plum spoke up. "You know, there's a lot of doom and gloom around here. But, well, I hold the books, folks, and in many ways this tour has enjoyed some financial successes. The last two shows were sell-outs. If Italy follows suit, we are going to be well in the black for the European tour. And that's despite the low crowds in Paris and Antwerp."

Heavy nodded. "I guess we have all been a little hard on ourselves. It's just that… well, this is so far removed from what we are used to."

Lacey leapt up off the couch, seemingly rejuvenated. "Now, that's more like it, boys. Enthusiasm! You know, there's an old saying in showbusiness circles. Something about going out in style…"

Plum chuckled. "One more show, and then the boat home!"

Klondike sat back behind his desk, cigar clamped in the side of his mouth. "Home…" he mused. "For us, home is the next town. The next stop. The next paying crowd."

They all sat in silence, as the colourful Imperial train chugged across the Great St Bernard Pass, cresting high above luscious valleys of green pasture land.

In less than an hour, they would be in Italy. And a date with destiny.

CHAPTER 27

Park Villa Borghese was a truly sprawling public facility, packed full of miniature forests and historic buildings, which seemed to sit every few hundred yards, like ships in a vast bay.

The beautiful wooded area was barely a mile from the central tourist and business complex of Rome – a world of greenery and tranquility so close to pure metropolis commotion.

The circus train had arrived at Grande Stazione Ferroviaria, in the heart of the city centre and, this time, all the equipment and trailers had to be transported across to the show ground at Borghese.

There, beside some ancient historic battlements and at the head of a giant, seemingly never-ending field of immaculately cut grass, the circus encampment began to take shape.

Within a few hours, the tent was being raised and the shanty town of trailers and midway stalls were up and attended.

To the park dwellers and Rome locals, it was an incredible sight to witness this well-oiled machine of a team of roustabouts construct a circus camp instantly, all around them. Many citizens gathered around the head of the field to watch the operation in full flow. Children happily approached and were rewarded with appearances from the clowns, who handed out posters and balloons.

The arrival and set-up, as usual, went without a hitch. But everyone – staff, performers, roustabouts – knew that this was only the opening act on this make or break final show of the European tour.

Many silently wondered if the circus would somehow find salvation now they had arrived in Italy.

The Addison International trade envoy worked out of an office in Strada Principale, central Rome, barely a mile from the wide-open spaces and greenery of Villa Borghese.

With plenty on their minds, Klondike and Heavy decided to walk across the city and get their bearings enroute to the office.

They had plenty to go through with Addison's man out here, whom they had been informed was an Italian who had lived in America previously.

Klondike scanned his street map of Rome, which was neatly folded into a pocketbook, and offered directions as they left the parkland behind and headed down a side street before arriving in a bustling city square. Traffic was everywhere, the cars all small and box-like, sirens blaring endlessly. Street traders offered them oranges, bottled water and what looked like cans of seafood.

Klondike and Heavy wandered along the bustling streets quietly, both trying to feel enthused. This was quite simply like nothing they had envisioned. Rome. The final date of their triumphant European tour. Instead of a glorious send-off, a season finale, both men felt like they were heading to the wake of an old friend.

As Klondike consulted his small map and gestured, the duo crossed the street and walked idly across a large square, full of coffee shops and outdoor stalls, where postcards and Italian flags were sold.

At Park Borghese, the surrounding buildings and fences had been covered in Klondike's Circus posters. Since leaving the general vicinity of the park, they had seen none.

They both looked up as they saw a giant Italian il Tricolore flag draped from a balcony on one of the square's monolithic skyscrapers.

"Remember our last time in Italy, buddy?" Heavy quipped as they watched the great flag flutter in the light breeze.

"Who could forget," Klondike mused ruefully. "Sat in a tank as we cleared building after building. The ghetto dwellers all cheering as we came out in Naples." He shook his head. "By that time, was getting kinda hard to tell the good guys from the bad. And to know what exactly we were doing out there."

"To think," Heavy whispered as they slowly began to walk again, "all these experiences we've been through, Kal. Two street punks from Hell's Kitchen. The Marines. The war. England, Germany, Italy. Then the circus. Ribbeck's World Circus. Then our circus. And then, after all our successes, we find ourselves back out here. England, Germany, Italy. And this time… this time nobody seems to want us."

Klondike nodded. "No cheering townships. That's for sure."

Heavy shook his head. He changed the subject as they headed down the main drag, out of the square. "You think Addison's man is gunna be able to help us?"

Klondike squinted down the road. "Well, he's the only sucker out here who has any chance. He'll have connections, pals, associates… hell, something. And, besides, he's all we have, Heav. We're alone out here. Again! There's no one. This guy, whoever he is, needs to stop whatever he has planned for the next three days and become our new best friend."

Heavy smiled. "Maybe he will save us. Can you imagine?"

"Our luck is due to change, old buddy."

They walked on, past a run of news stalls and advertising hoardings.

Klondike glanced again at his pocketbook map. "Well, it isn't far now. Looks like it's closer to two miles than one." He thought for a moment. "Say, do you think Addison's man is going to be a-"

He turned and paused, bemused. Heavy had stopped walking and stood five yards back, staring transfixed at the outer wall of one of the news stalls.

Frowning, Klondike waded back over to him. His old friend had a look of exasperation, his eyes wide in shock. "Heavy, what the…"

"Kal!" Heavy exclaimed, his eyes unwavering. "Look! Look at that!"

He pointed. Klondike followed the outstretched finger. It led to an outside wall of the wooden news stall. The construction was like a giant garden shed. Several battered old posters covered the oak. Klondike squinted. The main piece, in the centre of the bunch, was actually a circus poster. It advertised something called Circo Grande, the troupe name headlining the poster in extravagant purple letters.

Klondike looked at Heavy, then back at the poster. "Heavy, are you-"

"No, look, Kal!"

Klondike stared at the poster. There were pictures of clowns, trapeze flyers and the usual performers. It was a standard, traditional circus poster, much like their own. He had seen them a thousand times before. Looking at the pictures of the acts, Klondike studied each figure curiously.

Then, he saw it.

At the top of the poster, towering above the other talent, was a cut-out of a giant man dressed in what looked like spandex, possibly a wrestler's outfit. The grizzly, bear-like figure had wild brown hair, an unkept beard and looked more monster than man.

Klondike actually smiled. He felt an unusual rush of emotions – fear, desire, shock and relief. All hit him at once.

"Tarz!"

Heavy nodded, also smiling. "Damn straight."

Klondike couldn't take his eyes off the picture of the giant. "It's him alright. Only one man in the world looks like that… like a god damn Yosemite wart hog."

Heavy was nodding wildly. "After all this time, looks like we have a break. A clue."

Klondike's heart was beating like a jackhammer. "We've got more than that, dammit." He paced across to the stall's frame, and studied the poster earnestly. Heavy joined him, both examining the small print at the bottom of the poster, which usually contained the featured circus's official details.

"Circo Grande…" Klondike breathed savagely. His blood was pumping again now. He squinted at the writing at the very bottom, the poster's imprint. "OK. There's an address here. 112 Via del Corso. Jesus Christ, Heav! That's off the main square. I saw it back there. It's maybe five blocks away."

Heavy gulped. "What do you suggest?"

Klondike looked at him with a weird glint in his dark eyes. "After all that's happened during this tour, all the disasters. We've had no luck the whole time. Nothing! Well, now…" he gestured at the poster. "Now, the dice have rolled in our favour, pal. Now, we have something. This… this Circo Grande could be the answer. Hell, it all makes sense now. A rival circus company out here. Maybe one of the biggest in Europe. They see us as a threat. Try and buy us out. And then… then try to destroy us! My god! This could be it, Heavy."

Heavy looked at his old friend. "If nothing else, they may have some answers. If that ape Tarz works for them, they must know something. But…but what are we going to do, Kal?"

Klondike looked like a battle-hungry warrior from ancient times, nostrils flaring, eyes wide in fury. "I'll tell you what," he snarled. "We get some answers. Right now!"

"Wow, wow, wow," Heavy blabbered. "What, you want to just storm in there and confront… whoever runs this outfit? Just like that?"

Klondike smiled, feeling like he had claimed a long-overdue break. "Damn right. It's perfect, man. We catch them on the hop. Unaware. No meetings. No corporate get-togethers. We go in, and get some god damn answers. Finally!"

Heavy was concerned now, looking about him. "Kal, this isn't the OK Corral. We can't even speak the language. At least let's go to the camp and get some back-up."

But Klondike was beyond reason, his heart and head set on one thing – what he considered justice for his circus. And an answer to the mystery that had plagued them ever since they crossed the Atlantic.

"Every second counts," he said, glaring at Heavy like a man possessed. "Our show is on Saturday. We've still got to prepare for that. But first… first, we find out just what the hell is going on out here."

With that, he stormed off back towards the main square. Heavy looked pained, but quickly followed.

To what, he had no idea.

112 Via del Corso was actually a monolithic yellowstone tower that seemed to rise to the heavens.

Klondike and Heavy hurried along the street and stopped outside, in awe of the massive construction before them.

At street level, a giant, curved sign hung over an arched, old-fashioned doorway. It read: Courtinio and Co Intrattenimento…

Home to Circo Grande.

Klondike grinned as he read the sign. He was now beyond excited, beyond sanity almost. Revenge consumed him. Heavy was on guard, aware of the dangers. The whole escapade was happening too fast.

They waded inside the huge lobby. The marble-floored enclosure resembled a five-star hotel, with various doors leading out and a large reception desk at the far end, where a young woman in a business suit sat, staring at the newcomers with interest.

The duo marched across the marble to the desk. The woman seemed to back away into her chair.

“We’re here to see the boss of Circo Grande!” Klondike rasped at her.

The woman looked terrified, but regained her composure. “You have an appointment, signor?”

“Nope,” Klondike spat out. “But it’s an emergency. Just tell us what floor he’s on and we’ll do the rest.”

The receptionist baulked, pushing her wheely chair away from the desk towards the wall. “I am sorry, signor. Without an appointment, it is…er, no chance. You understand?”

“Yeah, I understand alright. Listen-“

“Kal!” Heavy had been studying a giant sign next to an elevator, which had headings in red lettering. He pointed towards the top of the list. “Look…”

Klondike joined him by the elevator doors and studied the writing. It was all gibberish to him, but he recognised the words Heavy pointed to. Officio esecutivo, Circo Grande.

Again, Klondike grinned like an alligator eyeing its next meal. “Perfect.” He turned back to the receptionist. “Never mind, lady.”

With that, he studied the sign again, and pressed the elevator’s call button. When it arrived seconds later, both men entered. Heavy pressed the button for floor 26. And up they went. Just like that.

As the elevator doors shut, the exasperated woman at the front desk reached frantically for one of the many telephones before her.

She said one word into the receiver. “Trouble.”

With a gentle “ding”, the lift doors rolled open.

Beyond sat a world of opulence, of wealth and prestige.

Klondike and Heavy peered out from the elevator. The penthouse room was immaculately decorated. Oriental rugs covered the floors, extravagant artwork lined the walls, and a library sat in one corner. What looked like old Renaissance antiques seemed to sit everywhere, porcelain figures and gold ornaments sprouting across the sanctum like everyday decor.

Klondike's wild confidence dipped slightly, but he knew not why. Unperturbed, he walked in angrily with Heavy. They both studied the ornaments and paintings with interest – it was hard not to.

Then, as they eyed the vastness of the huge room, both spotted simultaneously the ornate, mahogany desk in the far corner. It sat beside a large, cavernous open fireplace. Just behind it to the left sat a smaller enclosure, where two doors led outside.

On the desk were books and papers, with a pen and a glass of wine in place. It looked like someone was in the middle of some paperwork. All that was missing was a host.

The two newcomers studied the scene before them, like detectives eyeing a crime scene.

"Kal Klondike and Henry Brown!"

The shrill voice startled them both. It came from beyond the fireplace. They both looked over.

A small, tanned man with thinning brown hair and pointed features stood there, leaning an arm against a bookstand. He wore a white suit, complete with pink cravat, looking like an old-fashioned southern plantation owner. The older man seemed happy, gracious.

Klondike finally spoke. "Right. And you are?"

The man laughed. "Allow me to introduce myself. Carmine Courtinio. Owner and chief operating officer of Circo Grande. The biggest and longest-running circus show in Europe."

Klondike and Heavy glanced knowingly at each other.

"Well, Mr Courtinio, we have a problem," Klondike said slowly. The older man's cheerful manner unnerved him slightly. It wasn't the reaction he had been expecting. At all. Their surprise appearance seemingly had no effect on him.

Courtinio laughed once more. "You do indeed, Mr Klondike." He cleared his throat, and made his way slowly to the desk. "A disastrous European tour. Appalling reviews. Lower gate receipts than expected in Paris and Antwerp. And, unless my sources have failed me, a near riot after your last show in Geneva."

"You're well-informed," Heavy blurted.

"It is in my business to have the finest information, Mr Brown." Courtinio placed a hand in his jacket pocket and seemed to float before them. He was enjoying it.

"Now, listen…" Klondike began.

"I have been expecting you." Courtinio cut him off.

Klondike stared at him. "You what?"

"That's right," the smaller man said gently. He shook his head. "Maybe now you realise you made a grave error crossing over into Europe, my friends. Coming through the forbidden gate. Invading us!" He chuckled. "Look at you! Look at what has happened."

Klondike was, once again, reaching boiling point. "Listen, what the hell do you want with us? And what is your-"

Again, Courtinio cut him off with a shrill exclamation. "I have a way out for you, Klondike."

"You have a what?" Klondike was feeling dizzy.

Courtinio's face twisted into a sneer. Gone was the strangely friendly demeanour, replaced by a sadistic-looking gaze. "You are finished, Klondike. The show in Rome will form your epitaph." He held a hand aloft. "But I, Carmine Courtinio, the greatest circus promoter in the modern world, am going to save you. With this!"

He sprang to his desk and produced a file that seemed to contain several pages of text.

Klondike and Heavy were struggling to process the surreal exchange. Nothing had gone as either expected.

"What the hell is that?" Heavy barked.

"A contract," Courtinio murmured. "Placing I, Carmine Courtinio, as the new owner and manager of Klondike's Circus. You, Kal Klondike, will sign over your 79 per cent controlling interest. To me! And I will take over, merging your troupe with Circo Grande and…" more laughter…. "And then commencing the world's first ever global circus tour. America. Asia. Africa. The Middle East. Nothing will be beyond me. With your stars on my roster, I will have the greatest line-up ever assembled. And with my team managing them, they will be cheered across Europe, not booed!"

Courtinio stood proudly, as if he had just addressed a battalion on the eve of a great conflict. Klondike and Heavy glanced at each other, then glared wildly at the diminutive figure before them. It all felt like a bad dream.

"You're crazy!" Heavy bellowed.

Klondike looked disgusted. "What do you know about my circus?"

Courtinio nodded solemnly. "In the beginning, I thought you were a pitiful operation, my dear Klondike. They told me your troupe is the future. I was not convinced. But now… now I am wondering. I feel you have a lot to offer… to me, to Circo Grande. You, ah, worry me, no? As a competitor. Despite the mess you have gotten into out here."

Klondike's eyes hardened, as he stared at the strange little man hopping excitedly before him. "So, it was you! It was all you. You were the one! The one who targeted us. The negative press. The damn attacks. Turning everyone against us. It was all your doing, Courtinio."

To the shock and dismay of Klondike and Heavy, Courtinio merely stood there grinning. "Of course it was. I was eliminating a threat. And now, I am buying out what is left."

"You're delusional!" Heavy bellowed.

Klondike had heard enough. "Why, you rotten son of a bitch!"

Suddenly, he launched himself towards the Italian.

"Halt!"

Klondike froze at the command, which came from the small enclosure just behind the desk. A figure had emerged from one of the doors, and he was holding a revolver pointed at Klondike's chest.

Conrad Handel. He looked completely out of place holding a gun, with his bouffant hairstyle, reddish tan and stylish peach suit.

Klondike and Heavy felt a wave of anger cascade over them as they watched Handel come across and stand at the desk. The gun was firm in his grip. He was then joined by Tarz, who followed the German from the doorway and stood directly to the side of Handel and Courtinio, arms folded, face impassive.

Courtinio gently placed a hand on Handel's shoulder. Both laughed with glee.

“You see, Conrad,” the Italian was saying. “Our American friends saved us a lot of trouble. They came to us!”

Handel held the revolver in a steady grip, pointed straight at Klondike. “It’s get better and better, my Duce.”

“Indeed, it does, my dear Conrad.”

Klondike glared at the trio before them. Tarz stood smugly, his eyes locked on Heavy.

“You boys have caused a lot of trouble,” Klondike whispered savagely. Suddenly, they were trapped. Of all the turns for the planned showdown to take, he had never expected anything like this. He thought wildly, looking around him. His eyes caught sight of a small porcelain figurine placed upon an iron stand about six feet away. It was roughly the size of the knives he used to throw during his act. If he could somehow grab it and hurl it at Handel…

“And now,” Courtinio purred, interrupting all thoughts, “enough drama. And back to the contract. The ink is wet, my dear Klondike, and, as you can see, you have no choice but to sign. So, without further ado…”

Klondike stared at the gun. “You’re actually gunna shoot us?”

Handel looked across at him coldly. “You have broken into our headquarters. You stormed in. We shoot intruders out here, Klondike. No one will question it. Mr Courtinio is one of the wealthiest men in the city. We are untouchable.”

Klondike just stared at him, beyond dumbstruck. Heavy took a step forward. “You guys really are crazy. What in god’s name are you trying to pull?”

“It’s very simple,” Handel said calmly. “Sign over your operation to Circo Grande. Then leave Europe. Forever!”

Then something unexpected happened.

At that moment, as Klondike and Heavy faced the three madmen before them, there was a sudden movement in the small enclosure directly behind the trio.

A door opened silently, and a figure in a grey trenchcoat emerged slowly on to the carpet.

Klondike felt like his eyes were about to pop out of his head as he recognised the newcomer. A woman with swirling, tussled black hair and high cheekbones, her figure covered by the long coat.

It was Carla Selenzy.

As Klondike and Heavy stared beyond the three men to the shocking appearance of Carla behind them, she immediately made a motion, putting a finger to her lips. Her eyes were wide in fright. She lifted her other hand, and Klondike saw she carried a yard-long golden sceptre, no doubt taken from one of the many displays all around them. She held the ornament high, like a baseball bat.

Klondike returned his gaze to Handel, not letting on someone was behind the trio. He desperately tried to keep his features impassive.

It worked. Courtinio, Handel and Tarz were too fixated on their seemingly victorious act to notice their visitors' eyes enlarging.

Now, Klondike stared directly at Handel, then Courtinio. The silence was surreal. He watched, without changing his expression, as he saw the lithe figure of Carla creep up behind them, inching closer and closer, the sceptre rising.

Klondike realised he needed to stall them for a few seconds. Whatever was going on, it seemed Carla was somehow going to help. His mind was a whirlwind. How was she here? Now? What was happening?

"Alright," he finally stammered. He took a step forward, and slightly to his right, closer to the porcelain figurine on the stand. "You win, boys." He held up his hands, as if in surrender. "There's no way out of this. I can see that now."

He looked up, and couldn't help tensing as Carla stood behind Handel, the sceptre high above the German's head. She had crept up behind them like a wraith.

But Tarz caught Klondike's look, and turned slightly.

Then, it all happened at once.

Tarz let out a muffled roar. But he was too late. With a mighty swing, Carla brought the gleaming gold ornament down, smashing it into Handel's skull. The blow made a sickening, thudding sound. Handel seemed to catapult himself forwards, his head wobbling, as he plunged through the air, sprawling onto the beautiful beige and green rug before them.

Klondike's reactions were instantaneous. At Tarz's shout, he shot across two paces to the stand, ripped off the foot-tall figurine of a medieval lady, and gripped it behind his shoulder.

He took up his old knife-throwing stance, knees bent, left hand forward, right behind his ear, and hurled the figure with alarming velocity. He threw it without even thinking.

The china piece flew though the air and shattered into Tarz's face, slamming into his nose and mouth. The Hungarian giant let out a primal scream as the figurine broke into hundreds of pieces, while he went over backwards like a fallen redwood.

Carla screamed a second after hitting Handel. She backed away, shocked by her actions. The sceptre rolled across the carpeting.

Klondike and Heavy sprang into action. As Handel sprawled in a heap on the floor, Klondike and Courtinio both dived for the dropped revolver as it bounced across the rug towards the desk.

Heavy charged at the fallen Tarz like an enraged bull. He dived at the strongman, who was lying on his back, and sat upon his midriff before unloading two punishing right crosses into Tarz's jaw. The big man was roaring like a wounded rhino, struggling to move away his attacker.

As Klondike leapt for the gun, the surprisingly agile Courtinio rolled onto it half a second before he landed. The Italian led there, the revolver in his hands before him on the floor. From behind, Klondike encircled his arms around him, gripping the smaller man in a mighty bearhug. He squeezed with all his might. Courtinio wailed like a stricken hyena. He couldn't move the gun as Klondike frantically got his hands on the grip. Both men wrestled wildly, two pairs of hands on the gun, which was stuck pointing straight ahead. Courtinio fired the trigger, and a shot rang out, the bullet immersing itself in a volume within the library. Carla screamed at the explosion of the shot. She ran to the doorway, squatting down in horror.

The two men grappling for the gun crashed into the desk, both almost falling. Klondike squeezed again. Courtinio managed to free his right arm, before viciously slamming his elbow into his assailant's mouth.

Klondike's hold faltered. The Italian got a better grip on the revolver, both hands now encircling the handpiece.

Klondike realised the desperation of his situation. Grabbing again at Courtinio's waist from behind, he wrapped his long arms around the smaller man's midriff. Joining his hands in the middle, he got a firm hold. Then, he lifted the Italian into the air, so his feet were two feet off the floor and the head above his own.

Klondike eyed a small armchair directly behind them, and immediately had a plan. Running backwards as he carried Courtinio before him, he fell heavily into the chair.

Then, seated, he used his momentum to throw himself into a backward roll, sending the chair over flying, with both men upon it. The seat went straight over to the floor.

Klondike tucked his head into Courtinio's back and kept him in place. As the chair crashed harshly onto the floor, the back of the Italian's skull thudded heavily onto the polished floorboards. The smaller man let out a deafening wail on impact.

Klondike heard the gun slide across onto a rug. He released his grip as Courtinio led on his back, arms around his head in agony. Klondike snaffled the black revolver in triumph and finally stood up, reviewing the wild scene before him at long last.

Heavy had a semi-conscious Tarz in a headlock, and appeared to be sending the giant to sleep. Handel lay headfirst on the floor, seemingly unconscious. Behind, in the window enclosure, Carla sat there trembling, hiding behind a door, eyes wide in fright as she watched. Her sheer relief was obvious.

And, just before Klondike on the beautiful, vintage rugs led the man called Carmine Courtinio, his head in his hands as he rolled around wildly, spewing Italian expletives.

Klondike quickly regained a semblance of composure. He held the gun steady, pointing it at the fallen Italian.

"Alright," he yelled. His chest was heaving, and his vision was slightly blurred. The whole confrontation had been beyond surreal. He called to Heavy. "Alright, Heav. You can get off him now. I've got him and the old man covered."

With a grunt, Heavy tossed the giant, almost prone form of Tarz to one side. The Hungarian slumped, like a stricken whale. Heavy sat there, panting insanely.

Both men now stared inexplicably at the woman at the back.

Carla Selenzy.

She had emerged from nowhere, and, for some unknown reason, had saved them. From this bizarre nightmare they had unexpectedly walked into.

Carla slowly stood, shaking slightly. She nodded at Klondike, those beautiful ebony eyes showing something other than fear… victory.

Klondike kept the gun on Courtinio, who was on all fours now. But he couldn't help staring at the woman.

"Carla…" he breathed. They both glared at the aftermath of the surprise showdown. "Where did you come from? Why are you here? And why in heaven's name did you help us?"

Heavy rose to a standing position. "And where did you disappear to in the first place?"

She wandered helplessly, giddily across the fallen men towards them. Then, she held her hands theatrically in the air.

"I know," she gushed. "I know how it must seem. I will explain. Si, si, si. I will explain. Everything! You must just wait. One momento please. I beg you!"

She staggered to the desk, and immediately picked up the telephone.

Klondike kept the gun on Courtinio. Heavy was watching everything dumbstruck. "Who are you calling?" he wailed.

She looked at him innocently.

"The police."

Ten minutes later, the whole crazy episode had taken another unexpected turn.

After blabbering excitedly on the phone for several moments, Carla replaced the receiver and seemed to freeze all over.

Klondike and Heavy were still staring at her incredulously. On the floor around them, Handel and Tarz were unconscious. Courtinio was writhing around in agony, holding his head as Klondike deftly kept the gun pointed at him.

"Carla," Klondike breathed, trying to bring her back to life as she stood rigidly by the desk. "What the hell is going on?"

The Italian looked a far cry from the last time they had met. Gone was the confident charisma and bravado, replaced with a childlike innocence, borne of shock and guilt.

“Mister Klondike,” she stammered, quivering as she gazed at him. “It is ok now. All is ok. It is over.”

The two men gaped at her. “What is over?” Heavy cried. Then, without warning, he ran to her, held her arms gently and seemingly tried to prise the answers out of her. “What is going on, Carla? What are you doing here? Who are these people?”

Carla began breathing frantically, almost hyperventilating. Her eyes looked like they might pop out of their sockets.

“Heavy…” Klondike said calmly. The big man let her go and backed off. Carla began to breathe more easily. She ran her hands over her face as she stared in horror at the fallen men around her.

Klondike kept the gun on Courtinio, but looked straight at Carla.

“Miss Selenzy. Can you please explain what has happened here? In your own time…”

She nodded frantically. Another deep breath. Then, finally, she began talking, in a garbled, stop-start fashion.

“These men… they represent Circo Grande. They are the ones! They are the ones who went after you. The bad press stories. The people against you in Europe. The attacks! What happened to your equipment. It was them, all them.”

She looked down sadly at Courtinio, who was struggling to get into a sitting position as he moaned in pain. Klondike looked from him back to Carla.

“And you?”

The Italian woman continued looking down at Courtinio. Slowly, her glare turned from one of fear and pain to an icy stare of pure hatred and venom. It was an ugly look.

“Si,” she whispered tersely. “And me. It was all part of the plan.” She grimaced, and there were tears in her eyes. “For years, he has used me. Exploited me. Worked me over. He set me up… as a whore. A honey woman. A schemer. One to get men to do what I want… but really what he wants. It has been that way for too long.” She sniffed and wiped at her eyes. Then, she lurched towards the stricken Circo Grande boss. “Well, not any more, Duce! It all ends now! No more jobs, no more marks, no more operations. Now…now I strike back. I give you what has been coming to you. You dirty campesino!” She gestured around the suite. “All this wealth, all this grandeur. And look at you! You are nothing but a street rat, living in a world of corruption and filth!"

Klondike and Heavy stared at the riotous scene before them, then at each other. Both shrugged. It was an impossible scenario.

"Listen," Heavy said frantically, "this is all happening too fast. We need answers. Are you… are you helping us, Carla?"

"Si," she whispered, still staring at Courtinio. "I made my decision long ago. I have files, pictures, notes… all to be used against Circo Grande in a federal indictment. And now this."

"Carla!" Courtinio screamed. That had brought him round. "What are you saying?"

"Quiet!" Klondike shouted, aiming the gun at his skull. Then, he turned to Carla again. "Listen. We're about to be arrested, god damn it. And we're far from home, unable to speak the language. We're gunna be worse off than any of you guys."

"No!" she cried. "No, you are saved, Kal Klondike. And I am your saviour."

He stared at her dumbly. "What!"

"Is true," she said excitedly. "I know what to do. I can save your circus, Kal. I can! I have connections, people, everywhere! They will listen to me. All the work your circus needs… I will make it happen. And then on Saturday night, we will be a smash hit. You'll see!"

Klondike's head was spinning. "We? What are you talking about?"

She smiled beautifully at him and opened her mouth to speak.

Then, with a ding, the elevator door flew open and a group of eight uniformed policemen rushed into the suite, followed by a man in a black trenchcoat.

Carla squealed at them in Italian and seemed to direct proceedings. The cops, in their resplendent sky blue uniforms, hastily ushered Klondike and Heavy across to the side of the room. Courtinio was hauled off the floor and moved to a couch. A pair of paramedics arrived seconds later and tended to Tarz and Handel.

Klondike had deftly placed the gun on a tabletop as the police had bundled into the suite, and now stood quietly with Heavy by the bay window, one of the cops watching over them menacingly.

They watched as Carla blabbered wildly at the man in the trenchcoat for several minutes, gesticulating as she spoke. The men seemed in awe of her, possibly due to her celebrity status in the country.

Finally, the trenchcoat separated himself from the group and eyed Klondike. We wandered over slowly, glancing around at the displays dominating the great room.

Klondike looked at him. With thick greying hair, steel-rimmed glasses and a wispy beard, he looked more like a college professor than a cop.

He approached and casually lit a cigarette. "Detective Gianni. Rome Metropol." He said the words softly as he eyed Klondike and Heavy with interest. "You are the American circus people?"

Klondike nodded. "That's right."

Gianni smiled. "Quite a day you gentlemen are having?"

"Tell me about it, detective."

"Miss Selenzy has painted quite a picture. Her tale of what has happened here. It, er, defies belief, no?"

Heavy tried to grin. "You wouldn't believe what went down here, pal."

Gianni got serious. "Well, soon we will know the truth. For sure."

Klondike froze. "And how's that?"

With a queer look, the detective turned and pointed up towards the ceiling in the very far corner of the suite, by the library. Klondike squinted across, following the finger. There appeared to be a small, metallic box in the very far corner, where the walls met at the end of the building.

Gianni turned back to them. "Our dear Mr Courtinio was very advanced with his technology in this, er, private utopia of his. That, my friends, is a security camera. What is called closed circuit television." He smiled wisely. "Miss Carla has told us about what went on here. She mentioned how Mr Handel pulled a gun. Alleges there were threats to kill. As well as mentions of extortion and coercion. Well… all we need to do is examine the footage from this device and then…" he let the sentence hang theatrically.

Klondike felt his lips curling into a smile. "That is incredible," he whispered. "The whole thing was caught on camera."

Gianni dragged on his cigarette. "So it would seem."

Heavy looked past him as a weary Courtinio was questioned by two policemen. Carla seemed to be explaining events to the others.

"So what happens to us?" he blurted.

Gianni looked around idly. "You'll have to come down to the station, of course, until we straighten this thing out. But…" he seemed torn for a moment, choosing his words carefully. "We have been investigating Courtinio and Co Intrattenimento for several months now. Dear Carla is the latest in a long line of potential witnesses to report alleged wrongdoing. But by far the most significant."

Klondike nodded. "She said they have been using her. Making her do bad things."

Gianni turned and stared at Courtinio coldly. "That adds up," he said quietly. He tugged at his beard in thought. "A picture is beginning to take shape of how Courtinio runs his empire. And the whole thing, er… how do you Americans say? It stinks."

Despite the tension and the crazy encounter, Klondike had to smile. "I couldn't have put it better myself, detective."

Gianni also smiled. Then, he pointed to the elevator. "Come. We'll go down to the station now."

They moved towards the shiny champagne-coloured lift doors. As they went inside, Klondike glanced back at Carla, who was now surrounded by a ring of five cops as she again recounted what had happened.

She caught his eye, and smiled, raising her head and offering an angelic look.

As the elevator doors slowly closed, Klondike gave her a nod.

Then, they were gone.

Four long hours later, Klondike and Heavy were finally reunited with the seemingly ubiquitous presence of Carla. This time, though, they were huddled together around a grimy, plastic table in the basement canteen of the Roma Central Police Station.

All three had been questioned incessantly by Gianni and his fellow officers. The same questions seemed to be thrown at them continually. But, as the afternoon wore on, it felt like the police were satisfied with their stories.

Now, Heavy returned to the table in a far corner with three brown plastic cups of weak-looking coffee. Carla had just come down to find them, and now all three slumped in the tacky red vinyl seats.

Klondike could not stop staring at the woman he remembered as the 'Empress of Acrobatics'. She looked almost a different person in her trenchcoat and minus any cosmetics.

"You were saying," he mumbled, grasping the plastic coffee cup as if it held an elixir for eternal life, "something about saving our circus." He glanced at Heavy then back at the trapeze ace. "Care to elaborate?"

Carla looked haunted, but somehow free of some great burden. She sat hunched over the coffee cup. "It is true," she whispered. "I owe you sincerely, Kal Klondike. All of you. What I did was wrong and I am deeply ashamed. But… but maybe now you understand why I had to do it. How I had no choice."

Klondike nodded. "Yeah, we got it. That snake Courtinio built you into a star. A trapeze sensation. An angel of the air. Then, he started setting you tasks, errands, designed to ruin his competition. If you protested, he threatened to ruin you. Run you out of the business." He eyed her sadly. "That's a terrible existence for anyone, Carla. We're sorry you had to carry that burden."

She stared into nothingness, the bitterness bleeding out from her. "He used me. What happened with your circus, it… it has been the same before. Many, many times."

Heavy leant forward. "How did you know we were going to be there? In Courtinio's office? At that exact moment."

She stared at Heavy, her beautiful ebony eyes looking enormous as she looked over innocently. "It was all destiny. I was there to go through the rest of the Circo Grande season, with Handel and the lawyers. Handel was buzzed, to come into the office suite. They said there was trouble." She looked from Klondike back to Heavy. "I knew… I just knew it was you people."

Klondike frowned. "That madman Courtinio. He said he was expecting us. What did that mean?"

She nodded. "He came up with a plan to buy you out. Add your talent, your equipment, everything, to his promotion. He planned to attend the Rome show on Saturday, but I guess in his mind he wondered if you'd find him first."

Heavy shook his head. "Unbelievable."

"Carla, we are indebted to you," Klondike said. "Those guys may have shot us dead for all we know."

"I did what I thought was right," she murmured.

"Thank god," said Heavy.

"Alright," Klondike said tersely. "So how about Rome on Saturday night, Carla? You've got us excited now."

She smiled impishly, finally warming to the surreal happenings.

"I can arrange everything," she said dryly. She opened her hands out wide. "I have heard from Handel of all the misfortune you have suffered. And I have a plan." She cleared her throat, as the two men stared at her in desperation and a touch of bewilderment. "Dr Luciano, a master horse vet from Foggia. He will come and tend to your animals. If he can't cure them, nobody will. DeBrizi, the mechanic, will also come. He will do anything for me. This man, he will fix your motorcycles. No doubt. Zenga Electronics, right here in Roma, can rig you up with a new sound system. Right away. I have credit with them, so is no problem. And then, well, my home circus troupe over in Naples, Superstar Italia, can provide you with anything else you need. It is run by my old partners. They have already agreed to help out, in return for a mention at your show, some advertising at your big top, and a handful of tickets." She smiled widely, and it was the most beautiful look either man had seen in an age. As well as the most welcome.

"Carla…" Klondike breathed. "Is all this for real?"

"But of course," she gushed. "You have my word. It is the least I can do after the horrors I have caused you and your team. My friends, I am deeply ashamed of what I did. You can see now, I had no choice. This, this gesture, is my way of redeeming myself. Let me help you. Let me, us, my people, my contacts here, help you all. And give the Italian people a show to love!"

Heavy roared his delight. "I always liked her," he said to Klondike, laughing.

Klondike chuckled too, despite the crazy day they had endured. "Carla," he barked, "all is forgiven." He squinted at her. "Can you really deliver on all these promises?"

"But of course." She pouted. "That is… if you and your team will have me back? After all that happened."

"Jesus," he spat out, "you've just put together a blueprint for saving our circus. Five hours ago, we were crippled. Without hope. Now, hell, now we're motoring. Yes, we want you back!"

She giggled softly. "Just leave everything to me. I, well, I actually have a few ideas for the show, if you would care to hear them."

"More than anything," Klondike said. He looked around the grimy canteen. Policemen in those bright sky blue uniforms pottered about, casually gazing over. "But first, we just need to get outta this god forsaken place!"

As if on cue, Detective Gianni suddenly emerged from the swinging double doors at the back of the canteen hall.

Stroking his beard, he still looked disinterested and vaguely dishevelled.

Approaching the table, he took a moment to study the three unexpected visitors to his precinct.

"Ok," he finally mumbled. "We are holding Courtinio and his two associates for the full 48 hours, for further questioning. I am drawing up charges now. They mostly involve corporate corruption, which would appear to be his forte."

Gianni looked around idly. He seemed to think out loud. "He is one of the wealthiest men in the city. But he has left behind him a trail of dirt. It would seem no one thought of, er…covering the tracks."

Klondike looked up hopefully, feeling ready to burst. "So… do we have permission to leave, sir? We have much to do."

Gianni nodded. "So I hear." He breathed in deeply, and reached for a cigarette from a packet in his hip pocket. "Si. You may go. You are staying here in Roma until Monday, no? Good. If we need you, we know where to go. Five days is time enough." He held an arm aloft. "Go, my friends. Please go. We will be in touch. Probably with Miss Selenzy here."

They all stood, shook hands warmly with the detective, and exited the canteen.

At the front desk of the precinct, they rushed through the main doorway and out into the busy Rome street.

Klondike put an arm round Carla as they looked for a taxi stand.

“We’ve got you, Carla. Time to get to work. Hell, we’ve got the triumphant last leg of our European tour to plan!”

And that was the truth.

CHAPTER 28

The following 48 hours resembled an otherworldly whirlwind of activity for the men and women of Klondike's Circus.

The sudden and unexpected reversal of fortune that had befallen the troupe seemed to galvanise everyone, both talent and roustabouts.

Where the entire team had been lost and bereft of hope, suddenly the staff seemed emboldened and alive once more. From a deep abyss of despair and agony had arisen a new feeling of hope and salvation.

And the whole euphoria had emerged after that surreal encounter at the Circo Grande headquarters – an episode Klondike had struggled to relay to his people, such was its nature.

Now, as the glorious red and blue big top stood proud at the head of Park Villa Borghese, the circus encampment was once again ablaze with activity as various newcomers, sent to the camp by Carla, all went to work.

A team of veterinary surgeons had been treating the Range Riders' horses at the stable block, feeding them a nutritional supplement and some form of unknown stomach relaxant. Within a day, the horses were trotting around their enclosure again, happy to be healthy.

DeBrizi the master mechanic and his team of elderly workers had the Daredevils' motorbikes up and running again by the Thursday. The auto team had arrived in a giant motorhome that doubled up as a workshop, complete with a full holding of spare parts. A few alterations were made to the bikes, but Enqvist seemed satisfied that his machines were back to full standard.

Zenga Electronic arrived on Thursday morning with a high-tech sound system, to be loaned to the circus for the show. A gleaming amplifier and microphone were delivered to Heavy's trailer, much to the ringmaster's considerable delight.

And then there were the men and women of Superstar Italia, Naples' biggest circus, where Carla had become a star in the 1950s.

On the Empress of Acrobatics's word, the Italian troupe were only too happy to help out with just about everything. Rugged, grizzled Tuscany gypsies were the troupe's trusted roustabout crew, and all threw themselves into their work, assembling the midway, erecting the big top grandstands and generally doing anything Jim McCabe requested.

Superstar Italia's show featured a large ensemble of acrobats and dancers, who were keen to perform under the American big top. When Carla put it to Klondike, he was only too happy to accommodate the local stars, adding them to the Rockin Robins and Hightops showpiece acts as additional razzle dazzle.

As all of the circus's many troubles seemed to rapidly diminish, Carla simply went into overdrive. Having solved a seemingly endless list of problems for Klondike and his staff, she had already switched her attention to the show on Saturday night.

And Klondike and Heavy could see they had another winning hand with the dazzling trapeze queen on board. In essence, one of the biggest stars in Italian circus, willing to help out in whatever way they deemed necessary. A special guest star, to elevate the show to the highest stratosphere possible for the Italian fans. It was a match made in heaven.

But, before any of that, there was one more important episode to be completed. One that would be crucial for the whole upcoming extravaganza.

And it involved Klondike's two circus aces.

"So, you see now, it was all an act. A desperate, cruel, horrifying act. Where, truly, there was no choice. Refuse, and I would be back in the gutter. Bankrupt and ignored by promoters across Europe. So, I had to play that role. I just had to…"

Carla stood solemnly before them, like a children's storyteller, her arms wide and her eyes frightful as she said her piece. She swayed slightly on the sawdust, gazing up at the thousands of empty seats all around in the barren circus tent.

Then, her eyes fell down low, and focused on Shapiro and Olsen, who both sat before her in the front row of the empty grandstand. It felt eerie seeing them both together like this, separated by just two places on the bench seat.

About 18 yards away at the flap, Klondike and Lacey were nervously watching the whole drama unravel. Both held their breath repeatedly.

"I can only hope you will both forgive me for my actions," Carla continued, moving closer to the stand and holding her hands out before her. "Carmine Courtinio corrupted me. Used me as his whore. His instructions were to drive that wedge between you both. In heavens name, look at what happened. Surely you can see I was doing his bidding?" She took a deep breath, and there were tears in her eyes. "Well, I played that role for too long. Before too many men. Oh, so many poor souls. Now, it is over. And I am doing everything in my power to make your circus a success again." The eyes went wide once more, pleading, as she stared at the two men before her. "But, before that, I need to know that you both forgive me. I…I am begging you. Please allow me your forgiveness."

An uncomfortable silence followed. Olsen, in his green jacket and jeans, was stunned into oblivion. He slowly looked across at the man beside him. Shapiro, dressed in his orange tracksuit, sat, arms folded, his face an alarmed smirk.

"You played us real good, eh mamacita?" he whispered angrily. "Your finest performance yet, no? And for what? To cause only destruction." He shook his head. "Why, me and the dollmaker here… we made to kill each other that day on the train. All over you!"

"Which is exactly what the Duce wanted!" she cried in desperation. "Don't you see, Gino? He wanted Klondike's Circus to implode! To fall apart, from within. I was the dynamite, planted inside the walls of the big top."

Shapiro could not stop staring at her. He shook his head again, sadly this time. "Well, you had me, dearheart. You, er, consumed me. Yes, I said it! I'm not scared to admit the truth. Your act, your style, your skills…everything, dammit. Like no dame I ever met." He looked up at her as she hovered over them. "My compliments on your performance."

She shuddered, running a hand over her face. "You're wrong," she blabbered. "My finest performance will be on Saturday night, right here in Roma. Promoting you! Gino Shapiro. Klondike's Circus. With everything I have. I only hope this demonstration of payback will merit your respect and forgiveness."

Shapiro was torn. He ran a hand through his oily, black hair, seemingly in despair. "Well," he finally cried. "It is a start."

Carla seemed to lighten up at that. She turned eagerly to the younger man on the bleacher. "And you, dear Roddy? Please say you forgive me."

Olsen looked like a confused, lovestruck teenager, hands in his pockets as he gawked at the beautiful Italian. "Well, I , er, I don't know what to think anymore. This all feels like some bizarre dream."

Carla nodded. "For me, a nightmare."

Olsen looked lost. "My god, how I fell for you. I was under your spell, Carla. For real. It was crazy, looking back. And all so fast." He shook his head as he studied her. "And now, look at you. All this. The help, the innocence, the whole story about what happened to you. Now, you… you just seem so… so different. It's like it's not really you."

She nodded, quivering. "Attacking the Circo Grande bosses like that… striking back. It was a life-changing moment. It took everything inside me to take action. To betray the Duce. And side with Klondike. Side with you all."

Everyone was silent. At the flap, Klondike and Lacey watched, dumbstruck. Carla had simply transformed. The act had been dropped, and they were now glimpsing the real woman behind the mask, worn for so long.

With a deep sigh, Carla unexpectedly waltzed toward the grandstand and hopped over the front gate. Then, as if she owned the place, she slumped into the bench seat, tucking herself neatly between Shapiro and Olsen.

Klondike baulked. It was quite a sight.

"Alright boys," Carla said softly. "Judge me, my actions, after Saturday night, ok? We have a truly inspiring show planned. I am here to help make it work. And give your tour a grand finale. See what you think of my plans, and we will go from there, no?"

Olsen nodded thoughtfully, while Shapiro scowled. "As long as this isn't another act of yours, sweetheart."

She smiled, seemingly happier now. "I will be elevating all of us, Gino. After all…" a mischievous glint filled her eyes. "I'll be performing with the most esteemed partner. My favourite. The debonair king of the air."

Despite his anger, Shapiro could not help but smile. "You're still playing me! Even now."

She laughed. "No, this time it is all for real."

He shocked everyone by addressing Olsen. "What do you think, dollmaker? Do we let the Empress back into the kingdom?"

Olsen was taken aback at being addressed so warmly by Gino. He smiled at the woman between them. "Sure. Carla, from what you've told us, it sounds like you've been to hell and back. I'm not going to stand in the way of this, er, redemption, as you call it." He sniggered. "Gino's right. He and I did try to kill each other… all over you." He looked at the other two. "And now, here we all are, laughing about our next show. All together, like one big happy family."

Shapiro smirked. "Well, I'll sure as hell take this compared to the madness of Geneva." He eyed Carla in a mystical fashion. "After everything that has happened on this tour… hell, this latest drama seems, ah, somehow right." He finally smiled. "Let's see what you've got, Carla."

They all grinned. With that, Carla placed a hand on each man's arm, on either side of her.

As she began speaking again in a giddy tone, at the flap Klondike and Lacey stared at the scene with wild, bemused eyes.

Lacey softly linked her arm around his and gently tugged him out of the tent, away from the sudden, joyous reunion.

They walked slowly across a gravelled pathway, slipping away from the big top and heading for the trailers at the circus encampment.

"Well," Lacey whispered as they strode, "that went better than just about anybody on earth could have predicted."

"Damn straight." Klondike could not help glancing back at the tent entrance. "What in the hell is going on around here? First, that crazy dame saves us from a gunman. Then this! The two men who fought over her, almost to the death, now buddies with her… holding hands with her?"

Lacey nodded slowly. "The stars finally aligned."

"What's that?"

She smiled demurely. "Fate has played a huge role in our tour, Kal baby. We've had too much bad luck out here. Ever since London. And now... now our luck has changed. Finally, everything has fallen in our favour."

"Like the Braves in the '57 World Series..."

She stared at him blankly. "Right. As you and the boys would say, the dice have rolled in our favour."

He nodded. "And it's about god damn time."

Lacey looked over his bruised, scarred face, concern clouding her beautiful looks. "Jesus, Kal. How many times have you been hit on this tour?"

"Too damn many," he growled. "It felt good to knock that overgrown punk Tarz out, I can tell ya."

She shuddered slightly. "And you're convinced Carla is now a confederate of ours? A friend?"

He grunted. "If you had been there, at the Circo Grande offices, you would be convinced too, Lacey. It was unnerving, what played out up there."

"I can only imagine."

Klondike thought for a moment as they entered a small enclosure where several rows of trailers stood dormant in the afternoon sunshine.

"Y'know, Carla has some radical ideas for the show. And, despite all this god foresaken trouble we've had out here, now the focus has to be on the circus. Saturday night. That's all that matters, Lacey. The show."

She smiled wisely, having heard the words many times before. "Indeed, my dear tiger. Showtime is under 48 hours away. And things are really taking shape."

They both studied the Italian roustabouts from Superstar Italia, who seemed to be everywhere, carrying props and service equipment as they scurried around the midway.

"Just look at all this," Klondike mused. "We've been transformed. Revived. Brought back from the dead. And, dammit all, it's all thanks to Carla Selenzy... a woman we thought was our worst enemy. I can't believe it's real."

Lacey smiled smugly. "The stars. It's all in the stars."

Klondike gazed around mesmerically, a dreamlike expression dominating his rugged features. He seemed almost hypnotised.

Remembering an old line uttered by Corky and repeated by others within his troupe down the years, he spoke in a fascinated whisper.

"That's just it, Lacey."

She looked at him. "What's that?"

He smiled, gazing at the sky. "We are all stars. But together, we are the heavens."

Duster Williams held the reins with all his might as Goldie raced around the temporary practice enclosure set up by the stable block.

The amber palomino looked unrecognisable from the start of the week, when she had been weak, uninterested and barely able to move.

Now, the famous 16-hands high beauty galloped like a wild mustang, soaring round the corral in great circles as a crowd of roustabouts and cowboys stood watching in awe.

Williams let out several "yee-haws" out of pure relief and delight as he rode his beloved mount in the afternoon sunshine. Often during those grim few days since Geneva, he had wondered if he would ever feel this almighty sensation again.

But now, such notions had been vanquished as Goldie galloped faster than ever. It was as if the horse had found a new lease of life, as if the great beast knew herself someone had tried to nullify her powers. This was her way of proving her enemies wrong, it seemed.

Gently digging his silver spurs into her hide, Williams expertly slowed the horse down. Goldie downstaged through the gears, finally entering a trot. At Williams' command, she then performed her signature hind leg salute, holding her weight and that of her rider on her back legs for a full 20 seconds as Duster gleefully waved his stetson at the assembled camp crowd.

As Goldie landed again, the veteran cowboy slowly removed his legs from the stirrups, placed both hands on the leather horn before him and slowly stood up on the saddle. Goldie remained still as a statue. Williams smiled, checking if his mount still remembered their stage moves. She remembered, alright.

Williams stood tall upon the horse's back, stretched his arms high and punched the air. Then, balancing easily on the worn leather saddle, he vaulted into the air, hugged his knees into his chest and deftly landed in the soft gravel next to Goldie.

The assembled spectators clapped enthusiastically, before going back to their duties.

Williams lovingly patted his mount's neck, before grasping the reins and gently leading Goldie back to the portable stable block next to the corral.

"I'll be damned," he muttered as a Range Rider cowboy opened up one of the holdings for him. "The old girl is as good as new. I still can't believe it!"

The cowboy grinned. "That's the craziest transformation I ever saw. In anything, man or beast. Two days ago, old Goldie was sick as a yard dog. Like the rest of our hosses."

Williams looked at the animals in the stable holdings. All the horses were neighing and bobbing their heads. "What the hell is going on Red? It's like these mounts have been given some kind of wonder drug."

The cowboy, Red, looked mystified. "That doc…" he said slowly. "Something about that guy. What he was doing with the hosses. Ain't never seen nothing like it. Me and the boys been around mustangs and fillies our whole lives, Duster. And we ain't seen nothing similar. Hell, the only reason we let that guy treat em was because we was desperate. Weren't nothing else left to cling to. Just raw hope."

Williams nodded, intrigued. "I've heard about these kinds of people before. The Cheyenne used to have them in their villages in the old days. Horse healers. I just never expected to find one out here, in Italy of all places!"

Red chuckled as he wandered away into the stable workshop.

Williams kept patting Goldie, then looked up as a sudden roar of exhaust interrupted his thoughts.

Tip Enqvist was riding one of his motorbikes across a pathway towards the corral enclosure. The machine looked like it had just come off the production line with its gleamy new body parts.

And Enqvist looked equally reborn, clean shaven and with his whitish blond hair slicked back. He wore clean grey coveralls.

Williams smiled at the stunt rider. "I was just saying how Goldie and the other mounts are healthy and full of beans again." He eyed the bike under Enqvist. "Same could be said of your sickles, Tip."

Enqvist rolled his motor to a stop before the stables, turning in the saddle. "You said it, man." He turned off the ignition and looked down at the handlebars with satisfaction. "Me and my boys have completed a full test run. Looks like we're back in business." He patted the engine. "Kal was right, that mechanic from… wherever the hell he's from, he fixed our rides up real good. In no time at all. They know bikes, these Italian boys, I'll give em that."

Williams left Goldie in the holding and leant over the fence surrounding the practice ring. "It was all thanks to that woman, they say. The flyer. The one from Berlin. Who caused all that trouble. Seems like she realised she owed us one. And, boy, did she turn up with the trump cards."

Enqvist nodded vaguely. "A curious case, that Italian broad. A brash, ego-driven starlet, full of bravado and sexuality. But yet fragile and innocent underneath. And now our saviour, it would seem."

"From what I've heard," Williams mused, "a lamb in wolf's clothing."

Enqvist sniggered, removing a large hip flask from his pocket. He took a long pull. Then, with a curious gaze, he offered it across.

Williams looked away, shaking his head.

"After everything we've all been through out here," Enqvist began, "the highs, the lows, the crazy crowds… still, you resist the drink, eh? Still no urges, no thirst?"

The old cowboy looked around the corral wistfully. "I've realised I don't need a drink to feel alive. Not anymore. No, being out here, on the road again, performing in a big top… hell, that's all I needed. All my heart desired, to make me whole again. I… I can really see that now."

Enqvist grunted, taking another slow pull. "It won't last forever, man. That feeling."

Williams finally faced him, staring mesmerically. "It doesn't have to, Tip. Because, come Saturday night, out here in this wonderful country… we'll be the kings of the circus once again. I know it. I can feel it. Hell, it's been a rough old tour, but we're going to end it with a blockbuster. You'll see."

Enqvist shrugged. "Well, having Miss Carla on board is only going to help. She's a megastar out here."

Williams just kept on smiling. "She's brought along some trump cards. But she… she will be our ace."

That night, Klondike treated his inner circle to an extravagant dinner at Perla d'Oro, one of central Rome's most exclusive eateries.

Located at the heart of the Centrale district, the restaurant was a grand, traditional spot, complete with classic red and white tablecloths, dark oak tables and tiled floors. An open kitchen sat at the far end of the seating area, aside what looked like a miniature wine emporium.

Klondike, Heavy, Lacey, Plum and Bannion were led to a large, round table in a far corner, where they were instantly served ornate baskets of freshly baked breads and jars of olive oil, along with two giant jugs of a deep burgundy Lambrusco.

Lacey insisted they all stick with the restaurant's renowned "set menu", and ordered everything in modest Italian, to the welcome surprise of the others.

Soon, everyone settled down, sampled the wine and sour breads, and soaked up the pleasant, warming atmosphere that settled over their table. Each individual present could almost taste the relief.

After jokes were cracked, assurances made and another retelling of the story of Klondike and Heavy's adventure at the Circo Grande building was complete, the group slowly got around to business.

"OK folks," Klondike uttered, sipping his wine. "So, there is no getting away from this. Saturday's show is going to be like nothing we have put on. Anywhere. Ever."

Heavy chuckled, as he had for much of the past two days. "After what happened in Geneva, I'm glad to be relieved of announcing duties."

Plum glanced from Heavy to Klondike. "So, Carla is going to be a ringmaster extraordinaire. That is now official?"

"Absolutely," Klondike said.

"It is all so completely fantastic," Lacey gushed. Dazzingly dressed in a pink and black cocktail dress, lightly covered in a feathered scarf, she looked like a guest at a movie awards night. "It's beautiful. Here, within our circus, we have the biggest star in all of Italy. Known to all the fans, everyone. Beloved by our audience." She paused for effect as the others gaped at her. "Carla will be the face of our show on Saturday night. Ringmaster, or host, as we put it. The fans will love it."

Heavy smirked. "Yeah, just don't give her a megaphone to announce with. I don't ever want to see one of those things again, let alone hold one."

They all laughed softly. Bannion ripped a piece of sourdough bread off a mound in the basket closest to him. "You said something about new ideas, Kal."

Klondike nodded, his eyes alive and fiery. "That's right. Showstoppers. The kind we like. We've discussed this thoroughly with Carla – the expectations of the audience, the trends, what sort of things go down well in Italy. She recommended a few tweaks. I then had a few ideas on how to… elaborate."

Plum looked up quizzically. "What kind of tweaks?"

Lacey took over, as she often did. "The Superstar Italia's sublime group of dancers and acrobats will support the Robins and the Hightops for the opening acts. They are truly spectacular, and beloved out here. Then, it will be a case of our usual acts in their standard spots. Until, that is, we get to Gino's gig at the end."

Bannion nodded. "A repeat of Berlin? Get Carla doing her thing with Gino? Sounds like a winner."

Klondike leant forward eagerly. "Carla told us how Italian circuses tend to have a show-stopping finale, something truly spectacular, involving the top stars, right at the end. A surprise, a celebration, something unexpected."

Heavy and Lacey both had knowing looks. Plum and Bannion remained puzzled. "So, the Cadillacs and the parade?" Plum prodded. "The song. The grand finale."

"That will follow," Lacey murmured in a tantalising tone. "But, first, we are working on something else."

Plum gaped at them. "What? What is it?"

Klondike chuckled. "The funny thing is, Richie, you've seen it before. But long ago. Back in '58. When we first met, actually. You and Lacey were patrolling the midway with me, right before the first show of the season. Your very first show with us, in fact, Richie. After you and Lacey had joined me from Addison's office. That was back when I still didn't quite trust the pair of yous." He grinned at them both.

Plum looked puzzled. "All I remember is the foul smell. Horse manure mixed with cotton candy, with a hint of fried hot dog onion."

Klondike grinned. "Well, we all saw something special that night, before the show even began. I'd forgotten all about it until last night. I was trying to think of a special grand finale for Rome. And then… then the memory hit me, and an idea came to me. I asked Lacey and Heavy here what they thought."

Lacey smiled beautifully, like an enchantress. "It is all so fabulous."

Plum stared dumbfounded. Bannion spoke up. "Would you care to enlighten me and Richie?"

"You know what," Klondike drawled, holding his wine glass aloft. "It might work better as a surprise." He laughed again. "I want to see your face, Richie."

Plum and the Englishman both shrugged as everyone chuckled lightly.

"OK. And then Suzi will sing this opera?" Plum asked, moving on.

"Oh yes," Lacey said quickly. "Carla has got us the recording for our new sound system. The song is so moving, there will be tears in the audience."

Heavy chewed on a breadstick. "It will sure seem weird not closing out with Can You Feel The Magic Tonight."

Bannion nodded. "What is this opera called?"

Lacey gazed at them all mesmerically. Then, in a typical theatrical gesture, she raised her arms aloft.

"The song is called, Palcoscenico più Grandioso di tutti." She looked them all over with her entrancing violet eyes, building suspense. "The grandest stage of all."

The others all cheered together as one.

Then, as if on cue, a pair of waiters appeared carrying great plates of steaming hot linguini marinara.

Lacey held her arms out once more. "Buon Appetito."

"Billions of barrels of beautiful, bubbly beer were brought to the bar by the boy in blue pyjamas…"

Roddy Olsen said the words aloud. But his lips did not move. As he studied his jawline and mouth in his dresser mirror, his lips finally transformed into a thin smile of satisfaction.

"Perfect," Suzi called from the couch in the centre of the trailer. She was looking at him while flicking through a magazine, her legs tucked up against her frame.

Olsen nodded, looking at her in the mirror. "Good to see I haven't lost my touch after all that happened."

Suzi studied him. "After…after the drinking…"

"After everything. All that madness back there in Switzerland."

She put the magazine on a coffee table and hugged her legs. "I'm glad we've just put all that behind us."

Olsen finally stood, moving away from the dresser. The trailer looked clean and free of clutter, with a table and wooden chairs beyond the couch and the standard kitchenette at the rear. He felt reborn and rejuvenated, and his neat living quarters seemed to illustrate his new-found sense of normality.

"I let you down, Suzi," he said quietly. "You, Kal, Lacey, the fans… hell, everyone. I know that." He looked her over, moved as always by her sweet, innocent youthfulness. "I can't thank you enough for standing by me, supporting me. With your time, your care… just being here."

Suzi stood slowly and approached him in the narrow confines. "We support each other, Roddy. I look up to you. I'll always care about you." They looked at each other awkwardly. Smiling thinly, she tried to change the subject.

"With what you are attempting tomorrow night, in front of all those people, you need all the support you can get, buster!"

They both laughed. "And you," Olsen whispered, gazing into her deep grey eyes. "Singing opera. In opera land? Now, if you ask me, that takes real guts."

She waved a hand playfully through the air.

The joviality was suddenly interrupted by a sharp rap at the trailer door. Olsen looked at her cautiously. It was way past 10pm.

He slowly wandered across to the doorway, and opened up. He involuntarily stepped back in alarm at the sight of his visitor.

"Well, well, this all looks very nice and cosy, kids," said Gino Shapiro, casually leaning against the doorframe. He was dressed in a fluffy, white cardigan over his orange tracksuit.

"Gino!" Olsen said in alarm. "What are you doing here? And at this late hour."

"Relax, dollmaker." He appraised Suzi, who stood behind Olsen, as if on edge. "Darling girl, a pleasure."

"What do you want?" Suzi snapped.

Shapiro looked wounded. "Just checking in, you might say…" He eyed Olsen as if gazing upon a sacred idol. "On our golden goose."

Olsen rolled his eyes. "Here you go again, Gino," he muttered. "All the insults, the humiliation, the anger. Then, every once in a while, when it suits you, this! Adulation. Praise. Friendship." He shook his head, studying the trapeze artist. "When will it end? Will it ever end?"

Shapiro remained perched in the doorway, the light of a full moon illuminating the dark night outside, shining upon the rows of trailers and the midway beyond. He nodded, as if in understanding.

"That's not what happens. I respect you enormously, Olsen. You know that. Out there, under the big top, we are team-mates, yes, but we are rivals. For top billing. Is the same in every circus outfit in the world, my friend. We are rivals, yet we are team-mates."

Suzi had already had enough, folding her arms angrily. "Is there a point to any of this, Gino?"

"Si, always," he mused, still studying Olsen with majestic eyes. They seemed to sparkle. "Tomorrow, we roll, amigo. Together. Way up top. Now, I just wanted to look into your eyes. Real close, like this. With no bosses around. I wanted to see your eyes, Olsen." He leaned into the trailer, his gaze transfixed on the younger man. "I want to know… are you ready?"

Olsen turned away, away from the deep dark eyes bulging at the sockets. "Jesus, Gino. Back there in Geneva, you tried to kill me. You went after my voice box, man." He spun around, now glaring at the man at the door. "If Kal hadn't turned up when he did, we… we might have put each other out of action, permanently!" He shook his head in despair. "And now… now you act like we're friends again. After all that."

Shapiro nodded vaguely. "Come on, Olsen. It was the woman. Carla. She orchestrated all that back there. We both fell for her, went under her spell. That's right, I fell for her big time."

Suzi seemed to explode. "But don't you see how insane all this is? Carla is the one who has got you two together now. As partners. Performing this crazy stunt tomorrow, for a show she thinks is all hers. You're still under her spell! You just can't see it."

"No," Shapiro barked, "this is different. Carla has come up with a plan to save our show." He turned and waved across the circus encampment beyond. "And just look at what has happened out there already. We were on our knees when we arrived in Roma. Now, we are ready to conquer, like we used to back home. And it is all thanks to her."

Dizzying notions swirled through Olsen's mind. Several times over the past three years, Shapiro had approached him like this, offering praise and respect. Even a partnership. The surreal exchanges just made their peculiar relationship all the more bizarre.

He rested against his dresser. "I've said it before, Gino," he whispered. "If we could just get along, together, as one… well, the circus would benefit more than any of us could guess. Our craft would improve. The troupe too. Everything would just be better."

Shapiro folded his arms, gazing out at the moon beyond. He seemed deep in thought, rubbing at his chin.

Suzi and Olsen gaped at him, waiting for what was beginning to feel like a definitive address.

"You know," Shapiro mused, "I am wondering if you are right. Maybe… maybe now you are. And now, after all this time, I can see it."

Stunned, the other two stared with wild, unconscious expressions.

Olsen gasped. "What changed your mind?"

Shapiro nodded wisely again, the charismatic smile returning.

"Your eyes."

Then, he turned and disappeared into the night.

CHAPTER 29

The night of the big show finally arrived on a beautiful, warm May evening. And with it came an almighty assemblage of excited patrons.

Young and old, rich and poor, people from all cosmopolitan demographs. All flocked to the bright illuminations and colourful attractions of the circus midway now dominating the northern end of Park Villa Borghese.

The historic parkland was awash with excited fans, all jostling to get their tickets stamped and enter the world of fun. Many waved the now customary miniature Stars and Stripes flags.

The show was a sell-out, as had been widely expected. And the midway was packed two hours before showtime, with the Rome citizens, and others who had travelled from further afield, all clamouring to play the games, buy the treats and watch the circus clowns performing tricks across the entranceway.

Everyone seemed to gaze up at the monolithic big top as they entered the grounds, dazzled by its bright colours, impressed by its sheer immensity.

Posters of Carla Selenzy were draped across the booths and hoardings of the midway, along with the circus's regular pictures of Gino, Roddy, Corky and The Daredevils.

The trade was astonishing, as fans eagerly passed over their hard-earned lira to get their hands on cotton candy, hot dogs, popcorn, sodas, programmes, posters and signed pictures.

All in all, an electric atmosphere seemed to grip the circus grounds as the paying public spilled in.

Klondike and Lacey watched the spectacle from a fence that separated the staff trailers from the midway stalls.

The gruff circus boss, with the obligatory unlit cigar wedged in the side of his mouth, stared in awe at the crowds in the early evening sunshine. Lacey, wearing a light pink shawl over her summery dress, watched earnestly, trying to somehow calculate the midway take.

"I'll be damned," Klondike was muttering, "it's like old times out here."

Lacey giggled softly. "We better get Richie to check out the confectionary and merchandise stands. Look at those queues! The trade must be enormous."

Klondike watched idly as a small group of men in business suits, each carrying a stick of cotton candy, all gathered around a giant poster of Carla Selenzy stuck to a bollard, pointing up at her in something like enchantment.

"That crazy, mixed-up broad," he said, dumbstruck. "It's her, all her. She is responsible for all this. This turnout. These people."

"Circus royalty, baby," Lacey mused, rubbing his arm playfully. "They all love their Carla, as she might say."

Klondike thought it all over as he watched the giant queue of excited spectators pouring through the entrance gate. "Do you really think…" he whispered, "that, somehow, tonight, we will be saved? That this whole tour, all that we've been through in Europe, will be worth it, just for tonight?"

She looked at him, and they stared into each others' eyes. She spoke very quietly, yet still sounded emphatic.

"Well, we'll find out soon enough. After all, it's nearly showtime."

"Senors and senoritas…"

The excited hubbub of the big top audience was suddenly nullified by the loud exclamation, quickly followed by the shrill sound of trumpets playing a military march over the PA system.

A hush slowly descended across the thousands of fans that had filled the big top arena.

As the loud horn music blared out, every set of eyes in the grandstands stared towards the circus flap, the small enclosure wedged between two blocks of bleachers.

And there she was. Looking as majestic as a harlequin and as sacred as an angel, Italy's circus sweetheart emerged from the back and strode nonchalantly on to the sawdust.

Carla Selenzy looked every inch the superstar she was, wearing a dazzling, jewel-encrusted leotard in the tricolour green, white and red of the Italian flag. As was befitting her role as ringmaster, she wore a snug scarlet jacket over the top half of the outfit.

Endlessly blowing kisses to the cheering patrons, she finally made it to the centre of the arena, and the microphone stand.

"Good evening Roma!" she screeched into the mic, waving in a circle, as if to everyone present. "And welcome to Klondike's Circus, America's favourite entertainment extravaganza. And, tonight, for one night only, the greatest show in the United States is here, in Italia, for you to enjoy."

She paused as cheers and applause broke out across the big top.

Continuing, she cried into the mic: "Tonight, my fellow Italians, we are going to change the world! And make history. With the greatest circus performance ever seen in our nation. So sit back, prepare to be amazed, and enjoy the wonders and delights of America's Klondike's Circus. And so, Roma, are you ready?"

The audience seemed to roar as one. It felt like the opening whistle of a big city soccer match had just sounded, the supporters unleashing their wildest cheers.

"Alright then," Carla screeched. "It's showtime. Let's go!"

With that, she whipped off her jacket, the crowd whooping at the sight of her patriotic leotard. Then, sprinting towards the exit, Carla launched herself into a run of cartwheels, executing them with rapid velocity. After half a dozen, she expertly arched her body vertically and turned the cartwheels into back flip somersaults, flying head over heels again and again as she flew in a blur of red, green and white towards the flap.

At the same time that Carla had begun her cartwheels, the Hightops team of acrobats, all decked out in gold attire, began doing the same thing, but travelling towards the arena's centre. From high in the stands, the effect was dazzling, as a team of 12 gold flyers bled across the floor, while a multi-coloured exocet cut threw their centre.

The dazzling array of flips and flying bodies was mind-blowing. Then, the Hightops all came to a halt in the middle, before throwing themselves into a mass hybrid of gymnastics manoeuvres.

Almost immediately, they were joined by a team of 15 dancers decked out in sky blue and white lycra. The Superstar Italia crew.

As jazzy pop music blared out on the tannoy, the Naples crew performed an intriguing blend of dance moves and gymnastics.

One woman walked out with a girl stood upon her shoulders. Another pair of females raced onto the sawdust, taking it in turns to leapfrog over each other. One man walked out on his hands.

The two teams performed an incredible range of routines, and were soon joined by the Klondike's Circus clowns, who mischievously weaved in and out of the ensemble, trying unsuccessfully to copy the athletic moves. Several of the clowns mixed with the clapping fans, walking into the aisles of the grandstands to perform hand magic tricks.

At the flap, Klondike watched with interest, trying to phase out the deafening cheers and applause all around. He was attempting to understand the Italian team's routines.

As always, Heavy and Lacey were perched just behind him at the front of the enclosure, practically on his shoulders, it seemed.

"Whatya think?" Klondike drawled, almost to himself.

Lacey spoke, watching with her arms folded. "It's interesting. This set-up is almost the same as what we pulled in Geneva. Only this time… this time it seems choreographed." She watched as the Hightops performed their human tower set, while the figures in sky blue all did the splits and pointed up at the rapidly assembling line of bodies. "These Superstar Italia guys rehearsed a lot with the Hightops. But they have done it to put the spotlight on our guys. Everything is tailored to make the Hightops look good, to put them over."

Heavy nodded. "Yeah, they're like some kind of super-skilled support act."

The centre of the arena was a mass of wild, flying bodies as the Hightops transformed themselves to create their celebrated human dome. Incredibly, the Italian dancers all continued their routines beneath them – inside the dome!

Klondike smiled widely, glancing briefly up at the cheering fans all around. "We're back!"

The spectacular opening routine set the tone for an evening unlike any other.

As the dancers, acrobats and clowns all slowly receded from the stage, a dramatic orchestral tune sounded across the big top as the Rocking Robins and Flying Batistas arrived and performed their own incredible routines.

Again, the Superstar Italia dancers seamlessly moved rhythmically in the background, seemingly encouraging the crowd to cheer the performers in the centre.

Next up, the Showcase Revue burst onto the sawdust. As the weird and wonderful ensemble all scampered through the tent entrance, there was one notable difference this time around. As Gargantua somersaulted and vaulted his way across the floor, Goliath slowly followed – with Carla on his shoulders. The crowd heartily applauded the sight. When the giant finally reached the microphone stand, Carla reached down low to collect the mic and, perched on Goliath's mighty frame, addressed the audience.

"I always wanted to be the biggest star in showbusiness," she cried, to much laughter. "Well, I can tick that one off now! Why, I can almost see Sardinia from up here."

Then, with her usual theatrical flourish, Carla climbed fully onto the giant's shoulders, stood tall and launched herself into the air, arms wide, before landing with a gymnastic dismount.

She encouraged more applause as Goliath moved towards the grandstands and began high-fiving some of the fans, while Gargantua executed his usual handstands and somersaults.

When Rumpy Stiltskin joined the fray, bouncing across the floor on his six-foot stilts, Carla stood perfectly still and beckoned him towards her. Rumpy produced his scene-stealer, a full 360 degree somersault straight over her frame. The wooden pegs missed her skull by inches.

The spectators continued their wild applause, as Carla left the stage again and the Revue completed a lap of honour.

When Corky and his clown troupe entered the tent, the laughter that emanated all around was the most beautiful sound Klondike and his staff could recall hearing in some time. Such noise could not have been more welcome. It was the sound of joy and, for Klondike, of life itself.

Corky drew maximum cheers from the stands by engaging with the spectators, offering animal balloons and his seemingly never-ending supply of flowers, all magically emerging from his suit sleeves.

He followed the magic acts with a display of fast juggling, before mounting his unicycle and completed a lap of the floor while juggling fire sticks. Slowing down at the end of his lap, he "fire-ate" the pins, extinguishing the flames in his mouth, to the shock of all watching.

The human cannonball act drew mighty applause once again, as the fearless, veteran clown flew across the floor, like a multi-coloured dart, slamming into the safety net and bouncing to the floor again. As his clown pals dusted him off, the fans stood and applauded as one.

The group in the facepaint and pink, yellow and polka dot suits completed the obligatory lap of honour, jogging around the circular arena floor, still pulling flowers and handkerchiefs from their sleeves.

Carla again emerged to make her next introduction and, as she finished, was rewarded with a custard pie straight into her face, courtesy of Corky.

There then followed the electrifying, unmistakeable sound that many in the big top had been waiting for, longing for even.

It was the deafening roar of motorbike engines revving up wildly.

The Daredevils raced out into the cauldron of cheers, their bikes looking shiny and new, and the riders' yellow and black jumpsuits and helmets equally scintillating.

The stunt riders drove around the tent floor several times, and then launched into their usual initial stunts. The leapfrogs and wheelies were met with warm applause, but that was soon blown away by the cheers emanating from everywhere when the famous Globe of Death was spotted at the entranceway.

Still sat on its standard flatbed truck, it was manoeuvred towards an iron platform in the arena's centre, and slowly secured as the bikers whizzed past in great, loud circles.

Then, to each of the Daredevils, it was as if the past six weeks had never happened. The horrors of London and Antwerp, the screams and confusion, all were forgotten in an instant. Now, they were the subject of adulation again, from an adoring audience. And each man lapped it up.

The riders all entered the great caged sphere, one every minute, and raced around in their relentless, looping circles.

Enqvist knew exactly what to do as he finally drove his motorcycle up the small ramp towards the Globe's entrance door. Looking up all around at the cheering patrons in their thousands, he once again performed his trademark pose, removing his helmet, holding it aloft and pumping the air for several moments before preparing to enter the Globe.

After soaking up the acclaim, the Norwegian threw on his shiny helmet, placed his fists against the handlebars and, waiting for his mark, dropped down into the sphere.

For the usual full two minutes, the six riders roamed round and round in the great Globe. And this time, as in Berlin, the audience were truly in awe.

When the riders all emerged one at a time and performed their customary lap of honour, everyone was on their feet, their cries of delight and amazement banishing the shrieks and despair found at the start of the tour. Suddenly, the Daredevils were stars again, beloved in Rome.

As the troupe rode away towards the flap, Enqvist slowed slightly at the rear of the pack. Then, inexplicably, Carla suddenly raced from nowhere and performed a perfect leapfrog, vaulting high, spreading her legs and placing her palms on top of the rider's helmet to propel herself over the moving bike.

Acknowledging the applause with an outstretched arm, she jogged to the mic stand and made her next introduction.

"And now, my beautiful people, please give a warm Roma welcome to the man who can make anything talk. The Puppetmaster… Roddy Olsen!"

Looking like a Broadway stage star, Olsen emerged in his silver waistcoat and purple pants, carrying his trademark suitcase.

Reaching Carla, he stooped and kissed her outstretched hand.

"Good evening, Miss Selenzy," he said as she held the mic out.

"Wonderful to see you, Roddy," she gushed. "Now, I am very excited about this act, as I understand we are going to sing together, no?"

"Yes, that's right. A beautiful duet for our wonderful Italian fans. That beautiful old song, You Are My World."

She nodded, smiling.

The opening notes of the song boomed out from the tannoy. Olsen sang the opening line, followed by a verse from Carla.

Then, suddenly, another voice emanated from somewhere.

"Hey! Stop that singing! And let me out! Let me out!"

Shocked gasps emanated from the stands.

Carla looked shocked. "Why, Roddy, who, or what, is that?"

Olsen's shoulders slumped. "Let's have a look, shall we? It was coming from the suitcase."

Then, Olsen performed his time-honoured piece as he struggled to remove Rusty Fox from the suitcase.

"Yow! Don't put your hand there! What are you doing!"

Then, Olsen stood up again, with the fox puppet on his arm. Another cheer came from the stands.

Carla squealed with delight. "Why, Roddy, who is this? He is just adorable."

Olsen proclaimed: "Miss Selenzy. Ladies and gentlemen. May I present my very good friend, Rusty Fox."

The fox magically began to talk on Olsen's arm. "That's Rusty Fox, teen idol. Heart-throb. Popular with all the chicks. Even the ones I try to eat!"

The little fox turned to appraise Carla. "Well, hellooooo…" he crowed.

"Good evening, Rusty," Carla said, laughing.

"My pleasure," said Rusty. The puppet turned back to its master. "Hey, Olsen, beat it! I got a chick here. I mean, er, a real one. Not one for supper. Come on, beat it, man! I need to be alone with her."

Olsen rolled his eyes. "Er, how is that going to work, Rusty?"

"What do you mean?"

"Well, er, you need me. For everything. How will you whisper sweet nothings into her ear? You can't talk without me!"

Rusty looked from Olsen to Carla and back again. He groaned. "OK, you can stay, Roddy. Without you, Miss Carla here might find me a little, er, flat."

Olsen stared at his puppet. "You're a dummy!"

"Yes, but I was born that way. What's your excuse?"

The crowd laughed merrily at the comedy. Then, Olsen waved his spare hand through the air. "Listen, I've got a good idea. Why don't we all sing a song together?"

"Now you're talking," Rusty cried.

"What an honour," Carla said.

The music started up again and the trio – man, woman and puppet – took it in turns to sing a line each.

You Are My World ended with a high-pitched final note from Rusty, which had everyone cheering.

As the applause died down, Olsen made Rusty take a bow. The fox cried: "Thank you, thank you. It's so nice to be around beautiful, young people."

Suddenly, a loud, commanding voice emerged from the suitcase.

"Attention!"

Carla threw her hands in the air. "Oh my god, who is that?"

With Rusty still on his right arm, Olsen bent down and went back to his suitcase, this time emerging with Napoleon on his left hand.

The elderly, army character in the GI fatigues drew a round of applause.

"It's my dear old friend Napoleon," Olsen said, a puppet on each arm.

The old man took over. "US Army. Retired. Now stuck living out of a suitcase, with a damn warthog for company."

"I'm not a warthog, I'm a fox!" snarled Rusty.

Napoleon looked up at Olsen. "I wasn't talking about you, fox!"

"Alright, my little friends," Carla said, enchanted. "Now, I hear the three of you are all very good at singing… together!"

Olsen baulked. "All three of us?"

"Something very special," Carla said, pointing up to the stands. "For all of us here. Something to make us all proud."

Then, as she held her hands aloft, the most familiar tune imaginable began echoing from the speakers, down through the stands. Il Canto degli Italiani – the Italian national anthem.

Olsen and his two puppets all sang in perfect Italian, one line each. And, to the joy of Carla, the entire audience seemed to stand as one as a mark of respect.

It was a phenomenal moment, seeing the diverse characters of Olsen, Rusty Fox and Napoleon singing in Italian – with all the fans joining in.

A rousing ovation followed, with Carla kissing each of Olsen and his puppets at the conclusion. As she embraced Rusty, the little fox cried: "Carla, you're one foxy lady! We were made to be together!"

Carla laughed, before saying into the mic: "Now, Roddy, where is that famous Las Vegas lounge singer I've heard so much about?"

"Why, right here," came a smooth voice from out of nowhere.

With that, Olsen deposited Rusty and Napoleon into the case and came up again carrying the tuxedo-clad Tony Tan. Everyone laughed and applauded.

"Thank you very much," the crooner mumbled as Olsen set him down on a stool. "It's so great to be back here in… where the hell are we?"

Olsen whispered into the mic. "Rome, Tony. Italy."

"Ah. The old country. I like the wine here. And… the whiskey, the bourbon, the vermouth, the vodka, the rum, the gin, the brandy, the port. Oh, and the beer too!"

Olsen rolled his eyes. "I think you missed a few."

Tan noticed Carla. "Oh man! It's Sophia Loren!" he cried.

Carla giggled. "Oh Tony! You're too much."

"Thank you, Sophia. Most people seem to think I'm too little."

"Please, Tony," she pleaded, "your voice is renowned throughout your country. Please… treat us to a song."

"Well," the puppet drawled, "when in Rome."

With that, Olsen launched him into a whole new song, recorded multiple times by Italian-Americans down the years, entitled The Moon Is Blue In Turin.

The rendition was met with another rousing ovation, led by Carla beside them.

Then, Olsen produced all three puppets in his arms and bowed with them as one. He said a "Thank you" into the mic held by Carla, before manoeuvring each of the puppets' mouths to the mic for a thanks of their own.

Then, returning his 'guys' to the suitcase, he waved happily to the stands as he jogged off the stage. The ovation as he departed was immense.

Reaching the exit, Olsen was mobbed by Klondike and Lacey, who both hugged him wildly. Heavy placed a meaty arm around the youngster and led him calmly outside, singing his praises as they walked.

"Way to go, kid, way to go! They love you. What I tell ya? You're the crown prince of the circus."

They both chuckled. Truly, this time, Olsen could not stop smiling.

Following another loud introduction from Carla, Duster Williams and the Range Riders stormed into the tent on their horses.

The cheers were loud and full of delight as the cowboys performed their full repertoire of tricks and stunts, with several doffing their stetsons to the younger fans, who were seeing a TV western come to life.

Everyone shrieked and cried out as the cowboys stood on their saddles as the horses bounded across the floor. Then, as the riders leapt from mount to mount, landing upon the racing horses with ease and saddling up again, the cheers grew louder, reaching a crescendo of euphoria.

When Williams performed his solo spot, gasps of wonder filled the tent. The veteran star had Goldie perform several hind leg salutes. He then completed a vertical handstand atop the horse, his hands gripping the saddle horn with a firm hold. He dismounted by standing on the saddle and leaping on to the floor.

With a flourish of his hands, he removed his lasso and began his roping act.

Duster performed the giant circle loop, then manoeuvred the lasso into a smaller spinning wheel, which he jumped through back and forth, as the loop got smaller as he pulled more rope through his grip.

The falling hoop trick was next, as the lasso was thrown high into the air before falling neatly into a perfect circle around his feet.

Smiling widely, he turned to Goldie for the perennial crowd pleaser.

Holding his hand towards his trusted horse, he said loudly: "Put it there, partner."

Goldie stood on her hind legs, offered a hoof and the two – man and beast – shook hands.

As ever, delighted laughter echoed down from the bleachers.

Williams ran his arm round in a corkscrew motion and Goldie set off. He sprinted after her, expertly pulling himself on to the saddle and remounting the horse as she took off on a lap of the arena floor.

The rest of the Range Riders then joined in and, suddenly, the entire team were racing around in a giant loop again, with the cowboys performing saddle swaps and riding backwards as the act continued.

Then, the team slowed down and headed towards the exit. Each rider held his stetson above his head in a sign of acknowledgement to the fans, who cheered endlessly.

Duster rode at the back. There were tears in his eyes. Nearing the flap, he looked up at a group of teenage boys dressed in cowboy attire. He stopped Goldie and the beautiful palomino performed one last hind-leg salute in front of the youngsters in the stand.

"I love you," Williams screamed at the group. "Thank you. Thank you, each and every one of you. Everywhere, in the world."

He steered Goldie into the flap enclosure, still waving at the cheering patrons.

Klondike walked alongside him as he made for the exit, placing a hand on the reins.

"What can I tell ya, Duster," he said happily. "You're the greatest! They all love you."

He smiled up at the older man, feeling his emotion.

Duster wiped at his tears. "And I love them. Every last one of them." He looked down at the circus boss. "And you, Kal. And Miss Lacey. Hell, all your staff and crew. You… you people have given me a purpose. A reason to go on. To live!" He glanced back towards the stage floor. "And that, that feel of a live circus audience. That is what I am devoted to. Forever. I can see that now. I can feel it."

Klondike patted him on the leg as Goldie ducked through the flap and headed outside.

He watched in awe, as the old cowboy rode off towards the trailers, his frame soon becoming a silhouette in the early evening gloom.

"Thank you," he whispered quietly.

The big top audience were soon clapping happily again as Italian pop music began blaring out from the tannoy and, like a human exclamation point, Carla Selenzy burst out on to the sawdust.

Her dazzling array of somersaults and flips left many onlookers feeling dizzy.

She executed an artistic gymnastics routine, running at a lightning speed before throwing herself into a leap many Olympic high jumpers would be proud of. She landed on her hands and pushed herself off into another round of cartwheels, finally ending the routine with a flying vault and landing with the splits.

As the crowd screamed their amazement, the Italian Empress of Acrobatics performed her usual leap on to the trapeze support rope, jumping high with a pirouette before clasping ahold of the dangling rope and hauling herself up.

Carla pulled herself up a distance of 25 feet in mere seconds.

Then, she arrived at the hastily assembled high-wire platform, which stood pristine in the arena's centre. Two giant bright red derricks sat with the 20-yard long, coiled plastic wire running between them at the summit.

Smothering chalk from a small box on the platform into her palms, Carla prepared herself. As the entire audience quietened completely, a drumroll sounded on the tannoy.

And then it began. Carla executed a handstand on the thick plastic wire and turned her body to face the far platform, opposite where she was now poised.

One hand reached past the next, over and over, as she slowly maneouvred herself across the high wire. Her tiny frame remained straight and firm, barely quivering at all, as she guided herself across.

The big top remained deathly silent as everyone watched the outrageous stunt. To many, it was the most surreal, foreign sight they could have imagined, let alone witnessed.

Then, just like that, the upside-down Carla was at the other end of the line, her legs sloping forward like a contortionist until they rested on the far platform, before the rest of her frame followed in a slick movement. She stood vertical again.

As thunderous applause followed, Carla smiled beautifully to "her people", raising her palms high and waving to all sides of the arena.

Then, instead of darting back down a support rope, she bent down and picked up a cordless microphone from the platform she had arrived on. It was time for a special introduction.

"Thank you," she screeched. "And now… ladies and gentlemen, get ready to be amazed by the superstars of trapeze. The world's number one high-flying act, direct from America. First, the queen of the skies, Miss Penny Fortune. And, our star act… love him, cheer him, never forget him. Please welcome the debonair king of the air, the one and only Gino Shapiro!"

A dramatic classical tune boomed out from the speakers.

Shapiro and Penny strode out, soaking up the ovation as it bled down from the stands.

As they relinquished their fur-lined capes and confidently began climbing their tall ropes, Carla began encouraging the crowd to cheer louder from her perch atop the wire platform, raising her hands upwards and whipping everyone into more of a frenzy.

The trapeze showcase exploded into action as the two flyers hauled themselves up to the tent's stratosphere.

Shapiro performed his trademark array of leaps and jumps. All the moves were on show tonight. There was the double and triple roll, the helicopter spin, the turtle somersault, the standing fall and the long dive. Each jump followed the last in a seamless blend of human aerobatics.

He was propelled to the rings by Penny, who hung upside down on the first ring in the very centre of the trapeze rig.

After the array of vaults was complete, Gino and Penny completed a move they had practised all week, a feat of synchronised trapeze. Both executed handstands on their respective rings, before allowing themselves to swing around in a 360 degree arc, at the exact same time. Manouevering their powerful wrists and arms in tandem, side by side, the fearless duo began spinning round and round on their rings, getting faster with each swing. As jaws dropped across the audience at the twirling pair high above, they soon snapped shut in shock as both released their grip, being propelled a good 12 feet into the air. They performed a somersault in tandem, before landing on their rings again, in the sitting position. The moves were completed in perfect synchronic timing.

Again, the tent exploded with applause. Below on the platform, Carla started screaming Gino's name into the mic, with the crowd joining in instantly.

The two flyers waved enthusiastically from their rings, before diving on to their tall ropes and lowering themselves downwards.

While Penny dropped to the ground, Shapiro slithered down to the high wire platform and joined Carla.

Giving the Empress a mighty hug, he rubbed some of the chalk onto his stockinged feet and stood at the edge of the great wire.

The drum roll returned on the sound system. Everyone held their breath. Carla patted Shapiro on the back, smiling devilishly.

Then, the master trapeze ace held his arms out wide and walked simply across the wire, one foot falling directly in front of the other, like a pre-programmed machine.

The wire walk was performed with the smoothness and grace of an Olympic gymnast, the carefree action belying the dangers and risks at stake.

As he passed the halfway mark, something truly unexpected happened. At the far platform, a door in the floor decking suddenly opened up. Then, of all the figures to appear, Roddy Olsen climbed out, with Rusty Fox sat upon his shoulders.

The crowd gasped in shock. Olsen held up a hand and picked up a tightrope walker's pole from the platform edge. Holding it out horizontally at waist height, he looked across at Shapiro.

Gino had stopped walking across the high wire, merely standing there, suspended high above the sawdust, in an incredible display of balance and nerve.

The act had gone without a hitch so far. Olsen had first entered the structure secretly when the roustabout crew had moved the platforms into place earlier. The inside ladder and trapdoor led him to the top.

Now, the ventriloquist stood poised on the edge of the high wire, the fox puppet on his shoulders. Then, he took a step forward, holding the pole steadily. As he moved, the sound of Rusty letting off a frenzied scream reverberated around the arena. The comedic touch was a welcome relief amidst the unbearable tension.

At the flap, below and across the sawdust, Klondike, Lacey and Heavy all stared at the high-wire in rapt fascination, their feelings overwhelmed by fear, desire and ecstasy.

Seeing Olsen up there, so high off the floor, and with no form of protection, anywhere, was too much for Lacey, who looked like she might faint.

On the wire, Shapiro had begun retreating backwards as Olsen joined him on the coiled plastic, inching forwards. The height, the thinness of the wire and the sheer lunacy of the escapade seemed to have no effect at all on Gino, who crept back and forth up there with zero emotion.

Shapiro and Olsen began making gesticulations at each other, Gino waving a hand as if to ask the other man to move. Olsen screamed in Rusty's high-pitched voice, telling him to dismount.

Then, inexplicably, Carla joined them on the wire. She walked five paces effortlessly and then, to the sheer incredulity of all present in the tent, leapfrogged over Shapiro's head, flying up and over him in one graceful, fluidic motion, before landing in front of him, poised perfectly on the wire.

The almighty gasp from the audience as she dropped on to the wire again was possibly the loudest, most frenzied any of the circus folk had ever heard. Then, just like that, she was between the two men.

Smiling widely as she maintained her balance, she pulled the mic from a holder on her hip and said into it: "Well, my dear Rusty, how are you finding it up here?"

She held the mic up to the puppet, above Olsen's head.

"Somebody, please, get me outta here!" Rusty yelped. She laughed.

Olsen had been creeping across the wire very slowly, but had still made several paces towards the centre.

Then, as Carla inched backwards with Gino just behind her on the congested wire, a new sound emanated from below.

"Watch out up there!"

Every pair of eyes in the stands dropped down. There, in another inexplicable sight, was Corky the Clown. He was seated on the tallest unicycle anyone had ever seen. And in his hands were four large pins. He grinned manically up at the wire above him. "Cos here comes the high juggle!"

With that, Corky began hurling the pins upwards in the highest of juggling throws. Incredibly, the pins flew above the trio on the high wire, coming back down the other side and into the spinning hands of the clown.

It was a truly surreal sight for all to behold. Shapiro, Carla and Olsen, plus Rusty, all stood perched on the high wire, far above the ground. Just beneath them, Corky sat, wheeling frantically on his giant cycle, with his juggling pins somehow encircling the performers above.

As the trio on the wire all held their positions steadily, Carla screamed into the mic, holding one hand aloft in celebration.

"È il più grande spettacolo del modo!" She screeched. "It's the greatest show on earth!"

With that, Corky cycled towards the far side, his pins magically moving in a great circle with him. Then, four of his clown pals brought a giant red crash mat across to the ground under the wire.

Carla, Shapiro and Olsen all waved to the audience. Then, linking arms together, the trio jumped down as one, landing on the inflatable crash mat in a dignified sitting-down action, before bouncing several feet into the air again.

With a flourish, all three then stood and soaked up the standing ovation that practically raised the roof on the great tent.

Penny ran over and embraced Shapiro.

Then, in another surprise, Enqvist appeared on his bike, revving his engine for effect. With another big leap, Carla vaulted on to the back of his motorcycle and held onto Enqvist's shoulders as he cruised to the edge of the arena. Then, as the stunt rider began a slow lap of the floor, Carla stood to her full height on the back of the saddle, and spread her arms wide, floating through the air like an angelic bird.

It was all too much for the cheering fans, who were at a level of ecstasy by now, such was the non-stop action before them.

As Shapiro, Olsen, Penny and Corky all gathered in the centre of the floor and waved at the fans, Carla's voice once again emanated around the big top, as she talked into the microphone from her latest perch on the Daredevils' motorbike, whizzing around the sawdust.

"And now, ladies and gentlemen," she said breathlessly from the bike, "please welcome songstress supreme, here to sing us out tonight, the enchanting Miss Suzi Dando…"

Suzi finally waded out on to the arena floor, looking resplendent as ever in a white evening frock.

She reached the microphone stand, greeting her fellow performers.

The crowd waited. Suzi took a deep breath.

What followed was truly remarkable. With her slender physique, childlike features and youthful innocence, nobody present in the circus would ever have marked her down as a classical soprano.

The youngster stood at the mic stand, firing out the much-loved Palcoscenico più Grandioso di tutti in captivating fashion.

The Italian was faultless, as was her poise and range, holding the high notes with merciless authority.

She had studied the opera all week, and had been determined to make the song her own.

And then the grand finale was suddenly in full flow. As the enchanted audience swayed gently to the music flowing from the speakers and Suzi's beautiful singing, the Cadillac convertibles slowly rolled out from the flap enclosure.

The eight cars all began their lap of honour, the traditional show-closing parade, with the Daredevils and the Range Riders bringing up the rear, riding on their respective mounts. Enqvist pulled alongside his team at the back, still carrying Carla, who was punching the air in celebration as she waved to the fans.

Corky mounted his unicycle again, and peddled around alongside the Cadillac carrying the clown troupe.

In a break from tradition, Shapiro, Penny and Olsen all jumped into the last, orange convertible as it rolled past. The three of them all stood on the back seat as usual. Penny grinned mischeviously and, bending down, joined Shapiro and Olsen's hands together, before raising them up high. The duo stared at each other as the car cruised past the grandstands. The fans applauded warmly as the stars went by, hand in hand. Both nodded at each other. They maintained the pose for the entire lap of honour.

Then, in the centre of the arena, Suzi reached the dramatic climax of the operatic song, holding her last high note for what felt like an eternity. As she finished, she held her arms aloft in triumph. The cheers that followed were full of pride, respect and unbridled joy. Suzi smiled uncontrollably, arms still high. Then, with a hop and a skip, she raced over to that last Cadillac and leapt up into the back, where Shapiro and Olsen helped her aboard, now raising her arms aloft.

Everyone stared at that gleaming orange vehicle as it crept along by the edge of the sawdust. The fans stared entranced at its occupants, feeling like they were glimpsing immortals.

Truly, it was a wonderful moment for all concerned with the circus.

At the flap, Klondike and his team stared in a dreamlike haze as the cars rolled across the floor back towards them.

From the thunderous applause streaming down from the bleachers, to the beauty of the cars in the parade, and then beyond to the cowboys on horseback and the stunt riders on the bikes, with the wildly gesticulating Carla at the back… the whole ensemble looked otherworldly.

Klondike shook his head in wonder. “I’ll be damned,” he muttered in awe. “The parade has never looked more beautiful. More inspiring…”

“More fitting,” Lacey whispered at his shoulder. “This was the reason the grand finale was invented. For its majesty, its grace. Such a suitable way of closing a show.”

Heavy joined in. “This is what it’s all about. This, right here,” he stammered.

Plum had been sat in the bleachers nearby, but now came scampering over, beaming like a baby. “Kal!” He bellowed in a high-pitched whine. “You were right! I do remember. Roddy on that high wire. Before our first show. Out on the midway.” He laughed uncontrollably. “I’d forgotten all about it with everything that’s happened. Wow! What a time to bring that one out!”

Klondike put an arm happily around the smaller man. They all watched the end of the parade, as the cars began floating past them towards the exit.

“I thought you’d like it, Richie,” Klondike said.

“Man, what a surprise! I still can’t believe it.”

Klondike could not stop smiling. “We needed something special to close out the biggest show of our tour. We got thinking. Then, hell, then we remembered. The kid loved the idea, despite the risks.”

Lacey placed her forehead on Klondike’s shoulder. “Thank god it all went without a hitch. My lord, seeing Roddy up there on that wire… I can’t tell you!”

Heavy was watching the parade knowingly, a wisened grin on his lips. “Nothing is beyond that kid, nothing I tells ya.” He eyed Klondike now. “Put him and Gino together and… wham! You’ve got yourself a show, man. The show of shows.”

Klondike nodded. “Ain’t no one gunna argue with that.”

The management team all applauded and offered praise as the Cadillacs passed them and headed out to the field.

The orange car carrying Shapiro, Penny, Olsen and Suzi was last, and Klondike patted each of the performers as they rolled by. Each of them looked awestruck, as if this performance had surpassed anything they had ever experienced.

Then, the Range Riders and Daredevils passed by, and the stage was bare once more – except for one figure dressed in the colours of the national flag.

Carla Selenzy had hopped off Enqvist's bike just before the end of their lap of honour and was walking slowly to the flap, mic in hand.

Lacey happily placed her arms around Klondike and Heavy as they all watched. Plum hopped about excitedly behind them.

"You know, boys," Lacey purred. "I think this whole night will live long in our memories. So far from home, after this adventure in Europe." She shook her head. "What a way to end it all."

Klondike looked up at the still-cheering crowds encircling his arena.

"There's just one more thing to be said," he drawled.

They all stared out to the sawdust. Carla had stopped just before the flap, and now held the mic to her lips for the final address.

"Thank you so much for joining Klondike's Circus tonight. We hope you have enjoyed the glamour, the razzmatazz and the wonder. And we hope you can feel the magic tonight. Until next time, goodnight everybody and…"

She closed her eyes and screamed into the microphone.

"God bless Italia!"

CHAPTER 30

The historic harbour at Port Naples had never witnessed anything quite like it.

As a magnificent blue and white liner bobbed majestically at the waterfront, a huge, resplendent red carpet made up of sheets of fine baize attached to a steel walkway led up to the ship's gangway point.

The Floating Top had enjoyed a leisurely cruise across the Mediterranean after its Atlantic crossing six weeks earlier, and after taking on supplies and fuel provisions at Calais, the mighty ship was all set for its return voyage to the States.

A large, excited crowd of onlookers surrounded the harbour's edge and the extravagant red creation, many waving their miniature stars and stripes flags as they looked towards the large merchants pavilion in the centre of the dockside.

A group of dignitaries were waving to the assembled crowd, which included members of the Italian national press and TV camera crews. Several of the suited figures shouted grand proclamations to the onlookers.

Hanging from the pavilion's roof was a giant banner, with painted crimson letters saying: ARRIVEDERCI, KLONDIKE'S CIRCUS.

As if to complete the grand set-up, a small brass band were playing old jazz tunes in a gazebo at the edge of the waterfront.

Finally, a deafening dock whistle tooted, the sound reverberating through the watching crowd. Then, the Naples dignitaries all led the way down towards the red carpet get-up. This was it.

The spectators let out a mighty cheer as the stars of Klondike's Circus emerged from the pavilion and walked happily towards the ship before them.

Slowly appearing amid the frenzied fans, the performers were visible at last, waving and grinning at the assembled citizens. And what a send-off it was.

Gino Shapiro and Roddy Olsen led the way across the harbour, pacing slowly up the bright gangplank towards the liner, waving non-stop to all who cheered.

Penny Fortune, Suzi Dando and Corky were next, with the clown back in facepaint and a loud pink suit as they made for the ship.

The Daredevils all walked up together in their yellow and black jumpsuits. Then, a huge cheer erupted from the onlookers as Duster Williams emerged with the Range Riders, all dressed in neat country and western-style suits with boot ties.

Gargantua, Goliath and Rumpy Stiltskin were next, followed by the Hightops, Rocking Robins and the Flying Batistas.

The clown troupe made their way to the ship by mingling with the crowds, once again handing out balloons and performing hand magic.

The performers all boarded the ship at the gangway, before moving along the deck to the stern rail and watching the epic scene they were about to leave behind. Many in the crowd blew kisses, while others waved their handkerchiefs.

A lone woman in a dark green trenchcoat suddenly emerged from the masses, waving up at Shapiro from the dockside and calling his name. She wore a headscarf to disguise herself, but he knew it was her.

"Carla!"

She looked up at him longingly from the stone harbour base. He leant over the edge of the ship's rail, as if ready to dive overboard into the cold Mediterranean waters.

"Where have you been these past two days? I, well, I looked everywhere for you."

She blushed. "Loose ends, darling. So much to tie up. Everybody wants to see me."

He smiled in the sea breeze. "Everybody wants a piece of their Carla, eh?"

"That's right," she called back up to him. They stared at each other awkwardly.

"So this is goodbye," he said sadly.

She shook her head. "Arrivederci. But only for now. Until you return. When we shall meet again. And, bueno, perform again."

Shapiro was incredulous. "When will that be?"

Carla smiled devilishly. "You must return to Italia. After Saturday night… there is no doubt. Every town here wants your circus. They all want you, Gino, with me… up there, on that wire."

He smiled, glancing across at Penny by the rail, who watched the proceedings with a wry smile. Then, his gaze fell back down to Carla on the harbour's edge.

"Carla, my darling," he called. "You are the greatest!"

"Our partnership was the greatest, Gino. Always remember that."

The two stars merely gazed at each other, yards apart, one at sea, the other on land. She blew him a kiss. He opened up his jacket and patted at his chest.

"You're in my heart," he whispered to himself.

As Carla stared up at the man by the ship's rail, a newspaper reporter suddenly recognised her, rushed over and began firing questions towards her. She slipped back into character, making grand gestures as she spoke.

Shapiro smiled sadly. He turned, nodded to Penny, then noticed Olsen, stood watching just behind him. The two men stared at each other.

With a heavy sigh, Shapiro approached the younger man. He shocked them both by placing an arm around Olsen's shoulders.

"Come," he said. "Let me buy you a drink. We have a long road ahead, no?"

Olsen forced a smile, and the duo walked slowly towards the canteen.

A ship's whistle sounded. All the performers were now onboard the Floating Top, mingling happily on the deck, still waving at the fans who had come to see them off.

At the harbourside pavilion, Klondike and his management team had wandered out on to the veranda leading to the walkway. They had enjoyed the surprising reception put on by the Naples regional authorities, and had watched with pride as the large gathering cheered the talent boarding the ship.

It had been three days since that glorious Rome show, and the circus had made national headlines. Word of the extraordinary performances under the American big top had spread rapidly across the nation, and circus fans had wanted to catch a glimpse of these otherworldly stars, even if it was just to say goodbye and witness their departure.

Klondike casually leaned against a wooden pillar on the veranda and lit a cigar. His gaze went from the majestic Floating Top sat on the waters before them, out to all the people looking up at it in awe.

Heavy and Plum ambled over to join him.

"It's funny," Heavy muttered. "Ten days ago, I couldn't wait to get away from Europe and see good old USA again. But… but now, hell, I feel sad leaving."

Plum nodded. "These people have embraced us. Loved us. Given us salvation, after all we went through on this tour."

Klondike exhaled a long cloud of smoke. "We arrived six weeks ago in Southampton. Excited, intrigued and hungry to deliver to circus fans on the other side of the world." He looked out to sea and shook his head. "We've been through pain, heartache, despair, near disaster… and now, on the last stop, elation." He looked at his old lieutenants. "You couldn't have made it all up."

Jack Bannion wandered over, smiling as he glimpsed the Floating Top docked at the harbour.

Klondike smiled broadly as the Englishman came over. "And you," he cried. "You, Jack Bannion, were an ace card in our game out here." He offered his hand. Bannion shook it happily. "I can't thank you enough for all your help and advice out here, Jack."

Bannion patted him on the chest. "Hell, are you kidding Kal. I've had the absolute time of my life on this tour. Jesus, all the adventures we've had. I never, ever thought all this possible." He cackled. "And to think I imagined this would be a mundane, low-key circus tour through the old continent. Blimey! I thought I'd just be babysitting a touring show, giving guided trips and the like." Now, he eyed Klondike earnestly. "Thank you, Kal. Thank you. For giving me the time of my life."

Klondike tentatively raised an eyebrow, cigar in mouth. "You know, there's more of that back in the States. Much more. If you're interested?"

Bannion's face broke into a euphoric smile. "Normally, I'd say let's talk about it. But there's nothing to talk about. I'm in all the way, mate."

Klondike grinned, patting him on the back. Bannion joined Heavy and Plum in making a start for the gangway leading to the liner. Klondike continued smoking, enjoying the atmosphere and the ocean breeze.

"Kal! Look at this!"

He turned in surprise. Lacey was rushing towards him across the veranda, clutching a newspaper. As always, she made quite the impression, wearing a caramel fur coat paired with a black beret.

"Lacey!" He barked. "Where have you been? You missed the send-off these guys have put on for us. It was really something."

She practically collided with him as she raced over. "I was talking to some of the dignitaries, local Naples magistrates. But, look at this!" She pushed the newspaper into his hands. "Look!"

Klondike held the paper before him in shock. The publication was called Il Gazettino. It's front page banner headline screamed: Circo capo la cardiac cospirazione!

Klondike stared not at the bold headline, nor the text flowing beneath it. Instead, his steely gaze rested on the giant picture that occupied half of the front page, sitting vertically alongside the story.

It showed an older man in a tanned suit being led into a police car, his hands cuffed in front of him. Klondike would never forget that smug, soft-skinned face.

"Courtinio!"

Lacey grabbed ahold of the paper. "I managed to understand most of the article, but the locals back there helped to translate everything." She looked at him, her eyes wide in shock. "You won't believe it."

Klondike frowned. "They nailed him."

Lacey stared at the picture of the Circo Grande boss in handcuffs. "After an investigation, it appears Carmine Courtinio has been charged with eight counts of criminal activity. But the main charge involves his conspiracy to further his circus – and put ours, as well as several others, out of business. Apparently, the ploy had far-reaching tentacles, involving politicians, city officials, the media, TV celebrities… you name it, the list is endless."

"It's just like Detective Gianni said. He was up to his neck in corruption."

Lacey nodded, her eyes still on the picture. "Well, it appears his team made the charges, and intend to make them stick. The story says they are alleging all sorts – bribery, fraud, intimidation." Her giant eyes flicked up to him, and she noted his stern expression. "And also charged are his right hand man, Conrad Handel, and one Konstantin Tarzech, also known as Tarz the Strongman. I think it's fair to say his performing career is over."

Klondike snarled, still gripping the paper. "And what about Courtinio?"

Lacey moved back a pace, pulling on a pair of leather gloves. "His trial is set for later this year. But, due to the severity of the charges, he has been remanded into custody for the duration of the wait. No bail."

Klondike nodded. "And what does that tell you, huh?"

She rubbed his arm. "That he is going to jail."

"Well, the police have practically got a full confession from him on that damn security video he had in his office. I don't see how any fancy lawyer can dodge around that."

Lacey smiled beautifully and gently gripped his hands. The smooth leather of her gloves on his skin made him tingle. "All this, the indictment, the trial… it's all thanks to you, Kal. If you hadn't tracked him down, confronted him like that… why, he'd still be running this criminal empire. Exploiting others."

Klondike chewed on his cigar, which had gone out. "I'm just glad we turned the tables on him. That deluded old man almost ruined us. For good. Thank god we found him, before it was too late."

Lacey could not stop looking into his eyes. As always, he found it unnerving and overpowering, making him look away like an embarrassed kid. Her look was one of admiration. Deep, and highly felt.

"Alright," he finally blurted. "What now, my lady?"

She chuckled, before theatrically gesturing towards the red carpet, and the Floating Top beyond. They could see the performers and staff all spread across the open deck as the ship bobbed in the water.

“Our cruise ship awaits, Sir Galahad,” she purred mischievously.

He squinted down at the liner. “Next stop, New York.”

“We’ve conquered Europe,” she said. “Well, in a matter of speaking. Now, it’s time for our domestic season. And all the fun that comes with that.”

He turned towards the walkway that led down to the improvised red carpet gangplanks.

“Any plans for our return voyage?” he quipped.

“Yes,” she replied. “Lots of rest in my cabin.” She looked at him and rolled her eyes. “And no more meetings, baby. This gal has seen enough drama and contingency plans to last a lifetime. Please! Let’s just enjoy the journey.”

He smiled. “Aye aye, captain.”

With that, Lacey linked her arm through his, and the two strolled gently down the gangway towards the Floating Top.

And a passage out of this new world, and back to their own.

EPILOGUE – SEVEN DAYS LATER

"Land ahoy!"

It was the most welcome sight anyone onboard could recall seeing for some time. It was home.

Slowly emerging through the Atlantic sea mists, a greyish block of land could just about be seen jutting out into the ocean, like a welcoming arm.

New York City. Finally, they were back.

The Floating Top had sailed from Naples across Europe back to Southampton, where it had undergone a quick stock take, replenished fuel and supplies, before setting sail again for the States, from whence it had come weeks earlier.

Now, the circle was complete. The voyage over. The European tour in the past.

The staff and performers from Klondike's Circus had all very much enjoyed the return trip home. The ship had bounded along at a leisurely pace, the weather had been glorious, and the mood onboard was genial and calm after the highs of that last show in Rome. Now, everyone looked forward to getting back on to home turf, reuniting with family, friends and associates. They all surely had a tale to tell.

The Floating Top slowly crept across the mild Atlantic swells, nearing the New York harbour with each passing minute.

Klondike stood at the bridge, watching the helmsman as he guided the great liner along with a deft hand at the wheel. Alongside him, Lacey and Heavy looked out the massive bridge window towards the ever enlarging New York landscape slowly emerging before them across the water.

"There it is," Heavy said quietly as the ship rocked slightly beneath them. "I can just about see the Statue of Liberty from here."

Lacey giggled. "I can almost make out the bright lights of Broadway!"

Klondike sniggered. "And I can see the train that's going to take us 3,000 miles back to California!"

Lacey shuddered. "Oh, Kalvin! Come on, let's have some time in the Big Apple. We've just travelled across the world on this ship. The last thing on Earth any of us want to do right now is contemplate a two-day train journey."

Klondike had to laugh. "I miss our holding camp."

She rolled her eyes. "I'm sure it will still be there. Trailers and all."

Heavy pointed out to sea. "Looks like we've got company."

They all looked out towards New York harbour, which was slowly coming into view. Amid the various ships, yachts and leisure cruisers scattered across the waterfront before them, like traffic holed up at a parking lot, a tall, silver launch was making a beeline towards them.

As it drew closer, Klondike saw the words HARBOUR MASTER'S OFFICE printed on its starboard transom. He knew all incoming crafts had to be inspected by the harbour officials before entering the city's jurisdiction. The helmsman had already stopped the Floating Top's engines.

Five minutes later, the harbour launch had pulled up alongside them. A smartly dressed official and two men in work clothes, one carrying a briefcase, climbed down a ladder from the launch and moved up the gangway steps, finally entering the bridge.

The lead man, who wore a blue suit with a Navy cap and carried a clipboard, walked up to Klondike and the helmsman, offering a brief salute.

"Welcome to New York, sir," he shouted. "The harbour master sends his complements. I am David Thompson, deputy head of the NY harbour office. We're here to inspect your ship and check your papers."

"Right," Klondike drawled. He opened a drawer at the bridge controls and pulled out a wad of sheets. "There you go."

Thompson was impassive. "I will need an inventory for your ship, sir."

"It's right there, chief."

The harbour official flicked through the papers, then grinned to himself. "Ah, of course. You are the circus people."

Klondike smiled. “Right.”

“I remember your departure from here.” He continued checking the papers, then addressed Klondike again, pointing at his two companions, who loitered on the bridge wing. “My team will conduct the inspection, sir. It won’t take long. Just relax, and before you know it you’ll be back in New York.”

Klondike nodded his thanks and leant against the control panel, watching Lacey and Heavy.

“Hell, maybe you’re right, Lacey. It’s not everyday you get to see those bright lights of Broadway.”

She gaped at him. “You want to stay on for a bit?”

“What can I tell ya? Me and Heavy are from New York, remember. It’s not often we get a chance to look around. And, hell, every time we come back so much has changed.”

Lacey probed further. “You want to take in a show?”

“I was thinking more a ball game.”

Heavy chuckled. “Now you’re talking!”

Klondike laughed, enjoying the banter. “We can do both. Hell, Lacey, it’s about time we took you to a baseball match.”

She huffed dejectedly. “Alright. But I’ll take you both to a show of my choice. Agreed?”

“Agreed!” the two men chimed together.

A few minutes later, the harbour official returned to the bridge with his companions. “OK, people,” he barked. “Everything appears to be in order here.” He looked up at Klondike and smiled. “Welcome back home, Mr Klondike.”

They shook hands. Then, with a final goodbye, the harbour team ambled down the gangway steps to their launch and pulled themselves up their boarding ladder.

In seconds, the launch’s motor had rumbled into life and it pulled away from the Floating Top at an agonisingly slow pace, as if merely being dragged along by a wave.

As he watched the officials board their craft again, Klondike turned to Lacey and Heavy. “Well, that’s the bureaucratic duties outta the way. We are home free, folks. New York, here we come!”

The three of them wandered out on to the bridge wing, breathing in the salty sea air and enjoying the sunlight. The sea looked a luscious emerald green in the morning light.

Klondike studied the harbour master's launch as it gently reversed away from the ship, knowing it would then turn around and speed back to port.

His eyes roamed to the launch's bridge, sat behind a giant window at the head of the boat.

There seemed to be several figures gathered around the navigation controls. At the wheel stood a tall, well-built man with dark hair and a wavy beard. He looked like he'd be better off working as a longshoreman at the dock rather than driving a ship. Then, next to him was a woman with long blonde hair. As he stared, she turned around and faced the Floating Top.

Klondike froze all over. He felt like he was seeing things. He had to be. It was sea sickness, surely, making him delusional.

The woman stared right back at him. It was her. She had long, straight hair. Angelic, pointed features. Fair, pale skin. And cold, dark eyes.

In shock, Klondike grabbed at the railing before him. His body seemed to spasm. Heavy and Lacey studied him.

"Kal..." Lacey said in alarm.

"Oh my god!" he blurted in astonishment. "It can't be! It's her! Yes. It's... it's Jenny Cross!"

The other two glared at him. They looked at the launch. Then back to him again.

Klondike was transfixed, staring at the woman. She looked back at him, across the water. Their eyes met. It was impossible. Jenny Cross was here!

Then, something extraordinary happened.

The woman raised her hand and gave a wave. Klondike frowned. The way her hand had moved. It was not a greeting. It was a wave goodbye.

Klondike felt himself consumed by a ripple of fear and panic, rocking him to his very core. One solitary word escaped from his fraught lips as he stared at the departing launch.

"No!"

Then, it happened.

A deafening boom emanated from deep within the ship's bowels. It came from way down, amidst the engines and inner mechanics of the great behemoth. A loud, devastating noise, like an atomic blast at a military testing range.

Then, in an instant, the entire ship lurched manically, knocking every single person on board off their feet. The rumble felt like an earthquake, minus the build-up and the initial shocks. This was an almighty jar that erupted in an instant. An explosion.

On the bridge wing, Klondike, Lacey and Heavy were sent flying. Klondike flew back into the bridge area, slamming into the control panel with the seated helmsman.

Lacey and Heavy fell in a great, undignified bundle, rolling over each other as they slipped down the gangway, tumbling endlessly as they cried out in alarm.

Stunned, Klondike sat up on the bridge floor. He felt bumps and bruises all over him, and could feel blood pouring from a gash in his forehead.

Immediately, he realised the ship was listing badly. The entire craft seemed to be sat at a seventy degree angle. Even worse, he felt himself moving downwards. His heart pounded. The ship was sinking. And at a rapid rate.

In a daze, he clumsily pulled himself up to a standing position in the bridge. He struggled to keep his balance, such was the extent of the list.

He gazed in horror out of the central window pane. The sea was barely eight yards below him, eating up his ship as it plummeted down into the depths. He felt panic take over, as he stared in shock at the surreal sight all around him. He grabbed the barely conscious helmsman, and hauled him on to the wing, resting him down on the gangway. The man moaned in agony.

Then, with a cry of alarm, he saw Heavy and Lacey leaning uneasily against the railing. Both gripped the holdings in desperation as the plummeting ship rocked back and forth.

"Kal!" Heavy screamed. "What the hell happened? We're sinking! We're going down!"

Klondike stared at him in terror. In his maddened state, he realised the crew, his staff and just about everyone onboard was now out on deck, many diving into the water as it swallowed up their domain.

Within seconds, the water level had risen over the deck, which slipped under the waves at its grotesque angle.

Klondike clung on grimly. He shimmied his way across the lurching gangway to Heavy and Lacey. They both stared at him in abhorrent shock. Lacey was shuddering. He put an arm around her.

"Everybody hold on. We're going under."

"Kal..." Lacey said in a spasmodic, shock-induced tone as she shivered uncontrollably in his arms. "What happened? You said you saw Jenny Cross..."

Klondike watched hypnotically as the water level rose over the metal gangway, covering their feet. "It was her," he stammered wildly. "Those men... they weren't harbour authorities. They planted a bomb. It must've been in that case the two others were carrying. They put a god damn bomb in our hold. It's taken half the ship off!"

"Kal!" Lacey screamed. "I'm... I'm slipping!"

"Hold on!" Klondike yelled.

Then, in an instant, a gentle lap of the ocean swept over them and, suddenly, they were no longer attached to the ship, but were floating free. The trio clung to each other in desperation, slowly drifting away from the wreck. The ice cold water hit them like a shock wave.

Within seconds, the Floating Top was completely submerged, the only sign a ship had just occupied the surrounding space a smattering of aerials and masts that stuck out above the water line. Then, they too disappeared below. The liner was gone.

Klondike stared in despair at the scene of horror that now played out all around them, everywhere. People were floating all across the water in a huge circle encompassing about 50 yards. Never-ending screams pierced the air endlessly. The ship's passengers clutched various pieces of debris and damaged equipment. Several wooden crates floated to the surface. But that was it. Everything else – the whole of the circus's mighty haul of equipment – had been sent to the bottom.

Everybody just floated in desperation and panic, grabbing ahold of whatever they could – be it human or material.

Clowns, cowboys, dancers, roustabouts... they were all treading water in panic, everyone's face a mask of shock and fear.

The whole thing – the sinking of the mighty Floating Top – had taken just minutes. And now, everyone was in the water, fighting for survival.

Never in his wildest nightmares could Klondike have envisioned such madness and horror.

Now, as he treaded water while clutching desperately to Heavy and Lacey, he looked around dumbly at the ocean-bound chaos.

Then, slowly, he turned his head in the water, and squinted into the sun, looking towards land, so far away.

He managed to catch sight of the fleeing silver launch. It was speeding away now, in full flight. In seconds, it had blended into the myriad of boats and vessels scattered across the vast harbour. Gone.

Klondike grimaced, his head bobbing in and out of the sea, filling his nostrils with salty water.

"Oh my god, Kal," Heavy wailed as he kept his head above water. "It's gone. The ship. Everything. It's all gone!"

Lacey somehow managed to speak as she bobbed between them, held in place by the men's strong grip.

"What is happening?" she blurted between gasps.

Klondike looked at them both, then turned again towards the shore, trying to pick out that silver launch. With a grunt, he looked behind him, surveying the almighty mass of struggling humanity and charred debris.

When he spoke, his gnarled voice came in a pained whisper.

"The end of the world," he said.

"It's the end of our whole wide world."